STARGÅTE SG·1™

FEMALE OF THE SPECIES

Geonn Cannon

FANDEMONIUM BOOKS

An original publication of Fandemonium Ltd, produced under license from MGM Consumer Products.

Fandemonium Books
United Kingdom
Visit our website: www.stargatenovels.com

S T A R G Å T E
S G · 1 ™

METRO-GOLDWYN-MAYER Presents
STARGATE SG-1™
BEN BROWDER AMANDA TAPPING
CHRISTOPHER JUDGE CLAUDIA BLACK
with BEAU BRIDGES and MICHAEL SHANKS as Daniel Jackson
Executive Producers ROBERT C. COOPER & BRAD WRIGHT
Developed for Television by BRAD WRIGHT & JONATHAN GLASSNER

WWW.MGM.COM

Print ISBN: 978-1-905586-83-7   Ebook ISBN: 978-1-80070-038-3

To Sarah and Kate,
for the inspiration and cheerleading.

Historical note:
The events of this book take place during
season 10 of STARGATE SG-1 between the
episodes "Talion" and "Family Ties"

PROLOGUE

DANIEL JACKSON missed Jaffa. They were big, scary men in suits of armor carrying big, scary sticks which shot balls of fire. They were soldiers trained from childhood to engage in a war. It was easy to return fire on a group of Jaffa without thinking too hard about the consequences. Even knowing Teal'c, Bra'tac, and so many other Jaffa, it didn't change the fact that the Jaffa they ended up fighting were soldiers before anything else. Followers of the Ori, however, were just ordinary people. Misguided, confused farmers, merchants, husbands and wives who believed lies about a better life and thought they were doing the right thing. He was also affected by his time as a Prior, where he saw first-hand just how people were swayed to the cause.

He stood in the alcove of a tavern entrance, the hood of his robes up to conceal his features as much as it was to protect him from the rain. The clouds had moved in just after the team arrived, transporting in on the outskirts of town instead of using the Stargate. Rumbles of thunder echoed from the mountains, indicating the worst of the weather was yet to come. It was still peculiar to think he was standing on an alien world without traveling through a wormhole. The human race was capable of moving between solar systems and galaxies on ships they built themselves, and he was one of the people who did it enough that it was routine. Not only that, he was recognizable enough on those backwaters that he had to worry about being spotted loitering. With that thought, he stepped out into the alley and moved north. He passed the windows of the tavern and glanced inside. Cameron Mitchell and Vala Mal Doran were inside soaking up the local gossip, but he didn't spot them. He didn't change pace as he continued across the town commons where the Stargate stood stoic and forgotten on a stone dais. Merchants had left carts all around it, their storefronts covered with thick hides, and the DHD was surrounded by crates. It had already been relegated to an artifact of another time, a darker era when the Goa'uld could arrive at any moment and begin wreaking havoc. Once it held horror. Now it was just a piece of the landscape no one had bothered to move.

Daniel saw Samantha Carter across the square, a peasant cap pulled low over her ears. She locked eyes with him and nodded once. He dipped his chin in response and made his way over.

"Anything?" she asked.

"From what I could hear through the door, the Prior went back to the ship this morning. Everyone in town is pretty much onboard with Origin."

He looked past her as he reported his findings. The upper curve of the Ori warship loomed ominously above the town. It stood in darkness like a mountain, its metallic face polished to a shine due to the rain. A majority of the windows glowed with soft yellow light, and he wondered how many soldiers from the Ori galaxy were inside preparing for battle.

Sam said, "As much as I hate to say it, we may need to just walk away from this one. There's no point telling them the Ori are bad if they're not willing to hear us out. There are other worlds out there which may be on the fence."

"Choose our battles," Daniel said.

Sam shrugged. "There's only so much we can do, Daniel. If we focus on places that are more likely to turn against the Priors, then eventually they'll lose power and this world will be saved anyway. It's not abandonment. It's triage."

"I suppose." He looked toward the tavern. "It just feels like we should be gathering more victories after deploying Merlin's weapon."

"We don't even know for sure it eliminated the Ori. It certainly hasn't seemed to slow down their Priors. A lot of these worlds never recovered from the downfall of the Goa'uld.

They're latching on to something that seems familiar."

"And as a bonus, it doesn't require playing host."

Teal'c appeared in the tavern door. He paused for a moment to find Sam and Daniel and then made his way over to them. "I believe we should begin preparing for immediate departure."

Sam said, "Meeting not going well?"

"Colonel Mitchell and Vala Mal Doran attempted to talk reason with those who have already been swayed by the Prior. The conversation escalated."

Daniel said, "With Vala involved, why am I not surprised?"

"They are on the verge of being arrested as heretics. The town leaders intend to use their imprisonment as a symbol of their dedication to the Ori."

"Yeah, that's as good a cue as any." Sam reached under her shawl and gripped her radio. "This is Colonel Carter to the *Odyssey*. We're going to need extraction, ASAP."

The response was broken and full of static. "*— rter, the storm … — terfering with our instrum — …too many signals in town. W— …quire a lock…*"

Daniel said, "That didn't sound good."

"We'll need to get clear of the storm. Teal'c, we may need you to get Cam and Vala out of the tavern." Teal'c inclined his head and turned to retrieve the rest of their team. Sam turned her attention to the sky. "The storm moved in from the north. If we go to the south, we might be able to get ahead of it."

"Colonel Carter," Teal'c said.

She looked back to the tavern. The light within had grown brighter in the past few seconds, and the flames that suddenly began licking the window frame were a big clue as to why. A crash was followed by a yell, and then someone ran from the door and disappeared down a side street. Sam had no doubt he would return shortly with reinforcements.

"Crap," she muttered.

Mitchell ran out, followed by Vala, who had both arms over

her head for whatever meager protection they might provide from projectiles being thrown by the angry patrons. Mitchell indiscriminately fired his zat above head level to clear their pursuers before he bolted across the clearing. Sam and Teal'c took cover behind the nearest options: a fruit cart for her and the brick corner of a building for him. Daniel moved deeper into the alley, handgun drawn but aimed at the sky as he watched for anyone who might be coming up behind them. Vala scurried behind Teal'c and grabbed his biceps with both hands, using his body as a shield. Mitchell hit the ground next to Carter and scrambled onto his knees.

"So much for the friendly banter of the local bar."

"It always worked on *Cheers*," Mitchell said. "No one threw oil lanterns at people on *Cheers*. What's the extraction plan?"

"The storm is interfering with *Odyssey*'s sensors. We have to get clear of it."

Mitchell looked at her like she was crazy. "That's a hell of a lot of running."

"You have a better plan?"

"The Stargate!" Vala said.

The tavern door opened. Carter and Mitchell rose from behind cover and laid down suppressive fire. The barflies who had escaped the flames spread out and took cover of their own. Sam scanned the adjoining streets and alleyways for the man who had left in case he had returned with reinforcements.

Vala repeated, "We can use the Stargate!"

"It's too exposed," Carter said. "We wouldn't have cover while we dialed. It's too risky!"

"But as soon as it's open, these people will scatter! It's probably been years since they saw it open. Some of them may never have seen it. If you cover me while I dial the SGC, they'll be stunned by the Gate opening. We can get through before they recover."

Sam looked over her shoulder at Vala. "We're not risking it. We'll make a run for the edge of town. When the *Odyssey* gets a clear signal, they'll transport us up. It's the best option."

Some of the locals had relatively primitive projectile weapons, and Sam ducked back behind the cart as a few lead slugs impacted the wood with hollow thuds.

Vala rolled her eyes and slapped Teal'c on the shoulder. "Cover me, Muscles!" She pushed away from him and gracefully dived behind the cover Sam was using. She waited for a lull in the fire and then ran for the DHD.

"Damn it, Vala!" Sam shouted. She rose onto her knees and sprayed the ground with bullets to cover Vala's six. Mitchell also lit up the brick wall behind their foes with multiple blasts of the zat. He was careful not to actually hit any people, clearly unwilling to risk inadvertently hitting anyone with two shots.

At the far end of the alley where he and Teal'c had taken cover, Daniel saw movement. A group of locals were approaching in darkness. He couldn't see clearly enough to make out weapons, but he doubted they had shown up to the fight unarmed.

"Uh, guys? We're being a little bit surrounded here."

Vala whipped the tarp off the DHD and began dialing. A man spotted her and took aim, and Mitchell took him out, an obvious exception to his rule of no direct hits. The man convulsed and fell back into the mud. The fire within the tavern was now fully involved, spreading around the door with thick black smoke rising from the roof. Daniel was forced to open fire on the people advancing on his and Teal'c's position. Vala finished inputting the address and pressed the center dome with both hands.

The commons filled with blinding blue light which reflected off the raindrops and briefly diminished the fire's brilliance. As Vala predicted, the locals hit the ground at the sight. They dropped their weapons to cover their heads. Mitchell retrieved his GDO from a pocket of his vest and entered the code before waving to Daniel and Teal'c that they were clear to go. They made a run for it, and Mitchell shot the muddy ground to discourage anyone from trying to be a hero.

"Vala, go!" Daniel shouted.

She stepped around the DHD and hurled herself into the shimmering blue pool. Daniel followed Teal'c to the Gate and, before diving through, heard Sam sending one last update over her radio.

"*Odyssey*, this is Carter. I hope you're reading this. We're retreating through the Stargate. Repeat, we are retreating through the Stargate. Clear orbit and return to Earth."

If there was a response, he missed it as he dived through the event horizon.

~#~

Sam came through without breaking stride, yanking off her cap and holding it by her side as she advanced. Vala stood at the base of the ramp with the rest of the team. She stepped between Mitchell and Teal'c in the hopes they would protect her from Sam's rage. Rain from the alien storm dripped off Sam's clothes as she pushed past Mitchell and Daniel, ignoring General Landry's approach.

Vala worked up an expression that she hoped was a mixture of naïve hopefulness, pride, and confusion. "Well, that all worked out!"

"You disobeyed a direct order," Sam snapped. "You put yourself and the rest of the team at risk."

Vala's expression consolidated into anger. "I'm the one who got us out of there in one piece! You ought to be thanking me."

"If you had gotten shot —"

"You and Colonel Mitchell were —"

"That's not the point! The point is that you were reckless. *Again*. You're only lucky that it worked out this time."

"*Again*," Vala said, mocking Sam's tone.

Sam bared her teeth and took a step forward, but Teal'c put an arm across her chest with a hand on her opposite shoulder, holding her back. Mitchell cleared his throat, looking between the women before looking to Landry.

"Things got a little heated back on the planet, sir," he said.

"I can see that." Landry put his hands up. "We can save the analysis for the briefing. For now I'm sure you'd all like to get into some dry clothes. We'll contact the *Odyssey* to let them know you've all made it home in one piece."

Sam said, "Thank you, sir." She stepped around Vala, stopping just short of bumping her arm in the process as she continued out of the room.

Vala watched her go and then looked at Daniel for help. "Come on, you were there. We were surrounded. There was no chance we'd be able to get clear of the storm. I did what needed to be done and hey! Look! We made it home in one piece."

"Yeah," Daniel said, "but in situations like this, the ends don't always justify the means."

"Orders are orders," Mitchell added.

Vala felt betrayed. She turned to Teal'c, begging him with her eyes. "Not you, too."

He inhaled, appeared to consider saying something, and in the end followed Daniel out of the room. Left alone at the base of the ramp, Vala faced General Landry. He offered an expression of sympathy without support, shrugging as he followed the others from the room.

"It's certainly going to be an interesting briefing," he said.

Vala watched him go. She looked up at the control room, where Sergeant Harriman had been watching the whole thing. She held her arms out to either side, hoping maybe he would throw her a pity nod, but he instead pivoted in his chair to focus on something out of sight. Vala gaped at his disloyalty, dropped her arms, and marched from the gate room with her head held high.

The team might be angry at her, Landry might take their side, and even Walter might disagree, but she knew that she'd done what needed to be done. She'd gotten the team home safely and she wasn't going to feel bad about that.

CHAPTER ONE

WALTER HARRIMAN understood there were greater problems to be dealt with on the base. Aside from the fate of the entire world being at stake on a daily basis, they also had to worry about the IOA, various threats from within the government, and maintaining tenuous relationships with allies who were becoming more and more independent. He was the one who put the schedule on General Landry's desk every day, so he knew there were a dozen higher priority issues that needed to be dealt with. But how could they be expected to work on any of them when there wasn't a decent cup of coffee to be had on the entire base?

He'd determined that the least-objectionable coffee was in Daniel Jackson's office, but recently SG-1 had been on-base too much to risk sneaking in. One of the airmen maintained a carafe in the briefing room that was passable on good days. Walter sniffed it as he came down the steps into the control room, grimacing before he brought the cup to his lips. It was not a good day. He curled his lips and put the cup down as he resumed his station behind the dialing computer. The other sergeant looked at him.

"They figured out space travel, you'd think they would be able to swing a decent dark roast."

A klaxon interrupted any response his quip might have received. He focused immediately on the monitor as the Stargate came to life, the iris sliding into place as a precautionary measure. Walter hit the PA key and turned to the microphone: "Unauthorized off-world activation!" The whole base knew his warning and jumped into action.

He scanned for a GDO signal. It was imperative to respond to those as quickly as possible. If an SG team was coming in hot, they might be running full-speed toward that barrier waiting for him to open the door. His palm sweated as the screen remained blank. General Landry descended the stairs behind him and stopped just behind his chair.

"Someone coming home early?"

"No IDC yet, sir," Walter reported. The screen flickered. "But we are receiving a signal."

Landry moved closer so he could see. A message began scrolling out, numbers with the occasional letter thrown in. Walter tried to make sense of it as the message appeared but there didn't seem to be any pattern to it. Finally the block ended with a series of dashes followed by four words: VIAXEIRO and VALA MAL DORAN. Once the full message had been delivered, the Stargate shut down.

Walter looked up at Landry, who looked annoyed and intrigued in equal measure. "I suppose we should get Vala down here to see if she knows what this means."

"Yes, sir."

Landry walked away and Walter's eye fell on the cup the General had left behind on the control panel. Steam was still rising from it, and he could smell even from this distance that it was even better than Dr. Jackson's stash. His fingers itched to reach out and take it. No sense in letting fresh, hot coffee go to waste. And whatever the message was, it would probably require Landry's full attention. He might not even think about the coffee until it had gone cold, and —

Landry came back and retrieved the cup. "Walter!" he said, "Find Vala. Now."

"Yes, sir, on it, sir."

He headed to the wall-mounted phone. Maybe when his shift was over he could run by Starbucks.

~#~

In the weeks after Vala's flagrant disobedience of Sam's orders, the team managed to give each other space without blatantly avoiding one another. Sam took the opportunity for a trip to Washington so she could brief President Hayes about her experiences in the alternate universe. She was gone longer than anyone predicted and, putting aside the fact it may have been a long debriefing, Daniel got the impression she opted for a mini-vacation in her old stomping grounds. He also heard a rumor that Jack was taking a vacation from Homeworld Security around the same time she was scheduled to be in town.

Teal'c tried to distract himself with a "peaceful summit" which turned into a slaughter orchestrated by a Jaffa named Arkad. He led a group of Jaffa who had been swayed to follow Origin. Teal'c killed him and, with his death, the movement was believed to have collapsed. Teal'c was still recovering from the beatings he'd taken while seeking his vengeance, and Mitchell had a few scrapes and bruises of his own from trying to stop their teammate from doing anything rash.

Daniel was enjoying the time alone, frankly. No Vala bouncing around his office trying to get his attention, no missions trying to figure out the best way to convince people the Ori were just as bad as the Goa'uld had been, no listening to Teal'c recap movies Daniel barely remembered from his childhood. He needed time to himself so he could process his recent experiences as a Prior. It was part of a grander plan, and he'd never actually been brainwashed to the enemy's way of thinking, but he'd undergone a fundamental physical change. Sometimes he wondered if the constant changes they went through - Sam blending with a Tok'ra, his ascension and return, Jack's repeated death and resurrection at the hands of Ba'al - would wreak havoc on them down the road.

His theory that he was being avoided was disproven when Mitchell knocked on the wall outside his office door. "Yo, Jackson. Siler is offering lunch. Beer, wings, the whole nine yards, on him. Apparently it's been a week since he's been hurt, and he thought that required a celebration. You in?"

"Uh, maybe. Did he say where they're going? I'm still not really welcome in O'Malley's."

Vala's voice echoed through the corridor. "Dan-iel!"

He closed his eyes and pressed his fingers to his temple. "On second thought, it sounds like we're about to get busy."

Mitchell stepped aside as Vala appeared, arriving at such speed that she had to slam into the door just to slow herself down enough to get into the office. She wobbled on her feet a little and shook her head as she stumbled over to where Daniel was sitting.

"Daniel. Ow. I need your help. I need you to convince General Landry to send SG-1 on a mission. It's a matter of life and death."

"What mission?" Daniel said.

"It's a rescue mission. A mission of mercy! SG-1 does those all the time, right?" She looked behind her and finally noticed Mitchell. "Oh. Hello, Colonel Mitchell. You can help convince him, too. The two of you, how could he say no?"

Mitchell enunciated when he asked, "What… mission?"

"Calm down and use your words," Daniel said.

Vala sneered at him. "Don't you patronize me! This is a serious matter. My friend Tanis Reynard needs my help. She sent a distress signal. She's been arrested and she's being held in a horrible prison where there's no hope of escape. We have to go break her out."

"Tanis Reynard?" Daniel said, glancing toward his computer. "Tanis Reynard… why do I know that name?"

Mitchell said, "Tanis Reynard, the Hebridian prisoner who killed her guards when their ship crashed on an uninhabited world? SG-1 ran into her four years ago. She and her cronies tied up Carter off-world and tried to use the SGC computers to find new planets to pillage."

"Well." Vala flipped her hair out of her face and rubbed her arm where she'd run into the door. "We all have pasts we're not proud of…" She looked at Daniel. "So you've met Tanis?"

"No, I haven't had the pleasure." Daniel gathered his notebooks and stood up. "I was, ah, somewhere else that year. So, Cam, you mentioned beer and wings?"

Vala watched them go, desperate. "Wait! She's in trouble. You can't just walk away because you had some disagreements in the past."

Daniel stopped in the doorway. "Vala, this goes beyond disagreements. SG-1 encountered her while she was a prisoner. She was literally escaping custody when their paths crossed. The fact she's in prison again makes it sound like she hasn't changed her ways."

Mitchell said, "Sorry about your friend. But the SGC really isn't in the business of helping guilty people escape prison."

"But she's not guilty!"

"How do you know?"

"Because she's in prison!"

Daniel and Mitchell looked at each other, then turned to continue their departure. Vala growled and ran between them. She put her hands on their chests to keep them from advancing to the elevator.

"Tanis Reynard and I worked together for a very long time. She's careful. She plans her crimes out, and she doesn't take unnecessary risks. She would never have gotten caught for something she actually did which means she's been imprisoned unjustly. And she's in one of the worst prisons the galaxy has to offer, and the SGC most certainly *is* in the business of helping people in those situations. You can't just abandon her because she's done bad things in the past. Look at Teal'c! Look at me!"

Daniel closed his eyes and sighed. Mitchell's shoulders slumped.

"I'll let Siler know we're passing on the wings."

Vala beamed and hugged both men tightly around the neck. Daniel tried not to think of how much it felt like a noose and patted Vala on the back.

Besides, all they had to do was present her concerns to

Landry. There was very little chance he would actually okay the mission.

~#~

"Vala is running the briefing?"

Daniel shrugged, clearly unable to argue with the skepticism in Sam's voice. They were seated next to each other at the table, with Teal'c and Mitchell across from them. The Stargate loomed over Mitchell's head, and Sam wished she could jump through it to avoid whatever was about to happen.

"General Landry agreed to hear her out. And since SG-1 is the team that would go, he wanted us to get all the information at the same time."

"Yeah, but why is he even entertaining the idea?" Sam asked.

"I'm sure he has his reasons."

Vala came into the briefing room, trailed by General Landry. She stopped at the head of the table and smiled at the team, then realized Landry was glaring at her.

"Oh… I just thought… since I was running —"

"No," Landry said, shooing her.

Vala scooted around to Daniel's other side. "Okay. Right. Hello, everybody. I've gathered you here because one of you is a murderer."

Sam closed her eyes. "Vala…"

"Sorry. I read somewhere that if you're going to speak publicly, you should open with a joke. But I see that must not apply to every situation." She shifted her weight from foot to foot. "So let's just move on. My friend, my partner in crime, a woman who saved my life on multiple occasions is in trouble. She's been captured. Locked away in an inescapable prison. She cried out to us for help."

Mitchell said, "I want to hear more about this 'inescapable prison' part. Vee-a-jero?"

"V-ya-shero," Vala corrected. "The Viaxeiro Caldera is the worst prison in the entire universe. Growing up, every little thief is warned not to screw up or they'll be sent there. It was built on a drifting planet that wanders between solar systems, out in the middle of nowhere."

"A rogue planet?" Sam sounded intrigued in spite of herself.

"How would life even be possible there?" Daniel said. "No light or heat…"

"Possibly an artificial atmosphere," Sam suggested. "Not being exposed to ultraviolet light would make it easier to retain a hydrogen-rich atmosphere. That would trap enough heat on the planet's surface to sustain life. Or if it kept a moon when it was kicked out of its solar system, the tidal forces—"

"Colonel," Landry warned.

Sam winced. "Sorry, sir." To Daniel, she said, "Suffice to say, it's not something we've encountered before. But it is possible."

"That's right. No one on the outside can stage a rescue and no one on the inside can plan an escape. If you don't know where you are, you don't know where you can run. Only the people in charge of the prison know where it can be found at any given moment so they can send more prisoners, guards, supplies, you know, that sort of thing."

Daniel said, "It's an oubliette. A dark place where people are sent to be forgotten."

"Exactly!" Vala said. "But if anyone can find this place, it's SG-1."

Teal'c's expression didn't betray his position on the matter. "We do have a certain aptitude for escaping from inescapable prisons."

Sam said, "Usually when we don't have a choice. We escaped from Hadante because we were arrested by the Taldor. We risked entering Netu in order to save my father. This time we would be choosing to enter this prison to save a woman who, the first time we met, had just killed her jailers and then planned to leave SG-1 for dead so she could use the Stargate to loot the galaxy. I'm sorry, Vala, but she doesn't sound like a candidate for this kind of risk."

"Normally I'd agree with that assessment," Landry said, "but something Vala said stuck out to me."

Vala's posture straightened slightly, wary but proud. "Something *I* said…?"

"This Tanis Reynard woman has been out there surviving the past two years since the Goa'uld fell. She knows the criminal underworld like no one else."

Sam realized where he was going. "The Lucian Alliance."

"Bingo. They're in a tailspin now, thanks to the coup against Netan you all helped orchestrate. Homeworld Security is trying to put an operative into the Alliance undercover, but they can't get past the secrecy of everyone involved. I called General O'Neill, and he thinks this Tanis woman might be an invaluable source of information. She could give us the intel we need to finally plant a mole in the organization."

Sam was stunned. "General O'Neill actually agreed to the rescue mission?"

"Not exactly. A team was able to decipher the rest of the message and determined it's a gate address. General O'Neill thinks it's worth a look. See what you find and make a judgment call from there. If you decide to continue with the rescue, we'll offer Miss Reynard a nice cozy cell here at the SGC in exchange for what she can tell us about the Alliance. There's an opening tomorrow at 0800, you can leave then."

Vala said, "Oof. Eight o'clock in the morning…?" The team all looked at her. She flashed a smile. "It's fine! I'll go to bed early. No problem."

Sam still didn't think the mission was worth their time, but she knew it was futile to argue. The meeting was already over and she'd lost her opportunity to change the general's mind. "Yes, sir."

Landry dismissed the team and returned to his office. Daniel headed for the elevators. Mitchell made a break for the stairs.

Teal'c was still recovering from injuries sustained in his fight with Arkad so he was too slow to escape her. Sam had almost made it out of the room but stopped on the stairs, guilty about leaving Teal'c to face the brunt of Vala's attention.

"Muscles! Listen, I just wanted to say thank you for the vote of confidence in the meeting."

"I was merely stating a fact. We have indeed escaped from many situations which were, to that point, considered inescapable."

Vala bumped her fist against his shoulder. "That's the spirit!"

Teal'c inclined his head. "Our past victories have no bearing on future performance. It would only require one failure to lose everything."

Vala's smile wavered as he stepped around her. "Right. But I have the utmost confidence in all of us." She turned and Sam hurried down the stairs before Vala could spot her. She could hear a frustrated grunt followed by Vala shouting, "I wish you all would stop walking away and leaving me in empty rooms!"

CHAPTER TWO

VALA IDENTIFIED the address from Tanis' message as Pezjena, a lawless world where smugglers and mercenaries could meet up with allies and potential clients. Sam didn't think they would get very far in their standard uniforms, which meant they would need to sign out some of what Daniel called 'undercover rawhide.' The past few years had seen a rise in missions where teams needed to be incognito, so whenever possible they were asked to bring back clothing which could help them blend in. The SGC didn't exactly have a wardrobe department, so it was all filed in the archives. Sam didn't mind playing dress-up, but she was annoyed it would mean dealing with Major Hagman.

Hagman, when he was still a captain, served very briefly as a member of SG-1 after Daniel ascended. His disastrous first mission had proven he wasn't cut out for the field and he was reassigned to the base archives. Sam felt he blamed her for the fact he hadn't been given Daniel's spot on the team. Either that or he was just a lousy judge of women's fashion. She put in a request before leaving the base and, in the morning, opened her locker to find a low-cut peasant blouse and a dress which would greatly hamper her ability to run.

"Damn it, Hagman." She glanced at the locker next to hers and, after a moment of internal debate, opened it to see what the guys had been given.

She had already changed into the trousers and was buttoning the shirt when Daniel came in. He faltered at the threshold but continued inside when he saw that Sam was putting clothes on and not taking them off.

"Hey," he said.

"I'll be out in a second." She reached into her locker and retrieved the brown flat cap off the top shelf. "Hagman has given me this hat before. It's actually not bad."

"Give me a boonie hat any day," Daniel said. "Actually, I think I lost my last one. Do they still make them?"

Sam smiled. "This is the military. We still make everything, whether we use it or not." She shut her locker door. "Hagman forgot to give Mitchell an outfit."

Daniel looked at her slacks, the cuffs of which had been rolled up. "Hm. Strange."

"Yeah, I guess they still think we're a four-person team."

She was at the door when Daniel said, "Ah, just a second." She held the door open with her shoulder and turned back. "Is everything going to be okay between you and Vala?"

"Why wouldn't it be?"

"We haven't really gone on an official mission since... you know, Vala running through a hail of gunfire to the DHD against your orders."

Sam came back inside and slumped against the wall. "Oh, right. That."

"To be fair, she was probably right about the fact we wouldn't have made it out of town. We might have been taken prisoner, handed over to the Ori army..."

"And we would've found a way out of it, and maybe gathered more intel about whether Merlin's device worked or not. Vala took an unnecessary risk. All it would've taken was one bullet from those villagers and she'd have been dead and we'd have been captured anyway. She never would have–" She cut herself off and wrinkled her nose, looking at the ground instead of finishing her thought.

Daniel had known her far too long to let it sit. "She never would have done that if Jack was the one giving the orders."

"You know he never would have let her get away with half the things she does," Sam said, keeping her voice low in case anyone overheard. "I'm fine with Mitchell taking command. But if Vala's ignoring my orders on a regular basis, then I might as well get busted back down to Major and start calling Mitchell 'sir'."

"Vala is still getting used to this whole team thing. She's been on her own since she was a kid. Just give her some time to adjust."

"She's had time, Daniel. The universe isn't getting any safer, despite our best efforts. When she makes decisions on her own, it's not just her life on the line anymore. We need to count on her when the chips are down. If we can't do that… maybe SG-1 should go back to being a four-person team."

"Are you talking about Vala leaving or you?"

Sam sighed. "I guess we'll see when the time comes."

~#~

Vala was well practiced in the art of going off-world, but she was still getting used to the idea of leaving and then coming back to the same place. Normally after spending this long in a single place she would either be looking for an escape hatch or waiting for a mark to chase her out of the solar system. She still liked to make sure everything was in order before she left so, after she changed into the lovely little leather outfit that had been delivered to her, she spent a few minutes cataloguing her things. She didn't know if the airmen searched her quarters when she was off-world but she wouldn't put it past them. She didn't have anything illicit on the base but, if someone were to search, she didn't want them finding anything questionable.

She'd spent the entire night thinking about Tanis. They'd been partners, they had each other's backs, but Vala hadn't even thought about the other woman since she came to the SGC. Yes, she'd had other things on her mind, but still. Tanis had been more than a friend, she'd been the first true partner Vala ever had. She trusted Tanis more than anyone else in her life. She credited that bond with opening her mind to the possibility of home. It was what she believed prepared her for coming to the SGC and finding a family.

And now Tanis was in the worst prison anyone had ever conceived. Part of her horror was knowing just how easily it could have been her in that situation. She and Tanis were very much part of the same flock… no, how did people on Earth say it? Birds of a feather. They were both thieves and confidence artists, they pressed their luck, they lied and cheated and stole their way across the galaxy. And yes, Vala had been caught a few times, but she always managed to talk her way out of it eventually. There was no negotiating out of Viaxeiro, however. Tanis was counting on her and, since she had the means to help, she couldn't turn her back.

There was a knock on the door. "Hello." She turned and smiled when she saw Teal'c. "My dashing escort, here to make sure I don't get lost on the way to the Stargate. How chivalrous!"

Teal'c assumed a relaxed pose just inside the door. "Colonel Mitchell wished for me to ensure you were not delayed."

"He's just annoyed that I'm sometimes tardy."

"Perhaps you could counter his expectations by arriving early."

"You'd like that, wouldn't you?"

Teal'c said, "I believe we would all find it a pleasant change."

Vala harrumphed, closed her drawer, and threw her shoulders back as she walked from the room. "Very well. Escort me if you must."

~#~

Teal'c closed her door and fell into step beside her with his hands clasped behind his back. Vala seemed appreciative of the outfit he'd been given, though it seemed fairly standard to his eye. He wore a high-collared brown tunic underneath a matching vest, and that was covered by a long coat with a heavy mantle across his shoulders. Vala tugged at the hem of her own jacket in what he took to be an attempt at looking imposing. They stopped at the elevators and Teal'c turned to face her.

"May I make an inquiry?"

"Of course. You can ask me anything. I'm an open book."

Teal'c raised an eyebrow, skeptical, but let the comment pass. He followed her into the elevator. "Do you believe there will be a conflict between yourself and Colonel Carter on this mission?"

"Sam? No. I don't see why there would be."

"On our last mission, you disobeyed — "

"Oh, *that*." She waved a hand dismissively behind her head. "That's ancient history. Sam's forgotten all about that. I'm sure she won't bring it up again."

Teal'c thought it prudent not to mention the concern was whether she could be trusted to follow orders. Vala had been in the wrong during the last mission, even if she did get them home without harm. Colonel Carter issued orders and they should have been followed. If Vala couldn't understand the difference, he wasn't confident this mission would go more smoothly than the last one. Regardless, he was unconcerned. The team could work together even when they weren't on the best terms. It had been nearly a decade, and there had been dozens of missions where one of them was angry at another or some grudge was being held when they went through the gate. They were always able to put it aside and focus on their work. Hopefully the same would hold true this time.

They arrived at Level 28. Teal'c let Vala lead the way into the gate room, where the rest of the team was waiting. Sam stood at the base of the ramp, Mitchell waiting near the back wall under the observation window. Teal'c approached him.

"So, you talk to her?"

"She believes she did nothing wrong. In her opinion it is Colonel Carter who must adjust."

Mitchell looked annoyed. "Yeah, Jackson said Carter felt pretty much the same way."

"I must side with Colonel Carter."

"Well, of course. Hell, this is a military unit even if the majority of it is civilian. When you're out there in the field, you might as well be honorary officers. You take orders whether you like them or not. Jackson's figured that out."

"Daniel Jackson has had many years of experience. I believe if you asked General O'Neill, he would say there was a…" He searched for the proper phrase. "Learning curve."

Mitchell said, "Sure. But we're dealing with the Ori on one side and the Lucian Alliance on the other, and who knows what fresh hell is out there waiting to rear its ugly head next. Vala might not have the luxury of a grace period."

Landry's voice came from the control room above. "SG-1, you have a go. Godspeed."

Sam turned and nodded to him. "Thank you, General. Hopefully we'll be back before you can miss us."

CHAPTER THREE

A STRONG wind hit them as soon as they stepped through the Stargate. Sam regretted the fact that she didn't have her goggles and turned her head so she could get a clear view of their new location. They were on a circular stone platform with a pair of wide walkways leading away at sharp angles. The walkways were the upper stretch of ramparts that protected a city of orange-roofed buildings. Behind them was a steep drop to a rocky shoreline. Sam admired the setup. In peace-time the Stargate would be a nice decorative piece of art, but in the case of an invasion, defenders could attack from either side and drive their enemy over the edge.

Teal'c also took a moment to admire the layout, as Vala walked to the DHD and rested her elbow on the upper curve of it. She scanned the city and then spun to face the team.

"Welcome to Pezjena! If it can be bought, sold, stolen, fenced, bartered, or lost, you can find it here. Services also rendered for a reasonable fee. The majority of people here are Lucian Alliance or at least hope to be. Their planets suffered after the Goa'uld were defeated so they set out into the universe to make their fortunes in whatever manner presented itself. That manner was usually criminal, no matter which planet's laws you use."

"Theft is theft," Mitchell said.

"Exactly. It's common throughout the galaxy, people have something and someone else wants it. Once someone has a thing, they want to keep it. This breeds conflict."

Daniel looked out across the spread of buildings, homes clustered within the safety of the walls before following the slope of the cliff to a larger, palatial estate. "This is a pretty siz-able town, Vala. Are we supposed to just walk around asking people if they know anything about Tanis?"

"Of course not, don't be ridiculous." She started walking

down one of the promenades, and the team had no choice but to follow her. "Tanis and I came through here all the time. We knew who offered the best deals and where to get the best drinks. I know exactly where to look."

Mitchell said, "We're going to stick out like sore thumbs if the five of us go tramping in there all at once. Jackson, you go with her and — "

"No. Not Daniel. Sam."

Sam wanted to refuse on principle. "Why me?"

"People would think he's a mark. No offense, Daniel, they'd think that about any man I walked in with. But you especially. You're not exactly the best liar."

"I don't know if I should be offended or relieved."

Mitchell said, "And you think people will buy Carter here as a fellow thief?"

Sam glared at him over her shoulder. "I swear, if you call me Mary Poppins again…"

Vala rolled her eyes and turned around, walking backward without breaking stride. She pointed at each man in turn. "Teal'c is a Jaffa, which would raise far too many questions. Daniel isn't believable as being my equal — "

Daniel pulled a face. Vala ignored him.

"And the last time you, Colonel Mitchell, tried to pull a fast one on the Lucian Alliance, you got the entire team captured."

Mitchell said, "Hey! One, the Stargate got stolen in the middle of our escape. That's not my fault. And two, you weren't even there! How'd you know about that?"

"The base talks." Vala hooked her arm around Sam's and pulled her close with enough force that Sam almost tripped over her own feet. "The truth is that out of everyone on the team, Sam is the only one who is believable as my new partner in crime. She's smart and resourceful, and she's pretty enough that anyone will overlook their misgivings just to keep her in the room."

Sam narrowed her eyes. "Thank you…?"

"You're welcome." She flipped her hair out of her face and looked at the men. "Now, boys. You hang around outside in case there's any trouble. Feel free to discreetly ask around for anything anyone might have heard about Tanis or Viaxeiro."

"Who exactly put you in charge?" Mitchell asked.

Teal'c said, "It is only reasonable for Vala to take the lead, as she is the most familiar with this world and its inhabitants."

Vala beamed at him. "I knew you would have my back."

He raised an eyebrow and said nothing.

Mitchell sighed. "Fine. There's no point arguing. Sam will go in with you and we'll hang around outside. If there's any trouble we'll come running."

The promenade widened into a cobblestone square filled with people. Sam realized another benefit of the Stargate's high-ground placement was that new arrivals could be seen from anywhere in town. Everyone they passed took a moment to check them out, scanning for weapons or something worth stealing. Fortunately Teal'c was imposing enough that no one made an attempt to pickpocket the team as they cut a path through the crowd. Vala led them with her chin held high, unwavering in her confidence.

Mitchell fell into step beside Sam. They shared a look and he broke off. Daniel and Teal'c followed him and the three men were soon absorbed by the crowd.

Vala gestured at a tavern up ahead. "This is where we're going. It's called Lon'may. They serve drinks and snacks but it's mostly a place where people can meet up with other people. Neutral ground to work out deals without worrying about being stabbed in the back."

"You mean that figuratively, right?"

"Hm?"

"There's no actual stabbing risk in this city."

"Uh."

"Vala…"

"No. Very little risk of stabbing." She pushed through the door and muttered, "Some light zatting at the absolute worst..."

Sam rolled her eyes and followed Vala inside.

She'd been in a great many bars and taverns in her time with SG-1, both on Earth and off. The majority of them seemed to use some kind of universal blueprint. It was probably hard to advance the science of people buying alcohol and sitting to get drunk. Here, the bar was a recessed pit in the center of the room with a rail around the edge where customers could place their orders. Sam saw five or six people down in the pit preparing the drinks. Most patrons were seated at tables along the wall, but more than a few chose to stand in random clusters as if this was a cocktail party instead of a business.

Vala kept her head down, her face turned in a way that appeared casual but kept anyone from getting a full-on look at her.

"Worried about being recognized by the wrong person?"

"One doesn't gain a reputation by making friends. Well... you do... but then you occasionally have to betray them, and feelings get hurt."

"Right."

They managed to reach the center of the room without being spotted. Vala rested her elbows on the rail and scanned the room. Sam stood behind her and tried to look like she belonged.

"Well?"

"I'm looking," Vala said. "Patience. The odds that Tanis' contact will be here at the same time we show up are astronomical. We may have to wait for hours until I see anyone who looks even slightly familiar. And the odds of that person being the one we're supposed to meet..."

Her voice trailed off.

"Oh... no," Vala said in a small voice.

Sam tried to spot the source of Vala's sudden mood shift.

"What's wrong?" A waiter had moved away from one of the far tables to reveal its occupants to her. One man was sitting with his back to the corner so he could see the whole room. He was small at the shoulders and wide at the waist, wedged behind his table with a woman on either side of him. He had a small mustache that obscured his lips, the white hairs stained by the orange drink which had just been refilled.

Vala put her hands on Sam's shoulders and tried ushering her away from the bar, toward the door. "It would appear I made a grave miscalculation. A completely innocent mistake, anyone could have done the same in my situation, so I really don't think this should count against me. No harm, no foul, that's what humans say, isn't it? But we really have to go back to the Stargate *right now* or there will certainly be much harm and several fouls."

"A miscalculation?" Sam said, struggling to keep the irritation from her voice. "What miscalculation?"

Vala was frantic. "Tanis' message. She wasn't telling me to come save her, she was warning me to stay away."

Sam muttered a curse. She and Vala headed for the exit, but they'd only taken a few steps when they were stopped by a bellowing man with a voice loud enough to rattle the mugs hanging from the ceiling.

"Vala! Mal! Do-raaaan!"

The room became deathly still. Heads turned toward them, and the door was suddenly blocked by a pair of men who weren't even bothering to conceal the weapons on their hips.

Vala cringed and shrank into herself. "Damn." She moved her face closer to the lapel of Sam's shirt. "Colonel Mitchell, Daniel, Teal'c, if you're listening, your assistance would be greatly appreciated." She spun around and faked a laugh, spreading her arms out wide. "Jebauth! Jebauth Kavma, is that you? Why, you are half the size you were last time you graced me with your presence. It must be all that clean living! Well, it's been wonderful catching up, but my companion and I have a pressing engagement somewhere far, far away from — " Strong arms grabbed her from behind. " — here."

Sam started to protest, but she was grabbed as well. She rocked her head back into the jaw of whoever was behind her and stepped out of his grip. She pivoted and planted her foot in the man's gut, kicking him away as two more lunged forward to take his place. By the time they were close enough to grab her, Sam had freed her zat from her belt and fired once at each attacker. Vala called out a warning but it came too late. Sam's hand was hit by a wooden club, forcing her to drop the zat, and she was swarmed from all sides.

The large man had spent the scuffle getting out from behind his table. He laughed heartily, clapping his hands as he approached them.

"It's good to see you're still attracting lively partners, Vala," he said.

"Kavma," Vala said, sounding offended, "What is all of this? Surely we could talk about this. It's probably just a silly misunderstanding."

His eyebrows rose. "A misunderstanding? You and Tanis walked away with half my storehouse and left me with a ship full of worthless baubles. Perhaps the misunderstanding is that you meant to take me for everything. Is that what you mean?"

Vala laughed nervously. "We all make mistakes."

"I suppose we do." He rested his hands on his stomach. "And the true measure of a person is how they respond when it comes time to pay for those mistakes. I knew when that message got dropped in my lap it would be the perfect bait to draw you here. I altered it so you would think it was a cry for help instead of a warning, and then I added this address so you would fall right into my lap when you came running. I heard you were hiding out with the Tau'ri, so I made sure it was sent their way." He looked at Sam. "I don't know who you are, but if you're associating with Mal Doran here, then you're definitely guilty of something. So I'm not going to lose any sleep about detaining you as well."

"Now wait a minute…" Sam started to struggle, but the hand on her right arm squeezed and pinched a nerve. Her hand still stung from being hit with the club, and she wasn't confident she could hold or aim a weapon at the moment.

"Look at the bright side, Vala," Kavma said with an unctuous smile. "You can now consider your debt to me paid in full. Say hello to Tanis when you see her."

"You can say it yourself when —"

Whatever else Vala intended to say was cut off by a blast of Sam's zat. Vala's body went rigid, her eyes rolling back in her head in a manner that made it seem like she was more exasperated than pained. The charge passed through her body and someone standing behind her kept her from hitting the floor. Kavma looked at Sam again.

"As I said, stranger, this isn't personal."

"You son of a—" Sam bit off the word as she was hit with her own weapon. The person holding her let go, so as not to be affected by the blast, but grabbed her again as her legs became rubbery and she fell into unconsciousness…

CHAPTER FOUR

THE MERCHANT pulled the shawl from Daniel's grip, dropped it back down on the table, and used two fingers to motion him away. Daniel tried to placate the man. "It's not for me, it's for my friend. We are… ah… we're buying…" He waved his hands, obviously trying to think of a way to explain. "We have to supply a large number of people with outfits for any number of unpredictable situations…"

Cam stepped forward, slapped some of the currency Vala had given him on the counter, and grabbed an appropriate number of items from the display.

"They're for his wife," he explained.

The merchant didn't look happy, but he finally gave up on trying to stop them from buying. Daniel looked annoyed that he'd never been able to get his point across. They had waited outside the pub for a few minutes until they started getting curious looks from the locals, so Cam suggested browsing a little so they didn't stand out quite as much. It was Daniel who suggested buying some "non-Tau'ri" clothes for future covert missions.

Cam opened his pouch and stuffed the clothes inside. "These guys don't care why we're buying this stuff. Just keep your mouth shut and leave the money."

"We're not supposed to draw attention to ourselves. Three men buying women's clothing might make us stick out in someone's mind. A story might make it seem less remarkable." Daniel sighed and looked for Teal'c. "So what do you think the odds are that this will turn into a real mission?"

"You mean whoever Vala came here to meet is reputable enough that we risk going to an inescapable prison to save someone who once took SG-1 prisoner? I'd say not very good."

"General Landry did have a point," Daniel said. "We

could use whatever inside information we can get on the Lucian Alliance. We may have kicked over the anthill when we sent those bounty hunters after Netan, but the ants are still there."

"Story as old as time." Cam had moved closer to a fruit stand. He picked up something small and red, sniffed it, and scratched at the rind with his thumbnail. "You knock out the guy in charge, create a vacuum, and the guys underneath him rush up to fill the space. All you can do is hope the new guy in charge is better than the one you took out. Even better is if there's a group, like the Lucian Alliance, who are so disorganized they're too busy fighting themselves to cause trouble for everyone else."

Daniel said, "That's a bleak outlook."

"I'm not saying I like it, I'm saying it's what we're dealing with. The Lucian Alliance is a mess. They're cleaning house. There's no reason for us to go out of our way to go after them." He held up the fruit. "Do you think this rind is edible or do I have to peel it?"

Before Daniel could answer, Teal'c reappeared from wherever he'd gone. "I believe something is transpiring at the tavern."

"Again with the taverns," Cam muttered. He reached under his cloak and put a hand on the butt of his gun. "Hopefully nobody in this one decides to start throwing lanterns."

Browsing stalls had taken them far down one of the side streets, but they ran back to where they had split off from Sam and Vala. Everyone else also seemed drawn to the noise, so their attention wasn't conspicuous in and of itself. They arrived back at the tavern in time to see a flash of light in the doorway. Cam almost resisted the urge to groan, slowing down as he realized rescue was futile.

"Ah, hell, that was a transport beam wasn't it?"

"Maybe it was for someone else," Daniel suggested hopefully but unconvincingly.

They entered the bar and looked for their teammates,

but any hope was dashed. The other customers were milling around in an awkward silence. It was too soon after the scuffle for normal conversations to have resumed. A large man was shuffling toward the back of the bar. He laughed and slapped someone on the back, swaying his head from side to side with the body language of somebody who had just won a standoff. Cam made his way over to the man, slapping him on the arm. The man turned and straightened his back, revealing just how much bigger he was than the colonel.

Cam tried not to look intimidated. "Hey. There were two women in here earlier. One blonde, the other probably loud and obnoxious."

The man's face hardened into a sneer. His eyes tracked from Cam, to Daniel, to Teal'c. "More friends of Vala Mal Doran...?"

"Friends?" Cam said, thinking on the fly. "Friends?! No, we're not friends with her. We've been tracking her across seven systems waiting for the right moment to take her down. She walks in here and suddenly she vanishes. Did you help her escape?"

The man laughed. "Who are you?"

"Me? We're bounty hunters. I'm Lee Majors." He nodded at Daniel and then pointed at Teal'c. "Burt Reynolds. And the big guy... well that's Don Johnson."

"Jebauth Kavma, but you can just call me the man who stole your bounty out from under your nose. Trust me, my friend, I deserved the victory more than you did. For you, Vala Mal Doran was a job. For me, it was personal. I have been waiting for this day for years." He clapped a friendly hand on Cam's shoulder. Cam did his best not to flinch. "Come, we're all friends here. Let me buy you a drink!"

Cam twisted away from Kavma's grip. "That's all right. We don't need a drink. What do you mean it was personal?"

"Vala stole from me. She and her little friend incurred a debt. The bounty on their heads more than made up for what they took."

Daniel said, "Her little friend? Do you mean the blonde woman?"

"No, she was new. I don't know who she was, but she probably deserved to go as well. Whoever she may be, she's associating with Vala Mal Doran. Guilty by association, yes?" He gave a hearty laugh.

Cam and Daniel looked at each other. Daniel closed his eyes and nodded in silent agreement. The message had been a trap, and Vala walked them right into it. Cam bit back a sigh and focused on Kavma again.

"The bounty on Mal Doran and Reynard. Who set it up?"

Kavma started to answer, but then slowly narrowed his eyes on Cam. "If you are bounty hunters who have been on Vala's trail, should you not already know this information?"

Daniel said, "We're… independent contractors."

"What did you say your names were?"

Cam motioned for Daniel to start for the door. "You know, I think we're just going to mosey on out of here. You won, fair and square, so there's no point in dwelling on the past…"

Someone rushed Teal'c from behind. He must have seen the attack coming just in time because he put up his elbow, catching the man in the chin. Another customer grabbed Teal'c's other arm and twisted it. Teal'c spun on the ball of his foot and punched the man in his sternum. Daniel pulled the zat from his belt and managed to get off two shots before he was shoved hard against the railing. His weapon tumbled from his grip into the pit, where the bartenders kicked it out of his sight.

Kavma's hand shot out and closed around Cam's throat. Air suddenly became a luxury. As Cam's feet were lifted off the ground, he saw Teal'c receive a blow to the abdomen which sent him to his knees. He was still recovering from a brutal battle, and his opponent had gotten a very lucky blow. Others noted the weakness and focused their attack on Teal'c's midsection. He was fending them off as best he could, but there were too many.

"I think you are Vala Mal Doran's friends, Lee Majors," Kavma growled. "And perhaps I will fetch a very good price for you as well."

~#~

Teal'c was almost on his knees. Brutal fists pounded against him, blood from reopened wounds seeping through his clothes. He couldn't get his arms free to fend off the attacks, so he did the next best thing. He wrapped his arm around the closest attacker and pulled him close, squeezing him so tightly against his chest that the man couldn't draw breath. Suddenly every blow intended for Teal'c was striking the other man, giving Teal'c time to breathe. He straightened with a primal shout and threw his weight forward.

He knocked a trio of men over the railing, and they fell on top of the bartenders who didn't scatter quickly enough. He kept his left arm around his human shield as he spun and lashed out with his right hand. The mob backed up now that they had seen what he was capable of, and Teal'c dropped his now-unconscious battering ram to the floor. With visible effort he forced himself to his full height, drew the zat from his belt, and aimed it at Kavma with a hand which didn't shake.

"Release him. Now."

Daniel had his back against the wall, hands raised. "I would suggest doing what he says. You just had your debt repaid. It would be a shame if you weren't around to enjoy that, don't you think?"

Kavma considered the argument for a long second. Mitchell's eyes were unfocused, and he was slapping fruitlessly against Kavma's wrist. Finally, the big man relaxed his grip. Mitchell sucked in a deep breath and hit the ground, stumbling back upright as Daniel was also released.

"The ship that took Vala Mal Doran and her friend is already gone. You would not be worth the effort to call them back. But if I ever see your face in this establishment again — "

"Trust me, that won't be an issue," Mitchell croaked. He

rubbed his throat and backed away. "Lee Majors will never set foot on this planet again, you can count on that. Burt, Don… let's go."

Daniel offered Teal'c an arm, but Teal'c refused. It probably would have weakened his threat if he needed help walking, but he'd been hurt badly during the scuffle. Every eye was on them when they cleared the door, and from the looks they got in the square, it was obvious that sounds of the fight had traveled. Teal'c saw sunlight glinting on mostly-concealed weapons as they passed but he didn't meet anyone's gaze in case they took it as a challenge.

"I'll go dial the Gate," Daniel said, an acknowledgment that he was the most unscathed of the group. "I assume we're going back to Earth so we can regroup."

Cam said, "Yeah. We need to figure out our next move. Because right now, Carter and Vala are en route to the worst prison in the galaxy, and rescuing them is definitely a mission Landry and O'Neill will sign off on. We need to figure out a way to get them back." Daniel hurried up the stone path to the Stargate. Mitchell looked at Teal'c. "And hopefully Landry has some idea of what our first step should be 'cause, Teal'c, buddy, I don't even have a clue where to start looking."

CHAPTER FIVE

SAM KEPT her head down, chin on her chest, even after regaining consciousness. She was sitting propped up against the wall, legs stretched out in front of her, with her hands enclosed by something heavy and metallic. She knew she was aboard a ship; she could feel the vibrations in the hull and hear the hum of engines somewhere to her right. People were moving around on the opposite side of the space from her but no one was speaking. She tried to determine how long she'd been unconscious. She'd never heard of anyone being knocked out by a zat for more than an hour, but there were people who only reported losing stretches of ten minutes. And in situations like this, a lot could happen in ten minutes.

Someone kicked her boot. "We know you're awake, Vala's friend. No point faking."

She raised her head and looked up to see a small man with a misshapen head looming over her. Behind him she got a sense of the room she was in: cramped, stacked with unmarked crates and oddly-shaped. It took a moment for her to realize that the slope of the ceiling and angle of the walls indicated they were being kept in a hidden compartment. They were probably aboard a ship normally used for smuggling. This time, she and Vala were the cargo.

Her jailor had a small black mustache over twisted, puffy lips that seemed to plump up when he smiled. "You were a bonus," he said with either a lisp or an accent. "It wasn't personal against you. We didn't even know Vala had taken up with a new partner. But you surely knew this was a risk when you started working with her. You got a name?"

Their most recent encounter with the Lucian Alliance had proven SG-1's names were well-known throughout the galaxy, but it seemed their faces weren't quite as famous. She knew Mitchell or General O'Neill would be able to come up with something witty or clever on the fly, but her mind was a blank for pop culture references. She said the first name that came to mind.

"The name is Fraiser."

He put a hand flat on his chest. "I am Nyoman, and I am afraid that is the extent of our politeness, because you have no reason to be polite to someone in my position. You see, I am tasked with escorting the lady Mal Doran - along with anyone unfortunate enough to be in her company - to a place called Viaxeiro. It… is not a nice place."

Sam said, "I'm familiar with it."

"Mm-hmm," Nyoman said. "Its reputation is quite well-known in your circles. Criminals, I mean to say." He reached up and touched his bulbous forehead with two fingers. "We're not taking the most direct route to it. There's not exactly such a thing as a direct route to Viaxeiro. That's part of its appeal. But we're also being sure no one can follow us. Cautious-like. So hopefully you'll be nice and snug for the trip."

She smiled tightly up at him. "I doubt my comfort is high on your list of concerns."

"You may be right there, Fraiser," he said as he walked to the door, "but feel free to complain as much as you want. We'll be right out here ready to cater to your every need."

The door hissed shut behind him.

Vala said, "Quick thinking on the fake name."

Sam had to lean forward to see her. She was on the other side of a protrusion in the ship's hull. She was lying on her side like a dropped doll, her hands bound like Sam's but her cuffs were connected to a second pair on her ankles. She pushed herself up with a quiet grunt, flipped her hair out of her face and opened her eyes.

"Fraiser. Isn't that a television program?"

"She was a friend," Sam said. "You don't happen to recognize that guy, do you?"

"Nyoman? No." She squirmed in an attempt to find a more comfortable position. "Afraid not. He's unimportant, anyway. Just a lackey deliveryman, hired the same way Kavma was."

Sam said, "Great. And I don't suppose you have any theories about who could be behind this?"

"Oh, suspects? I have suspects. It's quite a list."

"I'll bet," Sam said. "How long have you been conscious?"

Vala said, "Only a few minutes. Long enough to overhear their plan includes taking us through at least three Stargates."

Sam closed her eyes and bumped her head against the wall behind her. "Fantastic. So much for Cam and the others following our trail."

"We still have the implant tracker chip thingies!" Vala's cheerful voice sounded forced. "The one your doctor implanted in my arm. They can just transport us out of anywhere we go."

Sam kept her eyes closed. "That's assuming they have the slightest idea where to look. And if this Viaxeiro place is as inescapable as you make it out to be, I'm sure they have some method of blocking the signal from getting through even if the *Odyssey* did miraculously show up in orbit. We're going to be just as trapped as Tanis."

Vala's smile collapsed. "Oh."

"Yeah."

"Well… on the bright side…"

Sam opened her eyes and glared across the room.

"Right." Vala withdrew. "Not in the mood for bright sides. Got it."

"If they're planning to take us through multiple gates, that will be our best opportunity to escape. Do you know how many other people are aboard?"

"At least three," Vala said. "There's probably more, but not many. I've been on ships like this before. They're cramped with a crew larger than six. If there were that many people running around we'd definitely hear them."

Sam said, "Okay. So three to five, let's say. Not the worst odds, but…"

"I don't recommend it."

"As you so helpfully pointed out when you suggested this mission, SG-1 has been captured a few times before."

"Yes, SG-1! As in you, two large men, and Teal'c. The odds are slightly more in your favor as a group. I, on the other hand, have more experience being captured alone or with one other woman. Trust me, Samantha, these aren't men we want to cross. We should wait until we get to the prison when we have more time to plan."

"Vala, if we have a chance to avoid being sent to the prison, we have to take it."

"It's a bad plan," Vala said.

"It's our only shot. We can't guarantee what will happen once we're at Viaxeiro."

Vala grunted in frustration, baring her teeth. "Could you please just *listen* to me for once? This is General O'Neill's cabin all over again!"

Sam furrowed her brow. "What are you talking about?"

"I told you it was unwise to traipse through the forest hunting those creatures, and that a better plan would be drawing them to us. Then, I pointed out how odd it was for a creature to attack us the way it did. You all ignored me and nearly got poor General Landry torn apart! And did I say anything? Did I even offer a very well-earned 'I told you so'? No. I did not."

"Vala…"

"Not to mention I put my very life at risk to warn the SGC about the Ori attack. I made that plan all by myself and I think it worked out fairly well, all things considered. But that is a whole different matter!"

"Vala, you—"

"No! I'm speaking. At the cabin, if Mitchell or Daniel had suggested waiting until morning to go after the creature, you all would have at least *considered* it. But no, because it came from me, someone who is now an official member of your team with a fancy arm patch and everything, it was dismissed out of hand. I'm not just going to drop it this time. You may be an astrophysicist and a colonel in the Air Force, but this is *my* area of expertise, and we're dealing with my life just as much as yours, so I'm going to call the shots."

Sam said, "Are you done?"

"Yes."

"I was going to say you're right."

Vala huffed. "Oh."

Sam sighed and looked toward the door. "You do have a lot of experience with saving yourself from situations like this. And you have been a full member of the team for a while now. We can't count on the rest of SG-1 or the SGC for backup. So— why do you think it's a bad idea to try escaping?"

"These people obviously set the trap for me. They didn't expect you and don't know what you'd probably be worth to the right bounty hunter. So if we make a fuss, you're going to be the one they attack to make sure I stay in line."

Sam scowled. "That's a fair point."

"Mm-hmm. It'll be much safer for both of us if we wait until we're actually at the prison to make our escape. There has to be opportunities. Prisoner drop-offs, staff that comes and goes, supply ships. Between the two of us, we should be able to fig-ure out a way to hijack one of them and find our way home."

"You claim Viaxeiro is inescapable, but you're equally cer-tain there's a way out?"

"Never thought anyone could use a Stargate to blow up a sun. I don't think anything is impossible when you're involved. Escaping right now is just needlessly dangerous. We should wait until we're at the prison where you'll have time to think of a solid plan." She rested her head against the wall. "You'll figure it out."

"No one bats a thousand all the time. One of these days I'm bound to come up short."

Vala chuckled under her breath. "I have faith."

"Yeah?"

"I spent my entire adult life avoiding prison or capture of any sort. Here I am, walking into the place parents use to scare kids into staying on the straight and narrow, and I'm calm as can be. Why? Because I'm going in with you. So I know I'm not going to be there long. This is just another adventure, part of being a member of SG-1."

Sam had to smile. "I wish I had some of that confidence."

"It's okay. I have more than enough for the both of us."

Sam chuckled. There was a change of pitch in the engine noise, indicating they had just drastically reduced speed. Sam's good humor faded.

"Okay, moment of truth. You're absolutely certain escape is the wrong move?"

"One hundred percent," Vala said. "We're completely out-matched right now. The smarter move is to cooperate until we have more information."

The door opened and Nyoman returned. This time he was accompanied by two larger men carrying Goa'uld pain sticks. He smiled at Vala.

"Ah, so good you've joined us. We're about to arrive at our first destination. Are you ladies going to cooperate or are we going to have to use some… persuasion?"

The goons were clearly hoping for the latter. One of them twirled the stick between his thumb and forefinger, eager for the chance to use it. Sam envisioned several versions of the next few minutes, all of which would require taking out all three men without one of the pain sticks making contact with her skin. There was also the fact that, if she attacked them, one of the men might be clever enough to threaten Vala instead of joining the fray. She would be helpless if she was jabbed with those sticks. Vala's plan to just go along with their transport went against everything she believed, but she couldn't deny it was the right thing to do.

"We'll go quietly," Sam said.

Nyoman beamed. "Excellent news! On your feet, ladies."

The goons, disappointed, put down the pain sticks and moved to help Sam and Vala stand up. One clamped his hand on Sam's elbow while the other bent down to unlock Vala's feet. He pulled her up and closed his hand high on the shoulder near her neck, then squeezed hard enough to make Vala's entire body twist.

"Watch it!" Vala said. "Don't want to bruise the merchandise."

Nyoman said, "We're supposed to bring you in alive. No one said anything about unmarked. You just keep that in mind."

They were marched out of the cramped closet and into a corridor. Two more men were armed with pistols she'd seen the Lucian Alliance carry. Just a few weeks ago, SG-1 had been targeted by the Alliance because Netan was sick of them messing with his plans. Bounty hunters descended on Earth in the hopes of cashing in on the high price the team would get. Sam knew that the solution they'd come up with hadn't been permanent, but she'd hoped it would be a little longer before she had to deal with bounty hunters again.

Nyoman urged them forward, around a corner to a large hatch which was standing open to the emptiness of space. Sam saw the shimmer of a force field, but the sight was still enough to make her blood go cold. Her "fight back" scenario now included a moment when Nyoman decided to cut his losses and order the force field to be dropped.

"What is this?" Sam said. "I thought we'd landed."

"Neutral territory." Nyoman put a hand on her shoulder and pushed her forward. "We don't trust the fellows we're meeting, and they don't trust us. This is a compromise. We let go of you, they deliver our payment, and they're free to snatch you up."

"And if they don't snatch us up?" Sam said.

"Not really my problem as long as I get my fee, love."

One of the goons opened a panel on the wall and withdrew a pair of bizarre facemasks. Each one was comprised of two eyepieces with a rubber seal over a circular metallic lock that would fit over their nose and mouth. He handed one to Nyoman and began to put the other on Vala.

"Get that thing away from me!"

Nyoman sighed. "This is a breather. It won't keep you alive, but it'll stop you from dying just long enough for the other ship to pull you aboard. That's all it is."

Sam nodded slightly. No point in fighting, and it was the only way they'd survive what was about to happen. The ironic thing was that she'd done this before, just from the other end. She used the rings to pull General O'Neill and Teal'c out of a malfunctioning glider using the same risky maneuver. She was sure Jack would appreciate the tables being turned, if she lived long enough to tell him about it.

Nyoman moved them closer to the open door and stood between them. Sam could feel the energy of the force field on her bits of exposed skin. She knew that what was about to happen was survivable, but she also knew enough about the science to be wary. Vala looked at her, eyes magnified to a comical size by the lenses. One of the men responded to a chirp from the control panel and moved to read the screen.

"They're ready to initiate the transfer."

Nyoman put his hands on their shoulders. "Well, my dears, it's been lovely having you as guests on my ship. Thank you for not making our time together any more difficult than it had to be. I would wish you fair travels until our paths meet again, but whether you die in the next few seconds or actually make it to your destination, I doubt we will ever meet again in this cycle. So I will simply say, good—"

The end of the word was cut off as they were shoved through the force field. The energy momentarily buzzed in Sam's ears, like a static shock from touching a doorknob spread out over her entire body. She was suddenly and unexpectedly weightless, hands still bound as if she were praying. She twisted and saw Vala floating nearby. A freighter loomed above them, huge and immobile. There was no sign of the rings being deployed. If she and Vala drifted too far from each other, or if they were exposed to the vacuum for too long, or…

She counted off the seconds in her head as she waited for the rings to deploy. She got to nine before she began to panic. At thirteen, she saw the bottom of the ship open and braced herself for a sudden return to atmosphere. They vanished in a flash of light, off on the next leg of their journey.

CHAPTER SIX

CAM'S GRANDMA swore by her hot toddy remedy for a sore throat: honey and ginger mixed in a tall glass of warm tea. Of course, when he got older he realized that his grandma always used whiskey when she made it for herself, and he wasn't exactly suffering from a real sore throat, but the mixture still helped. He wasn't coughing as much as he had when they first got back from Pezjena. Landry was understandably annoyed that they'd managed to lose both Vala and Carter, therefore necessitating the rescue mission. Landry wasn't too keen on the mission in the first place. Now that they were being forced to do it, he was grumpier than usual.

The worst part was that for the moment, they couldn't do anything at all. The ship which had taken their teammates was no doubt long gone from the planet even before SG-1 had gone into the bar. In the time it would take the *Odyssey* to get to the system, any hint of a trail would've been a distant memory. It wasn't like they could just waltz back into the tavern and start asking questions. He hated being on the base with only part of his team. They needed to be out there kicking down doors and getting answers, but he didn't even know where to start.

Faced with no other possibility, he took his hot toddy tea down to the infirmary to check on the one imperiled member of his team whose whereabouts he actually knew. He arrived just as Carolyn Lam was walking toward her office, and he quickened his pace to keep up with her.

"Doctor Lam."

She turned around and her eyes immediately went to the coffee cup in his hand. "Is that for me?"

He was thrown. "No. Why would I bring you coffee?"

"Sometimes people bring me things." She continued on

her way, marking something on the chart she was carrying. "Nice people."

He chuckled. "I'll keep that in mind. I was actually just going to check on Teal'c. How's he doing?"

She sighed and stopped. "Well, technically, he's doing better than you are, since he actually agreed to be checked out."

"I'm fine."

"Dr. Jackson said you were lifted off the ground by your throat."

"He... exaggerates."

She looked pointedly at his bruised neck. "Really."

He tugged at the collar of his uniform in a futile attempt to cover the bruises.

Carolyn sighed and looked at her chart. "Teal'c is in pretty rough shape, despite what he might say. He never allowed himself to completely heal after the peace summit attack. Then he ran off and almost got himself killed by Arkad."

"He also got in a brawl with me."

Carolyn raised an eyebrow.

"Oh, come on, I did a little damage."

"Of course you did." She folded her arms with the chart against her chest. "Look, Teal'c's been through a lot recently. He spent a century with a symbiote which took care of every injury he got and I think he's still getting used to the idea that his wounds won't heal as easily anymore."

Cam's expression darkened. "Yeah, that's a pretty tough pill for anyone to swallow. I'll talk to him."

"Good luck."

"You have to understand, it's not as easy as... just... taking it easy. When you're in the thick of things, you don't always have time to think about how dangerous it is. Sometimes you've just got to throw yourself into the fire and hope for the best. It's easy to sit here at the SGC and count scars and tell us we're pushing ourselves too far when you haven't actually seen what we're going through out there."

"Are you saying I don't understand you?" Carolyn said, her voice was light, but Cam could tell she was offended.

"I didn't mean that. And I'm not implying anything about your mettle or whatever. But we're on the front lines. We're going to get a few bumps and bruises along the way."

"Well, if you aren't careful, one of these days you'll get a bump or bruise that you can't come back from." Carolyn started back toward her office. "Oh, and Colonel…"

"I'll let one of your nurses check me out before I go."

She said, "That's all I ask."

Cam continued into the main room of the infirmary, where Teal'c was resting in one of the beds along the far wall. Compared to the last two times he'd been laid up in the infirmary, he didn't look bad at all. There was a darkening bruise on his chin and a bandage on his upper arm. Most of the damage was from previous injuries which were aggravated by the brawl. Carolyn was probably only keeping him in the infirmary so long as a punishment for getting hurt yet again. It was the SGC equivalent of a time-out.

Teal'c turned his head slightly at Cam's approach but gave no other indication he was no longer alone. Cam took a seat next to the bed and waited. Teal'c waited.

"So…"

"I assure you," Teal'c interrupted, "anything you are preparing to say has been said, at length, by Dr. Lam and her staff."

Cam said, "Oh, I don't know. I probably have a few insights they don't have. I know what it's like to be lying in that bed, man. You're hurting like you've never hurt before, and you think it might not ever get better. You think, this is what it's gonna be from now on. This pain. Feeling weak. And then one morning you wake up and it doesn't hurt as bad, so you're ready to jump right back in and prove you're the same guy you were before. I hate to break it to you, buddy, but you're not the same guy you were before. I never knew you when you had… when you were, uh…"

"Junior."

"What?"

"O'Neill referred to my symbiote as Junior. I believe the name made it easier for him to discuss."

Cam said, "You're probably right about that. Anyway. I have no doubt you were a big, badass Jaffa in those days, but I've only known you on tretonin. And you're still the biggest, baddest guy I've ever served with. But you need to give yourself time to heal. Especially after the things you've gone through lately. You were in a coma for two weeks, and Lam thought you might never walk again. And then you picked a fight with a guy who was stronger and more brutal than you ever were. He ran you through with a damn sword! And you're still not giving yourself time to heal."

Teal'c worked his jaw for a long moment before he responded. "Arkad taunted me during our fight. He called me soft… frail. I believe he spoke the truth."

"Come on, man."

"He was not referring to the tretonin. He spoke instead of my time among the Tau'ri. I found it difficult to counter his argument. I am no longer the warrior I once was."

Cam sighed. "So what if you're not? What does that even mean? That you're not out there choosing which people to slaughter so others can survive? You made a lot of choices in the name of the greater good back in the day, and to me, that makes you a greater warrior than anyone with a higher body count. Anyone can kill. You found ways to save people. And sure, you had to kill sometimes. But you're not that man anymore. You were a conqueror, now you're a soldier. You're a diplomat. You're a politician. You're still doing the same thing you always did. You're still fighting to help people, just without as much bloodshed."

Teal'c said nothing.

"The point is, we need you out there as much as we always did. You think you're just the muscle? We just want you around to bust heads? You're so much more than that. You're the comic relief."

He turned his head and raised his eyebrow.

Cam sighed. "Okay, that was a joke. But I'm dead serious. Teal'c, you're the guy who stood up against false gods and knocked them off their pedestals. You were one of the first dudes to turn against a false religion, turn against a man you were taught to worship as a god, and you got to see him die. We're out there dealing with die-hard Ori worshippers who need to hear that from someone who has been there. You might be the only hope we have of convincing them they have a chance, and you're not going to do that by busting their heads."

Teal'c locked his gaze on the ceiling.

Cam put his hand on Teal'c's shoulder. "The point is, it was never about how much punishment you can take or how many guys you can fight at once. You are still the same man. Just like I'm the same guy I was before the crash. We're just fighting in different ways now. Come back when you're ready."

He waited for acknowledgement, but Teal'c continued to stare at the ceiling, unmoving. Cam took a deep breath and stood up. "I'm going to go see if Jackson's come up with any bright ideas. I'll come check on you later."

He was at the door before Teal'c spoke. "Colonel Mitchell."

"Yeah?"

Teal'c still wasn't looking at him. "Thank you."

"Any time, buddy."

He wasn't sure if he'd actually gotten through or if Teal'c simply appreciated the effort he'd taken. Either way, he knew one pep talk wasn't going to permanently solve anything. But if it kept Teal'c in the infirmary until Dr. Lam agreed to release him, then he'd take it as a victory.

~#~

Landry couldn't say he was happy. But he also couldn't be overly upset, since the parameters he laid out gave SG-1 final say in whether to continue with the mission. In a way, they were doing exactly that. They chose to go ahead. He just wished they weren't being forced into the choice. He hated the fact that two members of the team were now God-knew-where in the clutches of God-knew-who, but that was simply how things seemed to go at this base. He couldn't predict how or where a mission could go wrong. He could only trust his people to do the best with the hands they were dealt. That didn't mean it would be easy to explain to the IOA how he'd lost track of someone as important as Samantha Carter. He wanted to have a plan before he even revealed the situation.

Unfortunately, Daniel wasn't of much help on that front. "Even if we sent in another team he wouldn't recognize, I highly doubt this Kavma guy would be forthcoming with information. Trapping Vala and Tanis to hand them over to this prison was personal for him. He did it because Vala had stolen from him. We're not going to convince him to help us."

Landry went to the carafe by the window to refill his mug. "Assuming he wouldn't just lie and trap the rest of SG-1 the way he did Carter. Guilt by association, I think he said."

"Right," Daniel said. "Well, we don't necessarily have to worry about tracking them. We know exactly where they'll end up, we just don't know where that is."

"So all we have to do is find the unfindable, inescapable prison and have the *Odyssey* swing by to pick them up. We can beam them out, or put boots on the ground. Either way, we'll get them back." He hefted the carafe. It seemed emptier than it should've been, but he couldn't imagine who would dare to sneak coffee from his office. "When you put it like that, it sounds simple."

"Doesn't it?" Daniel said.

Landry took his coffee back behind his desk and took a seat. "I could try explaining to them that the purpose of this mission was to prevent situations just like this. If we had assets inside the Lucian Alliance to turn to, maybe they could provide leads we could follow to find this damn prison." Daniel's posture changed slightly, just enough that Landry could tell he'd had an idea. He raised his eyebrows. "Dr. Jackson?"

"Well… we don't exactly have an asset within the Lucian Alliance. I wouldn't necessarily call him an ally, either."

"What would you call him?"

"Someone who is willing to listen to reason under the right circumstances."

Landry said, "And you know where to find him?"

"Not exactly. But he has to be easier to find than Viaxeiro. After the *Odyssey* was captured by the Alliance, Vala worked with SG-12 to come up with a list of gate addresses that used to be Goa'uld strongholds but are turning into bases of operation for the Lucian Alliance. Uh, shipbuilding facilities turned into chop shops, weapons manufacturers turned into arms dealers, that sort of thing. Major Escher has been assembling a whole dossier on the Lucian Alliance since we first learned of their existence. I could check in with him to see if he knows the best place to start. I think it's worth the effort of looking, sir. If Vala's right about the prison's reputation, then the man I'm thinking of will be able to point us in the right direction."

"Don't leave me in suspense, son. Who is this man?"

"Odai Ventrell."

Landry's smile faded. "The bounty hunter who took Colonel Mitchell and Vala hostage at his high school reunion?"

"The bounty hunter who was trying to collect on a bounty, but let us go when we gave him a better payday. He listened to reason. It wasn't personal, it was just business. I think we have a good chance to convince him to help us."

"Out of the goodness of his heart?" Landry said.

"We'll negotiate. Find something he wants that we're willing to give. I mean, this is Sam and Vala we're talking about. He might ask for something big in return for his help, but considering what's at risk…"

Landry considered it. "Violent?"

Daniel hesitated before answering. "To a degree. But when

he took everyone hostage at the reunion, he didn't kill them or threaten them." He winced. "Well, he did threaten them. But when he thought Sam, Teal'c, and I were surrendering, he ordered us to come down unarmed. That indicates he wasn't interested in a firefight. I think it's a calculated risk."

"As much as I hate to say it, I agree. We're not going to find this prison if we only deal with nice people. This Ventrell sounds just gray enough for me to approve the mission. You'll go with Mitchell. I want Teal'c to remain here, just this once."

"You mean Carolyn wants him to stay."

Landry held his hands out, helpless. "Who knew she could pull rank on me?"

Daniel smiled. "Jack used to have the same problem remembering that. Never get on the base doctor's bad side." He stood up. "I'll go find Mitchell to let him know we're shipping out. When is the next window?"

"We'll squeeze you in as soon as you have a gate address. No need to make Colonel Carter and Vala wait any longer than necessary for their rescue."

"Right. I'll let Cam know."

"Good luck."

Daniel left the office and went to find Mitchell. He couldn't help but feel they were bound for disaster. Sam could take care of herself, and Vala was savvy in her own way, but the odds were stacked against them. They were trying to break their friends out of Alcatraz with the added difficulty of not knowing where in the ocean Alcatraz was. They had their work cut out for them and it seemed like failure was all but guaranteed. There was only one thing he was absolutely sure about—he did not want to be the one who told Jack they'd lost Sam.

CHAPTER SEVEN

OTHER THAN the impromptu spacewalk, Sam and Vala's transfer was rather mundane. Sam held to her promise not to make trouble. The men and women who had been charged with taking them from one place to the next were silent and businesslike. Sam and Vala remained bound, escorted from a ship to a Stargate, through a dark building to another ship, to a shuttle, to another planet where they were shoved through another Stargate. Now they were waiting through their longest stop, which also turned out to be their last, on what Sam had finally decided was a space station. A few members of the crew had ventured out while the rest stood guard.

Sam spent the whole time watching for an opportunity to present itself. All it would take was one lucky break. If she could overpower whoever was guarding her the next time they used a Stargate, she could punch in the address to a friendly world. It didn't matter how twisted their trip got, she just needed seven glyphs and the smallest of openings.

But she couldn't act. She couldn't guarantee Vala would be able to escape with her in a situation like that, and she wasn't going to abandon her.

Eventually they were taken from the station to another ship. She'd lost track of how long they'd been in transit when their latest captor strolled into the cabin where they'd been placed. Sam braced herself to be led out of the ship to another temple or cracked stone dais overgrown with weeds, but the man knelt in front of her and slid back a panel on her restraints. She watched as he punched in a code and the metal released its grip with a quiet puff of air. She pulled her hands free and flexed her fingers.

"So I guess this means we've arrived at our destination."

"At last," Vala said. She was lying on her back with her legs stretching up the wall, boots crossed at the ankles. She rolled to one side and sat up on her knees, holding out her arms to have her restraints taken off as well. "If I had to be marched up another stone dais to another Stargate, I was going to absolutely scream."

The captain of their current ship came in. "You are now inhabitants of the prison Viaxeiro. Your safety is your own concern. The staff is only here to prevent escapes. You are not sentenced. You are here for the rest of your miserable lives. If another inhabitant decides to end your stay at the end of a blade, then that's one less person to keep an eye on. They will most likely not harm you directly, but they will also not come to your aid. Do not expect them to."

Sam said, "Sounds cozy."

He pushed up his sleeve and checked a screen strapped to his forearm. "You are Vala Mal Doran and her apprentice, Fraiser. Correct?"

"That's right," Sam said.

He punched something on the screen and covered it with his sleeve again. He motioned to the henchman, who grabbed the shoulder of Sam's jacket and shoved her toward the door. She stumbled slightly but managed to remain upright. Vala avoided the silent man's hand, glaring at him as she followed Sam out of the room. The captain and his goon followed them to the open door of the vessel. This time they'd actually landed and, through the open door, Sam could see a stretch of sandy ground lit by an unnatural red-orange glow.

The captain stopped them on the ramp and looked back into the ship. "Clear?"

"We're… oops! Spoke too soon. We've got one."

"Hold one mo', ladies. Can't let you out yet. But you can enjoy the show." He pointed outside. "Consider it a warning."

At first Sam didn't know what she was supposed to be looking at. Then she saw movement, a woman running full-speed toward the ship.

Sam leaned closer to Vala. "I thought this place was supposed to be escape-proof."

"That's the story, anyway."

The captain asked his crewman, "How close do you figure they'll let her get?"

"Not much further than this."

The woman was close enough now that Sam could make out the details of her clothes. She was only about a hundred yards from the ramp when her foot came down on a dune and her entire body went rigid. She was frozen in place, arms tight to her chest, face frozen in pain as she seized. She didn't even manage to scream before her body went limp. She collapsed in a heap, arms out to her sides, completely still.

"Sensors under the sand," the captain explained. "Trip enough of 'em while going the wrong direction, you get fried. Turns a life sentence into a death sentence." He smiled at them. "My advice is to keep going forward until you hit the wall."

Sam and Vala exchanged a look.

The captain said, "Welcome to Viaxeiro, your new home for the rest of your miserable thieving lives. Get the hell out of my ship."

~#~

Sam distracted herself from despair by focusing on the specifics of where they were. The ship had dumped them on a large stretch of open land resembling a salt plain. The ground was flat and featureless, covered with a thin layer of minerals that crunched under their boots as they walked. She tried to spot the landmines that had killed the woman, but they were either buried deep or camouflaged. The sand seemed to shine due to the brightness of the glow overhead, and Sam wished she had goggles or some kind of eye protection to block some of the glare.

Unfortunately, they hadn't been left with much of anything in the way of gear. It was the first time since being abducted they'd had a chance to take inventory, and it seemed as if they'd been stripped of all the weapons and gear they'd brought from the SGC. Sam was particularly worried about the loss of her GDO. Without it, even if they got to a Stargate, they wouldn't be able to open the door to get through.

But there was no point thinking about that while they were still trapped. A few minutes earlier, they'd watched the vessel which delivered them rise off the surface. The sand kicked up by its launch covered up the dead prisoner's body, effectively burying her. There had been a frisson of energy along the ship's hull once it reached a certain altitude and then, in an instant, it was gone through the barrier. Sam could see a wall which looked manmade looming in the distance. With no other options, they began walking toward it.

"What did you call this again?" Vala asked, putting up her hair to get it off her neck. It wasn't particularly hot, but they'd been walking long enough for her to sweat. "Plan-um? Planet-oid?"

"Planemo," Sam said. "It's a rogue planet. It was probably pushed out of its solar system by the gasses released by other planets forming around it. Once it's free of the star's gravity, it just drifts through the galaxy." She tilted her head up to look at the sky. "There shouldn't be anything to support life on this rock. Air, atmosphere, gravity: it all has to be manufactured somehow. Someone went to a lot of trouble to make this one habitable."

As they got closer, Sam could see that there was definitely a wall cutting across the landscape. She estimated it ran for at least three miles in either direction before curving out of sight. It was broken into segments by large beehive-like structures. Wide tri-barreled guns poked out from each guard tower, aimed at the sky. The wall was only about seven feet high, more symbolic of a border than an actual barrier. A series of archways ran along its length, all but one of them bricked up or covered by iron latticework. When they were close enough to make out details of the structure, Sam could see small windows carved into the stone at regular intervals. A shrill whistle sounded, followed by a hollow boom deeper in the… prison? Structure? City? Sam wasn't entirely sure what she was walking into, but she was prepared for anything.

"It's enormous," Vala said. "How are we ever going to find Tanis in a place like this?"

Sam looked at her. "Vala…"

"What? We're still going to rescue her, right? That much hasn't changed. And look, we're here now!"

"Yes, if we have the chance, we'll explore the possibility of freeing Tanis. But right now, our priority is getting ourselves out. If the opportunity arises before we can find her, we're going to leave without her. Is that understood?"

Vala pushed her bottom lip out, arms crossed over her chest.

"Vala? I have to hear you say it's understood."

"Or what? You'll leave me to rot in here, too?"

Sam closed her eyes and bit back a sigh. "We have no idea what we're walking into here, Vala. We have no plan, no backup, and no idea how we're going to get home. Until we can answer those questions, my priority is keeping the both of us alive. The welfare of Tanis Reynard isn't even on the first page of my to-do list. I'm sorry if that hurts your feelings, but that's just the way it has to be."

Vala pouted for another few steps. Finally she said, "Understood, Colonel."

Sam knew the matter wasn't settled, but Vala had surrendered the battle. That was good enough for the time being. She saw movement in one of the portholes carved next to the unbarred entrance. Seconds later she saw someone drop down to the ground on the other side of the wall. The woman's shouting echoed off the buildings around her.

"New condemned! New condemned!"

Vala said, "Looks like they're going to know we're coming."

"Maybe they'll bring us a fruit basket. If Tanis is part of

our welcoming party, we should try to be sure that she sees you first."

"Why?"

Sam said, "It's been a long time, but there's a chance she'll recognize me from our run-in. We weren't exactly on the same side that day. She may hold a grudge."

Vala nodded. "That's true."

A crowd had gathered by the time they passed through the opening in the wall. Fashion seemed to be vaguely uniform, with slight variances accounting for different worlds and cultures. One woman seemed to be wearing a toga underneath a handknit sweater, while another wore leather pants under a matching top with a series of straps crossing her shoulders. Sam scanned the crowd and noticed something else was uniform about their fellow condemned.

"Vala..."

"Mm-hmm?"

"Is this a women's prison?"

Vala slowly looked at the women around them. "It would certainly seem to be, based on the evidence before us."

Sam stepped in front of her. "You never mentioned that. Not in the briefing, not during the hours we spent being shuffled back and forth to get here. Not once did it come up."

"Why is it important now?"

"It's making me question why you insisted on meeting Tanis's contact with me and none of the guys. It makes me wonder if you knew it was a trap all along."

"I am offended at the implication —"

Sam cut her off. "We'll discuss this later."

She faced forward again as a tall woman stepped through the gathered crowd. Her curly red hair was piled in a knot at the back of her head, several strands falling loose along the side of her face. She wore a bright orange blouse with a black Cossack collar. It was cinched at the waist with a black belt which held a sheathed knife. Two women approached with her, one on either side, dressed alike in black-and-orange uniforms. They eyed Sam and Vala carefully as the older woman bowed a greeting and spread her hands to indicate the city.

"Welcome to Viaxeiro. My name is Lokelani Kiir. Who might you be?"

"I'm Fraiser," Sam said. "This is Vala."

Lokelani looked at her with newfound interest. "We know of the great Vala Mal Doran. You have quite a following here."

"A following, hmm?" Vala threw her shoulders back and lifted her chin as if posing for a painting. She smiled at Sam. "I have fans."

Sam rolled her eyes.

Lokelani motioned for them to follow her. She turned and began to walk away without making sure they complied, but the uniformed women waited to bring up the rear. Sam caught up with her first, and Vala nodded and waved to the people she passed who were now whispering and smiling at her. Sam ignored her and focused on the layout of the city. It looked like a thousand other planets SG-1 had visited over the years, with blocks of apartments and small stone buildings she assumed were either stores or some other place of business. There were domestic touches like benches and plants growing from clay pots which indicated at least some of the women considered it a home instead of a cage. People came out onto rooftop balconies and stared down as they passed, eager for a glimpse of the newest arrivals.

"It looks like you don't get a lot of new neighbors around here," Sam said.

"Oh, it's common enough," Lokelani said. "But the novelty never really wears off. There are about a thousand of us here, give or take. Older prisoners die off, the young and impetuous try to escape, and the number stays relatively the same. But we all remember when we were new. We remember how frightening it was to arrive in a place that is called inescapable, told this is where we'll spend the rest of our lives. It helps to be greeted by a friendly face. We've made this world into something unique, a place where we can coexist with one another."

Sam said, "What about the guards?"

"Oh, they're around." Lokelani pursed her lips and nodded her head to the right, indicating a man in an armored blue vest, sleeveless and snug at the throat. A helmet obscured most of his face, but he was clearly male. It was the first man Sam had seen since leaving the ship, and also the first person carrying a weapon. She didn't recognize the design, but the object strapped to his wrist so that it rested against his palm was clearly intended to be used like a taser. He ignored them as they passed. "They tend not to interfere with us any more than they have to. Their purpose is to prevent escape attempts which, as I'm sure you can guess, aren't very difficult to thwart."

Sam said, "The shuttles always land out in that wide open space?"

Lokelani nodded. "No one could cross that distance without being seen, so no one could get to the shuttles before an alarm went up. A few have tried, but they all failed. Their punishment was swift and cruel. According to the lookouts, you saw what happens to anyone who tries to escape."

"The landmines," Sam said. "So the punishment for escape is instant death?"

"Not always. If an escapee is caught early enough, the guards can make examples out of them."

"Okay. Message received."

"So for the most part, the guards simply laze about until their shifts end. They don't interfere with us unless they have to. That is why I established the Cai Thior." She indicated the uniformed women who had silently flanked Sam and Vala. "They maintain order. Settle disputes. Ensure the safety of the condemned, although I don't like thinking of them as such. We are neighbors and fellow citizens. We didn't get the choice of where we ended up, but that's no reason we should act like animals."

Sam watched the bored-looking guards. "They don't seem very alert."

"Of course not. They have nothing to be alert for." Lokelani looked at Sam again and smiled. It was a rather cold smile, at odds with her otherwise friendly disposition. "We've gone to great lengths to make this world comfortable for its inhabitants. Why would we attempt to escape when we have everything we need right here?"

"No men," Vala muttered under her breath.

Lokelani stared at her again, and Sam wondered if Vala was risking her celebrity status. "There are sacrifices which had to be made in the name of peace and solitude, yes. Fraiser… I'll leave you now so you may take in your surroundings. While you are exploring, we will prepare a place for you to stay. Only temporary, until you find a place that suits you better."

"We appreciate that," Sam said. "Thank you."

Lokelani touched Sam's shoulder and started to leave.

"There's one other thing," Sam said. Lokelani paused. "We think someone we know was sent here, maybe a few weeks ago. Her name is Tanis Reynard."

Lokelani's smile wavered. Her new expression was impossible to read. "There's a wine district not far from here." She gestured to the right, again using her lips and chin, a move Sam assumed was cultural. "You can normally find Miss Reynard there at this time of day."

"Thank you," Sam said again.

"Settle well," Lokelani said.

When she was gone, Vala moved closer to Sam. "Thank you for asking about Tanis."

"Sure." Sam was still watching Lokelani and the Cai Thior women. "Did something seem off about her to you?"

"Well, she's not a fan of Tanis, that's for sure."

Sam nodded. There was still a small crowd of people around, watching them while keeping a modest distance. Sam wondered what these women had done to deserve confinement. Every person they'd seen so far, presumably with the exception of the guards, had committed a crime so heinous they were thrown into the deepest, darkest dungeon in the universe.

"Welcome to the island of misfit toys," she said under her breath.

"What's that?"

"Never mind. Come on."

They started walking. The streets were narrow and without any rational arrangement. Some points were wide enough for two cars to pass each other, while others were so tight that Sam could have reached out with both hands and touched a building on either side. Occasionally the street would widen into a common area, where prisoners had created community gardens, somehow forcing plants and vegetables to grow despite the apparently arid ground.

Vala stuck her hands in her back pockets as they walked. She finally broke the silence. "So what changed your mind about Tanis?"

"We just found out there are two different levels of authority to worry about. The guards who were assigned by whoever runs this place, and also the internal force run by Lokelani. I still believe our priority should be escape. The best way to do that is with allies, and right now Tanis is as close as I think we'll get."

They paused at the corner. Sam was about to ask which way Vala thought they should go when there was a sudden shout from their left.

"You! Carter!"

They turned and saw a flash of movement, a slender brunette woman shoving a bystander out of the way as she charged toward them. She grabbed the baton of a guard as she passed, flicking her wrist and making its tip spark with energy. Tanis Reynard yelled again and lifted the weapon high over her head as she closed the distance between herself and Sam with long, loping strides. Sam reached helplessly for a weapon but she had nothing. She brought her fists up and prepared for a fight.

Just before Tanis could swing the baton, Vala stepped forward and smashed a clay pot on the back of her former partner's head. Sam stepped out of the way and Tanis hit the ground hard, arms splayed, face covered by her hair.

Sam stood over the unconscious woman. Vala stepped up to stand beside her and regarded Tanis with a tilted head.

"Well," Vala said, "it definitely seems as if she remembers you."

"Lucky me."

A blonde woman in a dark brown sleeveless top muscled through the crowd. She kept one hand by her side, so expertly hidden from view as she got closer that Sam knew she was holding a weapon. She moved like a fighter, jaw set and shoulders squared. Everyone on the street moved to get out of her way, and a circle of empty space cleared around the scene. She didn't take her eyes off Tanis until she was within striking distance, and only then did she look at the two new arrivals. Sam held her hands up in what she hoped was a universal placating gesture.

"Sorry," Vala said, "hello. This was just a misunderstanding, I swear. Tanis and I really are very good friends. This is, uh, Fraiser, and my name is Vala Mal Doran."

The blonde looked harder at her, narrowing icy blue eyes. "Vala? *The* Vala Mal Doran?"

Vala's grin reappeared. "I'm the one!"

The woman looked at Tanis. Some of the aggression faded from her posture. "She's going to be pissed when she wakes up."

Vala said, "Then let's make sure she wakes up someplace familiar, shall we?"

Tanis's friend lifted the hem of her shirt and secured her weapon somewhere out of sight, then motioned for Vala to help her.

Vala winked at Sam. "See? Now we have *two* friends."

Sam sighed and crouched to help them lift Tanis' limp body.

CHAPTER EIGHT

THE BLONDE introduced herself as Shein Pranassa as Sam helped carry Tanis off the street. Surprisingly, no one seemed concerned about what had just happened. Even the guard, who retrieved his stolen baton after it fell from Tanis' grip, didn't seem particularly interested in the altercation. The indifference to violence was the first thing Sam had seen since her arrival to remind her this was a prison and not just an oddly feminine border town from any number of worlds she'd visited in the past.

With little help from Vala (she insisted she was clearing the path, though no one seemed to be in their way), they carried Tanis a few blocks to what Shein called their "cold-water" because it lacked amenities like heating, hot water, or electricity. Sam expected something similar to a prison cell but was instead directed down a flight of stone steps, which led into a cavern blocked off by a heavy steel door. Shein used a key to let them in, revealing a spacious and sparsely decorated room. The walls were striated with geodes that shone a pale blue and provided enough light to see. It was a hell of an apartment for someone who was supposed to be in prison. Sam couldn't help but think Cassie would kill to have a dorm room this size.

Sam lowered Tanis onto the bed which filled an entire nook on the far wall. Shein sat on the mattress to examine the wound and clear out any shards of pottery. The thief looked different from their last encounter. Her hair was much longer, fuller. Even unconscious she seemed somehow stronger than she'd been on that abandoned world where her prison ship had crashed. In just four years she'd gone from random crony to a leader. As dangerous as she was back then, Sam knew she had only become more fearsome and a bigger threat.

Shein was almost finished applying a bandage when Tanis

grunted and began to stir. She opened one eye. The defensiveness vanished from her face when she saw who was tending her wound. "Who the hell hit me?" she growled.

"Hi!" Vala said, stepping forward with her hand raised in greeting. "Sorry about that. But I seem to remember you have a pretty hard head."

"Vala?" Tanis sat up, gently swatting away Shein's hands. "Damn it, I went to a lot of trouble warning you to stay away. You know how much it cost me to get that message out?"

"Yes, well, unfortunately I got a maliciously-edited version of the message you originally sent."

"Even if the entire thing had been gutted, you should have realized what I was trying to say," Tanis said. "The name Viaxeiro should be enough to make you run full-speed in the opposite direction."

"That's what you get for thinking I'm predictable."

Tanis finally noticed Sam, who had been trying to blend in against the stone wall. She shot to her feet and reached for a weapon on her belt. Vala jumped forward and put her hands on Tanis' shoulders to hold her back.

"Wait!" Vala said. "This is Samantha Carter of SG-1... She—"

"I know who she is. What is she doing here?"

"I'm a member of her team. I'm a member of SG-1 now."

Tanis looked at her with betrayal in her eyes. "You're *what?*"

"I know, I can hardly believe it myself some days," Vala said. "But when they thought you were in trouble, they leapt into action to come save you with no regard for their own well-being."

Sam said, "That's not entirely—"

Vala shot her a silencing look over her shoulder, but her eyes shifted to one side and the admonishment turned to surprise. "Look out!"

Sam moved just as Shein grabbed for her, the other woman's

hand closing on the empty air Sam had just occupied. She bared her teeth, shifted her weight, and thrust her other hand forward. The dim light of the room glinted off a blade. Sam crossed her hands at the wrist and hit Shein's arm, forcing it up and away from her torso. Shein was thrown off-balance and Sam managed to twist one arm behind her back. She pressed Shein against the wall as gently as possible, but with enough force that she couldn't get free. Sam looked at the bed, the last place she'd seen Shein, and tried to figure out how the woman had gotten behind her.

Tanis was smiling, proud even though Shein had been thwarted. "Now you know why they call her Mist and Shadows on seven different planets."

"Guess I won't be adding Tau'ri to that list."

"There's still time," Tanis said. She still hadn't stopped glaring at Sam.

"Tanis has told me all about what Samantha Carter of SG-1 did to her. I'm no fan of do-gooders."

Vala sighed and waved her hands. "Look, can we just put a pause to all this hostility? We came here as friends! We set out on this mission to save you, and just happened to get caught up in a net."

Tanis pointed at Sam. "She and her friends humiliated me. They had me lead Pender and Corso into a trap. I told you that I made sure they ended up in a deep dark pit? That's because I *had* to. They both would have killed me if I'd given them the chance, all because of her and SG-1."

"You were criminals," Sam said. "You tried to use our computers to find new worlds to loot."

Vala patted the air with both hands. "Let's just say mistakes were made on both sides. But that's no reason we can't all get along now. We've all done things we're not proud of in the past, right? Sam, I tried to steal your ship. But you've all forgiven me for that. Bygones! Right?"

Tanis relaxed slightly. Vala gestured for Sam to let go of Shein.

"Good!" Vala said. "We're making progress. We're all friends."

"You still haven't said how you got here," Tanis said.

Vala said, "The original plan was to help you escape."

"So you and the ribbon girl here got yourselves captured?" Tanis arched an eyebrow. "Brilliant plan there, Vala. I'm starting to feel really lucky we parted ways when we did."

Sam caught Vala's eye. "What's a ribbon girl?"

Vala turned and spoke sotto voce. "It's a cultural thing. Just assume it's a compliment and move on." She cleared her throat and tugged at the hem of her jacket. "Professional courtesy, Tanis. We used to be partners. We watched each other's backs. I thought you were calling for old times' sake. Trapped in the worst place the galaxy has to offer and you can only think of one person to save you. I had the resources of the SGC at my disposal so of course I came running to the rescue. You're welcome."

Tanis said, "I appreciate your intentions, but you really just screwed yourselves over in a monumental way. You're here now, and there's no getting out."

"That's why I've brought Samantha along. You've heard of Hadante? Netu? Samantha here found ways to break out of both of them."

"Well, I had help," Sam said. She was momentarily distracted by the sneaking suspicion Vala really had known it was a trap and went barreling in regardless. She dismissed it to analyze at a more appropriate time. "And just from my first look around this place, I have to say I'm not liking our odds."

"You've barely even investigated!"

Sam looked at Tanis. Shein had moved back to sit on the bed and, once again, Sam hadn't seen her move. "Do any ships come closer to the city, or do they all land out in the salt plains?"

Tanis shook her head. "We watch them come in, we watch them go out. When they drop off supplies, the boxes are left at the landing site. We have people go retrieve them once the ships are gone and the landmines are disabled. If anyone goes beyond the walls while the ship is still here, the landmines get reactivated and changes their minds real quick-like."

"The landmines can be disabled?" Sam asked, with as much hope as she dared.

"Not by you," Tanis said. "Lokelani knows how, but I doubt she would do it for you just because you asked nicely. To her, this place isn't about justice. It's about power."

"Are there any spaceworthy vessels on this planet?"

Tanis shook her head again. "Nope. There are a few land-based vehicles, but nothing that can fly. Basically, if it can leave the ground, you won't find it here."

"And I suppose I shouldn't even ask about a Stargate, since there's no possible way a lock could be achieved on a rogue planet."

Vala said, "That's not the Sam Carter I know! Come on, where's that can-do attitude?"

"Your new pal is right, Vala." Tanis moved forward and stood in front of Sam. She smiled smugly, thumbs hooked in her belt. "In fact, there's a sort of poetic justice to this. Four years ago, the Tau'ri found me on a rock with no hope of escape. Now she's the one who doesn't have a way out. It's almost worth everything just to be here and see her trapped like this. All that self-righteousness and you still ended up in here with the rest of us lowlifes. Funny how life works out, Major Carter."

Sam kept her face neutral. "It's actually Colonel now."

Tanis' smile widened and she shook her head. "Not here it isn't."

Vala cleared her throat. "And actually, she gave her name as Fraiser because, well, the whole Tau'ri-as-prisoners thing would draw more attention than—"

"She can call herself whatever she wants," Tanis interrupted. "It doesn't matter in here. Come on, Shein. Let's give our new friends some time to settle in. Don't touch our stuff. The door will lock automatically when you leave." She brushed past Sam.

"Sorry you got caught up in this, Vala. I really did intend the message as a warning to stay away. As for you, Tau'ri Carter or Fraiser or whatever you want to call yourself... welcome to your new home."

~#~

Daniel felt bad when he knocked on the door of Major Escher's office. The desk was covered with notebooks open to pages full of quickly-scribbled notes and diagrams. A message board across from the door was covered with photographs connected by stretches of red string that linked each person to someone else. To an outsider it would look like the room of an unhinged conspiracy theorist, but Daniel knew the threat Escher was tracking was all too real.

Escher himself looked exhausted when he gestured for Daniel to have a seat, then quickly moved to relocate a pile of binders and notebooks from the chair.

"Sorry about the mess," Escher said.

"Are you kidding? This is pristine and catalogued compared to my office. Thank you for shifting your focus on such short notice."

Escher waved him off. "It's Colonel Carter. No one on the base can count how many times she's saved our bacon. All of SG-1, really. So I'm happy to help."

Daniel said, "So you were able to find Ventrell?"

"That depends on how you define 'find.' I know where he's been and where he's most likely to be, but beyond that it's mostly guessing." He shuffled the papers on his desk and somehow divined which notebook he needed from the bottom of the stack. "After the situation in Kansas, SG-12 was assigned to identify the bounty hunters who had been sent after you. Colonel Carter was able to cover up her sniper easily enough, but we had a very hard time explaining the woman who was hit by the bus when she came after you."

"Right." Daniel winced. Sometimes he still saw the woman being hit. His brain didn't seem to care she'd been on the verge of taking him captive or even killing him. A life was a life, and that was a horrifying way to die. "I imagine it was hard explaining a corpse without any identification or discernable footprint."

"We've actually gotten pretty good at creating false identities for aliens who have come to live on Earth. It's a skill I never thought would come in handy without turning to a life of crime. Uh, anyway, we gathered intel on the bounty hunters and were able to determine where they came from and where they got the order to capture you."

"There's a whole planet of bounty hunters?"

"No, there's a planet where bounty hunters go to find clients, and vice versa."

He turned the notebook around as he handed it to Daniel, who skimmed what was written as Escher summarized.

"Their records called the planet Far Scythia. I'm sure you'll recognize the name…"

Daniel closed his eyes. "Uh, nomadic Eurasian tribe. One of the first to master the art of mounted warfare." He looked at the notepad again. "You're thinking this place was founded by their descendants."

Escher nodded. "Displaced by the Goa'uld, and then however many centuries removed. Your would-be assassin had the gate address programmed into a device we found on her body. My team was going to explore it further when there was an opening on the schedule, but I would say SG-1's needs take precedence right now. I'm just basing this on what we've seen, but the people who came after you were freelancers. Freelancers need jobs, and jobs seem to come from Far Scythia."

"Thank you," Daniel said.

"Whatever you need, Dr. Jackson. Bring them home, okay?"

Daniel stood and patted Escher on the shoulder. "We're going to do everything we can. It just got a lot easier thanks to you and your team."

He and Mitchell had both already changed into their more comfortable blue BDUs, and he was reluctant to change back into covert clothes for the next leg of their journey. He looked at his watch as he left Escher's office, painfully aware that it had now been over a day since Sam and Vala were taken. He assumed they were already at the prison, suffering indignities he couldn't even begin to predict. Escher's comment proved that the whole of the SGC, not just SG-1, weren't going to rest until Sam and Vala were brought home safe. Daniel was ready to do whatever it took to make that happen.

He just wished he didn't have to do it in leather pants.

CHAPTER NINE

CAM HITCHED up his belt, unsure if his pants were too big or if they were just designed to be this awkward. He looked around and didn't see any of the other patrons struggling with their pants, but they also didn't seem to be wearing buckskin. They had arrived at Far Scythia ten minutes earlier with their weapons concealed, but it quickly became apparent that no one cared about showing they were armed. They'd been surprised to discover the Stargate was just one part of a large complex located between a fleet of land vehicles - glass eggs tilted on their sides with two large wheels at the back and a concealed third wheel under the nose - and a landing strip which reminded Cam of an Air Force base. It was an airport, bus station, and train depot all blended into one noisy hub.

A Prior was standing in an intersection where pedestrians couldn't help but pass him. Daniel averted his gaze as they neared his makeshift pulpit.

"Hallowed are those who — "

"Yeah, blessed are those who walk in the path," Cam said. "We gave at the office."

They joined the flood of people pouring out into the main city, choosing one street at random so they could get the lay-out of the city before looking for Odai. Cam jerked at his belt again.

Daniel offered a commiserating smile. "It could be worse. Hagman told me that the last world they visited didn't have mass-produced clothing but they did have chitons and shenti."

Cam said, "I know what a chiton is. Shenti?"

"Egyptian. Wrapped skirt."

"What, like a kilt?"

"Sort of."

Cam decided to stop complaining about his pants. "I'll tell you what really feels wrong. Going on a mission without Teal'c or Carter."

"And Vala," Daniel reminded him.

"Right, of course, and Vala, but I have to admit, I'm still getting used to that. I'm talking about the old-school, the varsity crew. I went through a lot of trouble putting SG-1 back together, and now it feels like it's falling apart again. But it's worse this time, because it's not by choice."

"We'll get Sam and Vala back. As for Teal'c… if things go south, would you really want to risk aggravating his injuries?"

"I gave him a big speech about how he's more than just a big scary guy who beats people up for us, but right now I kind of miss having him as backup."

Someone bumped into Daniel from behind. He reached out and grabbed the offender before he could disappear into the crowd and snatched his zat back from the man's weaker grip. The pickpocket sneered at him, pulled free, and ran. Daniel returned the weapon to his hip and looked at the other people surrounding them on the street. Thugs and criminals, all.

"I don't think having one more person on our side would make much of a difference. A team of marines probably wouldn't make much of a difference. Who knew there was this much crime in the galaxy?"

"Goa'uld fell," Cam said, "people saw an opportunity."

"Yeah, I'm having a hard enough time with guilt over bringing the Ori here. I really don't need more guilt about helping to create the Lucian Alliance."

As they passed an alley, a man with heavily-bandaged hands reached out to them. His fingers couldn't quite reach Cam's pant leg, but it was enough to catch his attention. The man had used soot to draw markings on his face like those of a Prior, but there was a scar on his forehead where long ago he had sloppily attempted to give himself a Jaffa tattoo.

"Quick hands, you got," the man said. "Lots of quick hands here, but you still quickie. You look for something? Want to hire? You tell Sanda, he find it for you faster than you find it yourself, even with quickie hands."

Cam said, "What's that gonna cost us?"

"Depend on how difficult," the man said with a shrug. "I find quickie, you don't give much. Take me all day, though, valuable time costs."

"Sorry, buddy," Cam said. "We don't have… whatever you use for cash here."

"But…" Daniel reached into his pouch and withdrew a candy bar. "We have this."

He held it up so Sanda could see it before handing it over. He demonstrated how to open the wrapper. Sanda sniffed it and his eyes widened with recognition.

"This is xoclah," he said suspiciously. He looked around and used both hands to cover his treasure. "You give whole piece…?"

Daniel looked surprised. "Yeah, the whole thing."

Cam said, "We've got more where that came from if you're quick about helping us."

"More?" Sanda tried to contain his excitement. "Who? Who look?"

"Odai Ventrell," Daniel said.

The man muttered the name a few times as he backed away. "I find, I see, I be back!" He turned and fled through the crowd.

Cam said, "So apparently it works on Abydonians, Unas, and random street urchins."

"Chocolate has been cultivated for millennia all over Earth. It makes sense it would be one of the things people kept when the Goa'uld kidnapped them. Candy is easier to pack than coffee, so I never leave home without a handful of bars in my pack. If you ever need coffee when we're off-world, go to Sam. She keeps enough in her gear to make Starbucks an intergalactic brand if they knew about it."

"Good to know. But I give good odds he just comes back with some buddies and mugs us for the rest of our chocolate."

"I figure it's worth the risk if it saves us the trouble of wandering around this entire city for someone who might not even be here. Besides, you saw the markings on that guy. He obviously throws in with whoever is in power at the time. I'd say that candy bar bought us at least a few hours of loyalty."

Cam said, "Uh-huh. And what happens when Ventrell walks in and recognizes us? You never did give Landry a clear answer about how you plan to get him on our side."

"I'm hoping inspiration will strike in the moment. Time is kind of against us here. We don't have the luxury of thinking things out in advance."

Cam laughed. "Boy, if anything could be the motto of this team…"

~#~

They claimed an empty table at a nearby bar where they could wait. Everyone around them was too concerned with their own deals to pay them much attention. Cam saw credits being passed under tables and several more blatant transactions happening in plain sight with no concern for witnesses. One man exchanged a poorly-wrapped parcel shaped like a severed hand in exchange for a small wooden box.

"There are only two reasons I'm not killing one of you and taking the other captive."

Cam sat up straighter at the sudden voice coming from behind them. Odai Ventrell had a distinctive cadence that was unmistakable even in the clamor of the bar. He stepped into their line of sight, making sure they could both see the blaster on his hip before he took a seat on the other side of the table. He leaned back and glared at them as if they were wasting his time.

"One," he continued, "I'm not sure which one of you would bring the biggest payday, so I'd hate to kill the valuable one. And two, I'm not aware of any current bounties on SG-1's heads. Now, I could just take a risk and auction Dr. Jackson off to the highest bidder. I'm sure there are plenty of Goa'uld still around with a lot of time on their hands."

Daniel cleared his throat. "We, uh, appreciate that you're willing to hear us out."

Odai's smile was cold. "I'm not hearing anything out. I just couldn't believe two members of SG-1 were actually looking for me. I had to see it for myself."

"We're here because we think you can help us," Daniel said.

"I have absolutely no interest in helping you. With anything."

Cam said, "Hey, you owe us. We're the ones who gave you the idea to go after Netan. You had to get a lot of clout from being the guy who cut the head off the snake. So to speak."

"You'd think that, wouldn't you? But no. Netan has a lot of lieutenants who were annoyed I tried to jump the line. By the time I convinced them to leave me alone, I had pretty much just broken even. But I'm feeling generous, so I'm not going to take it out on you. If you'll excuse me." He placed his hands flat on the table and pushed himself up. "Next time you come looking for me, I'm going to gamble on someone making your capture worth my while."

"Colonel Carter and Vala have been captured," Cam continued as if Odai hadn't spoken.

Odai leaned down and met Cam's eye. "Why should I care?"

Cam knew the moment had come for a brilliant idea, but he couldn't think of anything. Their best chance of getting Sam and Vala back was about to walk away, and he had no clue how to convince him to help. He glanced around as if inspiration was written on the walls of the bar. Odai chuckled under his breath and straightened up.

"This has been a strange encounter, gentlemen. I'll be sure to tell the galaxy that SG-1 has been trimmed down to three members. It's been a rough few months and they could use the good news."

He started to walk away. Cam noticed the beaten, weary look of everyone in the bar, along with Sanda's makeup, and the Prior trying to hold court near the Stargate. In an instant, he knew how to convince Odai to help them.

"It must be difficult to operate with the Ori breathing down your neck."

Odai stopped, but didn't turn around. Cam twisted in his seat and addressed the man's back.

"You want them gone? Just like the Goa'uld and the Replicators? SG-1 is your best chance of making that happen. But we only have a chance to do that as a unit. We need Sam and Vala. You help us, you're helping rid this galaxy of every Ori ship and Prior."

Odai remained where he was, unmoving and silent. Then finally his shoulders sagged and he shook his head.

"Ah, damn it," he said under his breath. He looked at them again, clearly angry he'd been outplayed. "What do you need from me?"

~#~

The underground cavern Tanis and Shein called home was part of a honeycomb of other residences all connected by a narrow corridor. Sam left and wandered until she found a set of steps leading up to ground level. She climbed it, then found a ladder on a side of a building which could get her even higher. She didn't check to make sure Vala had followed her, but every now and then she heard a grunt or muttered exclamation which proved she was there. When she got to the roof, she walked to the far edge and sat down. She planted her feet flat on the stucco material of the roof, crossed her arms on her bent knees, and rested one hand on top of the other. Vala sat down beside her, legs folded in front of her.

They stared out over the city together. There was no unifying architectural style, no hint that the city had been planned in any way. Styles merged and morphed into each other. Small ovoid pods clung to tall cylindrical towers. Flat slate roofs marched in a line with domed buildings. Turrets, pyramids, gables, and pagodas. It was clear that everyone who came to Viaxeiro built homes as needed, bringing their own distinct tastes and styles. From up high, the pattern of streets called to mind an ant farm with just as much reasoning behind its twists and turns.

Vala finally broke the silence. "So? What's the plan?"

"I don't know." It felt good to say. She so rarely got away with saying it but, in this case, she didn't have any other true answer.

"I get it," Vala said, still sounding annoyingly optimistic. "You need time to think through your options."

Sam laughed. "What options, Vala? You heard Tanis. You saw what those landmines can do. Even if we could evade the guards, there's no way we can get to a ship. If, and it's a very big if, the SGC somehow manages to locate this rock and mount a rescue mission, there's nothing we can do from this side to help them unless we decide to overthrow their leader with no weapons and no backup beyond Tanis and her assassin girlfriend."

Vala stared at her in disbelief. "So… that's it? You're just going to sit here and play the damsel in distress? Wait for the big strapping men to come rescue you? That is not the Samantha Carter I know."

"It's the only option we have right now. I don't like it any more than you do, but look around us. We're stuck in a city surrounded by people who ignored the fact we knocked Tanis out and carried her away. These are bad people. The worst of the worst. If any of them find out who we really are, they might just kill us out of spite. There could be people who got sent here because of SG-1."

"All the more reason to be proactive! Listen, let's brainstorm. How did you get out of Hadante?"

"We had a Stargate. And on Netu, we had rings, we had ships, we had people on the outside waiting to pull us to safety. We had *options*. Right now, we have nothing. Even your friend Tanis is resigned to staying trapped here. I don't know her well, but she doesn't seem like the sort who would just give up and stay in prison."

Vala said, "No. But neither am I. If you're not going to come up with one of your brilliant plans, then I suppose it'll have to be up to me." She stood up and brushed her hands over the seat of her pants. "This is the perfect opportunity to prove myself to you. I'm a brilliant strategist. I'll get us out of this mess and the next time SG-1 is in a sticky situation, you'll turn to me for ideas."

Sam shook her head, smiling ruefully. "I wish you luck, Vala. Really."

Vala turned to leave but didn't even make it a single step. "Oh. Samantha."

Sam turned to see Tanis had just finished climbing up to the roof. Shein was right behind her, bearing the scowl which had become her default expression upon discovering Sam's real identity. Sam stood up as well and wished she'd taken the time to find weapons. There were no clay pots on the roof for Vala to improvise with if Tanis decided to attack again.

"Someone said they saw you climb up here, 'Fraiser'," Tanis said. "Hope you don't mind us crashing the party."

Vala said, "Just so long as it stays a party. We're all friends now. Right?"

"I'm not going to go that far." Tanis kept her eyes on Sam. "After we left, Shein and I got to talking."

Shein nodded at Sam. "You're really a member of SG-1?"

"We both are," Sam said.

Shein looked at Tanis before she continued. "We used to hear a lot about SG-1 on my world. Back when the Goa'uld were still around. There were even actors who traveled through the gates to reenact some of your greatest adventures. They gave us all hope even when we were worried about the Jaffa coming to attack at any moment. I always thought that if SG-1 could just come to our planet, it might turn things around. Then you took the Goa'uld out and things just got worse."

Vala said, "You can't blame her for that!"

"I'm not," Shein said. "Hell, the Lucian Alliance was the opportunity I'd been waiting for. There's no way I was going to let someone put a snake in my head, but with the Alliance I had a chance to make my own name. It got me out into the universe. Got me here, too. But that hasn't been without benefits." She glanced at Tanis, smiling at some inner thought before she continued. "That's not the point. I spent years hearing about the great SG-1 and the miracles they pulled off."

Tanis, standing to one side with her arms crossed over her chest, muttered, "All right, c'mon. Ease up on the flattery, eh?"

Shein said, "You want off this rock? Maybe Tanis and I could help you out."

"I thought you two were perfectly happy here."

"We are," Tanis said. "We don't want you to take us with you. We want you to earn our help before you go."

Sam narrowed her eyes. "And how exactly would we do that?"

Tanis said, "We want you to kill Lokelani Kiir."

CHAPTER TEN

"SO? ARE you in or out?"

"With what?" Vala said. "The thing you mentioned up on the roof? You couldn't have been serious. Or maybe I misheard you."

"It was a clear enough directive," Tanis said. They had relocated back to the cold-water room. Shein had secured and locked the door and was now leaning against it. Sam had reluctantly followed along and now sat with her elbow on their dinner table, watching the exchange.

"Yes," Vala said, "but I could've sworn you said 'kill'…?"

Tanis arched an eyebrow and dipped her chin. "What, you've gotten soft? I'd hate to offend any delicate sensibilities you've acquired with the Tau'ri."

"We didn't kill!" Vala said. "I mean, we didn't… well, we tried very hard to make sure no one was killed in our jobs."

Sam said, "Tanis wasn't always so conscientious about body count."

Tanis glared at her. "We were prisoners. They were our jailors. We were trapped on a planet with no apparent hope of escape. If we thought they would have agreed to peace —"

"Yeah," Sam said, "but you never tried approaching them about peace, did you?"

Vala stepped between them before the debate could get heated again. "Regardless of the past, we definitely don't kill now. Why do you want Lokelani dead?"

"She's a despot," Shein said. "She was probably the first person you spoke to when you arrived, right? Introduced herself, told you the rules of the place."

"Rules she came up with herself," Tanis added.

Shein nodded. "She's been here longer than anyone else. She uses that to her advantage. She gets to know people as soon as they come in, feels them out, finds their strengths and weaknesses, and figures out the best way to use it for her own benefit. Right now she has her cronies asking around about Vala and... I keep forgetting, what did you say your fake name was?"

Sam said, "Fraiser."

"Hold on," Vala said. "How could she have been here longer than anyone else? This place is a death sentence, right? There's no way she could have outlived everyone who was here when she arrived unless — "

"Unless she's a Goa'uld," Tanis said.

Sam sat up straighter. She hadn't felt anything but an unquantifiable unease when they met the woman, but secret Goa'uld infiltrators weren't much of a problem these days. It had been so long since she'd had to pay attention to that odd little twinge that she accepted she might not have noticed. "You know that for a fact?"

"We've pieced it together." Tanis walked closer to the table. "Where I come from, we have a saying: the clever hawk hides its claws. We think she was exiled about a hundred years ago. She acts like she's the same as all of us, has the story she tells people about her crimes — "

Shein recited, "Ship captain responsible for a smuggling run across four systems."

"Drugs, food, people," Tanis said along with her, their voices monotone but perfectly in sync. "You name it, she ran it."

Tanis continued, "But people talk. The older condemned know that she was here when they arrived. They also know she hasn't aged in that time. We even found one of the oldest condemned who claims Lokelani used to have a different face."

"New host," Sam said.

"There's no shortage of potential hosts here," Tanis said. "Lokelani makes sure the condemned who know her secret are well taken care of so they won't spill the beans. Also, it helps that they're all completely terrified of her. She can be kind when she wants to be, but I wouldn't cross her. People have disappeared. No one is brave enough to ask where they went."

Sam said, "So you want to take her place."

Tanis grinned and shrugged. "What's life worth if you aren't crossing the line? I'm perfectly content to stay here, just like I told Vala. I've been running around my whole life and I'm starting to get sick of ending up in crappy prison cells. Viaxeiro is supposed to be the worst of the worst, but once I was here, I realized something. If no one has ever escaped, then no one has ever reported what it's actually like here. All the rumors come from the officials who lock us up, and they have an incentive to make it sound as bad as possible. Maybe no one has ever escaped because *no one wants out.* I have more freedom here than I ever had out in the wilds. And I don't have to worry about getting caught because I'm already locked up. Plus Shein is here." She looked at the blonde and then quickly looked away. "There's just one thing ruining it."

Shein said, "A damn Goa'uld running the show."

"A damn Goa'uld running the show," Tanis echoed, shaking her head in disbelief. "I finally find a place I could settle down, and I have to live under one of those eyeshiners? No thanks."

Shein pointed at Sam. "After we left, Tanis told me about who you are. SG-1, Goa'uld killers. I figured if anyone could help us out, it's you."

Tanis said, "If you get rid of Lokelani, we'll get you out of here."

"Why should we trust you?"

Tanis laughed. "Why would I want a member of SG-1 as a neighbor?"

"Two members," Vala said.

"Yeah, whatever. I still doubt that. So? What's your verdict?"

Sam pondered the proposition. Shein reached for a bowl in the center of the table and retrieved a small piece of candy in a hard round shell. She squeezed it between her thumb and her first two fingers, cracking the outside. The inside of the candy looked like some kind of creamy, dark-black nougat covering a small nut. Shein plucked out the nut and passed it to Tanis, who took it and popped it into her mouth without looking away from Sam. Shein chose one of the largest shards and placed it on her tongue, chewing it thoughtfully as she watched Sam.

"Why don't you take care of her yourself?" Sam asked.

Vala, who had watched the exchange with the candy, said, "Leverage."

Tanis looked away. Shein pursed her lips and focused on the shards of candy still in her hand. Sam realized what Vala was saying. If Tanis went after Lokelani and failed, Shein could be hurt or relocated as punishment. Neither woman could make a move without putting the other one in danger, and neither of them was willing to take the chance.

"We were stupid enough to let Lokelani see our vulnerability," Tanis said, still looking at the wall instead of at Sam. "She doesn't even have to threaten us. We've seen how she operates. We know what she would do if either of us crossed her."

Sam thought back to a day on a Goa'uld mothership, a dire situation which had almost led to General O'Neill getting a lobotomy. Just because he wouldn't admit the real reason he'd stayed behind. Sam knew all about that kind of vulnerability, and she hated how much sympathy she felt for Tanis and Shein. She also thought about their chances of getting off this rock without help, especially now that a Goa'uld was allegedly in charge.

"How many Goa'uld have you killed?" Shein asked.

"Me personally…?"

"If you're talking about SG-1, it's fourteen," Vala said.

Sam frowned. "That doesn't sound right."

"The commissary staff have a chart in the kitchen."

Sam would have to look into that when she got back to the base. *If* she got back to the base. She was about to tell Tanis they would take their chances alone, but Vala spoke up first.

"Give us a chance to talk privately, take a look around to

confirm what you're telling us, and we'll get back to you with an answer."

Tanis raised an eyebrow. "You think I'm lying?"

"Well, darling, you know what they say." Vala flipped her hair. "Keep your friends close, but count your money when they step away."

Tanis grinned. "I suppose that's solid advice. Fine. You should probably get the lay of the land anyway. Go ahead, take your time. You know where to find us when you're ready to work out the details.

"Samantha, let's go for a walk, hm?" Vala moved to the door and gestured with her head for Sam to follow. Sam stood up and brushed by Tanis, waiting until they were outside with the door closed before she turned on Vala.

"What the hell was that?"

"I took initiative. I know Tanis better than you, so I knew exactly the right thing to get us out of the room without pissing her off. C'mon." She started down the hall.

Sam caught up with her. "We're not agreeing to her plan."

"It's a Goa'uld!"

"Allegedly."

Vala rolled her eyes. "We can at least investigate to see if what she's saying is true. And if it is, the possibilities are endless! If she's concealing the fact she's a Goa'uld, who knows what else she's hiding? She could have a ship hidden somewhere. Maybe it's cloaked in orbit and she has transport rings so she can come and go as she pleases. Hell, maybe her home is so big she has a Stargate hidden inside! When you're dealing with a Goa'uld, nothing is off the table."

Sam said, "Or Tanis made all that up and wants us to kill her competition so she can take over."

Vala pursed her lips. "I won't lie, that is a possibility. But this is what SG-1 does! Ride into town, see an injustice, make things right, then..." She pushed one hand out in front of her as illustration. "Back home again."

"Usually there are more of us in that scenario."

"Ugh, again with the 'just little old me.' Yes, Sam, we are but two members of SG-1. But that's almost half! With your brain, you can imagine what they would do if they were here and tell me what to do. I can fire a gun as well as Daniel. I can charm anyone as well as Colonel Mitchell. And…" She flexed her arm and looked down at her biceps. "I don't quite have Teal'c's muscle, but I can hit someone with a pot again, if it comes to that."

"On the ship, you said we were at a disadvantage because we didn't have the rest of the team."

"That was different. We would be punching up from a lower position in that case. Here, we're on even ground. We have time to think and plot and plan. We're not tied up in a little room. We can do this!"

They were back on the street, and Sam moved Vala closer to the wall.

"You know, the last time you volunteered me for something like this, you insisted I could use Merlin's device to take an entire village out of phase. I got an Ori staff blast to the gut."

"But everything else worked out fine! And you've healed up nicely from that!"

Sam rolled her eyes. "I have an alternate plan. We go to the other side of the city and pretend that whole conversation never happened. We don't have time to do a criminal's dirty work for her. We need to get off this rock. We'll get close to Lokelani and investigate. If we find evidence she has a way out of here, that's when we'll worry about making use of it. Tanis has made it very clear she doesn't plan to go with us when we leave, so we can't waste time thinking about her. The only thing that matters is finding the quickest route to a Stargate and getting home."

Vala's face had become stone. "I understand. I understand that you only see Tanis as a thief. Pretty telling."

Sam sighed. "Vala, you're a completely different…"

"Am I?" She shrugged. "I was just like Tanis. Worse, sometimes. So if you think she's nothing more than a thief—"

"Do I have to point out again that she's literally in prison?"

Vala held her arms out to either side. "So was I, from time to time! And so were you. And every member of SG-1. Tanis is in prison because she was tricked, not because she was tried and convicted in some Earth courtroom. She did what was necessary to survive. That doesn't make her a bad person. It doesn't make *me* bad, either!"

Sam said, "Lower your voice…"

"No! You don't respect me. That's fine. You know what, you go work on whatever brilliant plan you're sure to come up with, and I'll work with Tanis. We'll just see which one of us ends up leaving first." She started to leave, but then came back. She poked her finger against Sam's shoulder. "And when I escape first, I just may consider sending the *Odyssey* back here to pick you up. But don't count on it."

With another flip of her hair, Vala turned and stormed away. Sam knew it was better for them to stick together but, at the moment she was grateful for the opportunity to get away from the other woman for a little while. So instead of pursuing she walked in the other direction and thought about her options.

No prison was inescapable. Viaxeiro wasn't self-sufficient. Supplies were brought in and guards were sent out. Prisoners were dropped off by ships which then managed to leave. There had to be some way to utilize that. On Hadante, the prison had a Stargate through which the prisoners could receive food. On Netu, Bynarr had rings in his quarters which went down to the planet. Both of these were fatal flaws SG-1 used to escape each respective 'inescapable prison.' So far, Viaxeiro didn't seem to have anything she could employ other than Lokelani's control over the landmines, but that was useless if there was no one waiting to pick them up.

The end of the street widened so that the intersection was a large open egg-shape. Other prisoners had gathered there, and more than a few glanced at her as she joined them. She wondered if any of the Lucian Alliance bounty hunters had used photographs to hunt for the team, and how many of those bounty hunters might be incarcerated alongside her. She tried to keep her head down as she walked. She needed to find someplace quiet where she could think, rest, get her thoughts in order. She was never going to find a way out of the prison if she was constantly looking over her shoulder.

"Sri Fraiser!"

Sam was grateful she'd chosen such a familiar name. It had been shouted from a distance, almost lost in the din, but she still stopped and looked around for the source. The crowd parted to allow Lokelani to pass, flanked by two women in the orange uniforms of the Cai Thior. Sam wondered if the woman went anywhere without them as escort.

Lokelani was smiling brightly as she approached but Sam couldn't help but notice the women had weapon-like holsters on their belts. She kept her guard up and forced a smile. When she was close enough, Sam focused hard to see if she could detect the presence of a symbiote. There was nothing, but she'd lost a bit of faith in her ability to sense symbiotes. It wasn't a skill she'd been called on to use since the downfall of the Goa'uld. She had spent years ignoring the sensation whenever she was close to Teal'c when he still had a symbiote, so now it was difficult for her to pin down with any certainty.

"Lokelani. I… was just looking for you."

"I thought you might be." She briefly looked around the area. "Is Sri Mal Doran not with you?"

Sam said, "No, we thought we'd explore separately for a little while."

"Ah." Lokelani folded her hands together. "I am glad that I found you. It's something of a tradition for me to dine with newcomers. Not all of them, of course, but the ones I think are particularly interesting."

Sam raised an eyebrow. "Me? Interesting? I don't know

about that…"

Lokelani clicked her tongue. "You're far too modest. Most of the women who come here have long histories, reputations, that sort of thing. But not you. I've asked around and no one has ever heard of you, Sri Fraiser." She was still smiling, her features kindly, but her eyes were hard and searching. "I find that fascinating."

"Wouldn't that be proof I'm not worth getting to know? There's a reason I'm working as Vala's apprentice. I still need to make a name for myself."

"So you're a newcomer to the world of crime."

"That's right," Sam said. "I was only sent here because I happened to be with Vala when she was captured. Wrong place, wrong time."

Lokelani said, "A tragedy, to be certain. You must have had quite a life to end up here. I would love to hear the entire tale over… I'm sorry, what part of your meal cycle are you on? Mid-day? Evening?"

The interminable shuffle between ships and gates on their way to the prison meant that she'd lost track of Earth-time, but the mention of food made her stomach audibly growl.

"I think I would eat whatever you were willing to serve me," she said.

Lokelani laughed. "Most are, when they arrive."

Being invited in was definitely the easiest way to get a look at wherever this woman called home. Sam looked around to see if Vala had materialized in the crowd, but the only faces looking back at her were strangers. She gave up looking and resigned herself that she was willingly following a woman she knew she couldn't trust into a potential trap.

She had essentially found herself in quicksand, then, after alienating her only real ally, began digging herself deeper.

Not your best plan, Carter, she thought as she allowed herself to be led away.

CHAPTER ELEVEN

ODAI WAS still laughing, although he had stopped a few times to catch his breath. Cam and Daniel sat across from him and waited impatiently. Daniel examined the ceiling joists. Cam had his arms crossed and kept his eyes locked on Odai, features locked in a scowl. Odai's face was still red when the laughter finally tapered off and he could speak again. He reached for his cup and shook his head before taking a long drink.

"Okay," Cam said, "now that we have that out of the way—"

"No," Odai said as he put his cup down. "No, that's not out of the way. That's only out of the way if you move on to something less ludicrous. You say the name Viaxeiro again and I'm just going to start up again." He snickered and shook his head. "I've always heard the Tau'ri were some crazy *den jen rat n'key*, but this goes beyond the pale even for you."

Daniel said, "We're not asking you to help us break them out. We just need to know where it is."

"That, by itself, is a pretty tall order, Dr. Jackson. The whole appeal of Viaxeiro is that no one knows where it is."

Cam smiled. "Come on. Guy like you? You've got to have your ear to the ground. You know all the secrets no one wants you to know. Secrets are currency."

"Be that as it may, I can't help you. If I were you, I'd focus on taking down the Ori. It's just as impossible, but at least there you can go down swinging."

Daniel said, "Okay, fine. We don't have to know where it is. What sort of crime would hypothetically get someone sentenced to Viaxeiro?"

"Whoa." Cam cleared his throat. "Uh, Jackson? Can we take a second here?"

Daniel turned toward Cam and lowered his voice. "I'm only

asking hypothetically."

"We can't help anyone if we're stuck in the same prison as Sam and Vala." Odai's chuckle had turned into a full laugh, drawing Cam's attention. "Is something funny?"

"I'm just picturing you two as Viaxeiro prisoners. I shouldn't laugh." He nodded at Daniel. "With the right facial enamels, you would make a very fetching young lady."

Daniel frowned in confusion. "Why would…?" Realization dawned. "It's a women's prison."

Cam looked at him. "You don't think…?"

"That Vala knew it was a women's prison, expected to be taken prisoner, and that's why she insisted on going on ahead with Sam and not the rest of the team?" Daniel let his irritation show. "No, it hadn't crossed my mind. Sam's probably thrilled."

"Oh, yeah."

Daniel cleared his throat and looked at Odai. "You have to know something."

"Information is usually treated as currency in places like this." Odai raised an eyebrow. "You fellows have anything to bargain with?"

"I don't suppose you like chocolate," Cam asked.

"The Tau'ri would owe you a favor," Daniel said.

Cam said, "Whoa, now… let's not get crazy."

"A favor?" Odai said. "From the Tau'ri? Now that *is* intriguing. It might be nice to have SG-1 in my debt." He considered for a moment, during which Cam glared at Daniel and Daniel ignored him as best he could. "All right. Just information. Viaxeiro was created a few thousand years ago when everything was going particularly swell for Goa'uld. Even back then with the snakes running things, humans did okay for themselves. We worked as bounty hunters, lo'taurs, messengers, attendants. You ever seen a Goa'uld pleasure palace?"

Daniel said, "We're familiar with the concept."

"So there was work to be had. There was also crime, and

criminals had to be dealt with. Men could be put to death, sent to work camps, turned into hosts, any number of things. But people were more squeamish about that sort of thing happening to women. No one wanted to hand their women over to the Goa'uld, so they had to find a place to put their female criminals. A place where not even the Goa'uld could find them."

Cam said, "So they lassoed themselves a rogue planet?"

"It was a little more complicated than that, I'm sure," Odai said. "But essentially, yes. A group called the Overseers found the planet and set up the first colony. Then they invited anyone who had female prisoners to help populate the place. As far as I know, they're still running things. Sending supplies and arranging for prisoner transports."

Daniel moved to the edge of his seat. "Okay, now we're getting somewhere. These Overseers, how could we arrange a transport?"

"Jackson."

"Mitchell?"

"Can we have a sidebar?"

Daniel said, "We're talking in hypotheticals. Someone called up these Overseers and set up the trap Vala and Tanis fell into. Someone was waiting in orbit for the signal that Vala had shown up. So it stands to reason someone makes their living transporting women to this prison. We need to find them and convince them to help us. The easiest way to do that is to arrange a pick-up."

Odai cleared his throat. "That won't work."

"Why not?"

"Vala Mal Doran and Tanis Reynard are well-known criminals. They both have reputations. The Overseers knew who they were getting. What's your plan, to pick some random Tau'ri and tell someone to come pick her up? Won't work. There needs to be recognition or a warrant. There needs to be some indication beyond your say-so that the woman you're turning over belongs in Viaxeiro."

Cam said, "I guess it's nice to know the people who condemned our friends to life in prison have standards. Look, Odai, we're indifferent to one another. No reason to like each other or hate each other. There's got to be someone out there in this whole, huge universe who can help us."

Odai tapped his fingers on the table and worked his tongue against his front teeth. "A debt from SG-1," he muttered under his breath. He seemed to be calculating how much trouble such a prize might be worth. "I know some people who could help. They're going to be pissed, though..."

Daniel leaned forward. "Maybe we could owe them a debt, too."

Cam said, "Easy handing out the chits there, pal."

"They may settle for having you take the Ori out of the equation. Then again, they might throw me out an airlock for even bringing up their names in front of the Tau'ri."

"Hell, I like 'em already," Cam said. "Who are these scoundrels and where can we find them?"

~#~

Kimo hung upside down near the ceiling, her brown hair tied back out of her face and trailing out behind her head like a horn. Of course, upside down was relative in space. Her arms were out to either side and her legs were slightly bent so she could kick against the wall if she drifted too close to it. She looked toward the cockpit where Adamaris was still strapped in so she could keep an eye on their system readings. Life support was at the lowest possible setting. No circulating air, no gravity, no heat. She estimated if the patrol didn't find anything in five rounds of scans, they would move on to the next section. It was currently on the fifth scan.

Their ship hung under the bulk of a ha'tak which had been devastated in a long-ago battle. Dozens of gliders and vessels of an unidentified design hung motionless in the void. The patrol ship arrived just as they finished loading the last of their haul. Adamaris was quick enough to put everything to sleep before the first scan hit them. Now all they could do was wait patiently for it to get bored. She didn't understand why the Swaran Authority felt it was their job to police this battle-ground, but unless she wanted to pay a hefty fine and bribe the officials to look the other way, she would have to freeze and gasp for a little while.

Adamaris' normally brown skin was painted yellow and blue by the display she'd kept online to monitor the predator's prog-ress. She was also wearing an oxygen mask over the lower half of her face to regulate her breathing. Kimo had been a swim-mer when she was a child, so she was more capable of breath-ing in low-oxygen environments when necessary. It was just a matter of knowing when to breathe and when to hold her air. Adamaris watched as the sensor blip moved away from their location. She looked over her shoulder and gave a quick nod.

If they'd been daring enough to risk speech, Kimo would have chided her for tempting fate. As it was, fate saved her the trouble. The panel in front of Adamaris suddenly lit up with an incoming message. Adamaris reached for the screen but the communication alert sounded before she could cut it off. The silence was shattered by its hollow *pong*. It only went off three times, but that was enough for the patrol ship's sensors to detect an anomaly. Though it had been on the very edge of their radar range, now it had paused. Adamaris held her breath and let it out in a curse when the other ship started back toward them.

Adamaris tore off her oxygen mask and faced the controls. "Damn it," she said as she brought everything back online as quickly as possible. "Kee, you better hold onto something."

Kimo swam closer to the wall as gravity once again pulled at her limbs. It was a graceless descent, but she managed to hit the ground without getting bruised. The running lights at the base of the cargo hold glittered to life as she went forward to strap herself in.

"Twenty more seconds until we were home free," Kimo

said wistfully.

"Look at it this way," Adamaris said as she fired up the engines, "we're just shifting our luck to another day. In a few weeks or a few months, we're going to need the luck we just banked."

Kimo said, "That philosophy requires us to actually survive the next thirty seconds."

"Details."

Their communications rang with another alert, this time delivering a message they were unable to ignore. "*Unidentified vessel, you are currently occupying restricted space. Disengage your engines and await boarding by the Swaran Authority.*"

Kimo chose a sound file from their library and sent it back as a response. They couldn't hear it through their own speakers, but the crew of the Swaran ship had just received a blast of noise that would render them insensate for thirty seconds, give or take. Long enough for Adamaris to plot a course and get a nice running start. She turned the ship as Kimo plugged in a series of commands.

"Did I tell you about the dream I had last night?" Adamaris asked.

"No."

Kimo executed the command she'd just set. A harpoon launched from the back of their ship and impacted a piece of wreckage. Their momentum pulled the space junk along with them until Kimo released the tether to send it careening into another abandoned vessel. That began a chain reaction of gliders crashing into gliders, which crashed into the unidentified ships, which went spinning into the ha'tak, until the entire junkyard was a chain reaction between them and their pursuers.

Adamaris opened a hyperspace window and took them out of danger. "I was standing by a river," she said, "in the dream."

"Right," Kimo said.

"I think I was seven or eight years old, but I don't think it was a memory." She reached up and teased her short, spiky hair as she recalled the dream. "There was a bridge but I started walking straight through the water. I got about halfway across before the water was up to my chin and I realized I had made a horrible mistake. What do you think it means?"

Kimo thought for a moment. "The apparently easy way might not be safe, so you might as well take a risk and have some fun."

"Interesting interpretation."

"I thought so." She nodded at the console. "So who is going to receive my wrath for ruining our nearly perfect day?"

"Odai Ventrell."

Kimo raised an eyebrow. "Odai? Unless it's an invitation to his execution, I have no interest in what that *cra'tu* has to say."

Adamaris said, "He promises adventure." She raised an eyebrow and grinned evilly. "And it involves the Tau'ri."

"The Tau'ri?" Kimo said, suddenly intrigued. "What sort of job does he need?"

"Escort."

Kimo pursed her lips and watched the purple-and-black streaks washing past the ship. "We've never dealt with the Tau'ri before. It's always been a goal of mine."

Adamaris laughed. "You just want to see if Daniel Jackson is as cute as everyone says he is."

"He couldn't possibly be! But oh, to see him in the flesh… it might even be worth dealing with Odai Ventrell." She leaned forward and drummed her fingertips on the edge of the console. "How far away is he?"

"If we drop out of hyperspace and reroute, we could be there in about eight hours." She looked over at Kimo. "Might not be the safe path."

"But it should be fun," Kimo agreed. "Message Odai and tell him we're on the way." She twisted her chair around and stood to go into the back of the ship.

Adamaris looked after her. "Where the hell are you going?"

Kimo plucked at the lapel of her shirt. "If we're going to meet *the* Daniel Jackson, I'm not going to show up in these rags."

CHAPTER TWELVE

HE WAS NOT weak. Teal'c reminded himself of this fact even as he grunted with pain. He was Jaffa, with or without a symbiote. He stood up straight and put a hand against his side. He would fight through the pain and become stronger for it. His team needed him. Samantha Carter and Vala Mal Doran were in danger. According to their latest message, Colonel Mitchell and Daniel Jackson were involving themselves with very unsavory individuals.

"Oh, you have got to be kidding me." Carolyn Lam dropped her files on a bed as she hurried past so she could take Teal'c by the arm. "You are by far the most stubborn member of SG-1, and that is an extremely tight race."

"I cannot remain," Teal'c said.

Carolyn wearily said, "I know the spiel. You're fine. You'll heal better when you're on your feet and out in the universe letting people use you as a sparring dummy."

He placed a heavy hand on her shoulder. She looked at him.

"I am not fine, Carolyn Lam. I am, in fact, in great pain. I was hoping to be provided with some of your medication to assist me. But my injuries do not change the fact that I am a member of SG-1. If I were in their position, and they in mine, do you doubt they would do everything in their power to render assistance?"

She pressed her lips together and lowered her voice. "I understand that, Teal'c. I really do. But you have to understand that you've gone through two experiences which would have killed an ordinary man. You cannot keep going halfway in your recovery. There's only so much I can patch back together."

"I am aware."

Carolyn looked at the bed he had escaped. He could tell

she was weighing the odds she could convince him to stay there.

"Okay. I'll make you a deal. I'll help you get to the control room the next time SG-1 calls in with an update. I think one is scheduled in a few hours. If they say they need your help, then I'll sign off on letting you go through the gate and joining them."

"Thank you, Dr. Lam."

"Oh, I'm not letting you off the hook entirely. If you do go off-world, there's not a chance in hell I'm letting you go alone. Colonel Mitchell thinks I don't understand what you guys go through off-world. Going along will take care of you both at the same time."

Teal'c considered that for a moment before he nodded. "That is an acceptable compromise."

"Yeah," she said, sounding less than enthused. "I was just thinking I haven't gone on enough extremely dangerous missions. It's not like doctors on this base have bad luck or anything like that."

He looked at her. "I believe you are employing sarcasm."

"Astute." She guided him back to the bed and eased him down on the mattress. "Now, stay here and rest while you wait for Daniel and Colonel Mitchell to dial in. If I find out you've been sneaking around again, I'm going to strap you down in an isolation room." She offered her hand to him. "Do we have a deal?"

He took her hand in his. "Indeed."

Carolyn smiled. "From you, that's as good as a signed contract."

She walked away and Teal'c lowered himself onto the mattress. It was not, perhaps, the ideal arrangement, but he could make peace with it. It made no difference if Carolyn Lam accompanied him through the Stargate. The most important thing was that he would be there if his team needed him. He folded his hands over his stomach and closed his eyes.

If rest was what it would take to get him through the gate, he was going to be sure he got as much as possible.

~#~

Lokelani's home was definitely a point toward her being a Goa'uld. A far cry from the subterranean cold-water Tanis and Shein called home, Lokelani escorted Sam to one of the large buildings several blocks away from the city walls. If anyone ever did stage an invasion, this would be one of the safest places to be when it happened. She saw a flight of stairs clinging to one side of the building leading up to the roof, reminiscent of a fire escape without the safety railing. The façade was decorated by ostentatious carvings of animals Sam had never seen before. Lokelani saw her looking and smiled proudly as she opened the door.

"Lovely, isn't it? Amazing what art forgers with an endless amount of free time can produce."

Sam hadn't seen any other buildings so ornately decorated. "And they just randomly decided to honor your home with their work?"

"I do things for them, and they show their gratitude. We can talk about it all inside."

She dismissed her escorts with a quick sideways nod. The women returned the nod and vanished down a dark corridor that branched off the main hall. Sam had been watching them during the walk. They had never said a word and appeared so indifferent to everything that was happening that Sam started to wonder if they were some sort of automatons.

"Please, come in," Lokelani said. "I believe the cruelest thing about this prison is how our captors simply drop us here with no guide or hint about how things work. So I took it upon myself to take in the newlings."

The front hall was an open space larger than Tanis' cave. Lokelani continued across the polished tile of the floor to a large curtained doorway in the opposite wall. The curtain was pushed aside to reveal a comfortably adorned room with plush furniture.

Sam followed more slowly to examine the décor. A mirror with a gilded frame hung from one wall, flanked on either side by tall bronze vases.

"More forgers?" Sam asked.

Lokelani chuckled and shrugged. "I do enjoy surrounding myself with art. It helps me forget where I am and remember the places I will likely never see again."

"It's… nice." She was actually thinking it was a bit gaudy. The statement made by the decor was less 'prison cell' and more 'Goa'uld summer home.'

Lokelani opened a wooden cabinet near a small fire pit. "The ladies will take care of our meal. While we wait, would you like something to drink?"

"Water, if you have it."

"Of course. The temperature here can be rather balmy, depending on what you're used to. The shield which provides us with the atmosphere and light also regulates things like that." She poured herself a glass of something green and opened a second jar for Sam's drink. "I believe it's currently set to 'two degrees hotter than would be comfortable.' This is a prison, after all." She smiled as she brought Sam a glass of water. She gestured at one of the seats. "Please, Sri Fraiser, relax."

Sam took the water and sat down without taking a drink. "Sorry. I guess I'm a little wary of kindness in a place like this."

"Mm, wise." Lokelani sat in the center of a long divan. "A prison like this can be good for morale, but it also leads to idleness. Boredom. Honor among thieves is a credo which cannot be followed when everyone around you is a thief. Now where shall we begin? What would you like to know about this lovely little cage you now call home?"

"How to escape."

Lokelani slapped her leg and laughed heartily. "That is the first thing everyone asks and, sadly, the one thing I cannot answer. The irony is that if I could answer it, I wouldn't be here to tell you how I did it. But I'm glad that you asked because I believe it's good to get that question out of the way early. This prison is inescapable. Countless people have tried. They've been slaughtered in uprisings, and their fellow inmates were starved by a severe limiting of rations in the aftermath. For a while, our Overseers left the bodies of attempted escapees on the salt plains where new condemned couldn't help but pass them on the way in. I found that cruel, and disrespectful to the dead. So I had my ladies clear away the corpses as a kindness."

Sam narrowed her eyes. "You can turn off the sensors."

Lokelani regarded Sam for a long moment with an unreadable expression. Finally, she smiled and dipped her chin. "I have certain privileges which come with my position. Maintenance, that's all it is. The guards allow me a modicum of control in exchange for watching over things."

"That's a pretty big allowance." Sam thought of trustees in Earth prisons who were allowed certain freedoms, but she doubted any of them would have been given the keys to the front gates. "What if you decided to shut them off the next time a ship comes in? Let everyone go home?"

"They know I would never do that," Lokelani said. "I won't discuss this further. I hope you understand."

Not to mention you have this palace and a stable of slaves who look at you like a queen, Sam thought. She gestured at the opulence around her with the glass. "The people in charge… the Overseers… they don't mind you setting yourself up like this? Living it up in a palace, running your own private militia. You'd think they would want their prison to be more of a punishment."

"Oh, they have no idea how we live, nor do they care. They haven't set foot on this planet since they originally set it up, and that was so many generations ago, I doubt any of them even know what it looks like. They rely on their guards for reports, and as we don't make a fuss, they ignore us."

"So the guards can be bribed? Negotiated with?"

Lokelani shook her head. "No single officer has the power to sneak you aboard a ship. If you disabled one, stole his uniform, and boarded the return vessel in his place, you would be immediately discovered. They only recruit males, and the first thing that happens when they board the vessel home is they turn in their gear. All of their gear, including the uniforms."

Sam's hopes of simply disabling the sensors to escape were dashed. "Huh. That's... very thorough."

"Yes, I would say so. The few women who attempted such a plan were sent back specifically to tell the rest of us why it would never work. I don't want to destroy your hope, Fraiser, but this rock has been occupied by the most cunning criminals the universe has to offer since the Goa'uld were using Unas for hosts. Every possible angle has been explored, every weakness exploited. If there was a way out, it would not still be touted as inescapable."

"Alternatively," Sam said, "the Overseers might go out of their way to ensure that reputation survives. Maybe going so far as to cover up any successful attempts."

Lokelani nodded slowly, a professor humoring a slow student. "Yes. I suppose that is a possibility. Tell me, Fraiser, if you were the first woman to escape from Viaxeiro, how long would you keep silent? How long would you hold your tongue before using it to impress someone in a tavern or to sell your services to a client? Have you ever heard even a hint of someone making such claims? No. You have not. If there has been a successful escape, I would say the Overseers eventually caught up with whoever it was and ensured they were unable to brag by turning their conviction into a death sentence."

Sam grimaced and sipped her water.

"Here are your options, Sri Fraiser. You can live here in relative comfort, or you can put your life at risk by planning an escape that will at best be futile or at worst result in your death. I've made my choice and I'm very happy with it."

"You make a convincing argument."

Lokelani shrugged modestly. "I've had many years to perfect it. I'm sure you have many other questions. Such as accommodations. Space is at a premium and I'm afraid as new condemned, you and Sri Mal Doran will have to make do in one of the sub-service rooms we call cold-waters. They're actually quite nice. Once you've been here for a while, you can make arrangements to transfer into better living quarters."

"How long does it take to arrange something like this?"

Lokelani laughed. "Quite a long time, I assure you. Food, clothing, medicine, things of that nature are brought in by supply ships. Those items are delivered to the canteen by guards, and from there you can negotiate for what you need. There are people here who I'm sure will help you figure out that process." She tapped her fingers against the side of her glass. "It's natural to focus on thoughts of escape and return to your past life. To cling to who you once were. I want to tell you in the kindest way that it simply isn't possible. This is your life now. It's not one you've chosen, but it's only bad if you fight it."

"Just relax and accept it."

"Exactly."

Sam took another drink to disguise her sneer. It sounded an awful lot like placing a live frog in cold water and slowly raising the temperature. Before long the frog would be boiling with no idea what had happened.

Lokelani finished her drink and stood up. "Now... let's talk about you, Sri Fraiser. Like I said, I hear stories from the guards. Other condemned tell me things about their cohorts, rivals, partners, and so on. I've heard a story about every single woman sharing this city with me. But you... I've never even heard a whisper of your name."

"Well..." Sam cleared her throat and touched the cuff of her sleeve to her lips. "I told you before, I haven't been around long enough to build a reputation. I'm new."

"Yes, so you said." She leaned forward and fixed an unblinking gaze on Sam. "But in my position, it pays to know as much as possible. So tell me... who exactly *are* you?"

Sam drained her glass of water.

CHAPTER THIRTEEN

VALA EXPLORED the streets of Viaxeiro, trying to get her irritation under control. The town was nice enough, one of the nicer settlements she'd seen. She passed people sitting outside their homes, gathered in pubs, or participating in some sort of brutal game that involved maintaining possession of two different discs at the same time. She watched the game for a moment before recognizing a few of the players as former marks, at which point she quickly covered her face and walked in the opposite direction.

In a way, she was annoyed at herself for blowing up at Sam. Of course Tanis' plan wasn't ideal. She hated the idea of killing anyone, although that was tempered by the fact their intended target was a Goa'uld. They had such little regard for human life that she wasn't going to lose any sleep over one of them dying. She was certainly capable of arranging for one to die even if she didn't pull the trigger herself. And if doing it meant freedom for her and Sam, then it was a worthy endeavor.

Then again, it was another example of Sam dismissing her.

Then again *again*, Sam technically outranked her and therefore she had the final say.

Then again again *again*…

Vala growled and pushed her hands through her hair, shaking her head to dismiss her rambling thoughts. She retraced her steps back to where she'd started. Tanis was coming outside as Vala arrived and stood beside the building as she caught up.

"There you are," Tanis said.

"Here I am," Vala muttered. "Where's Shein?"

Tanis gestured toward the cold-water with her head. "Resting. I was hoping to chase you down. Get a chance to talk without Shein or… your new friend… listening in." She stuffed her hands in her pockets, petulant and barely bothering to disguise her irritation at who Vala had arrived with. "I can't believe you threw in with them. What happened to the Vala I knew?"

"Two years is a long time. I mean, look at you! Last I saw, you had a ship full of treasure and were on your way home. You were going to get a ship, win that big space race, go legit. What happened?"

Tanis smiled. "Like you said, two years is a long time. I was able to buy the best ship I could find. Oh, it was fast, Vala. There were times I thought it was faster than going through the Stargate. And the Loop of Kon Garat was still a few months away. So I decided to take the ship for a little test run."

"And you got carried away."

"No," Tanis said, "and then the Ori showed up, and our cowardly Serrakin occupiers decided it made more sense to bend the knee than to fight back."

"Oh. Right, I heard about that. I was a bit distracted around that time." She looked at Tanis. "Your people just gave in? I thought you had warships. A whole flotilla."

"We did. I presume we still do. But our leadership didn't want a war." She scoffed and shook her head. "Our planet went from being controlled by the Goa'uld, to the Serrakin, and now the Ori. I'm starting to think I was born onto a planet of milksops. All the more reason to remain here on Viaxeiro where at least I'm surrounded by cutthroats I can respect." She looked at Vala. "What about you? What have you been up to that you show up here with a Tau'ri?"

Vala feigned breeziness. "Oh, where to start…"

Should she bring up that she was at least partially responsible for bringing the Ori to this galaxy? Or that her daughter was their leader? She was already risking what remained of their friendship by being a member of SG-1. Revealing her connection to the Orici risked completely alienating Tanis. She decided to go with a broader version of the truth.

"I went to Earth because of Daniel Jackson. I figured without you to keep me company, I could use a new pet. I hadn't the slightest idea of the dangerous life he led! All I wanted was some treasure, and I ended up bound to him by the kor mak bracelets."

Tanis laughed. "I told you those things were more trouble than they were worth."

"Well, I had to stick around Earth and join them on missions, which means I was… I was with them when this Ori threat began. I couldn't just sit idly by and watch when I could actually do something to help. So that's what I did. I'm not doing it because I've suddenly turned over a new leaf! I'm still the same woman you knew. The Ori are just objectively bad guys, like the Goa'uld are, and I know SG-1 is the best chance we have of defeating them."

Tanis sighed heavily. "At least tell me you're making life hell for that Colonel O'Neill jerk."

"No, he's not on the team anymore."

"Dead?"

"Promoted."

Tanis shrugged as if that was the same difference. "I guess I have a little more respect, since you're not working with that guy." She smiled coyly. "What about that cutie, Jonas? Is he still around?"

"No… and what do you mean 'cutie'? I thought you were…" She nodded back toward the cold-water where they'd left Shein.

"I am. But cute is cute. If you thought teasing this Daniel guy is fun…" She grinned predatorily. "You would have eaten poor Jonas alive."

"Sounds fun."

They had reached the edge of the street and Tanis faced her. "So, the plan. Are you in? Shein and I have talked about this for a long time, but we didn't think the two of us stood a chance against her on our own. You always had a knack for making the impossible come true. And as much as I hate to admit it, Shein is right. Having a member of SG-1 on our side might make all the difference."

"Two members," Vala reminded her once again.

Tanis winced. "Sorry. I'm not ready to make that a reality yet."

Vala put her hands on her hips and looked at the sky. "The way I see it, Samantha doesn't want to agree to a plan that involves killing. Not lightly, anyway. But sometimes we have to do things we don't want to do. You have to convince us Lokelani is as bad as you say she is."

"Give her time," Tanis said. "Right now, you're new. She's going to be nothing but nice to you for a while. But eventually someone is going to make her angry, and that will be the last you see of that person. No one knows what happens to them, but vanishing is bad enough to keep me in line."

"How did you find out? You couldn't have been here long enough to discover her secret on your own."

Tanis shook her head. "I didn't. Shein has been here for a while. Long enough that she gained the trust of some old-timers who brought her into their confidences."

Vala said, "So this is third-hand knowledge?"

"It doesn't take much to see the evidence once you know what to look for. I bet that's where your friend Samantha is right now. Confirming the truth about what this place really is."

"And what's that?"

Tanis said, "This might once have just been an ordinary prison, but the Ori and your Tau'ri buddies have made it something else." She held her arms out to either side with a sardonic smile. "This is Viaxeiro, the last Goa'uld stronghold in the known universe."

~#~

Sam hated thinking on her feet. She could figure out gadgets and computer systems at the drop of a hat; that was easy for her. She assumed it was like most people attacked a jigsaw puzzle. She saw the mess in front of her and began rearranging the pieces until the bigger image began to make sense. Technology was always different but it all had to work because of the same physics. She might zap herself a few times or need a couple dozen attempts before she got everything in the right place, but she usually got there eventually.

But building a lie out of whole cloth, fabricating a story that made sense and might be believable to someone else as the truth, was harrowing. She'd been impressed with her own quick thinking for coming up with the name Fraiser, but now she had to create the character's backstory. She was given a little time when Lokelani's Cai Thior ladies - Guards? Servants? - brought in three trays of food. Sam really was ravenous, and she took the chance to examine the offering. She didn't know if the flat pieces of bread were intended for sandwiches or to be a tortilla, but she piled scraps of meat and vegetables onto it before folding the ends together and taking a bite. She was embarrassed by how quickly she devoured the makeshift burrito but not enough to stop her from making another.

Lokelani chuckled at the sight. "Transport can have that effect on people," she said. "Sometimes getting here takes hours, other times it takes days. We're only so much chattel to them and they often forget we have some very basic needs. Please, take as much as you wish."

Sam finished her second burrito and began making a third. She was aware Lokelani was staring at her in anticipation of a response to her question. Her patience would run out soon, and Sam had to give her an answer or risk suspicion. She folded up the third burrito, wrapped it in a cloth napkin, and placed it in her satchel.

"I don't have a reputation as a thief because, before the Goa'uld fell, I was an upstanding citizen. I was… I was a member of my planet's militia. And I started a relationship with my commanding officer. We were discovered when the Ori showed up and I was kicked out."

Lokelani frowned. "Whatever for?"

"Our, uh, militia has rules about that sort of thing. And since he outranked me, I was the one who got cut loose." She cleared her throat and wished she'd gone with a different lie. This one was much too close to reality for her liking. "That meant I couldn't join the fight when the Ori came, so I set out to find other ways to stop them. I met Vala and she took me under her wing."

"I see." Lokelani thought for a moment. "I feel Sri Mal Doran makes a habit of taking in strays. From what I hear, they're either potential marks or decoys she uses to make her own escape if a job goes wrong."

Sam said, "Hard to imagine a job going more wrong than this."

Lokelani chuckled softly and nodded her head. "You make a valid point. But the warning stands. Now that your association with her has led to this place, I would advise you to rethink your partnership."

"And fall in with you?"

"You could certainly do worse. Vala will be your friend for as long as it suits her needs. She'll support you and encourage you. But the moment you're worth more to her as a sacrifice, that's all you'll be to her. Every partner she's ever worked with came to regret it."

Sam knew that was a lie, given how Tanis seemed to be fine with running into her again. On the other hand, Vala was very open about the fact that most of her partnerships crumbled because of betrayal. She kept her voice neutral.

"It's interesting how you know so much about her reputation given the fact you're trapped in here. Exactly how long have you been a prisoner here, anyway?"

Lokelani waved her hand dismissively. "Time is extremely relative and difficult to measure here. Most planets use an orbital system, but Viaxeiro doesn't have standard days and nights. The light overhead dims for a while so we can sleep, and then brightens for a 'day' period. It takes some getting used to. And by the time you've adjusted it's hard to tell how much time has passed out in the rest of the universe."

Sam said, "That sounds like a very longwinded way of not answering my question."

Lokelani's smile never wavered. "I have been here a very long time, dear. And I've brought in other condemned, like you, and I've asked them for updates about the rest of the universe. I listen to their stories. I keep myself informed. I know all about how the Goa'uld fell and the rise of the Ori. I was told about the scourge of the Replicators. I know all about the meddlesome Tau'ri."

Sam took a sip of water to keep from reacting.

"Information is key, Sri Fraiser. Even here, even now, with no hope of ever rejoining the universe at large. One must always know where the chips have fallen. Just in case."

"In case…"

"This prison is ruled by a group called the Overseers. There's always a chance they will be toppled. If they are, we'll likely only find out when the supplies and guards stop showing up. At that point, things will get very interesting here."

Sam raised an eyebrow. "Meaning what?"

"Anarchy, Fraiser." Lokelani stood and went back to the bar to refill her glass. "The food would quickly run out, along with the other things brought to us by the ships. People will revert to who they were before. Thieves stealing from thieves, murderers killing to take what someone else has. That day is going to come, and keeping tabs on the state of the universe helps me prepare."

"Do you think such an overthrow is likely?"

Lokelani shrugged. "I hope not, of course. Would you like another drink?" Sam refused and Lokelani walked back to her seat. "But as I said, it's inevitable. Some said the Goa'uld would never fall. Those same people would have said the Alterans would never lose power, or the Five Races would rule until the Great End of Things. Power always changes hands. One simply has to be patient."

"I suppose that's true." Sam noticed that once again, Lokelani hadn't answered her question. "So it's inevitable. But soon…?"

"You would know better than I do," Lokelani said with her enigmatic smile. "You've been out in the universe while I have only hearsay."

Sam said, "I have to admit, before I was sentenced to Viaxeiro, I'd never even heard of it. Maybe the Overseers are immune to changes in power."

Lokelani said, "We can only hope, because life under a bootheel is occasionally better than trying to survive without order."

"I should probably go. Vala's probably wondering where I am." Sam put her glass down on the table and stood up. "Thank you for the conversation and the advice. I'll keep it in mind."

Lokelani stood as well. "I hope you do. If you should need assistance in finding a place to sleep, or if you simply wish to talk more, my door is always open. I hope the two of us can become very good friends, Sri Fraiser."

"Me too."

She held out her hand. Lokelani gripped her forearm in a manner that reminded Sam of how the Jaffa greeted one another. Sam gripped Lokelani's arm as well, and as soon as their bare skin made contact Sam felt something buzzing inside her. It felt like pins and needles but in a distinctly unnatural swirling pattern, as if a swarm of miniscule bees had been injected into her veins. She masked her reaction to it, but Lokelani tilted her head to one side.

"There's something…" Her voice trailed off and she shook her head. "I apologize. I had a momentary lapse of… no, I'm sorry."

"No apologies necessary." Sam dropped her hand. "I'll be around."

"I'm very glad to hear it."

Sam allowed herself to be escorted from the house, letting out her breath only when the door was closed behind her. Though her heart was pounding, she was careful not to run just in case Lokelani or one of her guards were watching from the window. She didn't want to give any indication of what she'd felt. She had to find Vala, Tanis, and Shein. She still wasn't onboard with the whole plan, but one very big piece had just been confirmed.

Lokelani Kiir was, without a doubt, the host of a Goa'uld symbiote.

CHAPTER FOURTEEN

TEAL'C AND DR. LAM arrived on Far Scythia not long before Odai's contacts were due to arrive. Cam greeted them at the gate and tried not to smile when he saw Carolyn's outfit. She wore a short cloak over a cotton blouse, brown leather pants, and a pair of knee-high boots. Teal'c was in a sleeveless jerkin, his tattoo concealed by a flat cap pulled low over his brow, and a heavy shawl around his neck and draped over one shoulder. He assumed the rest of their gear was in the satchel hanging off Teal'c's shoulder.

"Teal'c," Cam said. "Glad to see you up and around."

"I am fortunate Dr. Lam is able to see reason."

Carolyn glared at him, then reached over and knocked on his chest. It made a heavy, hollow sound. "I made sure he was assigned an undercover outfit which could conceal Kevlar. It's called a compromise. You didn't outsmart me, Teal'c."

"Why don't we all just agree to disagree about who won?" Cam finally allowed himself a smile. "Good to see you off-world, Doc."

"You say one thing about this outfit, and I'm taking Teal'c home."

Cam held up his hands in surrender and then motioned for them to follow. "Wish I had been there to see how you talked General Landry into letting you tag along on this one."

"No, you really don't," Carolyn said. "I finally convinced him that Teal'c's welfare was only part of why I was needed. We don't know what Carter and Vala have been through in this prison. They were probably zatted or drugged for the transport to the prison. And now they could be getting tortured for all we know. The general agreed… reluctantly… that it would be good to have a doctor on-hand when you pick them up. And if that doctor happens to be a woman, when you're going to a women's prison…"

"Good call," Cam said. "And you're right on time. Daniel's with Odai right now, and he just radioed to say his friends are due any minute. Hopefully they won't hit traffic."

As Cam led them through the crowded streets, a small vessel shaped vaguely like a horse with two thrusters instead of saddlebags rose into the sky from where it had been berthed. It angled back toward the city and put on a burst of speed that picked up dust and shook the windows of every building in the area. Carolyn dropped into a protective crouch, one hand over her head, and watched as the ship angled up into the clouds.

"Yeah, should've warned you about that," Cam said. "They've been doing that all day. Odai said a lot of pilots like buzzing the town."

Carolyn frowned. "I'm starting to rethink the whole 'flying cars' future I've always dreamed of."

"Yeah, F-302s are much cooler," Cam said.

Daniel was waiting with Odai outside his ship. The bounty hunter was holding a small black communication device, which he held up as Cam rejoined them.

"Kimo just radioed. They're coming in for a landing right now."

Cam tilted his head back and squinted into the sky. "You told them we're with you, right? I only ask because SG-1 and the Tau'ri don't always get the warmest reception."

"They know," Odai said.

A speck near the sun quickly grew into the size of his hand, descending until he could see sunlight glinting off the metal. It turned wide and dipped as it neared the docks.

"I can't help but notice they seem to be going a mite fast," Cam said.

"They are. They won't be able to…" Odai growled. "They're not landing."

Daniel said, "So they're not going to help us?"

"I didn't say—"

A beam shot out from underneath the ship and swept across the ground, taking up Teal'c, Carolyn, Cam, Daniel, and finally Odai.

~#~

For a moment, Cam was afraid he had gone blind. He blinked a few times and held up his hand in front of his face.

"— that," Odai finished. The word echoed off the walls of the cramped, dark room they suddenly found themselves in.

Daniel said, "Was that an Asgard transportation beam? I haven't seen one like that since — "

"Cimmeria," Teal'c said.

"Right." Daniel subtly patted his chest as if to make sure he was all in one piece. "It must be an old model, which would explain how they got their hands on it." He also thought it sounded similar to how Wraith Darts culled victims. He wondered if there was some connection between the two technologies but he didn't have time to ponder it as one segment of the wall behind them slid out of the way. Two women entered and the first, darker-skinned than her partner with short, spiked hair, aimed a finger at Daniel.

"You. Jackson?" He nodded, uncertain if he'd just singled himself out for execution. "Move over there. By the wall."

Daniel glanced at the rest of the team. "We're not here to cause any trouble, we just want — "

"Just get by the wall," the other woman said. Her brown hair was loose and messy, falling over one eye. It was hard to tell in the dim light if she was threatening him, but he didn't want to take a chance.

"Okay." He moved to where the first woman was pointing. He kept his hands up.

Odai said, "Kimo, what's going on? What is this?"

"Hush," the brunette said, moving to stand beside Daniel.

Kimo turned to face her partner and brought up both hands so that her fingers made a pair of sideways slashes. The dark-skinned woman - obviously Adamaris - aimed the small gray box and examined a screen on the back. She grinned and swept her finger over the glass. The box hummed, and a small holographic image of Daniel and Kimo appeared in the air.

"Perfect!" Kimo said.

"Is this really the best time to add to your collection?" Odai asked.

Kimo reached out and tapped the hologram. It slowly began turning. "I said hush, Ventrell. You ask us for help with the infamous SG-1, you have to know I'm going to get a freeze of the legend himself."

"Legend?" Daniel said.

Cam said, "Legend," but in a much different tone.

Teal'c remained silent.

"I wanted to get that out of the way before we got into the heavy stuff." Kimo shut off the hologram, took the camera from Adamaris, and gave Odai her full attention. "Now, to business. What mess are you getting us into this time?"

Odai nodded at SG-1. "They're looking for the Overseers."

"Willingly?" Adamaris said.

"Apparently some of their friends got sent to Viaxeiro. They want to get them out."

Kimo laughed and nodded her head. "Yes. Okay. Very good, Odai. Now whatever you really want from us is going to seem reasonable by comparison." She laughed and shook her head before repeating, "Viaxeiro," so derisively Cam thought about calling the whole thing off.

Daniel cleared his throat. Teal'c put his hands behind his back. Cam looked at Dr. Lam, who seemed to be distracted by the fact she was actually standing on an alien spaceship. Or maybe she was just wisely pretending to be distracted so she was less likely to be noticed. Either way, Kimo's amusement quickly faded as no one rushed to correct her.

"You can't be serious."

Odai shrugged and gestured at SG-1. "Don't look at me. It's their insane idea. I'm only going along with it because I want the Tau'ri to owe me a debt."

Adamaris said, "You realize they can't owe you anything if they die on this mission."

Odai began to answer, but then his features became quizzical. He looked at Daniel. "Damn it."

"We'll make good on our promise," Cam said, "but first he has to make good on his. Can you, or can you not, take us to the people who run this prison?"

Kimo said, "Absolutely not."

Adamaris said, "Technically yes."

They looked at each other, then spoke again to switch answers.

Daniel sighed and dropped his chin onto his chest.

"We can," Adamaris said. "But it would be ridiculous for us to agree. We have a contract with the Overseers. We bring them supplies, food stores, anything they need for their little prison. They pay us very handsomely for that service, and they also make us sign a very aggressive confidentiality waiver. If we violate it, they could send *us* to the prison."

Kimo was shaking her head. "I can't believe we wasted a whole day on this. Odai, next time you should be absolutely clear about what insanity you expect from us. It will save us all some trouble."

Cam said, "There has to be something we can offer."

Kimo held out her hands palm-up. "From what I hear, the Tau'ri can take care of themselves. Your home planet is self-sufficient. You don't have any far-flung colonies to worry about. You don't need anyone like us."

"Perhaps the Tau'ri do not," Teal'c said, "but the Free Jaffa Nation has great need of just such a service."

Adamaris perked up. "The Jaffa…?"

"Jaffa won't even talk to us," Kimo said.

Teal'c removed his cap to reveal his tattoo. "You speak with one now."

Kimo gasped. "The shol'va. I knew you were once a member of SG-1, but I thought… I'd heard you left them behind. Is it really you?"

Teal'c bowed in greeting. "There are a great many Jaffa worlds which struggle to provide for themselves in the wake of the Ori's arrival in this galaxy. They would welcome any assistance in preventing famine. If I were able to witness you acting honorably to help those in need, I would gladly recommend you to the High Council."

Kimo looked at Adamaris, who was showing the galaxy's worst poker face. "Kee, think about it. This won't make us rich, but it will certainly raise our profile. Higher paying jobs… picking and choosing our clients instead of being forced to work for anyone that can pay our bills. It's a ticket to an existence we can be proud of."

"What…" Kimo spoke cautiously. She obviously wasn't fully convinced by her partner's speech. "What exactly would be expected of us?"

"We're not asking you to personally attack these Overseers yourself," Cam said. He was clearly trying not to sound too eager, but it was clear Teal'c had gotten their foot in the door. "We just need to know where to find them. You get us there, we'll do the dirty work ourselves."

Kimo worried her bottom lip with her teeth.

Cam rushed to close the deal. "And as a bonus, we'll give you a pair of Jackson's glasses."

"What?" Kimo's eyes widened.

"What?" Daniel also said, but in a much different tone.

Cam lowered his voice. "Come on, I know you pack a spare on missions just in case."

Daniel said, "For emergencies, in case this pair gets broken."

"So don't break them."

"They aren't exactly cheap."

"Have Carter buy you some new ones as a thank-you for helping get her out of prison."

Daniel didn't have a response for that. He appeared to struggle to come up with something but, when he failed, his shoulders slumped and he nodded.

"Okay. Teal'c will put in a good word with the Jaffa, and I'll… give you my glasses."

Kimo stuck her hand out. Daniel opened a pouch on his jacket and took out his emergency pair of glasses. He hesitated - they really weren't cheap - and then gave them to her. She unfolded the earpieces and put the glasses on, smiling proudly as she blinked at them through the lenses.

"Wow. Foggy."

Adamaris grinned at her. "Then I guess we have a deal. But I have to warn you. The Overseers don't like surprises. It's not going to be easy getting you into their station."

"You just worry about getting us there," Cam said. "We'll focus on getting in."

"Okay, then," Adamaris said. "Come with me. I'll show you where you can strap in."

As they filed out of the room, Kimo fell into step next to Daniel. She had her hand out in front of her face to stare at her fingers.

"So why do you prefer to see things unclearly?"

"That's-that's not really how they work," Daniel muttered.

Kimo and Adamaris led them to the cockpit. A padded bench ran along the back wall where the team could sit. Odai chose a seat far from the rest of SG-1. Cam strapped in beside Carolyn and noticed the tension in her shoulders.

"Nervous?"

"First time on a spaceship."

"You've been on lots of spaceships."

Carolyn said, "*Our* ships, a puddle jumper. This is a completely different thing."

Cam tightened the strap across his chest. "Just sit back and enjoy the ride. It's going to be smooth sailing all the way."

Teal'c and Odai looked at each other, while Kimo and

Adamaris twisted in their seats to look back at Cam.

"What?" he said.

"You've never been on one of these down-and-dirty smuggler ships before, have you?"

There was a hint of anxiety in Cam's voice when he said, "Well, no…"

"I bet you've also never been on a ship that had seatbelts," Daniel said.

"I… no…"

Kimo grinned in a way that made them all nervous. "Hold on, Tau'ri. You're about to find out how we really fly out here on the edges."

Carolyn grabbed the straps of her chest restraints with both hands. Cam did the same just as Kimo kicked off their autopilot and gave the ship a new burst of speed. The team was pushed back into the cushions, Cam, Carolyn, and Daniel's feet lifting off the floor. Though he'd been in all kinds of ships and taken dozens if not hundreds of extremely rough rides, Cam hoped that whoever equipped the ship with seatbelts had also thought about putting in air-sick bags.

CHAPTER FIFTEEN

VALA AND TANIS spotted Sam in the crowd and hurried to catch up with her. Sam started to say where she'd been, but Tanis held up a hand to stop her. "Not out here. Back at the cold-water." Sam agreed; she didn't want anyone to overhear what she had to say. As far as she knew the Cai Thior were all wearing uniforms, but any of their fellow 'condemned' might be loyal enough to report anything that sounded like scheming.

Shein was at the small kitchenette preparing something that smelled like burning honey. She looked up as they filed inside but didn't speak until the door was closed and secured.

"Looks like everyone's back together."

Tanis said, "Seems Carter got herself an invite to Lokelani's inner sanctum."

Shein smiled and came over to join them. "Did she give you the whole spiel?"

"She certainly had a lot to say, yeah," Sam said. "But more importantly, I was able to confirm your theory. She is definitely a Goa'uld. I felt it when we shook hands."

Vala perked up. "Fantastic! That certainly solves a few problems, doesn't it?"

"Not really," Sam said.

"Oh, come on! SG-1 is the leading Goa'uld killers of the galaxy." Vala counted on her fingers. "Anubis, Apophis, at least seven Ba'als, Bynar, Cronus, Hathor, Nirrti, Ra, Tanith…"

Sam said, "Nirrti wasn't us."

"You were in the room."

"Wait." She tilted her head to the side. "Was that list *alphabetized*?"

"I have a lot of free time on the base," Vala said sheepishly.

"No, I wasn't judging," Sam said. "I actually approve. But back to the point, the majority of those deaths happened in battle conditions. It was either them or us. We didn't just roam the galaxy looking for Goa'uld to take out."

Shein said, "The way I see it, you don't have much of a choice. Either you get rid of Lokelani or you stay here for the rest of your days. Are you willing to do that?"

"I'm not willing to admit that's the only way out of here. I have to believe there's a way to escape without causing a riot."

Tanis had moved to the bed and sat on the tangled sheets. "I knew Tau'ri were ignorant, but I had no idea they were this naïve."

Vala said, "Hey, there's no need to be rude."

"You think you can find a quiet way to escape? Just slip out the back door, no one the wiser?" She nodded at the door. "There are a couple hundred people out there who fill their days trying to distract themselves from thoughts of escape. Some of them have tried, all of them have failed, but they all have it at the back of their minds. If there's even a hint someone is planning an escape, it'll get around. And if you suddenly disappear, they'll know it worked. There's going to be a riot regardless. The only thing you can control is what happens afterward. Bring down Lokelani and leave a better world in your wake."

"How will anarchy be better than what you have now?" Sam asked.

"She's not talking about anarchy," Vala said. "She wants to take over."

Tanis grinned. "The highest devil stands above the lowest angel."

"Better to reign in Hell than to serve in Heaven," Sam said.

"I prefer my version," Tanis said. "Someone has to be in charge around here. There are supplies from the Overseers to ration out, there are disputes to handle. Better me than an eyeshiner."

Sam said, "Sounds like a lateral move to me."

Tanis showed her teeth and clicked her tongue. Vala seemed horribly offended by the gesture but tried to cover it.

"What does that mean?"

"Just, uh, don't worry about it."

Sam considered showing Tanis one of Earth's offensive gestures, but decided not to.

"Keep in mind," Shein said, "that if we're in charge, it'll probably be easier to help you escape. Who knows what tricks and treasures Lokelani is hiding in that house of hers? The only people who ever spend time there are her Cai Thior guard."

"The uniformed women," Sam said.

"Right. They might be the only way in. By the time I realized they were the key, I had been here too long to start sucking up to Lokelani."

Tanis said, "And when I showed up, she made it abundantly clear in our 'welcome interview' that I wasn't the kind of person she would ever trust. She probably paints Vala with the same brush." She aimed her little finger at Sam. "You, though. She might be willing to trust you."

Sam considered that. "Yes, but we should keep in mind that Lokelani might have sensed that I'm a former host—she didn't say anything, but that doesn't mean she's unaware." She looked at Vala. "However, she did seem interested in rescuing me from Vala's influence…"

Tanis chuckled. Vala huffed.

Shein said, "You would be a perfect candidate with your military training. Lokelani loves a soldier girl."

"Mm. She's not alone," Tanis said, looking at Sam. Shein jealously snapped her teeth. Tanis pursed her lips at her in response. "Relax. She might be a soldier, but she's still one of the Tau'ri who locked me up. I'll work with her but I'm not her friend."

Sam smiled coldly. "Fine by me."

Vala said, "Glad we can all get along. Now… back to your point… we pretend to have a falling out, Sam goes to Lokelani and asks for help…?"

"She likes picking up strays," Tanis said. "If she thinks someone is helpless and pathetic, she'll swoop in to play savior. What do you think, Carter? Can you be even more pathetic?"

Sam said, "If you're offering to give me lessons based on your vast experience —"

"*Ladies*," Vala said with an exasperated sigh. "Don't make me be the referee, please. It's far too much responsibility and we'll descend into chaos."

Tanis scooted back on the bed, giving up the battle. Sam also withdrew and moved toward the wall. Vala began to pace.

"Okay, here's the plan so far. Sam and I get into a public biffo. Sam seeks refuge with Lokelani and joins her little group of not-Jaffa. That gets her inside the house where she can look for ways to get us home safe."

Shein said, "And for ways we can overthrow her."

"Of course," Vala said. "We'll need a way for Sam to keep in touch with us. Does Lokelani give her people time off? Nights when they can wander around unsupervised?"

Tanis rubbed her thumb along her bottom lip as she thought. "They mostly live at the compound where Lokelani can keep an eye on them."

"Her own personal army," Shein added. "Keeps them in line."

"And helps to prevent exactly the kind of conspiring we have in mind," Sam said.

Vala stood in front of Sam to grip her upper arms. "Yes, but now we have a plan! Which is more than we had a few minutes ago." She slapped Sam's shoulder. "Here for less than a day, and we're already making progress!"

"Go us," Sam said flatly.

"We'll find ways to communicate," Tanis said. "When I was locked up after my first encounter with SG-1, Corso and I were able to scheme about our own escape."

Vala cleared her throat and leaned closer to Tanis. "Maybe don't bring up the fact you betrayed the last person you conspired to escape prison with."

"What I'm saying is that communication is always possible, especially when you aren't literally under lock and key. You'll be part of the system, one step below our actual guards. You should have plenty of freedom to move around and give us updates."

"And while I'm in the belly of the beast," Sam said, "what will you be doing?"

Shein said, "We'll be talking with people who have been here longer than we have. Looking for vulnerabilities in both Lokelani and Viaxeiro. With the four of us working together, I think we have a real shot at getting out of this place."

Tanis laughed softly under her breath. When Shein looked at her, Tanis waved dismissively. "No, don't pay any attention to me. I was just wondering how many people condemned here have said the exact same thing."

"We have something they didn't have," Vala said.

"What?" Tanis nodded at Sam. "Her?"

"Yes, her. And the rest of SG-1. I guarantee you they are out there right now, tireless, leaving no stone unturned until they find this place. Unlike everyone else who has tried to break out of this prison, we aren't alone. Our white knights are right around the corner."

~#~

Cam's head was between his knees. It was taking all his strength not to slump onto the floor and stay there for the rest of the month. "I think I'm going to be sick."

Three different people around him said, "Again?"

With great effort, he sat up straight. He was green around the gills, eyes pleading for relief. "What kind of ship doesn't have inertial dampeners?"

"Oh, we have them," Kimo said. "They're just spotty and not very good."

Daniel said, "Are you going to be okay there, Shaft?"

Cam grunted. "Are we there yet?"

"Almost," Adamaris said. She fitted something in her ear and began working with the radio. "We need to give the engines a rest from time to time or they have a tendency to kind of… shake off."

"That's very comforting, thank you." He slumped against the back cushion.

Kimo turned in her seat so she was facing them. "The Overseers don't like people showing up unannounced, so we're taking this chance to let them know we're on the way." She smiled and stood up, patting his shoulder as she walked past him to the back of the ship. "And a chance for your stomach to catch up with us. I do apologize for the rough ride. Some people just aren't cut out for traveling at high speeds."

Carolyn snorted and covered her mouth with her hand. Cam glared at her, his irritation undercut by the fact he looked close to death.

"And why aren't *you* in the same boat, Doc?"

"Have you ever flown anywhere with my father?"

"No."

She smirked. "Airsick bags were for sissies. And surprising your daughter with an unexpected barrel roll is the height of hilarity."

Cam bent over double again at the mention of a barrel roll. Carolyn put a hand on his back, patted his shoulder, and looked at Daniel.

"Hey," she said. "Why aren't you puking your guts out, too?"

"Years of reading in cars, buses, planes…" Daniel shrugged. "I don't really get motion sickness."

Cam said, "No, this isn't motion sickness. I know motion sickness. This is something else. This is a motion sickness wrapped in a radioactive monster."

Kimo returned and handed Cam a small black canister. "Here, this should help."

"What is it?"

"Diamondgut," Kimo said. "It helps you deal with ships like these. I had to drink gallons of the stuff when I first started flying."

Cam uncapped it and took a drink. He gagged. "You sure that's not turned to coal?"

"Tau'ri," Adamaris said. "There's just no pleasing them. You better hold on tight, though. I just got confirmation from the station, and we've been cleared to continue on."

Daniel said, "Don't worry, Cam. I'm sure the next leg will be smooth sailing."

Cam took a deep breath and downed the rest of the diamondgut.

~#~

Ideally, Landry would never leave his post while any team was in danger. Jack had warned him about it, and said that George had felt the same way. "Walking away from that desk at the end of the day is one of the hardest things you'll have to do," Jack told him. "It might not seem like it, but when you've got teams out there in the line of fire, you're going to want to keep your butt in the chair until every last one of them is home."

Hank understood. It was almost midnight and he was still sitting at the desk, reading reports that could have waited until morning. The lights in the corridor were low. Occasionally he heard the voices of night shift officers as they moved about the base, but for the most part he felt like the last centurion, standing guard. Most nights he was able to trust he was leaving things in good hands, but this time was different. This time it was his daughter out there, with SG-1, walking right into the lion's mouth. He couldn't have chosen a better team to watch her back. But still.

The phone rang. It was two hours later on the east coast, but he didn't even question who would be on the other end of the line when he picked it up. "Speak of the devil."

"That's rarely a good way to start a conversation."

Hank laughed. "How are you, Jack?"

"Oh, no complaints. Pining for the days when I could shoot at the people irritating me." He paused. Hank imagined him staring out the window at the Washington Monument, lit against the night sky. "How late are they?"

Hank didn't bother to ask how General O'Neill knew SG-1 was off-world. "Technically they're not overdue at all." No response from Jack. "Not enough to be worried. What they're doing… what they're in the process of doing… is complicated."

More silence from Washington. "Well," he finally said, "they're good people. Whatever they're doing, I'm sure it'll all work out."

"Same here."

"Hank," Jack said, "it's late. Why don't you get out of that chair and go home?"

Landry smiled. "I'll leave it when you do, Jack."

"Fair enough."

When the call was over, Landry stood up and walked out to the briefing room. The gate room was always brightly lit, never night. He was fortunate they couldn't discuss mission details over the phone, and hoped he hadn't lied to Jack about SG-1's current situation. He also knew they couldn't exactly send regular updates where they were going. As for Carter and Vala, he could only hope they were safe wherever they'd ended up.

In a few hours or a few days, the Stargate in front of him would open again and he would be needed. At the moment there was nothing for him to do but go home, get some rest, and trust his people. He knew they would be trusting him to be ready when they needed him and that would require sleep.

"The light is on, SG-1," he said under his breath. "We'll be here when you come home."

He stood there a moment longer before he went into the office and began gathering his things to leave.

CHAPTER SIXTEEN

THERE WERE no nights on Viaxeiro, at least not the way Earth and most other planets experienced it. Tanis explained to Vala what Sam had learned from Lokelani, that the light from the energy field dimmed every fifteen hours, giving them approximately fifteen hours of darkness. It was never completely dark but it was close enough for the condemned who were used to a diurnal existence. Shein knew of an empty cold-water where Sam and Vala could get some rest and took them there. It was extremely spartan: two beds on opposite walls, barely enough space between the foot of each for someone to walk between. There was a glowing glass orb attached to the wall over each bed. Vala went to one of the beds and sat on the mattress, legs folded in front of her.

"We'll meet up again in the morning," Shein said. "We can work out the details of your fight to make sure Lokelani sees it happen."

Sam nodded. "Sounds good."

She held up a bag and tossed it to Vala. "Clean outfits. Hopefully by tomorrow, Carter will have one of the Cai Thior uniforms, but Tanis thought you might want something to wear just in case."

"Thank her for me."

Shein nodded and leaned against the door. "I believe you'll succeed and get out of this place. If anyone can do it, it's probably you. But if you don't, you might have to get used to sticking around here. Well, unless Lokelani puts us all to death for plotting against her. My point is, Vala…"

Vala's voice was soft, compassionate. "Tanis and I were partners in crime. That's all. You don't have anything to worry about."

Shein twisted her lips and kicked softly at the ground. "I just wanted to be sure I said it."

"Understood."

"Peaceful night," Shein said as she left, shutting the door behind her.

Sam went to one of the beds and sat down. She felt a lump in her satchel and took out the last burrito she'd made at Lokelani's home. She was still hungry, but she knew Vala probably hadn't had anything substantial to eat since they arrived. She walked over and placed it next to Vala on her bed.

"It's not much."

"Food?" Vala eagerly unwrapped the cloth napkin and tore into the bread.

Sam went back and sat on the edge of her bed. After a moment she lifted her feet off the floor and stretched out.

"What about you?"

"I ate at Lokelani's."

"No, I mean…" Vala swallowed her mouthful. "I mean, do you think we'll be successful?"

Sam said, "I have to believe. We plan for failure, but we can't let ourselves believe it's an option. That's how this works. Same with the rest of SG-1. We always believe we're going to win."

"Good," Vala said.

Sam lifted her head. "Why, do you not believe it?"

Vala sighed and looked around. "I've been in a lot of prisons, Samantha. Good ones, bad ones, all kinds. This is a good one. A rock in the middle of nowhere, no ships on the surface longer than it takes to off-load supplies…"

"There's always a way out, Vala."

"I know."

"And the rest of SG-1 is out there right now looking for a way to get here and help us out."

"I know."

Sam said, "So relax."

Vala said, "I'm relaxed. I'm very relaxed. I just wanted to say that I'm intimidated by this prison. And if I have to be trapped in here with anyone, I'm very glad it's someone like you. Now, you don't have to say it back. I know you have the whole of the SGC to choose from and you'd probably prefer it if I was General O'Neill or Daniel or something, but—"

"Vala," Sam said, interrupting the ramble. "I could have done far worse in terms of cellmates."

"Thank you, Samantha."

Vala finished eating and flopped down on her bed. Sam reached up and, after tapping on the glass a few times, figured out how to dim the light. Vala kept her light on.

"Samantha?" Vala asked after a few minutes. "Are you still awake?"

"Oh, God." Sam put a hand over her face and laughed. "I'm having a slumber party."

Vala pushed herself up on her elbows. "A what?"

"Never mind. But if you're about to ask if we can put on nighties and hit each other with pillows, you're out of luck."

"Now I'm *really* curious."

Sam shook her head, still smiling. "It's a thing on Earth. Pretty much exclusively in movies made by men. For men, too. A bunch of young women get together to spend the night at a house, and they strip down to their underwear, jump on the bed, and hit each other with pillows. It's very prurient." She looked at the door. "Come to think of it, women-behind-bars is also a big thing on Earth."

"So the men who make these movies only wish to see women as sexual objects or in a cage?"

"That's the long and short of it usually."

Vala snorted and dropped down onto her back. After another long stretch of silence, Vala said, "I'm sorry I kept the fact this was a women's prison from you. I really didn't know it was a trap. I wasn't trying to trick you. I only insisted on having you come with me because I thought it was a golden opportunity for you to see me in my element. Dealing with a criminal, crossing and double-crossing, that sort of thing. After the last mission when everything went — " She blew air through her lips and flashed her hands out in front of her. "I just wanted you to understand what I could contribute to the team."

It was Sam's turn to sit up. "Vala, I know exactly what you contribute. You're an amazingly strong, smart woman. And I know you hide that strength because it's always been better for people to underestimate you. I admit there are times when even I'm fooled by it, but that's my fault for not looking past the surface. For you to have survived the things you've been through? Host to a Goa'uld, imprisoned by the Ori, giving birth just to have the baby taken away from you to lead an army…? My God, even one of those things would be enough to bring a weak woman to her knees. But you're not only still standing, you're stronger and more dedicated than you've ever been. You don't have to tell me what you contribute to the team. I know your worth. And if sometimes I forget that, it's my problem. Not yours."

There was silence from the other bed for a long time. Finally Vala very quietly said, "Well. Thank you again, Samantha."

"You're welcome." She settled back against her pillow. "We should try to get some sleep. We have a big day ahead of us tomorrow."

"Goodnight, Sam."

"Goodnight, Vala."

~#~

The diamondgut helped, and Cam found himself actually enjoying the second leg of their journey. Teal'c seemed to be meditating and, after checking his vitals, Carolyn had fallen asleep with her head tucked against his shoulder. Daniel had a small notebook out and was holding it close to his face so he could scribble in the dim light. Odai was awake but staring blankly at the far wall, either daydreaming or conserving his energy.

Cam finally got bored of just sitting around. The drink Kimo gave him had settled his stomach enough that he was willing to risk unfastening his seatbelt. He moved up behind

Adamaris' seat to watch her fingers dance along the controls. It was difficult to understand what she was doing, but it seemed as if the ship required near-constant course correction. She rested two fingers on a glass dome set into the panel like she was tracing their route on a globe. When she reached over to push up a slider, Cam realized a buzzing sound he didn't realize he'd been hearing grew quieter.

"Looks pretty complex," he said.

"Takes a lot of training. Years of lessons."

He nodded thoughtfully. "And then years of experience to learn when to ignore those lessons."

"Whoa-hey," Kimo laughed, "he's a pilot after all!"

"The only downside to going through the Stargate is I don't get to fly much anymore. Well, and I get to see all these sweet ships I'll most likely never get a chance to fly."

Adamaris pushed away from the controls. "I can't stand in the way of a fellow windfoot. Sit down."

Cam hesitated. "I'm not going to crash us into an asteroid field or anything, am I?"

"No." Adamaris looked at Kimo. "No, right…?"

Kimo said, "No. Right now, it's clear enough so we'd only need one pilot anyway. I can cover if he makes any mistakes."

Cam didn't need any further persuasion. He dropped into the seat Adamaris offered and pulled himself closer to the console. Adamaris put a hand on the back of the chair and pointed to where he should put his hands.

"Take it easy. I know right now it feels like an explosion in progress, but you just have to be gentle and it'll respond. This thing is a wild animal, okay, and all you're doing is guiding it."

"Right." Cam watched the hyperspace streaks washing over the screen in front of him. He let out a slow breath and whispered, "Never gonna get old…"

Adamaris looked over her shoulder at the rest of SG-1, then leaned closer to Cam. She lowered her voice. "Sorry for everyone making fun of you earlier. Can I tell you a secret?"

"Sure." He didn't take his eye off the screen. "I love secrets."

"This ship isn't balanced right. Never has been. There's something wrong with its artificial gravity and, when we put on a significant burst of speed, it… well, it's hard to explain. But if you imagine the gravity of this ship like a bubble and space as a wave, they wash over each other."

Cam wasn't quite following, but he nodded anyway. "Okay."

"The thing is, it's so subtle that most people don't even feel it. The only people who are really bothered by it are pilots who can feel something is wrong but can't tell what it is." She patted his shoulder. "The only reason you were so green is because you know how a ship ought to feel, and this one was throwing you all the wrong signals. Truth is, Kee and I wouldn't let anyone touch the controls of this beauty if they didn't get a little tustle-tummy on their maiden voyage."

"Really?" Cam felt immensely better. "Well, how about that. So… wait, if it was just my senses fooling with me, why did diamondgut help? What was it?"

Kimo, who had been listening silently, laughed at the question. "Liquor." She looked over with an impish grin. "We got you a little drunk, windfoot."

Cam scoffed with offense, then shook his head and moved his hands across the controls. "You ladies are definitely trouble."

"And don't you forget it, Colonel Mitchell." Adamaris looked at the chronometer attached above the screens. "We've got a little ways left before we reach the Overseers. I'm going to the back of the ship to rest my eyes. Kee, let me know if we're coming up on any rough patches and I'll take over for the new guy."

"Will do," Kimo said.

Adamaris went into the back. Daniel looked up from his notebook to watch her go, then looked at Cam.

"See? Nothing to be ashamed about."

Cam said, "You tell anyone at the base about the fact I threw up because of space turbulence, and I'll fight dirty, Jackson. I know things about you. Shameful things."

Daniel smiled and went back to his notebook. Cam settled into the seat and smiled as he let his hands get used to the controls. He was well aware of the fact that Kimo was doing most of the actual flying, but that didn't matter to him at the moment. All that mattered was that he had an entirely new class of ship at his command. He wasn't going to squander that with silly details.

CHAPTER SEVENTEEN

THE FLOOR shuddered under their boots, prompting everyone to prepare for the end of their trip. Kimo returned to take over the controls from Mitchell. Daniel put away his books, Carolyn checked to make sure Teal'c didn't need any of his dressings changed, and Odai sat up straighter to stretch without actually moving very much. He rolled his neck and looked toward the front of the ship.

"It's about time."

"The Overseers are all about discretion," Adamaris said. "They can't exactly be under the radar if they're in the middle of every shipping lane in the sky."

When they had slowed enough for it to be safe, Daniel unfastened his restraints and got up to move behind Kimo's seat. The wild waves of hyperspace fell away to the normal starscape, and he scanned the vicinity for their destination, craning his neck to get a better look.

"That's no moon," he said, knowing it was what Jack would have done in his place.

The space station was shaped like an obsidian egg, studded at regular intervals with outcroppings he assumed were docking slips. Dozens of vessels were hooked up and, when they moved in closer, it was possible to see into the station where people were moving around. Kimo angled the ship toward the flattened underside of the egg. As she repositioned them, the bottom of the station was revealed to be a hangar. The station's gravity made it look like the ships were hugging the wall like houseflies.

Daniel closed his eyes and swayed a bit, unexpectedly queasy.

"You okay, Jackson?"

"Yeah, just-just trying to keep everything down. I apologize for mocking you earlier."

Fortunately it seemed as if Mitchell was on too much of a high to gloat. "Don't worry about it. Just try to talk through the nausea."

"So," Daniel said, "all these other ships…"

Adamaris said, "Couriers to pick up the condemned and take them to Viaxeiro, suppliers to bring food and clothing, and guards either going on- or off-duty. Prisoners get condemned on their home planet or caught by a bounty hunter. The prisoner is bounced around until they get dropped with one of the… hm. Kee, how many people like us would you say there are?"

"No more than ten."

"Right," Adamaris said. "One of the ten or so couriers who know how to find the Overseers' station. This is where they're officially condemned, and the pilot of the courier ship is given the current coordinates of the prison."

Mitchell seemed to file away that information for later, but Daniel focused on something else Adamaris had said. "Guards go off duty? So the guards are allowed to come and go?"

Kimo was already shaking her head. "If you think you're getting in that way, you're out of luck. Every battalion has a captain who knows what his men look like. Strangers won't be able to just throw on a uniform and slip aboard the ships unnoticed."

"That's a 'you' problem," Adamaris said. "We agreed to get you to the Overseers and we've done that. We'll do you one better and stick around for a while in case you need a ride back to a gate world. But it's not our job to get you to the prison."

Mitchell said, "That's okay. We don't want to cause you any problems."

"We do appreciate the ride," Daniel said.

Adamaris found an empty slot and guided the ship down.

~#~

Once the ship was secure, Kimo and Adamaris stood to give the team a proper farewell. Kimo had moved Daniel's glasses to her jacket pocket but, as she stood, she took them out and put them back on. She smiled at him and stuck out her hand.

"Just in case we're not the ones who take you home, I want to take this chance to say goodbye. It's been our joy to be your escorts, SG-1."

Daniel shook her hand. "And, as far as intergalactic thieves go, you're the nicest we've come across in a while."

"Ahem," Odai said.

"You tried to hand us over to the Lucian Alliance in exchange for a bounty," Daniel said without looking back at him.

Odai said, "Still. A little rude. I'm right here."

Daniel ignored him. "Enjoy the glasses, Kimo."

"I certainly will, Dr. Jackson. Good luck saving your friends."

"Thank you."

Cam looked at Carolyn and Teal'c. "So, Doc? Is he cleared to come out and play?"

"Under ordinary circumstances," she said, "not a chance. But given the fact it's Colonel Carter and Vala, I know nothing I could say will keep him from going with you. As long as I'm able to keep an eye on him…"

Teal'c inclined his head to her. "Thank you, Dr. Lam."

"Don't make me regret it, okay?"

Cam looked at Odai. "How about you?"

"I think I'll hang around, see if I can get a few jobs for these Overseers." He leaned to one side so he could see Adamaris. "They pay well?"

"They pay so well, sometimes I think they don't understand how money works."

Odai smiled at Cam. "I'll be fine. And this makes up for everything between us. You take care of the Ori and we'll consider our business done. The next time we run into each other, I don't want to hear anything about debts or favors."

"Sounds good to me," Cam said. "Good luck getting hired on."

Odai stood up. "Good luck on your suicide mission."

"Getting Carter and Vala out of the prison or stopping the Ori?"

"Well, if one of them doesn't do it, I'm sure the other will." He saluted to Adamaris and Kimo as he headed for the back of the ship.

Adamaris said, "We can't promise how long we'll be here. Someone might hire us as couriers and demand we leave immediately, or we could be here for days looking for a charter. But if we're here when you need to get home, you just call up. You're pretty fun passengers."

"Thanks," Cam said.

They walked through the back of the ship. Odai had left the hatch open for them, even though he was nowhere to be seen when they descended to the hangar deck. Cam took a moment to admire the rows of ships stretching out to either side - he thought he'd seen a few of them from an F-302 or the bridge of the *Odyssey* - before he began looking for a way into the station proper. The hangar was wider than it was tall, with a segmented roof which reminded him of a ribcage. A few other new arrivals were walking toward an opening in the far wall.

"So what's the plan, Jackson?" he asked as they began walking. "We knock on doors until we find the big boss, then ask them politely to grant a couple pardons?"

"I don't think that would work," Daniel said.

"Nor do I," Teal'c said, "in no small part because Vala Mal Doran is, in fact, most likely guilty of the crime for which she was incarcerated."

Mitchell scoffed. "Come on, man, statute of limitations! Besides, she wouldn't even have gotten caught if it wasn't for some goon she had a beef with setting a trap for her. If that's not extenuating circumstances, then I don't know what is. Entrapment, T, it's a thing."

"Be that as it may," Daniel said, "do you really think the people who took over a rogue planet as a prison and built *this* as their headquarters are going to be reasonable?"

"That… is a fair point," Cam said. They passed underneath the belly of a ship that reminded him of a Wraith dart. "So we don't go to the bosses. We can't sneak in with the guards. That leaves the supply ships. We find someone who could use a few laborers and, bang, we're at the prison ready to bust out the girls. Nothing to it. Be home in time for supper."

They had passed through the opening and now stood in a wide corridor that curved away to either side. Humans and humanoid aliens shuffled along the carpeting. Some moved with clear confidence that they knew where they were going while others moved slowly and consulted shining screens embedded in the walls.

"It's astounding anyone is able to maintain something like this in secrecy," Carolyn said. "Odai told me a little about its origins while we were en route. It has to be unbelievably old."

Teal'c said, "If they are anything like the Goa'uld, there is a high probability that those who have been incarcerated have helped increase the wealth of their jailors."

"So they arrest the criminals and keep their loot?" Carolyn said. "That doesn't seem right."

"No one's watching the watchers," Cam said. "They make the rules, they benefit from the spoils, and who's going to tell them no?"

She sighed. "I guess you run the risk of corrupt law enforcement no matter where you go. Nice to know humanity isn't unique in that."

Everyone else seemed to be moving in a clockwise direction, save for the people who were heading into the hangar, and Cam decided they couldn't go wrong by following the crowd. Once they got a better feel for the place he might suggest splitting up, but for the time being they needed to be a group. He was afraid if anyone drifted off on their own, they might never find them.

"A lot bigger than it looks from the outside," he said.

"The black-and-grey coloring probably helped create that illusion," Daniel said. "If it wasn't for all the ships hooked up to it, this whole place might have been next to invisible from the wrong angles."

Cam said, "The more I hear about this prison system, the less I like it. Maybe our best bet to get Carter and Vala back would be busting the whole place apart."

"That would be inadvisable," Teal'c said.

"He's right," Daniel said. "We have to assume that most of the people who sent prisoners to Viaxeiro had a good reason to do so. On Hadante, we thought Linea was a helpless old woman who didn't pose a threat to anyone. It turned out she was a mass murderer known as the Destroyer of Worlds."

Cam said, "And caused an entire planet to lose their memories and get younger. Right. All I'm saying is, Sam and Vala never even got a trial. They were picked up by some bounty hunter with a beef and sentenced to life in a secret prison. Tell me that sits right with you."

"Well, of course it doesn't," Daniel said. "We also have to assume that what some cultures consider a crime worthy of imprisonment on Viaxeiro isn't a crime by our standards. But unless we're willing to start making ourselves policemen of the universe, there's not much we can do about it."

Carolyn said, "What about this Tanis Reynard person? The whole reason we're in this mess is because Vala wanted to get her out. Are we sure she deserves freedom?"

Cam said, "I'm hoping Carter and Vala are making that evaluation right now. When the time comes to leave, they'll let us know if Tanis belongs in jail or if she's coming with us."

They were now walking along the outer wall of the station. They arrived at an open area with a carousel in the center. Men and women in brown overalls and orange shirts were sorting packages by the sticker on their sides. Through the portholes, Cam could see docked ships were attached to long transparent tubes like they used at the bank. Parcels shot through the tubes and arrived in an airlock, where they waited until one of the stevedores released it onto the belt.

"We need to get aboard one of those ships," Cam said, pointing through the glass.

"I agree," Daniel said. "Any idea how to get aboard them, seeing as their crew doesn't seem to actually come onto the station? I mean, if they planned to disembark, I imagine they would go to the hangar like Kimo and Adamaris did."

Cam thought for a second. "Okay. It's not a perfect plan, granted."

Daniel moved closer to the conveyer belt and cleared his throat. One of the stevedores glanced at him before going back to work. "No samples."

"Oh, no, I wasn't… that's not what I was…" He looked to the team for help and started over. "We, uh, we want to help. With the… the supplies, supplying… food. And whatnot." Cam sighed, sure Daniel could hear him even a few feet away. "What I'm trying to say is…"

Carolyn stepped around him and stared up into the sunken face of the worker. "I'm a doctor. Do you know what that means? A physician, a healer, a — "

He grunted and moved his head. Carolyn looked at Cam, who gestured for her to continue with whatever she had planned.

"Good. Because I know there's a lot of stuff moving to Viaxeiro, but I haven't heard a thing about medicine or doctors or nurses or anything that would account for the health of the people that have been sent there. Who do I speak to about booking passage?"

The man gestured vaguely. "On this ship?"

"On *any* ship!" Carolyn demanded. "I don't care who takes me there, I only care about the women who have been woefully neglected for far too long."

He shuffled away and touched a box on the wall. A red light around the box turned green, and he spoke a guttural language Cam didn't even try to make sense of. He looked at Carolyn and noticed Daniel and Teal'c also looked stunned by her outburst.

"That... uh, that was good," Daniel said.

Carolyn was suddenly sheepish. "Well, you weren't getting anywhere and I came up with that angle. I'm sorry I didn't have time to run it by you..."

Cam said, "We would've gone along with it. Well done, Doc."

"Thank you."

The stevedore returned. "Escort soon."

"You've been a tremendous help," Carolyn said. "I'm sorry if I was a little rough."

Another grunt, and he went back to shuffling boxes.

After a few minutes, the team was approached by a mechanical manikin mounted on a pole which moved via a track along the wall. It had a vague approximation of arms and legs attached to a torso that mimicked the station's shape. Its head was triangular with a single yellow light embedded where the face would have been. The light pulsated when it spoke.

"Medical-slash-humanitarian aid requesting travel permit to Viaxeiro."

"That's right," Carolyn said. "I'm Doctor... Who. These are my companions."

The robot said, "Please follow me." The body twisted on its axis and moved away from them. Carolyn looked at Cam again, and he gestured for her to lead the way. She'd gotten them this far, so why question it now?

Daniel spoke to Carolyn just loudly enough for Cam to hear. "You know, you're not as infamous as SG-1. There's no bounty on your head, so there's no reason anyone would notice if you used your real name."

"Everyone else gets to use fun fake names when they're on missions like this."

"Fair enough."

They followed the robot away from the processing center, deeper into the station where they hoped to find someone to give them permission to board a ship. Cam allowed a little optimism to seep into his outlook. It felt like they'd been running in circles while Carter and Vala were in danger, bouncing from one lead to the next but getting no closer to where they needed to be. Now, at last, he felt like they might be on the last leg of their search.

CHAPTER EIGHTEEN

VALA SPENT the evening staring at the carved ceiling of their cold-water. Someone, probably a millennium ago, had taken tools and painstakingly carved out this little hovel. The buildings outside had been constructed, decayed, and rebuilt all for the singular purpose of keeping women like her imprisoned. She kept her hands laced on her stomach, feet crossed at the ankles. Across the room, Sam had fallen asleep almost as soon as they said goodnight. She could usually do the same thing. It was a survival technique known to soldiers and thieves alike, the ability to sleep anywhere because they never knew when the next chance might arise.

She thought about seeing Tanis again after so long. It was like encountering a ghost, a remnant from her past life that she'd long thought buried and forgotten. Now here she was again, a memento of who Vala had once been. Before the Ori, before Adria. She knew she was a better person now. She wouldn't trade her current position at the SGC for anything. But there was a lingering, nagging doubt about how long the SGC would allow her to hold a position on their flagship team. She was an alien. A wildcard. She was not only a civilian, she was a civilian they couldn't control. She knew how much that terrified them.

What would happen if, one day, the IOA decided they'd had enough of her? Would they lock her up in that dreadful Area 51 she'd heard about? Or would they let her go back through the Stargate, back to her old life as if nothing ever happened? Vala didn't know if she belonged in that old life anymore. And even if she did find a way to slip back into her old role as miscreant good-for-nothing, she knew without a doubt her new life wouldn't just leave her alone. The Ori knew she was the mother of their Orici. They or their Priors or maybe Adria herself would eventually come looking for her as soon as she left the SGC. They would know she was vulnerable.

But on the other hand, if they knew she was vulnerable, they might not think she was dangerous... Her mind traveled along that tangent for a while. Eventually she must have slept, because at some point Sam moved from the bed to the small kitchen area. Vala kept her eyes closed until the room began to fill with a very familiar aroma. She sat up without opening her eyes, knowing her hair was wild, and sniffed the air.

"Is that... coffee?"

"It's one of the things I make sure I never leave the SGC without. GDO, extra rounds, and some coffee. It won't last forever, but I thought we had a pretty bad day yesterday, so..."

Vala kicked away the blankets and climbed from her bed, stumbling zombie-like toward Sam with one arm out. Sam placed a cup in Vala's hand.

"Did you know there's coffee on basically every planet I've ever visited?" Vala asked. "Earth's isn't even the best. I'll take you to Eritupina sometime."

"I'll hold you to that. And when we get back to Earth, I'll take you to Starbucks."

Vala rolled her eyes. "Oh, please. I've been on Earth almost a year. I've been to Starbucks." She sipped the coffee. Not the best, as promised, but still better than nothing. "Before I forget, I think I came up with a plan to capture Adria."

"Really?" Sam said.

"Mm. We'll have to erase my memories, though, and make new ones. Fake ones. So that I believe the SGC finally got sick of me and kicked me out. But really, you're just waiting for Adria to find out I'm vulnerable and come rescue me. Because I'll believe the fake memories are real, Adria will know I'm 'telling her the truth' and she'll trust me. She'll walk right into whatever trap you and SG-1 set for her."

Sam thought over the plan. "Wow. That could actually work. It puts you in an inordinate amount of danger, though."

"It's nothing the rest of SG-1 wouldn't do for the greater good."

"I suppose that's true. We'll talk about it more when we get home, but it's a good plan. We'll work out the details later. I think I could convince Landry to take the risk."

Vala covered her proud smile by taking another sip of coffee. "So have you thought about the current plan? The fight we're supposed to stage to get you in Lokelani's good graces?"

"It shouldn't be too hard to set something off."

"What do you mean?"

Sam shrugged. "You fly off the handle at the slightest provocation."

"I do not! I react as reasonably as one can in the face of unwarranted attacks."

"You're doing it right now," Sam calmly pointed out.

"Well, you're attacking me without warrant! I thought we had made real progress clearing the air, but clearly you still think I'm a liability to the team. I'm starting to think the true secret to SG-1's success is the sheer, unadulterated *arrogance* of you all!"

Vala huffed, catching her breath and waiting for a rebuttal. Sam silently stared at her over the top of her cup until realization dawned.

"Oh. Oh!"

"Yeah," Sam said. "I don't think picking a fight is going to be a problem. The real difficulty will be making sure Lokelani sees it and does what we want her to do. From what I saw yesterday, she's not easy to manipulate. I couldn't even get a straight answer out of the woman."

"She's had a lot of time to perfect her little game," Vala said.

There was a knock on the door and Sam went to answer. Tanis and Shein slipped inside, both women glancing at the cup of coffee Vala was holding.

"I thought it would be better if we met in here," Tanis said.

"Very few people know you're here, but word will start spreading soon enough. It'll be better if we're not connected to each other so we can work in secrecy."

"I agree," Vala said.

Sam went back to the small pot and took another pouch of coffee grounds from her pocket. Vala thought she was making more coffee for them, a petty jab at the woman she didn't like, but she was surprised when Sam took the two cups and handed them to Tanis and Shein. Even Tanis looked amazed by the small kindness.

"I had a little bit of Tau'ri *qahwa* when I was a guest of their infirmary," she said, her voice neutral. "It's quite good. Thank you."

Vala jumped on the thin thread of potentially common ground. "If you think what they have on the base is good, you should try the stuff they sell outside. It should be considered a controlled substance. If you ever make it back to Earth — "

Sam cleared her throat. "If she ever makes it back to Earth, she's never getting beyond the base."

"Come on, Samantha…"

"That's not negotiable just because she's your friend, Vala."

Tanis smirked. "Because no matter what I do, I'm still a criminal? Like Vala?"

"No," Sam said, "because unlike Vala, you've proven yourself to be untrustworthy on the base. But beyond that, there are any number of pathogens on Earth which you'd be susceptible to. There are rules that go beyond trust. Do you know how long it took for them to finally let Teal'c live off-base?"

"Oh, so you'd lock me up forever for my own safety."

Sam rolled her eyes.

"No, no, no," Vala said. "Remember the coffee? The kind gesture? Peace offering? Come on, let's just get through this, all right? We can make it work." She looked at Shein and spoke through gritted teeth. "A little help please?"

Shein held out her hands, shaking her head with a smile.

"I don't have an angle here. I'm just enjoying the show. I love it when Tanis gets all fired up."

Vala rolled her eyes. "All right, Tanis, fine. If you can't work with her, work with me. You know how good we are when we work together. Remember our last job together? We took on Wyrrick, one of the biggest arms dealers the Goa'uld had! We walked right into that party and walked out with a fortune, and he never even knew it was us!"

"Wyrrick...?" Sam looked confused. "Dysmas Wyrrick? What party are you talking about?"

Vala waved her hand dismissively. "Oh, it was just some silly little thing. It happened right before I came to the SGC. My last big hurrah with Tanis. Wyrrick threw a party and invited a who's-who among the Goa'uld —"

"I know who he is," Sam interrupted. "And I know that party. We were there."

"What?" Vala blinked in surprise. "We who?"

"We, SG-1. We were undercover. He had a piece of Kali's treasure that we needed to prevent a doomsday weapon from going off." She remembered a point during the mission when a locked door suddenly opened. They'd never figured out the reason for that bit of fortune. "*You* were there at the same time? Robbing him?"

Vala said, "We both were. How about that. Our fates intertwined once more!" She put one hand on Sam's shoulder, the other on Tanis'. "You see? You met four years ago, before Tanis and I became partners, before I had ever set foot on Earth. And two years ago, out of every planet in the universe, we wound up in the same place. And now here we all are once again. It was meant to be! We were destined to be here, now, doing this. So come on. Let's put aside our petty differences and agree that for the time being we're all going to tolerate each other for the duration of the mission."

Shein said, "I'm starting to feel left out over here."

"Don't," Vala said. "Because you're exactly what we need. I

trust Tanis and Sam, but they don't trust each other. And Tanis doesn't trust me the way she used to. But she trusts you. And you have no reason to distrust Sam… um… right?"

Sam and Shein looked at one another, trying to remember if they'd ever crossed swords. "She tried to attack me when we first got here," Sam said.

"I thought I was protecting Tanis. No grudge if no grudge."

Vala translated, "She'll forget it happened if you do."

Sam sighed. "Fine. Water under the bridge."

"There you go. You're the nexus. The go-between. You're the one who will keep us from betraying each other or becoming suspicious."

"I have an obvious bias toward Tanis, you know."

Vala said, "Yes, sure, of course. But for the sake of the mission…"

"For the sake of the mission," Shein said.

"I've worked with a lot of partners," Vala said. "Apprentices, mentors, all sorts. Some of them betrayed me or I betrayed them. But I've never had a partner I respected more than Tanis. And I've never been a team player but SG-1 is showing me it can work. This isn't the kind of job I normally would've taken on, but with you two in my corner, I think we can succeed."

Shein said, "Sounds fun if you ask me. Tanis, you've been saying since you got here that you wished you had a couple more people you could trust to have your back. Looks to me like they just showed up."

Tanis stared hard at Sam, who returned the stare without blinking. It was Sam who broke the silence between them. "Your goal is to stay behind and take over in Lokelani's absence. My goal is to make sure you stay in prison. Those obviously aren't mutually exclusive, so there's no reason for us to antagonize each other." She held out her hand. "Truce?"

"You forgot the fact that I want you to get out of here as soon as possible." She took Sam's hand. Vala could tell Tanis was squeezing harder than necessary, but Sam didn't flinch.

She also didn't seem to respond by tightening her own grip. She just met Tanis' gaze and let her decide when to let go. Vala admired the restraint. "Not to mention taking down a Goa'uld. I'm always up for that kind of fun, no matter who I'm playing the game with."

Vala put her hand on top of theirs. "Fantastic! Shein? Come on. This is a thing sports teams do on Earth. I think it's charming. Put your hand on top of mine."

Shein approached and did as she was told, but not without reservations. Vala pushed down, then back up, waving her fingers in the air as the other three women stared at her.

"Go, team!" Vala said.

Tanis looked at Sam. "We're all going to get killed, aren't we?"

"There's… there's a good chance of that," Sam muttered. "Yeah."

CHAPTER NINETEEN

TEAL'C KEPT track of their distance traveled as the robot led SG-1 from the outer edge of the station to the interior labyrinth of narrow corridors. They barely went a hundred meters before the escort turned them left or right or guided them around a bend which took them in another direction. He believed the intention was disorientation and confusion so they would not be able to find their way back to the hangar without help. Or, barring that, preventing them from retracing their steps if they should return to the station at some point in the future.

Eventually they took an elevator to an extremely narrow passageway which was flanked on either side by what he initially assumed to be glass walls. He could see ships angling past the station and coming in to dock backed by a spattering of stars and a distant nebula. But he quickly realized there was no part of the ovoid station which was this narrow, meaning the walls were simply viewscreens looking out onto the surrounding space.

The robot remained in the elevator car. "Please continue forward. The Overseers are expecting you." When the doors slid shut, Teal'c couldn't see a seam where they met.

Mitchell stepped forward and ran his hand over the metal. "Huh. Okay. I guess whoever runs the show will open this when it's time for us to go back up."

"If they let us go," Carolyn muttered.

"Rookie mistake," Mitchell said. "We don't say things like that out loud." He looked down the passage and pointed to the door at the other end. "I guess we forge ahead."

They could only walk two at a time, Mitchell and Teal'c in the lead with Daniel and Carolyn following. The doors slid open as they approached. Mitchell held up a hand so he could advance alone, pausing at the threshold to sweep the interior for any obvious threats. He didn't have his usual weapons available but there was a Beretta tucked into his belt. Teal'c was also armed with a zat, but he waited for a signal that he should draw it.

Mitchell finally motioned for the rest of them to enter. The space beyond the doors was immense and mostly empty, save for two tables with three seats each. The tables faced a tall stage with five raised platforms. The walls were concave and smooth, reminding Teal'c of the inner surface of seashells. Their footsteps echoed off the high ceilings as they approached the center of the room.

"Stand where you are."

The voice came from somewhere high above, the acoustics making it impossible to tell exactly where it started. The team stopped walking and five columns of blue light appeared on the stage. The light flickered before solidifying into the shapes of people in identical robes. Their upper faces were concealed by heavy veils. Teal'c could tell there were three women based on their physique and the shape of their jaws, but when they spoke their voices were distorted beyond gender.

"Identify yourselves."

"State your purpose here."

Mitchell said, "Hey, folks. We're —"

"You were not the representative who called this forum."

Mitchell looked at Carolyn. She looked terrified. He gestured for her to step forward and she reluctantly did so. Her bravado from earlier had evaporated in an instant.

"Uh. Hello. I'm… I'm…" She blanked and looked at Daniel, who mouthed the name she'd given. "Right. I'm Doctor Who."

"Doctor Who. Tau'ri transmission of a fictional adventurer."

There was a pause before a second Overseer said, "Identify yourselves."

"State your purpose here."

Carolyn nervously rubbed her hands together. "Okay, the truth. The truth… the truth is that we need passage on a supply ship. Any supply ship that's going to Viaxeiro."

Another pause. Then: "You have failed to identify yourself."

"Your continued evasion will result in expulsion from these chambers."

"Identify yourselves."

"This is your final warning."

Teal'c had been listening carefully to each statement, and he believed he had discerned what was peculiar about them. He paused beside Carolyn and touched her arm. "Do not tell them who we are," he whispered. "But continue to speak. Do not pause, do not give them an opportunity to respond."

"O-okay." She cleared her throat and began reciting. "We… we are Yankee doodle dandies. Y-Yankee doodle, do or die. We're… we're real live nephews of our Uncle Sam. We were born on the Fourth of July. We came to town riding on… a… pony. We stuck feathers in our caps and called it macaroni."

Teal'c strolled forward at a casual pace. He kept his hands behind his back and didn't address the beings standing on the stage.

"Buddy?" Mitchell said under his breath as Carolyn continued her recitation.

"I believe the phrase is 'pay no attention to the man behind the curtain'." He stopped at the base of the stage and examined it carefully.

"Yankee doodle, keep it up," Carolyn said, her voice now halting. "I'll keep it up as long as I can, but I'm running out of lyrics. Mind the music and the step…"

Teal'c removed the panel to reveal a complex array of electronics. He wished Colonel Carter were there. She would be able to make much more sense of what he was seeing but, as he'd hoped, he could confirm a few things just on sight. He had seen several versions of long-distance communicators when he served the Goa'uld. Since joining SG-1 he had also seen Asgard technology which served the same purpose. What he saw now was nothing like any of those. The fact that none of the figures had responded to his actions was further proof of his theory. All five were still listening to Carolyn's gibberish and waiting for a chance to respond.

He reached into the panel and found something that seemed important. He twisted it until it came free in his hand. One of the columns of light flickered and vanished. The other four seemed unconcerned. Carolyn stopped her recitation and raised her eyebrows at the apparent magic trick.

Mitchell said, "What the hell just happened?"

"It's like Cimmeria again," Daniel said. "Old technology. The people thought they were speaking directly to Thor, but it was just a holographic projection."

Teal'c said, "Indeed."

Mitchell stepped forward. "So... the Overseers are really just holograms."

"Programmed with generic responses," Teal'c said. "They process what is being asked and choose any one of several pre-set responses."

"It would explain how they've managed to keep the prison up and running for so long while maintaining the secret," Carolyn said. "No need to recruit more people when one of the Overseers dies or worry about the next generation giving away the secret."

"So we're sitting here talking to the alien equivalent of a Magic 8-Ball?" Mitchell said.

One of the voices spoke again, obviously registering a question. "Your request is not possible at this time. Leave this chamber at once, and you will find the transport waiting to return you to the common level."

"Teal'c, do you see a reset button on that thing?"

An Overseer said, "Expediency is required. Please leave at once or we shall be forced to — "

The four remaining columns suddenly vanished.

"Well done, Teal'c," Mitchell said.

"It was not my doing, Colonel Mitchell."

The lights in the room flashed red. The door through which they'd entered slammed shut. Mitchell jogged a few steps toward it then stopped. The entire room was bathed in the red light now, and the alarm was echoing loudly enough that they could hear it even through the walls. Mitchell drew his gun but kept it by his side with nothing to aim at.

"Jackson?"

Daniel stared at him. "Mitchell?"

"Come on, man, this is a classic SG-1 death trap. No exit, alarms blaring. Guards are going to be here any second. You've been in this situation a hundred times!"

"So have you," Daniel pointed out.

"But stuff like this is why I went to so much trouble to get the band back together! This is the sort of thing SG-1 lives for!"

"Or dies from," Carolyn said. She was trying very hard not to panic, but Teal'c could tell she was extremely anxious about what was going to happen next.

Daniel put one hand to his forehead. "This is usually the part where Sam would either do something brilliant or Jack would say something deceptively simple and it would trigger an idea. Neither one of those options is available to us. And unless you see something to translate or, or a puzzle to figure out, or someone to talk sense to…"

Carolyn began to pace. "I can't believe one of my last living acts is going to be singing Yankee Doodle Dandy to a bunch of holograms."

Mitchell looked toward the stage, then at the closed door. "We were brought here by a robot."

"Yeah?" Daniel said.

"We were brought by a robot to a room with holographic Overseers. How much of this place do you think is automated? And if there are flesh and blood people working here, do you think they know their bosses are just big columns of light? They keep everything else secret, so why not this?"

Daniel looked at the stage as well. "You're right. Teal'c, can you get those projections back up and running?" While Teal'c turned to work, Daniel touched Carolyn's arm and they started toward the stage. Mitchell followed them. "Dr. Lam, come on."

"Where are we going?" she asked.

"Hopefully we're going to hide in plain sight."

Mitchell, Carolyn, and Daniel climbed onto the stage. Teal'c finished replacing what he'd disconnected and the five Overseers reappeared. They seemed unconcerned by the alarm and resorted to what was obviously their standard response.

"Identify yourselves."

"State your purpose here."

Daniel waved his hand through the torso of one, then stepped up onto its platform. He turned slowly and made sure to keep his arms tight to his sides. "How does it look?"

"No overlap," Mitchell said. "Everyone inside."

Carolyn was completely enveloped by the Overseer she chose. Teal'c stepped into a beam and looked down to make sure his size didn't give him away. He crossed his wrists in front of himself and tried to remain as still as possible. He could see through the veil of the Overseer which turned the rest of the room into a hazy blue-yellow fog. When glanced to his left from the corner of his eye, he only saw the Overseers with no hint of anyone hiding inside of them. He took slow, shallow breaths, keeping his shoulders straight and his head up.

"You know," Mitchell eventually said, "we're going to look pretty silly if that door opens and it's a just bunch of robots."

"If that's the case, you better hope they don't have infrared or heat sensors," Daniel said.

"Crap," Mitchell muttered.

The doors slid open and, to Teal'c's relief, a pair of human security guards entered. They swept the area with their weapons before advancing slowly toward the tables in the center of the room. The younger one tapped a gauntlet on his wrist and the alarm fell silent.

"Identify yourselves," one of the Overseers said.

"State your purpose here."

The guard who spoke was older, with gray at his temples. "Our apologies, Auloi. We received an urgent alarm that you were under assault."

"The intruders stand before you."

The older guard glanced at the other, then turned and slowly examined the rest of the room. "Apologies, Kiunsu, but we do not see them. Perhaps they found a way to slip past you unseen."

"The intruders stand before you even now!"

The guards moved apart, scanning the far edges of the room. The younger one moved closer to the stage and glanced toward the panel Teal'c had pulled off. He frowned and turned to face it fully.

"Hey… something happened here."

He approached the stage and lowered his weapon. He reached out with one hand, pulled the panel open, and peered inside. "Your Eminences, did the intruders damage this?"

A bolt of blue light from Teal'c's zat hit the man, seemingly coming from the center of the Overseer's torso. Once his cover was blown, he stepped forward and fired again. The older guard was raising his weapon but clearly unwilling to aim at one of the Overseers even though it was obvious something unusual was happening. He was hit in the chest and collapsed without firing a shot.

The team emerged from cover. Teal'c ran to the door and placed himself in the frame, his foot planted against one edge to prevent it from sliding shut again. Mitchell and Daniel each went to one of the guards. The uniform was made up of jackets, padded vests, heavy belts, boots, and caps without brims.

Mitchell began undoing buttons on the older guard's uniform with a look of regret.

"Sorry, pal. You were just doing your job. But if it's any consolation, I've also lost my pants in the line of duty. More than once, actually."

Carolyn looked up at the Overseers, who were still looming above them on the stage. "What are we going to do about them?"

Daniel was transferring his things from his pouches to the guard's clothes. "What do you have in mind? If we disable the projectors, either people will still get sent to Viaxeiro or the whole system will come crashing down. We could be looking at an entire planet full of criminals being loosed on the galaxy. It would be a huge boost to Lucian Alliance's recruitment numbers."

She gestured at the stage. "But look at this. Women have been sent to this Viaxeiro place for centuries based on some algorithm? Who knows how many innocent people were condemned to life without parole because someone at the dawn of time decided what they did was a crime?"

"I don't think that's a possibility." Daniel had finished trading his clothes for the guard's. Mitchell was still fastening the last catches of his. "The Overseers just keep the prison running and make sure no one knows where it is. The individual worlds determine who is sent to Viaxeiro."

Mitchell said, "Like the separation between judges and wardens."

"I still don't like the idea of this process being automated," Carolyn said. "It's like these women are just being swept under the rug. Forgotten. No one deserves that, regardless of what crime they may or may not have committed."

"I agree," Daniel said. "But right now we need to focus on getting ourselves to Viaxeiro."

"And out again," Mitchell amended.

"Right."

Daniel and Mitchell dragged the guards behind the Overseers' platform and secured their wrists and ankles with zip-ties for when the zat blasts wore off.

"Major Hagman isn't going to be very happy when we come back without these clothes," Daniel said. "Have you ever seen the records he keeps?"

Mitchell said, "Yeah, he's just gonna have to get over it. We're going to look suspicious enough wandering through the halls without carrying luggage. Besides, it'll give these guys something to wear when they wake up. They deserve a little dignity, right?"

Teal'c started to follow but then looked back at the panel which concealed the controls. A thought occurred to him and he ran back to the panel.

"Teal'c?"

"If we do reach Viaxeiro, our chances of success would be greatly increased if any pursuit was delayed."

Mitchell said, "Or messing with the Overseers' program will tip someone off and we'll have people on our asses before we even get to the rock."

Teal'c hesitated. "I defer to your judgement on the matter, Colonel Mitchell."

Mitchell looked at the panel, looked at the Overseers platforms, and then down at the guards. Finally he came to a decision.

"All right, screw it. An extra monkey wrench in the works can't hurt. Knock 'em out, big guy."

Teal'c reached into the panel and ripped out as many of the chips and connectors as he could reach. There was a blinding array of sparks, followed by the light on the stage growing dim. He had no idea if he'd bought them an hour or cost them precious seconds. Either way, he hoped it would be enough to make the difference.

"All right, that should do it," Mitchell said. "Now let's get the heck out of Dodge."

Carolyn followed Daniel and Mitchell from the room. Teal'c let the door slide shut and jogged ahead of them. He checked the door for any way to force it open, but it didn't seem possible. Daniel had caught up and examined his gauntlet. Teal'c could see a small screen embedded in it glowing with small icons which Daniel scrolled through, clearly trying to make sense of them. "Hopefully one of these will…" The elevator doors opened. "Ah. Lucky."

"Very," Mitchell agreed. "Let's hope these uniforms have some weight when it comes to getting onto a supply ship."

They boarded the elevator and left the Overseers behind, silently waiting for their next visitor.

CHAPTER TWENTY

THE FIFTEEN hour cycle of darkness had ended, so the city was in full brightness when they left the cold-water. People were moving about the streets much as they had the day before. Sam watched them and tried to determine where they were going. A young woman brought a bag of laundry to a building where an older woman took it from her. She didn't expect a women-behind-bars type of scenario, but she had to admit she was surprised by how domestic the whole city had become. It was easy to forget they were in a prison.

Shein came outside and stood next to Sam. She squinted up at the barrier, then took a pair of goggles out of her bag. The goggles were oval, with glass blinders which would protect them from blowing sand. They reminded Sam of the goggles General O'Neill used to wear on missions and she became so homesick she had to look away.

Back in the cold-water when they were formulating their plan, Sam had asked Shein if she had any special skills they could use. "My eyes," she'd said.

She looked back at Shein and saw herself reflected in the convex lenses.

"What?" Shein asked.

"Just looking forward to getting out of here. I'm surprised you and Tanis aren't."

Shein sighed heavily. "That's because you came from somewhere nice. Hell, even I've heard of the Tau'ri. The Goa'uld had flying palaces of gold and they still couldn't leave you alone. Me, I came from a little nothing planet out on the far reaches. Goa'uld came there a long time before I was born, took everything worth taking, and then left the survivors to rot. We weren't even worthy to be hosts for them. By the time I was a little girl, the Tok'ra had shown up. They might have been more polite than the Goa'uld, but they were making the same pitch. Come with us. Let us put a snake in your head. Use your body like a damn puppet until you get killed."

Sam wanted to defend the Tok'ra, but she could understand how it could look. And they weren't entirely the most upfront people in the universe.

"I said yes just to get out," Shein continued. "I watched how the Stargate worked when they took me through to their planet. Once we were there, I knocked them out, took their weapons, and had one of them punch in an address where I could start fresh. The people I ran into tended to see me as a victim. It didn't take long for me to start proving them wrong. My planet made me a survivor, no matter what the circumstances."

"I can respect that."

"Even though I'm a thief?" Shein said. "I've been a sniper. I've killed people for money, and I didn't much care if they were good or bad. I know you're judging us. Me, Tanis… even Vala. You think you're better than we are because you've never had to resort to a life of crime."

Sam started to refute the claim, but Shein kept going.

"You're behind our eyes, Tau'ri. Seeing the same thing we've always seen. No one is coming to save you in time. You can't jump through the Stargate and bury it behind you to keep the bad guys from following. If you want to get home, you're going to have to come down in the gutter with the rest of us."

"I understand," Sam said.

"I hope so."

A woman came around the corner with a cart loaded down with what looked like broken mechanical devices. Sam watched the woman as she passed, then looked back at Shein.

"They let you have tech? Aren't they worried someone will rig some kind of communicator or call for help?"

Shein pushed her hair back out of her face. It was too short to tie back, just barely long enough to tuck behind her ear, and she seemed annoyed by its length. "They let us play with broken tech," she said. "It gives us something to do. Plus water purification and food prep would be impossible without it. But they don't let us have anything that can send or receive signals."

Tanis brushed past them. "Believe me, I've tried."

"And tried," Shein said, "and tried, and tried."

"No offense, Carter," Tanis said, "but if I can't figure it out, it's probably not something that can be figured out."

Shein said, "Tanis is the best techie I've ever seen. She may not have managed to make a beacon, but she did figure out how to repurpose a radio into a static-noise machine to help me get to sleep."

Tanis was turned away, letting her hair cover her face, but Sam saw a quick flash of a smile. She was pleased with her girlfriend's praise, but bashful of it at the same time. It was a completely unguarded moment of humanity and, for the first time since meeting the woman, Sam thought she could understand why she and Vala had become friends.

Shein continued, unaware of Sam's epiphany. "The barrier is too strong, so any radio signals sent from the ground just bounce back. Plus we have no idea where we are at any given moment or how fast we're moving, so we don't know where to aim a message even if we could get one out."

"So we stick to the plan," Sam said. "Shein, get into position."

Shein touched Tanis' arm as she passed. Tanis watched her go and then faced Sam. "You never said where I'd be."

Sam said, "That's because I didn't want you to be too excited about what I need you to do."

~#~

Fifteen minutes later, Sam was positioned in the doorway of a shop with Vala standing across the street from her. From Sam's position, she could see Shein on a rooftop two blocks away. Other prisoners moved around them with disinterest. It wasn't just that they were being ignored, it was as if their behavior was just part of the scenery. It made Sam wonder just how many escape attempts happened on a daily basis. She ignored that thought as it made her think of the success/failure ratio.

"All it takes is one successful escape," she muttered.

The women around her didn't seem to have escape on their minds. They seemed to be almost comfortable with their lives. It made a kind of bizarre sense to her. She'd seen many planets where the inhabitants were worse off, at danger from the Goa'uld, the Ori, the Lucian Alliance, or any number of threats that could sweep in with advanced technology and make life hell. It was probably why so many of these women had turned to lives of crime. All the talk about "worst of the worst, most hellish place you could ever end up" was manufactured by the people in charge.

Viaxeiro was a prison, yes, but it was self-contained. It was isolated and insulated from threat. She wondered how many women around her were happy to stay here in the "suburbs" of the galaxy. She could certainly see the appeal of it, if she'd come to this place by choice. The building across from her stakeout had little yellow flowers mounted in the window. She wondered how that was possible on a world without sunshine or weather patterns, but it only proved how dedicated the condemned were to make this place into a home.

Her reverie was broken by movement from Shein. She had raised an arm high over her head, an indication that Lokelani was on the move. Sam stood up straighter and watched as the woman tracked movement in the street below. When she dropped her hand, Sam left the stoop and began walking. Vala took that as her cue to move as well, hurrying to catch up.

"Hey! Hey, *Fraiser.* Where in the hell have you been?"

Sam stopped and turned. "I've been looking for a way off this godforsaken rock."

Vala held her arms out to either side in indignation. "When were you planning to clue me into these plans of yours?"

Sam laughed. "You? I wouldn't be here if it wasn't for you. I've had a lot of time to think since we got picked up, Mal

Doran. I think you knew you were going to get caught. You were just hoping to throw me to the sharks and get away while they were tearing me apart. Admit it. The only reason you took me on as an apprentice was to sacrifice me at some point and save your own skin."

"That is an outrageous lie!" Vala said, raising her voice. Now people were starting to take notice of them. Vala stepped forward and jabbed a finger against Sam's chest. "I gave you everything. You were a tiny little nothing when I found you. I took pity on you because no one else would be caught dead with you. Hah! Caught dead is exactly what they'd be if they were expecting you to watch their backs. What a joke you are. We walked right into that trap and you had no idea we were in danger until it was too late. I wish I *had* thought of throwing you to the sharks, because then you might finally have been of use to me." She jabbed Sam's chest again.

"Don't poke me again."

"Or… what?" Vala asked, punctuating each word with another jab.

Sam put her hands on Vala's shoulders and shoved. "The day I crossed paths with you was the worst day of my life, Mal Doran!" she shouted.

"You?!" Vala said. "It was my downfall! An epic career, untarnished by imprisonment, and after a few months with you weighing me down, look where I end up!"

"I seem to remember we were captured because of you, not me," Sam said, "and if you poke me again, I swear…"

"You'll what?" Vala said. "I hear a lot of talk but nothing to back it up. You want to take a swing at me?" She twisted her neck to present her jaw. "Come on! Take your best shot!"

Tanis said, "Don't you touch her."

Sam turned toward Tanis' voice, and Tanis punched her in the face. The blow was stunning, even though Sam knew it was coming. Her stumble was completely real, causing her to trip over her feet and land on the ground in a tangle of limbs.

Tanis pounced, grabbed the front of Sam's blouse, and hauled her up onto her feet. Sam clutched both of Tanis' forearms as she was shoved back against the wall of a building. The impact knocked the wind out of her so she couldn't warn Tanis that she may be overselling the fight, and she once again saw stars.

"Tanis, stop." Sam heard sincere concern in Vala's voice and hoped she wasn't about to ruin the con. "She's not worth breaking your hand."

Tanis let go of Sam, who slumped down to the ground. She touched her cheek and grunted with pain as she looked up at the brunette women towering over her.

"It might be a small planet," Tanis said, "but find a way to make yourself scarce. Because if you don't, I'll make you invisible next time I see you. Trust me on that."

She turned and walked away, leaving Sam in the dirt. Vala looked back once, but quickly turned away and slung an arm across Tanis's shoulders.

"It's going to be good to have a partner I can *really* count on again!" Vala said loudly enough that everyone could hear it.

Sam spit on the ground. There was blood in it, and she sighed heavily as she struggled to get back onto her feet as gracefully as possible.

Lokelani approached and extended her hand. Sam stared at it, then looked up into the older woman's serene, smiling face.

"Damn," Sam said. "I was hoping you wouldn't hear about it, let alone get a front-row seat." She clapped her hand against Lokelani's and allowed herself to be hauled up. There was another frisson of recognition, an awareness of the Goa'uld's presence, and Sam worried Lokelani felt the same thing. But she didn't react and Sam tenderly probed her jaw. It was probably going to bruise. She'd told Tanis to make it look real, and she'd prepared herself for the full brunt of an angry fist, but she was still surprised by how much it had hurt. "So I guess Vala Mal Doran doesn't take very well to cutting ties."

"No," Lokelani said, "it would seem not. But consider yourself fortunate. There are many others who suffered far worse fates upon leaving Vala's company. Do you have anywhere else to go? Do you know anyone else here?"

Sam tried to look pathetic and frightened. She glanced around at the crowd, most of whom were already getting back to their normal morning procedures. "No. Vala… Vala was pretty much it."

"Wrong." Lokelani smiled again. "You know me. Come. Let's go back to my home, and we can discuss options."

"Options?" Sam said.

Lokelani put a hand on Sam's elbow to guide her as they began to walk. "There is a hierarchy to this prison population. The guards, of course, are like the gods. Silent and unmoved by our plight, and yet we strive to not anger them. And then there is the Cai Thior," she said, nodding at the orange-and-black garbed women lingering at the edge of the crowd. "They are above the general prison rank. They're granted special privilege because of the uniform they wear. Because of who they serve."

Sam noted that Lokelani had placed herself one rung below a god, even though she hadn't said it explicitly.

"The women who wear the uniform of my Cai Thior are looked at with respect. They have dignity which every condemned quickly learns to recognize. Even Tanis Reynard and Shein Pranassa show deference to this uniform… as will Vala, unless she wishes to learn the consequences of disrespect."

Sam played dumb. "What… what exactly are you saying, Lokelani?"

Lokelani smiled at her. "I'm asking if you would like to change your outfit, Sri Frasier. Perhaps something in orange."

As they passed underneath Shein's lookout post, Sam lifted her head and saw the blonde sniper watching her. She gave the slightest of nods, and Shein vanished to report back to Vala and Tanis. Sam looked at Lokelani again and managed a nervous smile.

"I think I'd like that very much, Sri Lokelani."

CHAPTER TWENTY-ONE

CAM AND TEAL'C left the elevator first, just in case the other guards had somehow gotten free and alerted the rest of the station to what had happened. No alarms sounded and they weren't immediately surrounded by people with guns, so Cam motioned for the rest of the team to step forward. He scanned the faces of everyone they passed and tried to figure out which of them would be most receptive to offering them a ride.

"Okay, look for anyone carrying a lot of junk by themselves. Anyone struggling. We're going to have to work for our place on a ship, and given the secrecy of this place, only the most desperate person will agree to it."

Daniel looked back at Teal'c. "I don't want to throw a wrench in your plans, but I don't think Teal'c should be doing any heavy lifting."

"He has a point," Carolyn said, then immediately turned and raised a finger as Teal'c opened his mouth to speak. "And don't say that you can handle carrying a few hundred pounds, because this is exactly why I tagged along on the mission. I only agreed to let you into the field if you took it easy. Taking a job as a dockworker doesn't fit the bill."

Cam sighed. "Then what do you suggest?"

Carolyn looked around. "Well…" Cam could see she had come up with an idea, but he could also see that she hated it. "Suppliers aren't the only people who go to Viaxeiro. They also send prisoner transports."

Daniel was the first to realize what she was saying. "It *is* a women's prison."

"Whoa, whoa," Cam stopped in the corridor and turned to face them. "We're supposed to be getting our people out, not sending more people in."

"We're going to need a go-between anyway," Daniel said.

"Once we get to the planet, we'd have no reason to stick around. Sam and Vala would have no way of even knowing we were there. This way, we can send Carolyn in to let them know we're around."

Teal'c said, "If she is able to conceal a radio on her person, we could establish contact with Colonel Carter and Vala Mal Doran. We may even be able to devise a viable escape plan."

Daniel said, "At this point we're just guessing about what's happening on the planet. We need her in there, at the very least to let Sam and Vala know we haven't abandoned them. We get a ship, we drop her off, and then we stick around."

"What if whoever gives us a ride doesn't want us to stick around?" Cam asked.

Teal'c raised an eyebrow. "We convince them."

"Yeah. Okay, that was a stupid question. Doc, if you're not up for this…"

Carolyn rolled her eyes. "It was my plan."

"Right. Then I guess this is the plan we're going with."

"And if we're going to pretend I'm a criminal in your custody…" She held up her hands and tapped her wrists together.

Daniel looked down at the belt he'd taken from the guard. "Oh, right. Uh… here." He pulled a small infinity-shaped object from his belt and held it toward her.

Carolyn withdrew her hands. "Want to make sure you know how to open those before you stick them on my wrists?"

"Oh." Daniel examined the side of the device. "If Sam was here…"

Teal'c reached out and took it from Daniel. He examined them silently and Cam realized Sam wasn't the expert they needed in this case. Teal'c probably had more experience with alien restraints than the rest of the team combined. He didn't say anything and, after a moment, determined how they worked. He looked at Daniel's belt.

"There should be an oblong key."

Daniel searched the pockets and handed over a small object.

Teal'c inserted it into the side of the device, and the cuffs relaxed. He looked at Carolyn.

"I am confident I will be able to remove these."

"Thank you," she said, extending her arms again.

Teal'c secured her hands in the device. He checked to make sure it was secure without being uncomfortable and stepped back so he was bringing up the rear, leaving Daniel and Cam in the lead, with their supposed prisoner in the center. Cam examined the crowd again, but this time he was looking for something different. The people loading and unloading crates were of no interest to him. "Teal'c, were you paying attention on our way in? I thought I saw a food court or something, but I can't figure out..."

Teal'c brushed past Cam and began walking. The rest of the team fell in as he retraced their steps, pausing from time to time to examine the embedded tracks. There were multiple places where the tracks branched off so the robotic escorts could go anywhere in the station, but Teal'c seemed to know exactly which one would take them back to where they had started. Sure enough, it didn't take long before they found the area Cam remembered.

"Mind like a steel trap," Cam said, patting Teal'c on the shoulder.

Teal'c arched an eyebrow but said nothing.

The food court was a wide oval with food carts clustered at the narrow ends and a variety of tables in the center. Cam moved slowly among the diners. He didn't know exactly what he was looking for, but he hoped he would recognize it when he saw it. The vast majority of people looked human, but there were also aliens. He still couldn't get over a room full of very alien-looking aliens. Some of them had tentacles on their heads, some looked reptilian, while others were dressed head to toe in protective suits to defend against what was, to them, a toxic environment. He got the feeling it was something he would never get used to, like traveling through the Stargate, and he was fine with that.

A few tables away from him, a man was hunched over a plate to shovel something that looked like dry chips of beef into his mouth. He was older than most of the other people in the room, human by the looks of it, and didn't look like he could hold his own in a brawl. Everyone else was seated with at least three or four other people, crew members, but this guy was alone. A monitor had been propped up in front of him and he kept reaching up to tap the screen. Cam moved into a position where he could see what the man was watching. One side of the screen showed a woman lying on the floor in the fetal position, while the other side seemed to be a health monitor.

Bingo, he thought as he made his way over.

"Troublemaker?" Cam asked as he came up behind the beef-eater.

The man sat up straighter and locked a suspicious gaze on Cam. He was a wiry man, smaller than Cam but with strong shoulders which came from years of heavy lifting. He was bald, scowling, and looked like he wanted to jam his fork into Cam's gut. Cam kept out of reach, just in case.

"Who the hell are you?" the man growled.

"Lee Majors," Cam said, sticking with the fake name he'd used earlier. He sat across from his new friend and extended his hand. "And who might you be?"

The man stared at Cam's palm as if the target for his fork had shifted. He went back to eating his food, eyes shifting back to the screen. "Pemphero."

Cam dropped his hand. "Nice to meet you. So…? The woman on the screen. She a troublemaker?"

"Aren't they all?"

Cam chuckled low in his throat, wondering what any of the women on the base would do if they'd heard him say that. "Boy howdy, you don't have to tell me. Lock 'em all up, let them give each other headaches for a while, am I right?"

Pemphero snorted, neither agreeing nor arguing.

"Can't help but notice you're on babysitting duty here. Don't you have someone in your crew who could watch her while you grab a bite to eat?"

"Crews like to get paid," Pemphero said. "And I don't like cutting up my profits. This works just fine. She's drugged to the gills. No way she wakes up before I get back." He poked the screen with one finger. "I'm watching everything here. Heart, breathing, nervous system. It's physically impossible for her to regain consciousness before I finish eating."

"Thorough," Cam said. "But you know how it is with these women. As soon as they're conscious, they're always trying to find a way to trick you. I have this friend, right? A lady tried to steal his ship once. She knocked out the entire crew, save for him, and just walked away with it. He turned the tables on her a few times, but she still managed to get away. She was a wily one, boy, let me tell you."

Pemphero said, "You are irritating me."

"That wasn't the intention, big fella. In fact, I was hoping we could be friends."

"Friends have something to offer me. You don't."

Cam held up a finger. "Now that's where you're wrong, Pemphero. I have a couple of buddies who can help you out. We'll work as guards for your troublemaker here, and in exchange, you just have to take us where you're already going."

Pemphero looked skeptical. "You need a ride to Viaxeiro."

"Got a troublemaker of my own." He pointed over Pemphero's shoulder to where Carolyn was standing with the rest of the team.

Pemphero smirked and tilted his head to the side. "You're not my friend yet, and I'm not about to turn my back on you. Where I'm from, that's considered an old trick."

Cam chuckled and bobbed his head. "Yeah, it's pretty old where I come from, too. If you did turn around, you'd see we have a prisoner ready for transport. One little lady, no problems, no fuss. Counting me, there are three guys watching her, but she hasn't made a peep since we picked her up. But we have another problem."

"I assume you're getting to how this involves me."

"Exactly. See, we borrowed a ship to get here. We dock at the station and the second we're onboard, the damn thing fires up again and heads back out on autopilot!"

Pemphero laughed, sitting up straighter and resting his hands over his stomach, fingers lightly scratching the material of his shirt. His smile was condescending. "Oh, a recall device. I heard some Goa'ulds started using those when the Jaffa began rising up. The Lucian Alliance has been reprogramming them. Easiest way to steal a ship is to make it come to you. Bad luck for you, though."

"You're telling me," Cam said. "We're stranded here with Ma Barker and no way to deliver her. If we don't confirm delivery on this contract, we won't get paid."

"Ma Barker? Never heard of her."

"Neither had I, until the contract came along. Someone's paying a hefty price to make sure she never sees the light of day. I stumble over her, luckiest day of my life, and now karma's biting me in the ass. I'm sure it's happened to you."

Pemphero gestured at the screen with his head. "How do you think I ended up on a solo delivery? It wasn't by design, I assure you."

Cam leaned forward. "That's what I'm saying! I see you over here by yourself and I think, this guy could be the answer to our problem. And we could be the answer to his. If you take us to Viaxeiro so we can drop off *our* prisoner, we'll provide security for *your* prisoner."

"And half the bounty."

"Whoa, half?"

Pemphero raised his eyebrows. "The way I see it, right now you're looking at zero percent." He rested his elbows on the table. He had a sly and greedy look in his eye now, swaying a little in his seat as he found the upper hand. "You saw me and thought I would be a pushover? Desperate for your help? You thought you would play my savior. But I don't need saviors. What I need is a reason to give a damn about your problem. And that reason is money. You could pass on it, look around for someone else who might take less of a cut. I get the feeling you won't be very successful, though."

Cam pretended to consider the offer, when really he was weighing the options of getting on a ship with this man. He had been hoping SG-1 would easily gain the upper hand on a solo space pirate, but Pemphero was obviously a shrewd criminal. It wouldn't be easy to manipulate him. Then again, they really were pressed for options.

"When do you leave?"

"As soon as I finish my meal."

Cam looked past him to Daniel, Teal'c, and Carolyn. Daniel gave a questioning shrug. Time was running out. Someone could find the guards at any moment, and who knew what hell Sam and Vala were going through. He couldn't afford to be picky.

"Looks like we have a deal, Mr. Pemphero."

He extended his hand. Once again, Pemphero didn't take it. Instead, he hunched over his food and continued shoveling it into his mouth.

"I eat alone. Go away. If you see me leave, you're welcome to follow."

Cam curled his fingers into his palm and transitioned the gesture to a thumbs-up.

"Enjoy the rest of your meal."

Pemphero was already focused on the screen again. Cam stood and walked back to where the team was waiting.

"So?" Daniel said.

"He'll give us a ride. We let him take us to Viaxeiro. Once we're there, we can overpower him and take over the ship. I'm still Lee Majors." He looked at Carolyn. "I told him you were Ma Barker."

Carolyn shrugged. "I'll be honest, I was afraid you would call me Hot Lips Houlihan or something ridiculous like that."

"Oh, damn, that is better. Maybe next time."

Daniel said, "So now we wait until he's done eating?"

Cam nodded. "Shouldn't take very long. He, uh... he also expects half the bounty we're allegedly getting for Carolyn here." Daniel stared at him. "He wasn't biting! I had to sweeten the pot a little bit. He was our best, quickest shot of getting to the prison."

"He's not going to like us very much when this is all over," Daniel said.

Teal'c said, "We will burn that bridge when we have arrived at it, Daniel Jackson."

"Doc, when we get on the ship, we'll have to treat you like a prisoner. I don't know how far it'll go, but I get the feeling just putting some handcuffs on you isn't going to cut it. We'll be as gentle as we can with you."

"I understand," Carolyn said.

"Okay, then." Cam focused on the cluster of carts and shop-fronts that were selling food nearby. "As long as we're waiting, we might as well get something to-go. I'm half-starved over here. You think they'll have barbecue?"

CHAPTER TWENTY-TWO

SAM HADN'T really gotten a good look at Lokelani's home during her first visit. Now that she was back under different circumstances, she was led through the public areas to a smaller study that looked more lived-in. The walls were completely hidden behind shelves weighted down with books, scrolls, and loose pamphlets tied together with string. A table near the door was covered by a map. Sam could tell there were multiple other maps underneath the top one. She glanced down and saw it was a star map, but she couldn't tell much else without being obvious about her examination. Two of the guards had followed them through the house but stopped in the corridor.

"I don't think I thanked you properly back there," Sam said. "I get the feeling it's dangerous to show weakness in this place, and I looked pretty weak."

Lokelani sat on the edge of her desk. "We're not animals, Fraiser. Living in a prison doesn't erase our humanity. Yes, there are rogues who make us look bad. But the rest of us are just trying to build our lives and make the best of a bad situation."

Sam said, "But you still have people who try to escape. Vala and I saw one when we arrived."

"Oh, of course. None of us came here willingly. It's almost a rite of passage to test the boundaries of our new cage, and the guards assigned here by the Overseers do a good job of keeping those prisoners in check. But then there are others who realize what they have here. Peace. Prosperity they don't have to fight or risk their lives for."

"And yet…" Sam gestured at the guards waiting outside.

Lokelani smiled. "That's just common sense, dear. I've been here a very long time. I've built a very nice home for myself. The new arrivals, those like you who are still clinging to their old ways, might decide they want to live here instead of those dreary cold-waters. I assume you spent the night in one of them?"

"Yeah," Sam said. "This would definitely be an upgrade."

"It certainly is comfortable."

"I wanted to ask you the last time I was here." Sam nodded at the shelves. "Where did all of these come from?"

"Oh, I have so many sources. Compassionate jailors sometimes allow the condemned to pack before bringing them here. And the ships doing the supply runs will occasionally bring luxury items."

"And those come to you, and you decide who gets them."

Some of the kindness faded from Lokelani's face. "Someone has to. Imagine yourself wandering in a desert. You find an oasis, a source of shade and food and water. If you allow everyone to take whatever they want, the well soon runs dry and the tree is plucked bare of fruit. I serve the purpose of ensuring there will always be enough for everyone. No more, no less. The Cai Thior serve as guardians to protect the surplus. Have I satisfied your curiosity?"

"I'm sorry if I was prying. I'm just trying to figure out how this place works."

Lokelani smoothed her hands over the front of her gown. "The way this place works is simple. Someone has to be in charge to prevent this world from becoming chaos. To stop those sharks outside from devouring one another. I've elected myself for that role. If you have a problem with that, then perhaps I should leave you outside with Vala and her cohorts."

"No, no," Sam said, raising her hands in surrender. "You've made your point. I'm just... you know... I'm a little dense. Slow on the uptake."

Lokelani's smile returned, now patronizing. Sam had seen the same look on countless faces over the years, usually directed toward General O'Neill. His philosophy had always been that it was better to play the fool so people underestimated him than to lay all his cards on the table at the beginning of the game. Sam had no reason to let Lokelani know how smart she really was, so pretending to be an imbecile might work to her advantage.

"Of course you are. That's how you wound up in Vala's net in the first place." She stepped forward and looked past Sam into the hall. "Sukhan? Take Sri Fraiser upstairs. Find an empty room to her liking and provide her with a uniform."

The woman who responded was slightly older than Sam, with silver threaded through her dark braided hair. She was dressed in the same uniform as the other Cai Thior, but hers had the added element of a scimitar hanging from her belt. Sukhan bowed in response to Lokelani's order and faced Sam. Her eyes were a vibrant blue and, for a moment, Sam thought she saw something behind them. It was just a flicker and was gone before she could even confirm it had been there.

"I will show you the way," Sukhan said.

"Thank you."

Sam followed Sukhan out of the study and into a dark, narrow hallway. The walls crowded in on either side, brushing against her sleeves. She was led upstairs into a room she would've considered cozy at a resort on Earth. The bed was huge, with a spacious night table on either side. A tall armoire stood in one corner next to a writing desk. Sukhan walked to the wardrobe and opened it to reveal a rack of orange uniforms like the one she wore.

"Everything else you'll need is in the drawers below," she said. "I'm only guessing at your size. If you require adjustments, just let someone know."

"Thank you."

Sukhan moved toward the door but stopped. She looked down at her feet for a long moment before she met Sam's eyes.

"You don't remember me, do you?"

Sam tensed. "Should I?"

"I've been here for nearly five years. Before that, I sold weapons. My homeworld was very technologically advanced, and it was easy for me to find things just lying around that I could sell to more primitive worlds for whatever price I wanted. Before that... I spent a thousand years in suspended animation with my consciousness kept alive inside a virtual reality. I might still be in there reliving the same memories over and over again except, one day, we were given new memories."

"Oh my God. The Keeper's planet."

Sukhan wrinkled her nose. "We don't call it that. Would you name your planet after the man who had kept your entire race unnecessarily imprisoned?"

"Probably not." Sam still wasn't sure if she should be ready for a fight. "So I assume you know my name isn't Fraiser."

"I wasn't entirely sure about your name, but I know who you are. My people were close allies with the Tau'ri when I left. They probably still are. You were the great liberators who brought us back to reality. Back to a world unprepared for us, and which we were unprepared to maintain. We were forced to rely on whatever your people could bring us in order to survive. Some, like me, didn't like being so dependent on aliens after spending a millennia in prison." She looked around with a wry smile. "I guess I just sort of gravitate toward captivity."

Sam said, "Where does that leave us?"

"I don't know. I don't have any true loyalty to Lokelani. It didn't take me long to realize the best place to stand on this rock was at her side. But I'm not going to put my life on the line to protect her. Everything she told you was true, but a simpler truth is that people in Viaxeiro get by with their heads down. We don't make a fuss. I know you're lying. To what end, I don't know, but I assume it will only affect me if I become involved. So I'm not getting involved. I only wanted to tell you so you'd know I wasn't a fool."

Sam nodded slowly. "Noted. Thank you. May I ask you a question about this place?"

"Of course."

"How does the Cai Thior... exist? The guards should be afraid of you and the other prisoners should resent you. I know Lokelani has some influence due to how long she's been here, but I can't understand why she's allowed to have her own militia."

Sukhan chuckled. "Well, the prisoners are easy to explain. They accept us because we're like them. We understand what they're going through. So they prefer to deal with us rather than the guards because they feel we'll treat them justly. We're not faceless men sent here by some faraway Overseers who think of us as cattle and treat us accordingly.

"As for the guards," she continued, "look at it from their point of view. There are hundreds of women here, and this is a very large city. Lots of places to hide and hold secret meetings. If you were a guard, wouldn't it make more sense to have one group in charge instead of many smaller ones?"

Sam said, "I suppose that makes sense."

"The guards allow us to have power because it's preferable to all of the prisoners being equal. The other prisoners allow us to have power because it's preferable than dealing with outsiders who see them as less than human. And in that delicate balance, we thrive."

"I see. Thank you for enlightening me."

"Of course. I'll leave you to change." Sukhan stepped around Sam to leave, but she stopped on the threshold. "What I said earlier was not entirely true. I revealed that I knew the truth of your identity because I wanted to thank you. Nothing that happened on my world was your fault. You didn't destroy our habitat and, in fact, without your people we would have died during the first winter after we were released. Regardless of what came after, it's preferable to being stuck in that virtual hell. Thank you."

"You're welcome," Sam said.

Sukhan slipped from the room. Sam pushed the door shut and went to the armoire, checking the clothing to see if there was any kind of recognizable sizing chart. The inside of the jacket was marked with characters she couldn't read, but it seemed to be about the right size. There was also a sleeveless jerkin that she assumed went under it, and a variety of underwear that actually looked like it might be comfortable. She picked up one of the bras and examined it.

"Okay," she muttered, "an all-woman prison planet might not be *all* bad…"

She pulled out one of the uniforms and began to change, hoping Vala and Tanis were faring well on their end.

~#~

"You didn't have to enjoy it quite so much," Vala said.

"Sure I did," Tanis replied. "I had to sell it for Lokelani. Authenticity required enjoyment."

They were on the roof of a cold-water near Lokelani's compound, lying on their stomachs. Shein was down in the streets doing reconnaissance of the guards, making sure none of them were getting too curious about what was happening. Tanis was wearing a pair of sight enhancers which allowed her a view of the other building as clear as if she was standing beside it. She reached up to adjust the lenses. Sam had gone inside fifteen minutes earlier and as yet no one else had left.

Vala stacked one fist on top of the other, her chin on top of them both. "I know you think she's a bore, but she's saved my life more than once."

Tanis made a rude noise in her throat. "What the hell did they do to you on that planet, Vala?"

"They gave me a home," Vala said quietly. "They saw through all of my defenses, they saw the worst parts of who I am, and they still invited me in. And when I was at my absolute lowest moments, they held me up. Their kindness doesn't make them weak, it's what makes them strong." She turned her head to look at Tanis. "It's why you and I were so good together. We trusted each other. Yes, sometimes we got on each other's nerves, but we could always count on each other."

"Yeah." Tanis sighed. "That's one reason I didn't fight too hard when I was sent here. I tried doing the solo thieving thing, but it just wasn't fun anymore. I looked around for partners, but no one clicked. It was like they were playing music but I was dancing to the wrong beat."

Vala beamed. "I ruined you for other thieves!"

Tanis reached over and twisted Vala's ear.

"Ow!"

"You're still a brat."

"And you're still mean!"

Tanis took off the goggles. "I guess I just decided that if I wasn't going to do crime with you, then there was no point in doing it at all. Especially not with the Ori sticking their noses in everything. You run into one of those pasty-faced weirdos and you never need to see another. My past caught up with me, fair and square. If I tried to run, someone else would chase me down eventually. This is a nice enough place to retire."

"Plus you can't beat the company."

"Yeah." Tanis sighed and rolled her eyes. "Go ahead. Get out your jokes. Tanis Reynard, settling down like a tej'ro…"

"No, no. Maybe the old me would have mocked you a little bit. I might have thrown some of your own words back in your face, like how entering a marriage contract is an invitation to be a victim to a con down the road. Or how you don't want anyone to see you vulnerable, and a relationship is just an unending stream of defenseless days…"

Tanis said, "I remember!"

"So what's different about Shein? Was it just because she's, you know, convenient?"

"No," Tanis said immediately. "It's nothing like that. You know what I hate more than anything else? Going into a dangerous situation without a plan. I was dumped on this planet and surrounded by women as villainous as I am, and I had no clue how to defend myself. I decided to go on the offensive. Find someone, start a fight, prove I'm someone to be reckoned with. I chose wrong. The fight was over in seconds, and I was completely humiliated. Shein found me. Took me to her cold-water and made sure I could recover without anyone else picking on me. She told me how this place worked. By the time I was well enough to go out on my own, I didn't much feel like it."

Vala smiled wistfully.

"Look at you," Tanis said. "Miss Sentimentality."

"Hardly. Would you be more willing to leave if we could take Shein with us?"

She didn't know how that would go over with Sam and the rest of SG-1, but it was a moot point since Tanis was already shaking her head.

"I didn't expect a rescue, so I let myself consider what it would be like to have a home. To settle down in one place. I liked it a lot more than I expected. So if I'm going to eventually grow roots somewhere, this place is a lot nicer than my other options."

Vala thought about what awaited Tanis if she came to Earth: a cold windowless room deep underground. The SGC would treat her well, would take care of the basic amenities, but she knew they would never see her as anything but a threat and a villain. She pushed that aside and forced a smile.

"But it'll be even nicer if you're the one making the rules."

Tanis grinned, showing her teeth. "It's in my nature. Why bother to change this late in the game? I truly am sorry you got snared in the same trap. Getting that warning out to you was tough, but I wanted to make sure you were safe."

Vala said, "Honestly, if you hadn't sent the message, I never would have gone looking for you. Whoever set the trap in the first place likely wouldn't have gotten past the SGC defenses without you providing the note. On Earth they call that a Trojan Horse…"

"Wait, are you saying it's *my* fault you're here?"

Vala flipped her hair. "I'm only presenting the facts, my dear, but if your guilt arranges the story in such a way that—"

"I hope you and your Tau'ri friend both get thrown into the deepest, darkest pit this planet has and you're never pulled out."

"At least then we'd be spared any more of your 'helping.'"

"I'd forgotten how much I hate your accent."

Vala said, "*I* don't have an accent, darling, I merely speak properly."

"God, such a pretentious ass…"

Vala said, "I have a phenomenal ass."

Tanis had to smile. "Yeah. It's not bad."

Vala chuckled. "I've missed this."

"Me too," Tanis agreed. She pulled the goggles back down to watch for Sam or any of the other Cai Thior women. "So the Tau'ri… at least tell me there's potential romance for you there."

"Oh, yes," Vala cooed. "Although… well, he's more of a pet than anything else, but he's a lot of fun. His name is Daniel…"

CHAPTER TWENTY-THREE

"SPACE," MITCHELL muttered, "the dull frontier."

Teal'c raised an eyebrow and half-turned to face him.

"Yeah, that show probably wouldn't have done so well."

He was in the copilot's seat, while Daniel and Teal'c were seated in two overstuffed chairs which had been inexpertly bolted to the back of Pemphero's cockpit. Every time the ship shook or rattled, they were rocked roughly back against the cushion or shoved forward against the harnesses. The ship seemed unusually susceptible to space turbulence, a phenomenon Sam had once explained to Daniel but he couldn't repeat back.

Daniel had to admit Mitchell had a point. After they left the Overseers' station, Pemphero set a course and activated a small screen on his console which revealed a long string of text. He appeared to be reading a novel. Through the viewer ahead, they saw nothing but the familiar purple streak of hyperspace. Pemphero's hand was under his chin, lower jaw out, eyes barely open as he read. The screen seemed to be aware of his reading speed and scrolled automatically.

"Seriously," Mitchell said, "No little bags of peanuts or drink service…?"

"I didn't plan for passengers," Pemphero muttered, barely opening his mouth. "If you're bored, go watch the prisoners."

Daniel unhooked his harness. "You know, I think I'll do that."

He stumbled slightly when they were hit by another wave of solar energy, exacerbated by their high speeds - or something like that - and braced himself against the wall as he continued to the back of the ship. It was designed around a central power source, much like the Ori vessels. The corridors curved around the engine so that the inner wall vibrated from the engine and the outer wall separated them from the vacuum. The cockpit was perched on top of the ring, like the head of a turtle, and the prisoners were being kept in a holding cell at the back.

Daniel stopped at the force field that made up the edge of their cell. Carolyn was sitting against one wall, her legs folded in front of her. Her head was resting against the wall, eyes closed. She was still wearing the restraints. Daniel watched her for a moment and then backed up to leave.

"Dr. Jackson?"

"Sorry. I thought you were sleeping."

"Resting my eyes." She lifted her head and glanced at the other prisoner. The woman had still been unconscious when they arrived at the ship. "I figured we have no idea when we'll get another chance to rest, so I might as well take advantage of it."

Daniel nodded. "Jack felt the same way." He checked over his shoulder to make sure no one was eavesdropping. "I wanted to apologize…"

"Nothing to apologize for."

"We were rougher than we had to be when we brought you in here."

She raised her eyebrows. "Seriously, I'm fine. You had to make it look good for Pemphero."

"Be that as it may… sorry."

"It's appreciated. Any idea how long it will be before we reach Viaxeiro?"

Daniel shook his head. "He seemed to be settled in for a long haul."

"Like… Los Angeles to New York…?"

"More like Los Angeles to Moscow."

Carolyn winced. "Ouch."

"Yeah. We'll make sure you get fed and get a chance to get up and stretch your legs."

She nodded and rested her head against the wall. "I've been thinking about Colonel Carter's reputation on the base. One thing that everyone always talks about is her dedication when someone is missing. She figured out the gate mechanics when Teal'c was stuck in the buffer. She refused to give up when the gate was buried on Edora and General O'Neill got trapped. In fact, the only time they imply that she ever gave up hope was when you died."

"Which time?"

"The longest time, when you were ascended. General O'Neill and Teal'c are both on the record as saying they knew you'd come back sometime. Colonel Carter seemed to make peace with the fact you were gone for good."

Daniel smiled and looked at the floor, his shoulder against the wall. "Is that what you think?"

"It's not accurate?"

"No, I suppose it's… technically accurate that she gave up hope. I may not remember everything about that time, but I do remember that. I kept an eye on everyone when I was gone. When they needed me, I let them see me so I could offer advice. I never let Sam see me. I never revealed myself to her, never let her see the evidence that some part of me still existed. I did that because Jack wrote it off as a side effect of the torture he was under from Ba'al and the fact a Tok'ra had just been living inside his head. Teal'c also let himself believe it was just a hallucination. But I knew that if I showed myself to Sam, even for a second, even for the briefest of pep talks, she would have done whatever it took to get me back. She would have ripped open the sky and kicked the ass of every Ascended being who got in her way until she found me."

Carolyn smiled.

"Sam doesn't give up on her people. Not when there's a chance."

"That's good to know, Dr. Jackson. I think I can stand a little discomfort. For her sake."

He nodded. "Let us know if you need anything."

"Will do."

Daniel returned to the cockpit. "So, Pemphero. You been in the, uh… transport game long?"

The pilot didn't look away from whatever he was reading. "All my life. As soon as I could get around a ship without getting in people's way, my father was taking me along. People in my family have been taking criminals to Viaxeiro for as long as anyone can remember."

"Wow," Mitchell said. "You know, my pals here are old timers like you, but I'm sort of new to this whole thing. Who sentences women to this place?"

Pemphero rubbed a hand over the lower half of his face. "Well, to use my current transport as an example, she was caught raiding a Goa'uld armory and charged with desecrating a holy site." He chuckled and waved his hand at the screen. "Out here, you know, on the fringes, the Goa'uld hardly ever actually made an appearance. So their downfall really wasn't that big of a deal. That's one thing I've noticed on most of the worlds I've been to. Religion marches on even if the person being worshipped stops showing up."

"I've noticed that myself," Daniel said.

"Her defense was that their god had been killed, so anything he left behind was up for grabs."

Mitchell said, "I bet that went over well."

Pemphero scoffed. "She was labeled as a heretic. Not worthy of being incarcerated in their planet's fine institutions. That's where I came in. They commissioned me to exile her with all the other bad eggs. How about you?" He looked at Daniel. "What crime did this Ma Barker of yours commit?"

"Pirating music."

Pemphero thought for a moment and then shook his head. "I'm not familiar with that. Is it bad?"

Mitchell said, "One of the worst things you can do. Back where we're from, everyone from twelve-year-old kids to little old grannies are going down and they're going down hard. It's the only way they'll learn. She's definitely getting what she deserves."

Pemphero hmphed and folded his hands over his stomach as he faced forward again. "I've taken over four dozen prisoners to Viaxeiro. By the time I retire, I'll probably take four dozen more. I've never regretted any of them."

"Four dozen?" Daniel said. He hadn't thought much about how large the prison was, but if one man was responsible for that many transports, and there were multiple people dropping prisoners off… That implied a pretty sizable population. "You aren't concerned about them organizing? What if you show up to drop someone off and there's an army waiting for you?"

He smiled and rocked his head from side to side, dismissive. "There have been uprisings in the past. They're quickly put down by the guards. You know the landmines mean there's no way for them to get close enough to the ship to take it over. If the prisoners do try something, we have the authority to turn any condemned woman's incarceration into a death sentence."

Daniel shifted uncomfortably. He and Mitchell exchanged a look.

"You know," Pemphero said slowly, "it strikes me that a lot of this is information you should already know."

Mitchell said, "It's my fault. I'm the new guy. Skipped orientation."

Pemphero smiled. "Oh. Okay. Sure." He leaned forward and tapped the console.

"What are you doing?" Daniel said.

"In one hundred seconds, the back compartment of this ship will vent into space."

Mitchell said, "Are you insane?"

Pemphero held his hands out. "Ninety seconds now. Either tell me who you really are, or that woman you brought aboard is getting dropped off a little earlier than expected."

~#~

Before Daniel could speak, Teal'c rose from his seat and jogged from the cockpit. Pemphero moved to stop him, but

Mitchell shot one leg out and tripped the diminutive pilot. Teal'c was counting down in his head, well aware that he would be cutting it close. He arrived at the cell and wasted three seconds examining the control panel for the force field.

"Teal'c…?"

He ignored Carolyn's question and grabbed the edges of the panel with both hands. He pulled it free, cracking a section of the hull, and exposed the crystals that powered the field. He unholstered his zat, stepped back, and fired. With ten seconds left until the hatch opened, the field collapsed. Teal'c grabbed Carolyn and pulled her out. He moved around her, grabbed the still-unconscious other prisoner, and carried her to the corridor.

"Go!" he bellowed.

Carolyn ran toward the cockpit as the back wall of the holding cell split down the middle. The gap widened and the air was pulled out into the vacuum with enough force that Teal'c felt as if gravity had shifted. He could feel it battering his face and chest, making it impossible to take a breath or continue forward. It took everything he had to remain standing, but he couldn't fall without crushing the woman in his arms. Ahead, he could see Carolyn holding onto the entryway to the cockpit, her body parallel to the ground.

~#~

When the hangar opened, Mitchell and Pemphero both slid across the floor like hockey pucks. Mitchell braced one leg against the back wall, one arm wrapped around Pemphero's neck.

"Jackson!" he yelled.

Daniel ignored him, just as he was ignoring the incredible pressure on his chest. There was no more oxygen, and he could feel invisible hands trying to pull him from the chair and out of the ship. He knew Pemphero must have been planning for the force field to protect them from decompression. Now there were lights flashing all over the controls, but he had no idea which ones would save them.

Universal symbols, colors, flashing lights mean bad, he thought, falling back on the knowledge which had always served him well in the past. He pressed two fingers to the screen, jabbing blind near where the alerts seemed to be. He looked for symbols as his chest burned from the lack of oxygen. His vision blurred. Then he saw a small graphic that seemed to be doors. He slapped his hand against it and the invisible fingers released him. He heard bodies falling behind him as the hangar doors closed, and he let himself sag forward against the console.

He tried to take a breath; couldn't. It dawned on him that shutting the hangar door had only kept them from being expelled into space. The ship was now emptied of air. He gasped, clutched his throat, and spun the chair to look toward Pemphero.

The pilot had already wriggled away from Mitchell. He lurched forward, shoved Daniel out of the way, and punched a sequence of commands onto the display. There was a click, a loud whirr, and then air rushed back into the cockpit. Daniel drew in a deep and glorious breath. Pemphero breathed in with his eyes closed, as if savoring the best smell in the universe.

Teal'c put a hand on Pemphero's shoulder. He repositioned the smaller man, then punched him hard enough that Pemphero was unconscious even before he hit the ground.

Mitchell had crawled over to Carolyn to make sure she was okay. Teal'c had left the prisoner in the doorway, her chin resting on her chest. She had somehow managed to remain unconscious throughout the entire ordeal. Daniel coughed and sagged in the chair, while Teal'c stumbled back to his seat and dropped heavily against the cushions. The only sound in the cockpit was the whoosh of air being reintroduced and the coughing, panting sounds of SG-1 getting their collective breath back.

"Okay," Mitchell said, coughing into the bend of his elbow. "Next time, we work out a better story before we get on a ship. Agreed?"

"I can get behind that plan," Carolyn said.

"As can I," Teal'c said.

Mitchell got to his feet, still using the wall as support. "Jackson, you think you can figure out these systems before Pemphero here wakes up?"

Daniel turned the chair to face the console again. "I don't think I have to. When we got onboard, Pemphero uploaded something from the station. I think it was the current coordinates of the prison."

Carolyn said, "Unless he planned to make a pit stop first."

"I don't think so," Daniel said. "The prison is on a planemo, which is constantly in motion. I think the station automatically calculates where it is based on when the information is requested. The information wouldn't be accurate an hour from now, or maybe even five minutes from now depending on how fast it travels."

Mitchell said, "Really? So after jumping through all these hoops of finding Odai, finding the Overseers, finding someone with the right coordinates…"

Daniel looked out the view screens at the hyperspace waves. "Next stop, Viaxeiro."

CHAPTER TWENTY-FOUR

THERE WAS something comforting about putting on a uniform, even if it wasn't her standard BDU. The blouse was actually two pieces of cloth sandwiching a thin plate of metal. It was still malleable enough that it hung naturally off her frame and it didn't add much weight to the outfit. She hoped she would be able to take a sample of it with her when she left; armor like this could save countless lives. Once she was dressed, Sam adjusted the orange tunic, straightened the black cuffs, and made sure the belt was comfortably tight before she went to find Sukhan. Her search was actually a way to explore without Lokelani breathing down her neck.

The house—or to put it more accurately, stronghold—was three stories tall. She found a heavily-secured door which may have led down to a basement level, but she didn't feel comfortable trying to pick the lock until she had more time. She moved on and found a fully-stocked pantry which led into a kitchen where any number of professional chefs would feel right at home.

The contrast with the cold-water where she'd spent the night was jarring. There was definitely a hierarchy at play, and Lokelani seemed to be playing it perfectly to her advantage. Sam allowed herself a brief glimmer of hope. If Lokelani was lying about how many supplies were coming to Viaxeiro, then there was also a chance she was lying about the possibility of escape. She'd been in power long enough that she could have spread rumors to secure her position. It only took a few generations before a rumor became myth, and the myth could easily become gospel.

Just beyond the kitchen, she found a corridor which led across the courtyard to a smaller, much more modest building. The main room was sectioned off by long wooden tables that were filled to the point of collapse with boxes of food, tools, flatware, and other various items Sam assumed had been dropped off by supply ships.

Three Cai Thior women with small ledgers were cataloguing the items, but only one noticed Sam standing in the doorway. She was taller than the rest, older, and wore her long graying hair pulled back in a severe knot. She put down her book and offered a slow, appraising look.

"You must be the new arrival."

"That's right. I'm —"

The woman cut her off. "We are the Cai Thior. We are afforded certain comforts in exchange for our loyalty to Lokelani. Most of us have proven ourselves to her. But according to local gossip, you arrived yesterday. What makes you so special?"

Sam said, "She felt bad for me, I suppose. I didn't have anywhere else to turn."

Another woman, this one brunette wearing a pair of rudimentary spectacles, shook her head. "We are her strength. She would not choose someone out of pity. What is your real strength?"

Obviously playing the weakling wouldn't work with these women. Sam remembered something Tanis had said. "A clever hawk hides its claws," she said, squaring her shoulders and trying her best to look intimidating. "Lokelani saw something in me, but that doesn't mean I have to tell you what that is. When and if the time arrives when you need to know what I bring to the table, I'll be happy to demonstrate. For now, it looks like what you need the most help with is organization. I'm willing to lend a hand or I could just keep exploring my new home. It's up to you."

The older woman considered the reply. Finally she relaxed and gestured at the far table. "You can sort the extrinsic items. Writing tools, baubles, things which aren't absolutely necessary for living. Sort them into the appropriate boxes. My name is Aalid. The one with poor eyesight is Calyree, and she is Onora." The other woman, who had been silently observing with a judgmental look on her face, simply nodded and went back to her sorting.

"My name is Fraiser," Sam said.

Every time she said the name or heard someone else say it, she felt Janet watching over her. Janet, who never stood down in the face of tremendous odds, who could stare down generals and Jaffa without flinching. *I need a little bit of that steel spine, Janet,* she thought as she moved toward the table. Fighting was easy. Lying didn't come quite as naturally to her. She opened the first box and removed a set of homemade candles.

"So who sends these care packages?"

"People from home," Aalid said without looking up from her work. "Those who have loved ones incarcerated here."

Calyree said, "Bleeding hearts who fear for our humanity. Some believe that we deserve to be treated as humans no matter what our crimes may have been."

Onora finally spoke. "Usually it's people who believe that their own souls will be tainted if they turn their backs on us. A person's worth can be measured by how she treats her fellow woman. So they toss scraps into a crate, they gather up what garbage they can live without, and find a ship to drop it off. Then they can sleep easily until the next time their conscience nags at them."

Aalid said, "Part of our responsibility is ensuring no contraband gets through. Weaponry or communicators, not that they would do any good. No one could smuggle in a radio capable of punching through the barrier. Regardless, we confiscate any contraband we find to keep the peace." She patted the weapon on her hip to illustrate her point.

Sam translated the answer as 'to ensure Lokelani is the one with all the power'. "So how did Lokelani get the gear to start the Cai Thior? And how is this your responsibility? The guards are happy just letting you go through all of this and taking your word that there's nothing to aid in escape?"

"The guards have a singular purpose: no one gets out of the prison. Beyond that, they don't care a whit," Aalid said. "Quality of life, Fraiser, that means something even in a prison. The guards enforce the letter of the law. We add a more human element. We don't punish blindly. If an uprising began, the guards would be happy to let us kill each other and then pick off the survivors."

Calyree said, "Consider yourself fortunate, Fraiser. There is no place on this rock safer than where you stand right now, wearing these colors. No one will trouble you. If there is something you want or need, sooner or later it comes through here and you have first pick."

"That hardly seems fair."

"I've yet to visit a world with a fair system of distributing its goods. This is the way the universe works, Sri Fraiser. Just consider yourself fortunate to be on the side of plenty."

The women went back to their work. Sam watched them for a moment longer, trying to determine how complicit they were. Did they know their leader was a Goa'uld? Would they even care? She didn't want to take the risk of turning them against her if they did know. Her best option was to have a quiet conversation with Sukhan to feel her out on the subject. She had a feeling Sukhan could be her best asset in Lokelani's home.

She went back to sorting the items from the bin. Even if this plan worked and she was somehow able to find a way off Viaxeiro, it was going to take a while. They would have to be patient.

~#~

Teal'c had taken over the controls from Daniel. Pemphero regained consciousness to find he had been bound and secured to one of the bulkheads. He examined the restraints and decided it would be pointless to continue resisting or trying to get free. Cam watched him carefully anyway.

"Morning, sunshine." He held out the small silver bag he'd retrieved from his gear. "Want a little pretzel? They're good, but they make you thirsty."

Pemphero ignored the question. "So who is it? Hm? Your wife? Sister?"

"What are you talking about?"

"You think you're the first idiots to come digging for Viaxeiro? People always come. Sons, fathers, lackeys. All of them think they're going to be the ones to finally crack the code. They think they've got some trick nobody's ever thought of before. And you know what? They're all wrong. There are guards down there. They aren't there to keep the women *in*. Their job is to keep people like you *out*." He laughed and shook his head. "I'm just annoyed at how much time this nonsense is costing me. And so help me, if they damage my ship taking you out…"

Carolyn returned from the back of the ship. "The prisoner is awake," she said. "Her name is Koty'r, by the way. She's doing well, considering everything that's happened to her on this trip." She glanced at Pemphero, who snorted derisively and looked away. "I take it asking him for help hasn't been going well."

"We're making progress," Cam said, chewing on a pretzel. "We're friends now. Right, Pem?"

Teal'c turned away from the console. "I believe we are approaching Viaxeiro Caldera. At our current speed, we will arrive within the hour."

Cam crouched so he could face Pemphero. "You said you'd been here dozens of times. So if anyone would know where the weak spots are, it's you. Right?"

"Stands to reason," Pemphero said.

"If we send our friend down there, will you help us get her out? Along with our other friends who are already stuck down there?"

Pemphero held Cam's gaze for a long beat. "What exactly would be my incentive for helping you?"

Teal'c raised an eyebrow. "You do not appear to be in a position to negotiate."

"So you'll kill me if I don't help you?"

"Hey, man, you just tried to shoot me and all my pals here out into space…" Cam gave his most intimidating stare.

Pemphero grunted and rolled his eyes. "Fine. I know a few escape theories. If it gets you off my damn ship faster, then I'll help you. Under duress."

"We'll take it," Cam said. "Never expected you to help us with a smile, anyway." He slapped Pemphero's shoulder and pushed himself up.

"Okay, so we're doing this," Carolyn said.

"You still onboard?" Cam handed her a radio. "Because if you want us to work out that plan B…"

"No. No, this is the best way to get information to Colonel Carter and Vala." She looked hesitant but resolved. She tucked the radio under her belt and used her cloak to cover it. "I'm the only one who can go in, so I'm going in."

"With Koty'r," Pemphero said.

"What?" Cam said. "No, that would be an unnecessary complication. She's staying up here with us."

Pemphero shook his head. "Whatever you are planning, that woman is a criminal who was condemned to this prison. She deserves to be down there. You're here to save your friends, but are you willing to grant a pardon to a woman you don't even know?"

Daniel said, "It could be Linea all over again."

Cam closed his eyes and tilted his head back. After a ten-count, he dropped his chin and flared his hands out. He didn't like the idea of sending anyone to this prison, but she wasn't their responsibility. "Fine. We'll send her down, too. Happy now?"

Pemphero grunted. "No."

"Fantastic. Nobody's happy. The sign of a perfect road trip." Cam looked back at Teal'c. "Okay, buddy. Take us the rest of the way."

~#~

Shein signaled when a pair of Cai Thior women left Lokelani's, and Vala elected to follow them on patrol. She could have stayed put and let Tanis follow them, but she wanted a chance to get the layout of the city. If things went sideways, she and Sam might have to make a run for it without Tanis to lead the way. She wanted to know all the nooks and crannies and shortcuts that could mean the difference between freedom and remaining in the prison.

It was midday but whatever technology provided their atmosphere also maintained a comfortable temperature. The ground under her boots was a rough and uneven concrete, poured by inexperienced workers and marred by cracks every few steps. Still, it had a certain charm. Vala liked the crooked windows and the slapped-together buildings. These women, and the generations of women who came before them, had been dropped on an empty rock and left to die. They'd refused to despair and turned the barren wasteland into a home.

As they moved through the city, she paid special attention to the guards. The… official guards? True guards? The armed and armored men who were assigned to watch over the prisoners on behalf of the people who created it. Simple logic would imply animosity between the two forces. What kind of warden turned a blind eye on a militia being formed by the people who were supposed to be incarcerated? But the Cai Thior women were ignored by every guard they passed.

Was Lokelani really that powerful? Had she paid off the guards somehow, or did they just not care? It was probably a lot easier to stand back and let the prisoners police themselves. The guards could hang around and earn their pay without raising a finger or endangering their own safety. It was a neat little scam.

Vala watched the reaction of other prisoners as the Cai Thior moved through the marketplace. It was such a mundane area that it was easy to forget they were actually in a prison. The artificial sky was a pale red-orange overhead. Shops were open and doing brisk business with homemade trinkets, utensils, and other curios. She pretended to browse and found a brooch she thought Sam would like, as well as a hat she thought might look good on Teal'c when he was trying to blend in on Earth.

"Excellent items, both excellent items," the shopkeeper said, making her way over.

"Oh, I'm just looking. I don't have any money."

The old woman laughed and waved her hands around. "Are you new? No one here has *money*. We trade. You have food, you have skills. We can do a trade."

Vala looked toward the end of the market and saw the Cai Thior were about to disappear around a corner. She put back the brooch and hat.

"Maybe I'll come back for it later."

The woman picked up the hat, put the brooch into it, and waved them at Vala. "Take! If I need something at another time, I will know where to find you."

Vala hesitated. She didn't plan to be around long enough to pay off debts, but taking the items seemed like the path of least resistance. She took it, smiled gratefully, and hurried to catch up with her prey. At the back of her mind, she wondered what the generous old shopkeeper had done to end up in a prison like this. The women all around her who had made a home, who were resigned to the fact they would never see their families again... were their crimes really so horrendous it justified exiling them forever?

She knew it wasn't feasible to save everybody. They couldn't exactly set up a revolving door on the *Odyssey* and vet every single inmate. "And what was your crime? Ooh, sorry, gotta leave you behind, that's one of the crimes we don't like. Ta-ta!" Removing Lokelani from power was the best they could do. No matter how bad these people might be, no one deserved to live under Goa'uld rule.

Vala rounded the corner and nearly collided with one of the Cai Thior women. "Oh my goodness, I need to watch where I'm going!" she laughed, flipping her hair and swaying in what she hoped was an unthreatening manner. "I'm still trying to figure my way around this place."

The woman, a fierce blonde who looked as if she'd never been taught how to smile, narrowed her eyes. She was a full head taller than Vala, something that hadn't been apparent while tracking her, and suddenly it felt like staring at a statue come to life.

"Vala Mal Doran," the giantess sneered. "New condemned. You were involved in an altercation earlier today with the newest member of the Cai Thior."

"I was?" She feigned confusion, then realization. "You mean *Fraiser*? You recruited her? Did you need a human shield? Trust me, ladies, I've worked with her for a while now, and she's really not good for much else." The other Cai Thior was standing a few yards away reading the screen of a small palm-held device. "What is that? I thought radios didn't work on this hunk of rock."

"It's not a radio, it's a short-range messaging console." She put a hand on Vala's shoulder and urged her back the way she'd come. "It's of no concern for those of your ilk. Only the Cai Thior have access."

Vala twisted and tried to look past the tall woman. "Must be a pretty important message…"

"Again, it is none of your concern."

"I can be helpful, you know, I can make myself useful if—"

The tall guard shoved her. She nearly lost her footing but somehow managed to stay upright. She huffed, tugged at her blouse to straighten it, and lifted her chin haughtily.

"A simple 'your help is not required' would have sufficed. There's no need to be rude about it."

The woman with the radio approached and tapped the taller woman on the arm. "We need to go."

The taller woman aimed a finger at Vala. "Stop following us."

She spotted me? Vala thought. *Well, isn't that embarrassing.* She watched the women depart. She also noticed the official guards were also abandoning patrols and hurrying off the street.

"What's all the fuss about?"

"New condemned," someone said, barely looking up from her work at a kiln. "Newer than you, even. Someone's always comin' and droppin' folk off. You'll get used to it soon enough."

Vala raised an eyebrow. "But that means a ship is arriving! And a ship is a potential way out of here!"

The potter finally raised her head to give Vala a look of pity. "You really are new. You go ahead and try to escape, *usaq*. Guards'll put you down and it'll free up wherever you've been sleeping. That's how it goes 'round here. S'why it ain't over-crowded any more than it is. New ones always coming in, and foolish ones always tryin' get their way out." She shrugged and went back to her project. "We all get to decide how long our sentences are. Be smart. Take the life sentence an' be glad of it."

Vala suppressed a shudder at the thought. She jogged down the street and kept turning right until she found the wall. After that she simply had to walk north until she found the place where she and Sam had entered the city just one day earlier. God, it felt like it had been months.

Somehow word had spread that there was a new ship coming, as a crowd had formed near the arrival gate. Three of the Cai Thior were standing just inside the wall, watching the barren expanse. Vala didn't see any of the guards, but she knew they had to be inside the guard towers, where the tri-barreled guns were now swinging into position.

Minutes passed before Vala heard a shout from someone high up on the wall. "New condemned!" She and everyone else crowded around the barred entrances to watch the delivery. The energy of Viaxeiro's artificial atmosphere crackled along the egg shape of the ship's shields. Vala felt her feet itching to run toward the ship, to hop aboard and get back to civilization as quickly as possible. But she couldn't leave yet, not without Sam. There would be other, better opportunities down the road. They had to be patient.

The ship hovered in place for what seemed like an unusual length of time before the rings deployed. Two small bodies appeared in a flash of light, and they both fell over once the rings lifted back into the ship. One of them stood and hunched over the other, helped her up, and supported her as they started walking. The ship, meanwhile, lifted straight back the way it had come, enveloped by the force field and once again disappearing from sight.

A soft sound passed through the gathered women, and Vala realized seeing the ship was as important to them as welcoming their new neighbors. A ship meant people out in the wider universe hadn't forgotten them. It proved life went on, even while they were trapped in here. It was a fleeting glimpse of hope.

Vala looked back at the crowd. While she'd been watching the ship, more people had joined the crowd. She saw more Cai Thior uniforms and, to her surprise, one of them was being worn by Sam. She'd thought it would take more time to earn Lokelani's trust and get into the group. Their eyes met and Sam gave a quick, subtle nod. Vala returned it as Lokelani appeared. Vala ducked back into the shadows and put on her newly-acquired hat in the hopes it would keep her from being seen. There was no reason to hide from Lokelani, but there was also nothing to be gained by revealing her presence.

The two new condemned had finally arrived at the entrance. Vala glanced at them, certain there was no reason to give them much of her attention, but her eyes widened when she recognized one of them. She sat up straighter and looked across the way at Sam, who was now a few paces behind Lokelani. Sam had also seen the new prisoner's face, and she was trying to keep her expression neutral. She turned her head, found Vala, and raised her eyebrows.

Vala mouthed, "I know!"

Carolyn Lam was supporting a woman Vala didn't recognize, moving slowly due to the stranger's dazed and drugged shuffling. Lokelani approached them with a kind smile and went into the same spiel she'd used before.

"Welcome to Viaxeiro. My name is Lokelani Kiir. Who might you be?"

"I'm… Ma Barker," Carolyn said. Only someone who knew her would pick up on the exasperation in her voice. Either Mitchell had given her the sobriquet or she'd grown tired of using it. Either way, she was stuck with the alias for the time being. She nodded at the other woman, who looked like she was about to pass out again. "This is Koty'r."

Lokelani gestured to the Cai Thior, and two of them moved forward.

"Wait, don't hurt her."

"We're not going to hurt anyone," Lokelani said in a sooth-ing voice. "We're going to ensure that she gets the best care. She's obviously had a very exhausting trip. We'll find some-where she can rest and recuperate. Allow me to escort you somewhere as well. I'm sure you could use a change of clothes and something to drink."

Carolyn's relief was clear. "That would actually be great. Thank you."

Lokelani shooed the crowd away like they were curious chil-dren. She put an arm around Carolyn's shoulders as the Cai Thior took Koty'r somewhere to recover. Sam lingered until the rest of the Cai Thior weren't looking at her and found Vala again and smiled slightly. Vala winked and retreated until she was out of sight. It was impossible to know if Carolyn had seen them in the crowd, but that didn't matter much at the moment. What *did* matter was the fact her presence in the prison could only mean one thing.

The rest of SG-1 had actually found them. Escape suddenly didn't seem like such an impossible dream anymore.

CHAPTER TWENTY-FIVE

"DON'T TELL us it's impossible," Mitchell said, barely containing his rage. "Two of our friends are down there, and we just sent another one in with the promise we'd get her out again. I don't care how difficult it is."

Pemphero rolled his eyes. "I didn't say difficult. I said impossible. Is there a difference in your language, because there is in mine. Impossible means don't even try it."

Daniel said, "You said you had a way to get her out."

"I said I knew a few methods of escape," Pemphero said. "I've seen a lot of women try to escape Viaxeiro. Didn't say any of them actually worked."

Mitchell took a step toward the captain.

Daniel stepped between them. "Okay! Okay, look, mistakes were made. No one is saying we have to be friends. But why not make the best of a bad situation?"

"I have no interest in compromising with you," Pemphero muttered.

Daniel sighed, hands on his hips. "I don't want to play the 'you don't have a choice' card, but…"

Pemphero pushed out his jaw and curled his lip, but he didn't argue.

"Good. Now we're making progress. You told us that you know this place like the back of your hand after all the people you've transported. Was that a lie?"

"No. I probably know this prison better than the Overseers themselves."

"Great! And?"

Pemphero raised his voice. "And *escape is impossible*."

Daniel closed his eyes. He counted to ten in his head. Then he tried counting to fifteen. Then he gave up and opened his eyes to look at Pemphero again.

"Okay. Maybe you could explain why it's so impossible. This is a tough little ship, right? Kimo and Adamaris had a great ship, too. I'm sure everyone who transports prisoners for the Overseers have great ships. You're telling me that none of them are able to knock out Viaxeiro's defenses?"

"No weapons allowed on transport ships," Pemphero said. "And there are guns on the walls manned by guards who will shoot down anyone who tries to take off with a prisoner aboard." He sagged back against the wall, back slouched, knees bent. He looked like he was pouting. "If you want to make a suicide run, be my guest. But it's not going to do your lady friends a lick of good."

Daniel sighed heavily. "We're probably going to attract unwanted attention if we keep hanging around the planet like this. Teal'c, pull back but keep us in sensor range so we won't lose the place."

Pemphero sat up straighter. "What did you call him?"

"Crap," Daniel muttered. He pressed his thumb against the bridge of his nose and tried to remember the fake names Mitchell had given them. "Uh... Don Johnson?"

"You called him Teal'c." Pemphero flattened his feet on the floor and worked his shoulders against the wall to push himself up. "As in the *shol'va* who first stood against the Goa'uld? The man whose traitorous turn led to the Jaffa uprising and the eventual downfall of those blasphemous gods?" He looked at Cam and Daniel. "And that would make you SG-1, the Tau'ri who turned Apophis' ship into a bullet and slung it into his stronghold, destroying the whole planet. The team who flew into a minefield and snatched a prisoner from the beam transport. You faced the onslaught of Anubis himself in the skies above your planet and eradicated him and his unholy fleet with a snap of your fingers."

Daniel was surprised. "Well... I mean, there was a little more to it than that. And technically we missed when we tried to grab..." He coughed into his fist. "You know about all of that?"

"It is you," Pemphero said. "You *are* SG-1?"

"That's us," Mitchell said. "I take it you approve?"

Pemphero said, "I was born on a world ruled by Heru'ur. I saw his cruelty firsthand. When I was old enough, I joined a resistance against him but we never made any difference. At least not until his Jaffa began to abandon him. We heard he had been killed and that gave us the inspiration we needed to take back our planet. The Tau'ri may never have heard of my home planet, but just the same, they are responsible for its deliverance."

Daniel stammered. "Uh. Uh, you're welcome."

Pemphero looked at the three men again as if for the first time, reevaluating his opinion of each one. "When I said escaping Viaxeiro was impossible, that was before I knew I was dealing with the Merchants of Miracles."

"Damn, that might be the nicest nickname we've ever gotten," Cam said under his breath. "So you'll help us?"

Pemphero held out his bound hands. "Untie me and I'll do everything in my power to save your friends. If it costs my ship or even my life, I'll consider it a debt paid for everything you did to free my planet."

Daniel stepped forward and cut away the zip ties. "Hopefully it won't come to that."

"Come what may," Pemphero said, "if it's my time, I'll accept that. My *shol'va* friend, if you would allow me to take the seat, I'll move us to a safe distance while we debate the best course of action to save your friends."

Teal'c glanced at Mitchell for confirmation, then gave up the seat. Pemphero sat down and began moving his hands across the panels.

"You know, this would actually be the ideal way to go out." He smiled at the viewscreen as he angled away from Viaxeiro. "A hopeless mission with SG-1 of the Tau'ri."

Daniel drifted back to stand next to Mitchell. "Did we just trade a reluctant prisoner for a suicidal sidekick?"

"Trying to figure out which one is preferable," Mitchell said.

Teal'c joined them. "A fool willing to pay the cost with his life is a far greater asset than a beast who would rather dig in his heels than offer assistance."

"I bet that rhymes if you say it in Goa'uld."

Teal'c said, "It does not," at the same time Daniel said, "Not really."

Pemphero chuckled softly and shook his head. "No matter what happens, we're on the cusp of history. Either this is the end of SG-1, or the reputation of Viaxeiro Caldera will finally crumble."

"Still might be nice if we could tell which one you're rooting for," Mitchell said to Pemphero.

Pemphero laughed again and ignored them, maneuvering the ship to a spot where they wouldn't draw any unwanted attention.

~#~

This is fine, Carolyn told herself. She repeated it on a loop in her head to drown out the other voices screaming that this whole thing was a horrible mistake.

They had been taken to a small room where she was given water and a snack. The uniformed women doted over Koty'r, who seemed to be coming out of her drug-induced stupor faster than expected. After they had been given some time to "recover," the woman who seemed to be in charge - Lokelani—and the uniformed women who seemed to be her own personal Secret Service - Cai Thior—returned to take them on a tour of their new home.

And there in the back of the group was Colonel Carter. They made eye contact a few times during the brief tour of the city, but Sam hadn't made any attempt to communicate with her. Carolyn understood that. She probably had a cover to maintain. Carolyn was willing to let this play out with the knowledge Sam would step in if things got too hairy.

The real concern was Koty'r. The woman knew that something was fishy about how Carolyn had arrived at the prison. She might not know all the details, but she'd definitely seen enough to know that Cam, Daniel, and Teal'c weren't ordinary jailers. If she revealed anything, it could be disastrous. She caught Koty'r watching her a few times during their tour but she never said a word. The way her eyes darted around at the buildings they passed, Carolyn guessed she was taking in every detail and waiting for the right moment to act. It was a good reminder that everyone around them was some kind of criminal or another.

Lokelani was explaining the way the prison worked. Carolyn hoped she wouldn't be around long enough to need the information. When they arrived at a town square, Lokelani turned to address Carolyn and Koty'r.

"This place was designed as a prison. But through hard work and the dedication of every woman incarcerated here, we have turned it into a home. Whatever crime you committed to end up here, it doesn't matter now. It's a piece of your history. Move past it. Use this as a new beginning. And welcome to Viaxeiro."

"Thank you," Carolyn said.

Sam stepped forward. "Sri Lokelani, if I may?"

Lokelani appeared surprised but covered it well. "Yes, Sri Fraiser?"

Fraiser? Carolyn thought. *I suppose it's better than Colonel Mitchell's fake names.*

Sam said, "No offense, but you've all been here a lot longer than I have. I'm in a unique position of remembering exactly what it's like to arrive here and not know how anything works. I'd like to be the one to show these women around so I can share what I've learned while the information is still fresh."

"An excellent idea, Sri Fraiser," Lokelani said. "And just the kind of gesture I expect in our community. Thank you." She faced Carolyn and Koty'r. "This is Sri Fraiser. She was our last arrival before you, and I'm sure she can provide some valuable insight."

Carolyn nodded to Sam. "I appreciate your help."

Lokelani motioned for the rest of the Cai Thior to disperse. She stepped forward and gestured for Sam to lean in, lowering her voice. "Meet me when you finish showing them around, please."

"Of course."

A few of the Cai Thior eyed Sam as they followed Lokelani away down a narrow alley. Koty'r wavered between the two groups, uncertain of which she belonged with. Carolyn made a small gesture with her hand that the woman should stay. A few of the Cai Thior looked at Sam over their shoulders but Carolyn couldn't dissect their expressions. Were they friendly or antagonistic? Sam didn't give anything away, but she did watch them until they were out of sight.

"We should walk. At least pretend like I'm showing you around."

"Lead the way," Carolyn said.

Sam started walking. "I assume this means there's some kind of rescue or escape plan in the works? Otherwise this is a hell of a coincidence."

"The guys are on a ship nearby. Last I saw, the pilot was helping us, albeit forcibly. I have a radio in case we find a way to get a signal through the force field. Vala?"

"We thought it best to split up. Vala apparently has a reputation here."

Carolyn said, "I'm shocked. What about the rest of the mission? Tanis Reynard?"

"She's here. And she's not interested in leaving."

"What?"

Sam shrugged. "We're not exactly going to force her to come with us if she doesn't want to." She looked at Koty'r. "Who is this?"

"She's another prisoner," Carolyn said. "We hitched a ride

with the man who was delivering her. I, uh… I'm not exactly sure what we should do with her. She may not know exactly who we are, but she definitely knows something is up."

"I'm standing right in front of you," Koty'r said, rolling her eyes. "If I didn't know you were up to something before, I certainly do now."

Carolyn said, "Colonel Mitchell decided it was best to send her down to avoid a repeat of everything that happened with Linea."

Sam said, "What was your crime?"

Koty'r looked from Sam to Carolyn and back again, trying to determine if she could trust these odd women. Finally she said, "I desecrated holy sites for things to sell. People on my planet who never stopped worshipping the Goa'uld decided to make an example of me. Whoever you are, I'm not looking to make any waves. You want to leave me here, fine. You want to take me with you, that's great, too. But you don't have to worry about me ratting you out to the lady back there." She hunched her shoulders and shook her head. "Something about her rubbed me the wrong way."

Sam said, "She's a Goa'uld."

Koty'r grimaced. "That would probably be it."

"Wait," Carolyn said. "Are you sure?"

"I haven't seen any glowing yellow eyes or heard her voice change, but yeah. I'm sure."

"Could she just be a former host, like you?"

Sam shook her head. "It's hard to explain, but the feeling is different if there's a living symbiote."

Carolyn said, "So what's the plan?"

"Tanis claims she can help us escape if we help her depose Lokelani."

"Isn't that kind of going from the frying pan into the fire?"

Sam shrugged. "I have to admit, I don't like the idea of leaving a Goa'uld in charge. She seems to be running things well, but we haven't seen what happens to the people she disagrees with. Vala trusts Tanis. If she thinks this place would be better off with her in charge, I have to go with that."

"Okay then." Carolyn was a little surprised to hear Sam express such faith in Vala's opinion. The woman may have been a full member of SG-1 for several months, but the others had been slow warming to her. "So I guess being a member of this Cai Thior is part of your escape plan?"

"I thought it would be easier to figure out a plan if I got close to Lokelani. So we faked a falling out, and I ended up in this uniform."

"And Vala?"

"Working the other end with Tanis and Shein."

"Shein?"

"Tanis' girlfriend," Sam said.

Carolyn said, "Ah. Okay. Now her staying behind makes a little more sense. People will stay in all kinds of places for love."

Sam pressed her lips together and nodded quickly, obviously thinking about something specific. "Yeah."

"My part of the mission was to come down here, make contact, and let you know that the guys are working on a solution out there. And if you and Vala find a way out on your own, their ship is waiting to pick you up."

"Nice to know our ride is here," Sam said, looking up at the shimmering energy that made up Viaxeiro's marmalade sky. "Now we just have to figure out how to get to them."

CHAPTER TWENTY-SIX

AFTER PEMPHERO moved the ship out of sensor range he locked in a course that would have them following Viaxeiro on its journey. "It's easy enough to keep us in its tail," he explained. "Once you know where it is, you can work out its trajectory. Otherwise the Overseers would never be able to find the damn thing."

Teal'c said, "I find it difficult to understand how this planet's position has remained such a closely guarded secret if it is so easy to track."

"Not *easy*," Pemphero said. "You have to go to the Overseers to gets its coordinates, and they only unlock those for people they know or people who have been vouched for. They don't hand out the location to just anybody. And once you've got a job transporting prisoners to this rock, you don't give it up easily. Do you have any idea how much some governments pay for this service? The number of people I've seen retire younger than you." He pointed at Cam and shook his head. "If we actually pull this off and word gets out that I helped you, I'm going to miss the income."

Daniel said, "You probably have a pretty solid reputation among the criminal underworld. I mean, if you were entrusted with the location of Viaxeiro, you must have a lot of contacts."

Pemphero shrugged dismissively. He had sagged back in his chair, one foot propped against the console as he watched the stars through the view screen. "I know some people who might know people."

"Well... if you're so eager to help us out, maybe there's a larger part you could play. The Goa'uld may be gone, but the Lucian Alliance has been growing more and more powerful. And they kind of... ah..."

Cam said, "Hate our ever-lovin' guts."

"Part of what got us into this whole mess was the thought we might gain intelligence about the Alliance that we could use against them. Now, we've actually managed to get a look at the criminal underworld where the Alliance operates, and I have the feeling we'll be able to use what we've learned once we get back to Earth. But having someone like you on our side, providing information and maybe giving us rides to planets without Stargates..."

Pemphero considered it, raising one eyebrow and dragging his finger along his jaw. "So in a way, I would be an honorary Tau'ri."

Daniel blinked a few times and put on an awkward smile. "Sure."

"I'll think about it. Even if we don't get caught, I probably shouldn't risk showing my face around the Overseers after sticking my neck out like this." He grinned slowly. "Me, helping out the Tau'ri. Working with SG-1! I feel like I'm doing my family proud. Please, Dr. Jackson, tell me something about one of your adventures. Preferably a time when you stood against the Goa'uld."

"Uh." Daniel looked at Cam. "Uh... well. Okay... Teal'c and I went back to Abydos a year after the SGC officially started up..."

Cam noticed that Teal'c was standing at the back of the bridge, head slightly lowered with his arms crossed over his chest. He moved closer and lowered his voice so he wouldn't interrupt Daniel's anecdote.

"Buddy? What's on your mind?"

"I am considering our options. Carolyn Lam will alert Colonel Carter and Vala Mal Doran to our presence. They will therefore be prepared should we make a move to rescue them from Viaxeiro."

"What are you thinking, a kamikaze run at that force field? I don't think we'd be the first ones to try that, and Pemphero says they've got guards down there to discourage that sort of behavior."

Teal'c said, "Any escape attempt would require far more coordination between ourselves and the women of our team than we are currently capable of. We cannot so much as signal them of our intentions. They would be required to improvise immediately once our plan is in action, and that is only if they deduce what we need them to do."

"Wow. Never seen you so glass-half-empty, buddy."

"My concerns are merely practical, Colonel Mitchell. There is a reason no one has ever escaped this prison. Our odds are very low."

"Any suggestions on how we could improve them?"

"We could have delayed sending Carolyn Lam to the planet until we had a plan."

Cam sighed. "Yeah. If we'd known Pemphero was going to be so helpful, maybe we wouldn't have been so quick with the drop-off. But I thought it was important to let the ladies know we were up here as soon as possible."

Teal'c nodded once and faced forward. "There is no sense in weeping over spilled lactose."

"It's cry—" He narrowed his eyes, unsure if Teal'c had really gotten the idiom wrong or if he was just screwing with him. "Right. Well, Carter and Vala are pretty quick on the uptake. If we make enough noise, I'm sure they'll pick up on it."

Teal'c made a soft noise of agreement. "And we must hope our efforts are compatible with whatever plans they may already have in place."

"Yeah." He patted Teal'c's arm. "That's the spirit. Keep it optimistic."

Daniel was still telling his story. "—and, uh, since his bullets weren't working, Jack took his knife and flung it at Heru'ur's ribbon device."

Pemphero cackled. "Did it work?"

"Oh, yeah. Blade went right through his hand."

Pemphero rocked back in his seat and clapped. "Amazing!"

"At least we have a new fan. Kind of a nice change of pace."

Teal'c raised an eyebrow and said nothing.

~#~

Vala resisted the urge to skip back to the cold-water. Tanis was still in position to watch Lokelani's stronghold and didn't look up as Vala joined her on the roof.

"Carter just headed out with a couple of new arrivals."

"Those aren't just new arrivals," Vala said, dropping onto her stomach next to Tanis. She stacked her hands and rested her chin on them. "The dark-haired one is our friend. Dr. Carolyn Lam. If she's here, that means the boys aren't far behind. Rescue is right around the corner."

Tanis tensed. She sat up straighter and flipped up the lenses of her sight enhancers. "So I guess that means you're leaving soon."

"Well, we're going to do our best to follow through with the deal," Vala said. "I doubt SG-1 would willingly walk away while a Goa'uld is in charge."

"Right," Tanis said.

Vala looked at her. "Having second thoughts about staying behind? I'm sure I could convince Sam and the others to make room for Shein if you want to go."

"No, we're staying. It's…" She wrinkled her nose and swept her hand across the pebbled surface of the roof. "I… I sent you the message to warn you away, and I was pissed to see you show up, but I've really enjoyed seeing you again. Okay? You were the best partner I ever had. You're the only one I could still tolerate after going our separate ways. And if anyone else had shown up as a member of SG-1, I probably would've written them off immediately. Good riddance and don't get caught in my afterburners, you know? But I was able to look past it with you. That probably means something. And I'm going to miss you when you're gone, because after this, we probably won't see each other again."

Vala tried to keep her emotions in check. "I don't think I've ever heard you speaking so sweetly without ending it with an insult."

Tanis ignored her and flipped the lenses back over her eyes.

"You know, I wouldn't have gone to all this trouble for just anyone. Viaxeiro Caldera? Just suggesting it to the rest of the team was a huge gamble. I used so much of the goodwill I've acquired with them because I thought they had a chance to save you. Because I thought you deserved to be saved. You're the only person I've worked with I feel that way about. So what you were saying… what you didn't say… I feel the same."

"Glad to hear it," Tanis said.

"Nobody on SG-1 can insult me quite the way you do."

Tanis smiled at that. "Good to know I'm undefeated. Your friend, the new one who came in. Is she a good soldier?"

"Carolyn…? Uh… well… I know for a fact that she's made every member of the SGC bleed. And everyone, no matter their rank, is frankly frightened of her."

"Hmph," Tanis said. "At least the Tau'ri were smart enough to send a warrior."

Vala sheepishly looked anywhere but Tanis' direction. From the corner of her eye, she caught movement across the roof but didn't acknowledge the new arrival.

"So," she said as casually as she could muster. "That Shein… she seems pretty capable herself."

Tanis smiled. "She's more than capable, Vala. She could take you down in pretty much any sort of contest. Charm, pickpocketing, planning. I'm not saying this to make you feel inferior, because she's better than me at all that shit, too. I'd have been jealous as hell if I ever ran into her out in the real life. But here? Where we don't have to compete? I can respect her."

"Wow," Vala said, "I don't think I've ever heard you gush so much over a conquest."

"She's not a conquest." Irritation crept into Tanis' voice. "I told you, I'm here for good. I'm settling down. And Shein is a big reason for that." She flipped up her lenses again. "I've always been about taking things. Making them mine, possessing them. I don't want to steal Shein. I just want to be in her life. And I swear, if you mock me for this…"

"No, no, nothing of the sort," Vala said. "Nice to have it clarified."

Shein said, "It sure is."

Tanis twisted to see Shein standing a few feet behind them. She looked back at Vala and realized she'd been aware they weren't alone. She grunted and dropped back down onto her elbows.

"That was a nasty trick, Mal Doran."

Shein lay down as well. "And dangerous. What if you had badmouthed me? I'd have made you find a new cold-water to spend the night until I calmed down."

"All right, all right," Vala said, "enough flirting. Samantha is down there with Dr. Lam in the belly of the beast. What do you say we go catch up with her so we can brainstorm a way to remove Lokelani from power and get off this rock once and for all?"

Tanis pushed herself up and took off the magnifying lenses. "Sounds good to me. I hate being on surveillance duty."

Vala stood as well. She dusted off her clothes and looked at Shein. "We've got a ship out there with the rest of our team waiting for us to open the door. I'm sure in your time here you've come up with some plans to escape if you were ever granted the opportunity."

"Oh, lots."

"Preferably one that doesn't end up with a lot of corpses or half the prison escaping with us," Vala amended.

Shein's expression soured. "Oh. I'll have to think about that."

"Well, think quick," Vala said as they walked toward the

ladder which led to the street. "I'd hate to make the boys wait any longer than necessary."

~#~

Carolyn eyed a group of guards leaning against a building's wall. One of the men followed her with his eyes but didn't make a move to stop them. Koty'r followed them, remaining silent. Carolyn saw no reason to cut her loose yet. She waited until they had turned a corner before she spoke. "So what's the hierarchy here? Do those guards have authority over you, now that you're a member of Lokelani's little militia?"

Sam shook her head. "They're just ensuring no one tries to escape. Most of the prisoners seem happy to stay put, so they don't really have anything to do."

Vala came around the corner ahead of them, followed quickly by Tanis and Shein. Sam motioned toward a nearby alley. She led her small group into the alley and waited next to a long, squat dumpster until Vala joined them. Vala ran up to Carolyn and wrapped her in a crushing hug that impeded her ability to breathe.

"Dr. Lam!"

"Oh. Uh, hello. I wasn't aware we were at this level of friendship."

"She's a hugger," Sam said.

Vala said, "I'm just so glad to see you!"

"It's, uh, it's good to see you, too." She managed to wriggle free from the embrace. "Colonel Carter has been filling me in about everything." Tanis and Shein had stayed at the mouth of the alley to watch for guards, Cai Thior, or Lokelani. "I take it this is Tanis Reynard and…"

"Shein Pranassa," Tanis said. "You're Lam?"

"That's right. Uh, the name we gave to Lokelani was Ma Barker."

Sam said, "Colonel Mitchell's idea?"

"Yeah."

"Figures."

"Mm-hmm."

Koty'r lifted a hand. "Koty'r A'yiti. Not that anyone asked. But they said Tanis… you?" She pointed and Tanis nodded. "They said you would be in charge if all goes according to plan. Might be nice to get in good with the new leader. So if you need my help, you've got it."

"Why?" Sam asked.

Vala cleared her throat and whispered. "Samantha, isn't there a saying about animals being given as gifts that should keep their mouths closed?"

"No, we need to know why she's so willing to stay behind in a prison."

Koty'r said, "What prison? Out there, I see a town that's running smoothly. I don't see any temples to dead false gods. I don't see anyone sitting in the street begging for scraps. This place is a paradise compared to what I'm leaving behind. The only downside I can see is that there's a Goa'uld calling the shots. You want to change that. I'm in."

Sam nodded thoughtfully. "Okay. Do the guys have a plan in place?"

Carolyn said, "Well… they were mostly just playing it by ear. We've been going all-out just trying to find this place. All the team had to go on was rumor and innuendo. Couldn't really come up with a viable escape plan until they knew what we were dealing with."

"That's fair," Sam said. "Where are they now?"

"Staying out of sight," Carolyn said. "I think the plan was wait to see if you could pass along a signal or, if too much time went by, just charge the place. They're worried about the guards, though."

Tanis said, "The real threat is the landmines and the blasters on the wall. Even if you get across the sand to a waiting ship, those guns will blast you out of the sky before you even reach the barrier. But let's say you find a way around those obstacles. It doesn't answer the problem of Lokelani. I hate to sound like a petulant child, but you did give your word that you'd help get rid of her before you left."

"Right," Sam said.

"I've been thinking about that," Vala said, "and I just might have a solution. I was thinking that this prison has been around for… what… at least as long as the Goa'uld have been running around? And it's been populated exclusively by women like me and Tanis and Shein, people whose immediate thought is to find a way out. Generations of sneaky, clever women who made their living getting out of tough binds. And none of them have been able to find a way out."

Sam said, "You're not making me feel better about our chances here, Vala."

"No, but listen. *Why* haven't they been able to find a way out? Because… the only way out is crazy and dangerous and the sort of thing no sane person would even consider."

"Sounds like the Tau'ri," Tanis said.

"We do have a reputation for dumb ideas," Sam admitted. "What are you thinking?"

Vala blew air between her lips and pointed straight up. The women around her followed her finger. They saw clotheslines strung between buildings with curved rooftops, they saw small wooden platforms that served as balconies, with crawling vines of potted plants creating an elevated forest in the narrow alley. Someone with an open window was cooking a meal that made Sam's stomach growl idly. At first she couldn't figure out what Vala was talking about. When it did click, she snapped her gaze back to Vala's incomprehensibly smiling face.

"You can't be serious."

"It's just crazy enough it might work!"

"It's suicide," Sam said.

Carolyn looked between them. "What's going on?"

"She wants to find the force field generator and turn it off."

"That sounds really, really incredibly stupid," Carolyn said, her voice taking on a hint of panic. "Let's not do that."

"Just for a second!" Vala said. "What's the worst that could happen?"

"If the sky literally disappeared?" Sam said. "All the oxygen on this planetoid would immediately get sucked out into space, suffocating us all. The temperature would drop so fast we might freeze to death before we asphyxiated. And if we're unlucky enough to be close to a sun, anyone who miraculously survived both of those things would be hit with such a massive dose of UV radiation, they'd be burnt to a crisp."

Vala meekly said, "But... just for a second...?"

"That's why I said 'immediately'." Sam rolled her head and pressed both hands against her eyes. "Vala... I want to be more open to your plans. I really do. But this plan is just bad. Humans can't survive in a full vacuum. There..." She stopped short and her eyes swam out of focus as her attention turned inward. Vala could almost see words forming behind her irises.

"But...? Is there a but...?"

"There's..." Sam looked up at the sky again. "It would be suicide to turn off the force field entirely. But if we could *thin* the atmosphere..."

Shein said, "What is she talking about? Are they going to burn the sky?"

Tanis said, "They better not."

"No," Sam said. "The sky would still be there. Vala, do you remember the first time you left the base?"

"Daniel took me for ice cream at a lovely little parlor at the base of the mountain. There's — "

Sam waved her off. "That's not important. I mean when you were driving down the mountain. You said you could barely breathe."

"Right!" Vala said. "I felt as if I'd been running a marathon."

"The part of the world where our base is located has a very high elevation," Sam explained to the others. "The atmosphere is thin. People who aren't accustomed to it find themselves short of breath. There's something like seventeen percent less oxygen at that altitude. We can't turn off the force field, but maybe we can turn it down enough to thin the air. We knock it down to…"

Her eyes glazed over again but Vala snapped her fingers before she could completely drift away.

"You can do the math later! Would that work?"

"I think so," Sam said. "We would have to find a way to protect ourselves from the hypoxia, and the Goa'uld might be able to stay conscious, but the Cai Thior and the guards and all the innocent bystanders Lokelani might otherwise use as human shields would be taken out of play."

Tanis said, "And if you thin the atmosphere enough, you could get a radio message out to your friends. We'd just have to find a radio."

"Oh." Carolyn reached under her belt and showed them the radio. "Just in case."

Tanis looked excited. "Does this mean we have a plan?"

Sam nodded slowly. "I think we have the shape of a plan. Which is better than what we had a few minutes ago." She looked at Vala and nodded her thanks. Vala beamed with pride that she'd helped. "But it doesn't mean anything unless we can find the force field generator and figure out how to manipulate it. Carolyn, Koty'r, you go with Vala, Tanis, and Shein. See if you can find oxygen masks, life support systems, anything we can use to stay conscious when we take out the air."

"And you?" Tanis said. "Where will you be?"

"If anyone on this rock is going to know about the generator, it's Lokelani. I'm going to do my best to make her tell me where it is."

CHAPTER TWENTY-SEVEN

TEAL'C FAMILIARIZED himself with the controls of Pemphero's ship and used them to determine the area of space they were traveling through. They were currently skimming along the edge of a small planetary system which boasted three worlds capable of supporting life. They were well within the sprawl of the Stargate network, so it seemed likely that one of the worlds would have a Stargate. At the rate Viaxeiro was moving, however, he expected they would be out of range when the time came to make a daring escape. He scanned ahead for other systems and found something else instead.

"Pemphero."

The pilot had been slumped in his seat, dozing, but he was immediately alert. He moved his hands to the controls and watched the readout.

"A ship approaches our position," Teal'c reported.

Cam and Daniel moved forward and flanked Teal'c's seat. Cam craned his neck to look out the view screen as if something might be visible. "Anyone we should be concerned about?"

"No, no," Pemphero said dismissively. "Just a supply ship on its way to Viaxeiro. You can tell from the size. They need all that extra cargo room."

Daniel said, "What are they bringing in?"

"Standard rations, clothing, whatever the Overseers think they might need. There isn't a schedule. Sometimes you get two in a week, sometimes there's just one in a cycle. Feast and famine, it's the same all over now that the Goa'uld are gone."

"I thought you hated the Goa'uld," Cam said.

"I *despise* those gold-eyed bastards. But…" He sighed and cocked his head as he considered what he wanted to say. "The Goa'uld treated us all like cattle. But sick cattle doesn't do the butcher any good, mm?" He looked to make sure they were following him. "They weren't kind and they weren't generous, but they had a vested interest in keeping us alive. They didn't do it out of the goodness of their hearts, of course. Everything they gave us came with a cost. End the drought in exchange for a few potential hosts. That kind of thing. A lot of people are close to forgetting that part now that we have to scrounge for everything when times are tough."

Daniel said, "I suppose that makes it easier to fall into… less than moral choices."

"Mm," Pemphero said. "And falling in with the Ori makes a lot of sense, too. Same deal we had with the Goa'uld, but no threat of being turned over as a host. It's appealing."

Daniel and Cam exchanged a look. Pemphero grinned.

"Fret not, fellows, I'm not one of them. I found a niche that works for me and I'm happy here. I don't need to bow to anyone just because they have superior technology and fancier ships."

"Good to know." Daniel turned his attention back to the sensors. "Will they be able to see us?"

Pemphero shrugged and shook his head, indicating he didn't know. "Might, but could not. I'd have to know more about their ship to make a guess. But it shouldn't matter. Every time we make a trip to Viaxeiro, it's in a new place with different star systems and traffic patterns. If they notice us, they won't think it's unusual."

Cam narrowed his eyes. "The prison isn't expecting that ship to arrive at a certain time?"

"No one ever expects a ship on Viaxeiro," Pemphero said. "There's no way for them to know when someone is condemned."

"So if it was delayed, no one would ever know."

Daniel said, "What are you thinking?"

"I'm thinking that ship is going to land so it can offload some supplies," Cam said. "I think if we were able to get aboard that ship, it would be our ticket into the prison."

Pemphero said, "That prison is full of women, Colonel Mitchell. No matter how you arrive, you're going to cause a fuss. There's no need to sneak onto the supply ship. I could drop you down right now and get the same results."

Teal'c said, "Perhaps we would not have to be visible to enter the prison."

"You didn't happen to pack those Sodan armbands, did you?" Cam said. "Because radiation or not, those things would come in pretty handy right now."

"I did not." Teal'c turned away from the screen. "There is a tale of a war waged between Ra and Shaq'ran over a planet which bordered both of their territories. Both claimed it belonged to them but Ra was the first to establish a presence. He knew that he was at risk of an invasion so he immediately fortified his temple. But Shaq'ran was clever. He concealed himself within an offering to Ra. His Jaffa brought the alleged offering into a room of the temple allocated for these treasures, unaware that several of Shaq'ran's Jaffa were concealed within. They waited for their opportunity and then emerged, taking over the temple from within."

"A Trojan Horse," Daniel said. Teal'c looked at him. "We, uh, we had an army do something similar on Earth. Pemphero, is there anything on that ship which would be large enough to conceal us?"

"No," Pemphero said. After a moment, he said, "Not all of you. One…? Maybe. Possibly. I've seen some of the supplies being loaded at the Overseers station. There are usually crates that would be large enough to accommodate a human person." He looked at Teal'c. "I'm sorry to say you're out of the running, my friend."

"I'll do it," Cam and Daniel said at the same time. They looked at each other and, again in stereo, said, "Why you?"

"Because from a physical standpoint, there's no difference between us," Daniel said. "Same height, same build. But if we're choosing which one of us should stay on the ship we just hijacked and who should go down to the planet and be sneaky…"

"You think you're sneakier than me?"

"I'm better at talking my way out of a confrontation if I get caught. And if anything goes wrong on the ship, I'd much rather have you there to deal with it, because that situation is more likely to involve flying and-or fighting."

Cam thought about that for a moment. "Damn, that makes a lot of sense. All right. Jackson will be the one to go down. Probably for the best. Vala will be happier to see him anyway."

Daniel froze. "Wait, let's rethink this…"

"Too late. Plan is already underway. We've gotta figure out a way to hijack that ship before it gets to Viaxeiro." He patted Daniel on the shoulder. "Let's go be pirates."

~#~

Sam hesitated at the threshold before entering Lokelani's stronghold. There were no Cai Thior nearby that she could see and, even though she was wearing the uniform, she felt like a thief sneaking through the quiet rooms. She knew she was welcome, but was there a probation period? Would Lokelani expect her to have escorts until her loyalty had been proven? She didn't want to draw suspicions if it wasn't absolutely necessary. She decided to take the risk in order to gather intel. Knowing the layout of the house could be useful if they were required to fight in its rooms.

As she explored, she tried to mentally picture the layout of the prison. From what she'd seen, the city occupied a good patch of the planemo. Maybe a few square miles? Whatever was generating the force field had to be somewhere near the center in order to cover the outer edges. And it had to cover a space large enough to include the vast open desert where ships dropped off the condemned. That would require a staggering amount of energy. If it was true that the only people who came to the planet were prisoner transports and supply ships, then it meant that generator had been running without requiring service for… well, longer than she could calculate. If she got a chance to examine it, there was a chance it would revolutionize…

Lokelani stepped out of a doorway ahead of her and Sam's rambling thoughts immediately went silent. The Goa'uld had changed clothes again, now in a dark blue cloak with a yellow border. The collar was open to reveal a black blouse underneath. She smiled when she saw Sam.

"Sri Fraiser. How lovely to see you. I trust our new residents have found suitable accommodations?"

"They're settling in now, Lokelani, yes." There was something about her smile that made Sam uneasy. "I thought I would come back here and see if anyone needed my help. When we received word of the new arrivals, I was helping Aalid and two other women with the supplies."

Lokelani shook her head and reached out, putting her hand on Sam's shoulder and turning her around. "There's no need for that. Come." The hallway was just wide enough for them to walk side-by-side, but Sam still felt crowded. "I feel like I didn't quite explain to you just how treacherous Vala Mal Doran could be. The woman has a horrid reputation throughout the galaxy. I myself didn't know the full extent of it until a few moments ago."

"Is that so," Sam said.

"Mm. It seems that she's found herself conscripted into an army. I was hesitant to believe this at first, because Vala hardly plays well with *one* other person. An army would be unheard of. But you know what they say about rumors. If you feel enough raindrops, you must assume you are standing under a storm cloud. Have you heard that saying before, Fraiser?"

They had reached the end of the hall. Curtained doorways stood to the left and right, and a flight of stairs directly ahead led underground. "I can't say I have," Sam said.

"Well, perhaps it hasn't spread to the Tau'ri yet."

"I'm…"

Lokelani moved her hand to the back of Sam's neck and

squeezed. Sam hunched her shoulders and bit back a cry of surprise as Lokelani stepped in front of her.

"You were followed when you left this house. You were seen speaking confidentially to the new prisoners, and meeting with Vala Mal Doran and her cronies. Did you think I was a fool who would trust you completely? You are not Cai Thior. You are just a woman in a uniform until you have proven yourself. You failed your trial miserably."

"Does that trust go both ways?" Sam asked. "Does your Cai Thior know they're serving a Goa'uld?"

There was only a quick twitch of surprise on Lokelani's features, but she covered it quickly by widening her smile.

"Clever. And I suppose if it is true that Vala joined forces with the Tau'ri, it stands to reason that you are a member of SG-1. Female, blonde, with the ability to sense Goa'uld? It took me a while to recognize what I sensed from you. It's been so long since I was around a former host." Lokelani's eyes flashed gold. Her voice became a hollow echo. "Hello, Colonel Carter. I have been waiting for a moment like this for quite some time."

~#~

"I don't want to jinx anything," Vala said, "but I think things are going very well."

Tanis said, "What makes you say that?"

"Just a feeling."

The guards they were following had stopped, so Vala and Tanis moved to stand against a nearby wall. They had split up when Tanis noticed another pair behind them, curious about why such a large group of prisoners was wandering together. Shein had taken Carolyn and Koty'r, because she knew the larger group would attract more suspicion, and set out to lead them on a pointless chase through the city. Vala suggested turning the tables, following the guards to find where they might be hiding emergency supplies to use in the event of a riot.

"You and I have always worked well together, right?" Vala asked. "Whether we had time to plan or if we had to improvise, we always came out on top. And this time we have SG-1 backing us up! I know you have some issues with them, but they're on your side this time."

Tanis scoffed. "I'm starting to think those women we used to be are long gone."

"What do you mean?"

"Look at us!" Tanis said with a laugh. "I'm nesting in prison and you're hanging out with the good guys."

"That doesn't mean we've gone soft," Vala said. "SG-1... the Tau'ri..." She struggled for an argument that would work on her friend. "You hated the Goa'uld, right?"

"Any human without a snake in their head hated the Goa'uld."

"SG-1, Earth, the SGC, the people I'm working with now? The whole reason they started running around the galaxy in the first place was to stop the Goa'uld. They succeeded - yay! - and the universe became a much nicer place to be a criminal in."

Tanis said, "And now they're trying to take down the Lucian Alliance."

Vala rolled her eyes. "Do they have irritating morals that sometimes get in the way of a good time? Of course they do. That's what makes them the good guys. But they're just trying to give everyone a chance. You have to admit that we were always very self-centered. Working for our own goals and damn anyone else. The Lucian Alliance is the same way. The SGC isn't like that. They want what's best for everyone. The Ori are an incredibly dangerous threat. I know better than most what they're capable of. That's why I'm working with the SGC."

Tanis examined Vala's face for clues to what she'd just said. "What do you mean you know better than most?"

"Nothing," Vala said. "Forget about it. You weren't the only one that had adventures after we parted ways." She pushed away from the wall. "The guards are on the move again. Come on."

They were working on the assumption that the guards had some sort of protocol in the event of a catastrophic emergency.

According to Carolyn, the Overseers who kept the prison running were really just a bunch of holograms with a very basic AI program, but there still had to be precautions. Shein, working with Carolyn and Koty'r, would stage a false alarm which Vala hoped would send their prey running to whatever safety gear they might have stashed.

"As for you nesting," Vala said, "that's much easier to explain. You finally found a treasure you couldn't steal because it's inside you and it only exists when you're near Shein. You've never been content abandoning treasure. You're not settling down, you're protecting the score of a lifetime."

"Huh," Tanis said softly, not fully acknowledging the theory but also not ignoring it.

The guards had stopped again and Vala sighed wearily. "Do these dullards ever actually *do* anything or do they just wander?"

"The Overseers run a tight ship. No corruption, no perverts, no one who might cause problems. I suppose now it seems obvious that it was a computer system working to keep things running smoothly. But the end result is a bunch of armed men in uniforms who don't have much to fill their days. They're scenery."

Vala was about to respond but she was cut off by a sudden low moaning noise that echoed off the nearby buildings. Tanis had warned her about the horns, but she hadn't expected anything quite so unsettlingly mournful. It reminded her of whale song.

"Looks like Shein came through," she said.

Tanis nodded, watching the guards carefully. They lifted their heads as the sound of the alarm rose and fell in a peculiar rhythm. Shein's plan was to scale the exterior wall of the city and then drop down to the other side, out of sight. Based on past experiences, that would be enough to send up the alarm. Any guards nearby would investigate and the others would prepare for a worst-case scenario. Shein had only seen it happen once in the time she'd been incarcerated, but she was confident they would lead Vala and Tanis to a stockpile of gear they could use for Sam's plan.

The two guards consulted briefly before moving off in a hurry. Vala and Tanis pursued. Vala twisted to look over her shoulder and aimed a warning finger at Tanis.

"No killing!"

"No promises!" Tanis replied, grinning.

CHAPTER TWENTY-EIGHT

WHEN DANIEL was completing his PhD, he never dreamed that one day he would travel the galaxy exploring civilizations descended from the people he was reading about. Similarly, as a member of SG-1, he never dreamed the day would come when he would be crouching by a cargo hold waiting to hijack an alien supply ship on the way to a prison. Life could be funny that way.

He looked across the hatch at Mitchell. Teal'c was staying behind to keep an eye on Pemphero, just in case his enthusiasm was a ruse. He seemed sincere, but he had also risked his own life blowing the hatch when he discovered they were lying. Daniel didn't want to take the risk of being stranded just because the guy happened to know a few stories.

The floor pushed up against the soles of Daniel's boots, and he felt a twist of vertigo as they seemed to twist into a forty-five degree angle. Pemphero was lining them up with the supply ship, which was coming in at a slightly different trajectory.

"Aren't they also coming from the Overseers?" Mitchell asked, raising his voice to be heard. "Wouldn't they automatically be lined up with us?"

"We moved to stay hidden," Pemphero explained without turning away from the controls, "and I got creative about how I parked us. You'd be amazed how often people forget space is three-dimensional."

Daniel's stomach wished Pemphero had been more linear in his thinking. Even Teal'c reached out a hand to steady himself against the bulkhead.

"I'm sending out a distress call," Pemphero continued. "Their crew thinks my life support has failed and we're choking on the last bit of our oxygen. They'll send out an umbilical when we're lined up. Once it's secure you can open the hatch and slide through." He spun his chair to look back at them. "Are you sure you want to use those zats? Hardly anyone uses them anymore, and you'll be much more threatening with deadly weapons. I have some you can borrow."

He started to stand. Teal'c crossed the distance between them in two strides, placed his hand on Pemphero's shoulder, and gently pushed him back into the seat.

"They do not require more powerful weaponry."

"And you don't want me opening my weapon closet." Pemphero winked and nodded. "I understand, big guy. Playing it safe. SG-1 didn't get their reputation by giving weapons to the people they'd just met. But just in case this goes wrong and we need to arm up, the armory is in that wall. I'll let you get the guns out when and if the time comes."

Mitchell said, "How long until we're hooked up?"

"We're on a final approach now. Are you ready?"

"As ready as we'll ever be."

They both lurched as the ship came to a stop. Below, they could hear mechanisms snapping into place as they were connected to the other ship. Daniel looked at Pemphero to make sure he wasn't taking any precautions for another loss of atmosphere, then reached down and opened the hatch. A wave of air shoved up though the opening, just a quick puff of solid air that moved his hair and flapped the material of his shirt but was otherwise harmless.

Mitchell leaned forward and looked into the tube. He seemed to agree with Daniel's assessment that it would be a tight fit, but they could make it. He sat on the floor, dangled his feet over the ledge, and pushed off. The sound reminded Daniel of a waterslide: a quick zipping whistle as the material of the tube brushed over Mitchell's clothes. There was a quiet thump as Mitchell reached the other end. A moment later, the radio Daniel was holding crackled.

"All clear, Jackson. Come on down."

Daniel looked at Teal'c, who gave him a nod. Daniel took

a steadying breath and then went down the slide. He tucked his arms in against his chest and tried not to think about how obviously flimsy the tube was, and it was the only thing between him and the vacuum of space. Just one rip in whatever material they'd made it from and he would be dead before he knew what happened. Give him a trip through the Stargate any day.

After a few seconds which felt much longer, his feet hit the floor of the other ship. Mitchell put a hand on his shoulder to steady him.

"You okay?"

"Just a little disoriented." Daniel looked around and saw they were alone. "Where is everyone?"

Mitchell shook his head. He kept his voice low, just above a whisper, so it wouldn't echo off the walls around them. "Not sure. The place was deserted when I showed up. I think I can hear voices coming from that way, though. Can't tell how many there are."

Daniel took out his zat. "Let's hope they're willing to play along."

Mitchell said, "I like your optimism."

"Yeah, well," Daniel muttered. "Glass half full, glass half empty, you still don't want it spilled on your lap if you can avoid it."

They moved stealthily down the corridor. The voices of the supply ship crew got louder as they rounded a corner. The corridor dead-ended in a brightly-lit doorway. Mitchell stopped short so he couldn't be seen from anyone within, his back to the wall, and Daniel took a position opposite him. Cooking smells wafted to them through the open doorway. Daniel tried to remember the last time he'd eaten and willed his stomach not to growl at the scent.

Mitchell held up three fingers. He dropped them one at a time and, when he was holding up a fist, they moved forward together. Daniel nearly tripped over the edge of the door, but he turned it into a trot. He brandished his zat, holding it on the elderly man and teenage girl on his side of the room. He hesitated and looked at Mitchell, whose weapon was held on two women and a man who were all about the same age.

"Everyone stay calm," Mitchell said. "We don't want to hurt anyone."

The elder of the group smiled. "That is quite a relief, given that you are holding weapons on us."

Daniel said, "Uh, Cam?"

"Can this wait, Jackson?"

"No, I don't think it can. Look at their clothes."

All five of the people in the kitchen were dressed in black shawls with pale blue ascots tied around their necks. He didn't recognize the denomination, of course, but some things were universal. This was some kind of a religious sect. He lowered his zat.

"Jackson…"

"We don't need weapons," Daniel said. "These people are… uh, what do you call yourselves? Monks? Pilgrims?"

The elder said, "We are the Wayfarers. If the purpose of your deception was theft, we welcome you to take what you need from our cargo. All we ask is that you leave enough for us to make a delivery to the lost women of Viaxeiro. Do not ease your suffering by increasing theirs."

"We're not going to rob you." Daniel already had his zat tucked into his belt again. Mitchell reluctantly lowered his, but he kept it drawn just in case. "We apologize for deceiving you. It's just that we're a little desperate at the moment. We need to get into Viaxeiro because our friends have been wrongly imprisoned there. We came up with a plan to get them out, but it required us to be on a supply ship. Your ship."

The elder looked at the girl next to him. "I'm sorry, fellow travelers, but escape is impossible. Whether or not your friends have been wrongly imprisoned, no one leaves Viaxeiro. That is the law."

Mitchell said, "It's a law being upheld by a bunch of computers."

"Cam," Daniel muttered. "You're being a little O'Neill right now."

"I'll take that as a compliment."

"In this case, you probably shouldn't." He cleared his throat and faced the elder again. "We know about the prison's reputation. But we've already come this far. We have to at least try. And you can still make the delivery as scheduled, all we ask is that you put me in one of the containers."

Mitchell added, "And keep quiet about it to whoever picks up the supplies."

The elder said, "We have no contact with anyone inside the prison, so you would not have to worry about us telling anyone." He pressed his lips together and furrowed his brow. "It is our mission to aid those who are in need, no matter who they might be. But your intention is to free criminals from a prison."

"They were wrongfully accused."

Mitchell quietly said, "Well, at least two of them."

Daniel shot Mitchell a look. He shut up and focused on the three younger people.

"Hopeless causes, Father," the teenage girl said. "Blind fools who seek impossible gains. It is our calling to help those who cannot help themselves, even if we cannot see the purpose behind their actions. Whether they are doomed to failure or success, it is not for us to judge."

He put a hand on her shoulder. "Always the wisest of us, Moswen. You are correct, of course." He looked at Daniel. "We have your word that you will not interfere with our delivery?"

"Of course," Daniel said. "Yes, you have our word. We won't stand in the way. In fact, we need you to follow through as if everything is normal for our plan to work."

The elder nodded. "Then we will assist you. Have a seat and we will discuss what you need for the success of your mission."

Daniel sighed, relieved. "Thank you." He looked at Mitchell. He didn't say 'I told you so,' but he suspected his expression said it loudly enough to be annoying. "We really appreciate the help. Father…?"

"Kourash," the older man said.

"It's nice to meet you. I'm Daniel Jackson, and that's Colonel Cameron Mitchell."

Kourash stopped as he was about to take his seat. He looked at Daniel with suddenly cold eyes. Silence descended on the room like a veil, swallowing every sound except for the water boiling on the stove. The Wayfarers' faces had been serene but now they were hard and cruel. Their postures shifted to defensiveness as one of them moved slightly in an effort to block the exit. Mitchell brought his zat back up.

"Whoa, now. Let's not go standing in front of doors. What the hell just happened?"

"I have no idea," Daniel said. "Did we do something wrong?"

"Daniel *Jack*-son and *Cam*-uh-ron Mitchell of SG-1, of Earth," Kourash growled. "Killers of gods, blasphemers and heathens, intruders in the holy places!"

Mitchell backed toward the door. "Okay, really not liking the tone this meeting has taken, so we're just going to head out…"

"You are going nowhere!" Kourash shouted. "You are heretics who belong someplace much worse than Viaxeiro."

"We were getting along so well," Mitchell said, "then you had to go and start calling us names."

Kourash nodded at the women. "Disarm them."

Daniel wasn't sure if Mitchell intended to fight. He didn't want to make the first move, be it to surrender or fire his zat. He doubted these people had weapons, but he knew a fight would most likely results in a lot of unnecessary injuries to both sides. After a tense moment, Mitchell exhaled and relaxed his posture. One of the women moved forward and took the zat from him. Daniel handed his to the younger man, then raised both hands to shoulder height. The younger man handed the zat to Kourash.

"We really don't want to harm you," Daniel said. "We just needed to get down to the prison."

"To free more of your god-killers?" one woman sneered. She had taken a knife from the cutlery board and was aiming it at Daniel's chest. "We should release them from the airlock, Father. It would be a far more merciful death than any they gave to their victims."

Mitchell said, "Which one ticked you off? Apophis? Goin' old school, maybe, you used to kick it with Ra? Which Goa'uld did you follow?"

"We followed no Goa'uld," Kourash said. "Our offense is borne from your actions against the religion of billions throughout the galaxy. You judged their faith and, because it was found wanting in your opinion, you destroyed it. You desecrated temples, stole holy relics — "

"Most of which were stolen in the first place," Daniel said.

"You killed gods!"

Mitchell raised a finger. "Point of interest, by virtue of killing them, haven't we proven they were never really gods in the first place?"

Kourash waved the zat. "Virtue? You speak of virtue?"

"Bad choice of words, maybe," Mitchell said.

"All gods in all religions are but masks worn by the one true deity, the Entity at the center of All. It is that force which we worship, and whose hand guided you to us this day. You will finally be made to answer for your many sacrileges. We know you typically travel in a group of four. Sam-*un*-tha *Cur*-tear and the shol'va, Teal'c. You must have left them behind on your vessel as backup."

Mitchell didn't move, but Daniel could almost hear something click in his mind. "Yup. And if we're not back with a report about what we found, they're gonna get the heck out of Dodge."

"That is why you will summon them to this ship. We will capture you all without violence or bloodshed." He stepped forward, his eyes cold. "That is, unless you force our hand."

"No, you got us," Mitchell said. "We'll go quietly. I guess you'll escort us back to the hatch where we came in and we'll give them the all-clear."

One of the women said, "Wait. We will tell you exactly what to say to ensure there are no hidden messages in your speech."

Kourash said, "Good thinking, Avongara. You will say this and nothing else: The ship is safe. We could use your help down here."

Mitchell ducked his head, nodding in defeat. "Okay. You're coming with us, right?"

Kourash smiled condescendingly. "Lead the way."

Mitchell went first, with Daniel following. Kourash was right behind them with the zat ready. The rest of the Wayfarers clustered behind him, and the whole group moved down the hall until they reached the hatch. Daniel looked up through the umbilical, but it had twisted so much he couldn't see back into Pemphero's ship.

"Exactly as I stated it," Kourash growled quietly.

"Understood," Mitchell said. He cleared his throat and tilted his head back. "Carter, Teal'c! The ship is safe. We could use your help down here."

There was a long silence. Mitchell tapped his fingers on his thigh, watching Kourash. "It's a big ship. Maybe they're—"

"Call them again."

"With the exact same message?" Daniel said. "That would be more suspicious than any coded message we might send."

Before Kourash could respond, Teal'c called them from above. "Colonel Mitchell. Colonel Carter is occupied with piloting this vessel. Do you truly require both of us?"

"Yeah, T, tell her to stick the thing on autopilot. Could really use your help down here, buddy."

"Very well. I shall inform her."

Mitchell looked at Kourash. "So when they come down here, you're going to zat them? Have you ever had to deal with a pissed-off Jaffa? It's not fun, let me tell you. This one kicked my ass not long ago, and I'm still finding new bruises under the bruises that have started fading."

Kourash said, "Silence! You won't distract us with your prattling."

The Wayfarers circled the opening, weapons drawn. Mitchell glanced at Daniel, who allowed a quick, worried shrug. Teal'c now knew something was up, but the second he dropped into the ship he would likely be greeted by a hail of weapons' fire. They could only hope the warning had been enough.

CHAPTER TWENTY-NINE

TEAL'C KNEW he had mere seconds to devise a plan. Colonel Mitchell and Daniel Jackson were on the other end, but the request for Colonel Carter had to be a warning of some sort. They were in danger, and following their instructions would surely endanger him as well. He stood on the edge of the opening and gazed into the pipeline. It reminded him of childhood games, chasing *vierhiko* through the forests of Chulak. They were tiny beasts and easily frightened. When startled they would return to their dens, visible only as small holes in the ground.

Of course, he didn't have the option of flushing his quarry from this hole. And rather than prey cowering in its burrow, he was dealing with predators lying in wait.

Pemphero stepped forward and looked down as well. "Are you going down there?"

"My team is in danger."

"But going down there is going to put you in danger, too."

Teal'c looked at Pemphero and began formulating a plan. "Not necessarily."

~#~

Kourash glared at Cam. "You warned them somehow."

"I repeated exactly what you told me," Cam said. "How could I have warned them?

Daniel said, "Look, they're not hurrying because they think everything is fine. They don't think there's any reason to rush."

Kourash leveled the zat, his fingers tight around its grip. "If they do not arrive within the next — "

Whatever threat he intended to make was cut off by a sudden forceful jerk which pulled everyone off their feet. Cam and Daniel slammed into the ceiling of the tunnel along with the Wayfarers. Gravity seemed to have been turned off, and suddenly the entire group was clustered on the ceiling around the hatch. Kourash let go of the zat and Daniel had enough of his faculties to reach out and grab it. Cam kicked out one foot against the knife in the woman's hand, forcing her to drop the weapon. Kourash threw himself at Daniel, but his progress was halted when Teal'c emerged from the tunnel and grabbed the back of the older man's collar. He pulled with seemingly no effort and sent Kourash caroming into the far wall.

As quickly as it had left, gravity returned. The entire group hit the ground hard, but Cam was able to recover faster than the pilgrims. "Ah-ah-ah," he warned when one of them tried to get up. "Everyone just stay flat on your stomachs, hands on the ground with your fingers splayed. No one wants to hurt anybody here, okay?"

Daniel had banged his hip and knee when he fell, but he limped over to Kourash. The man was unconscious, but his pulse was strong and steady. He breathed a sigh of relief and looked to make sure Cam had the rest of the group under control.

"Thanks for the assist," Cam said.

Teal'c was wearing an oxygen mask and a thruster pack which he had used to maneuver through the umbilical without the aid of gravity. He pulled off the mask and dipped his head to Cam.

"Pemphero provided the inspiration. I only regret there was no opportunity to warn you of the depressurization."

"Hey, what's a rescue without a few bumps and bruises?" Cam rolled his shoulder. "We'll overlook it this time. For now, we should probably figure out what to do with these guys, check the ship to make sure there's no other crew. Either this thing is on autopilot or there's a flight crew somewhere. Be nice to know which it is."

One of the women glared up at Daniel. "When there were no more gods to slaughter, it stands to reason you would turn on their followers."

Cam said, "No one is killing anyone here, okay? Just calm down. We're going to borrow, *borrow*, your ship to save our friends and in a few hours we can pretend this never happened. Okay?"

She spit in his direction. "You will be made to pay for this!"

He resisted the urge to roll his eyes. "Great, we'll add you to the big book of bad guys we keep at the SGC." He patted Teal'c's arm as he walked past. "Good plan, big guy."

Teal'c looked at Daniel. "Are you injured, Daniel Jackson?"

"Nothing I can't walk off. Help me tie these guys up while Cam goes to see if they have any boxes big enough for me to hide in."

Cam was waiting at the end of the corridor. "Bet you never thought you'd say that when you joined SG-1."

"Yeah." He shrugged. "Although it was a pretty wild ride right from the beginning. One time my allergy medication prevented the outbreak of an alien virus. You roll with the punches on this team."

"Yeah, you got a point there. Okay. One box big enough for an archaeologist special delivery, coming right up."

~#~

Lokelani didn't pause to consider the sirens suddenly going off in the city. She adjusted her grip on the collar of Sam's uniform and urged her down the stairs. The Goa'uld was pressing something into the small of her back and, without knowing exactly what kind of weapon it was, Sam was reluctant to try escaping. She also had nowhere to run. The stairs led down into what seemed to be a large, unlit cavern with multiple cells carved into the walls. Sam could see movement in the shadows behind the bars but no one got close enough for her to see them clearly. It seemed like Viaxeiro had a typical prison structure after all, it was just kept well out of sight.

The sirens were still audible even through the thick stone. Sam looked over her shoulder at Lokelani. "You don't need to go check on that?"

"The Cai Thior will take care of whatever you set into motion."

"What makes you think it's my fault?"

Lokelani snorted. "Wherever the Tau'ri go, chaos is bound to follow in short order."

"It isn't always our fault," Sam said under her breath, channeling a little O'Neill-style petulance.

They reached the bottom of the stairs and Lokelani shoved Sam roughly toward the nearest wall of cells. She stumbled but managed to keep herself from falling. Now the prisoners had come forward, hands on the bars, looking out at their newest neighbor. Imprisoned inside a prison. This had to be some kind of new achievement.

"I guess these are all the other prisoners who have figured out your little secret."

"That, or they challenged my authority, or tried to kill me. There are multiple sins you can commit to end up down here."

Sam realized the endgame. "And when you get bored or this body is injured beyond your ability to heal, you just choose a new host."

Lokelani grinned. "It does keep people from asking too many questions. After a few years, I announce that I'm passing on my role to a worthy successor."

"This whole prison is just your own personal host farm."

"Don't be so crass," Lokelani said. "They're also my worshippers, willing or not. They obey me. They revere me. For centuries I craved this kind of adoration, a kingdom of this magnitude." Her shoulders sagged and she rolled her eyes. "But every little inch of ground I claimed, there was always some System Lord around the corner waiting to take it from me. It was exhausting. Then I heard about this place and started investigating. A protected haven, loose among the stars. New followers delivered on a regular basis. And best of all, no Goa'uld would ever think of this place as a prize. No one wanted it. So I took it. And I will not allow SG-1 and the Tau'ri to take it away from me now."

Sam said, "Do the Cai Thior know they're basically Jaffa without the pouch?"

"They know what they need to know."

Now Sam could see that Lokelani's left hand was gripping a circular red crystal set in a golden base. She recognized it immediately. "You're threatening me with a healing device?"

One of the prisoners said, "That thing hasn't healed in a very long time."

Lokelani laughed. "It's true. I've had many, many years to tinker. I didn't have much call for a healing device, as you pointed out, so I decided to make this useful." She lifted her hand. "Would you care for a demonstration?"

Sam took a step back. "I think I'll pass."

"I heard you were smart." She gestured with the device. "Get into the cell, Colonel Carter. You should consider yourself lucky. I treat my potential hosts very well, considering I may soon be walking around in their heads. As wonderful as it would be to take down a member of the infamous SG-1, it doesn't mean much if I can't brag about it."

One of the cages was open. Sam reluctantly moved toward it, her mind racing as she looked for an opportunity to fight back.

"What about Vala?"

"She's been a host before," Lokelani said. "It's uncouth to take a host another Goa'uld has chosen. Plus it just doesn't feel right."

"You know I've been a host, too," Sam pointed out.

Lokelani said, "To a Tok'ra. No one cares about that, dear. To answer your question, Vala is far too dangerous to just let her run around. I'll find someone with a grudge and tell the Cai

Thior to look the other way for a few hours. Vala Mal Doran won't be a problem for Viaxeiro much longer."

Sam was inside the cage. Lokelani kept the device trained on her as she pulled the barred door shut.

"You know Vala's reputation. You think she'll be that easy to kill?"

"I've always heard SG-1 was hard to capture," Lokelani said, "but look at what I have here: a caged Tau'ri. Get comfortable, Colonel Carter."

Lokelani took a moment to examine the other cages before she returned up the stairs. Sam gripped the bars and tested the strength of the door by rattling it against the lock.

"Are you really a member of SG-1?" a woman in another cage asked.

"Yeah," Sam said. "But she was wrong about one thing. It's not particularly hard to catch SG-1. As a group and on our own, we've all been captured too many times to count. The real trick is keeping us in the cage."

~#~

Vala gingerly hopped over one of the guards splayed in the doorway, pausing just long enough to make sure his breath still fogged up his mask. Tanis caught her checking and rolled her eyes as she dropped the third man to the ground.

"I know how to stop short," she said.

"I know, darling, I know. But who among us hasn't gotten carried away from time to time?"

Tanis shrugged.

They were standing in the threshold of a cramped storage room. Vala had let Tanis take care of the rough stuff by knocking out the guards as soon as the door was unlocked and then rushing inside to fight the one standing watch inside. Vala crouched down and grabbed the boots of the guard blocking the door and dragged him inside. Tanis pushed the door shut so no one passing by would get curious.

The room smelled like oil, dust, and men who had spent too

long in a cramped room with no windows. Vala wrinkled her nose as Tanis began searching the shelves.

"Look at this," she said, holding up a weapon Vala vaguely recognized. "Can you believe they have crap like this just lying around?"

"Tanis," Vala warned. "Be good. We're here to look for life support. Stuff we can use to stay awake when everyone else goes to sleep."

Tanis shrugged and put the weapon back. "It's just something to keep in mind when I'm running things. Nice little armory just sitting here… someone is going to find it eventually, and I'd prefer it not be someone looking to take over."

"Someone like you, you mean?"

Tanis said, "I'm not naïve. Even if this coup is successful, someone is going to decide they deserve to run things. So they'll come after Shein and me. It's the same thing on every world with a population greater than five." She picked up a plastic cone, sniffed it, then put it back. "I don't want to rule forever. Just as long as I can hold the throne. As it should be."

"Then I wish you a long and peaceful reign." Vala lifted a pair of goggles off the shelf and held them up in front of her eyes. "There has to be something here we can use…"

"Maybe they were just coming to get riot gear." Tanis hoisted a Goa'uld pain stick and jabbed the air with it. "I'm surprised these goons have managed to resist breaking out some of these toys."

"I'm not," Vala said. "Who would choose a planetwide riot over sitting around doing nothing all day? They might take out a few prisoners, but then they would be trapped here with all the rest. It would be chaos." She tilted her head to the side and pursed her lips. "You might consider you're risking the same thing."

"It's a non-violent takeover, thanks to the Tau'ri prude." She examined Vala carefully. "You asked me if I was sure about what I'm doing. Have you asked yourself the same question?"

"We've been over this."

Tanis said, "I want to be sure. I want to be absolutely sure that the Vala I used to know turned herself into this… crusading do-gooder."

Vala dropped her shoulders and rolled her head back. "For the last time, Tanis. Yes. There are bigger issues here. It's not just about the next score. People are dying because of the Ori. And if I can help stop them, then that's what I have to do."

"There have always been people dying. What makes this your fight?"

"It's my daughter," Vala said, finally giving up the truth.

Tanis went very still. "Your what?"

Vala closed her eyes. "It's a very long story. But I had a child. The Ori took her from me. They… they aged her rapidly. Then they made her into their leader, the figurehead of their war. She's the Orici. That's why I have to do everything in my power to stop the Ori from winning."

"I didn't know," Tanis said quietly.

"It's okay." Vala sniffed and swiped at her face as if she'd disturbed a cobweb. "I don't… um, I don't talk about it a lot."

Tanis nodded. "I understand. Something like that, it could make anyone join the good guys, I suppose."

"Sort of like you and Shein."

"Yeah." Tanis chuckled. "Caring about other people… what a way to go out."

Vala said, "We'll be the laughingstock of every tavern where we've run a tab."

"Good thing I'm staying here. Can't show my face anywhere else in the galaxy." She looked at Vala again. "So what's her name?"

"Adria."

"Oh."

"What?"

"Nothing. It's pretty."

Vala gasped. "Oh my G— I would not have named her *Tanis*."

"I didn't expect you to!"

"You most certainly did!" Vala said. "I saw the expectation in your eyes!"

"It's a good name!"

Vala rolled her eyes and went back to the search.

~#~

Lokelani was leaving the house as Sukhan arrived, and she paused to get an update. The alarms had stopped, but Lokelani could see the guards were still on alert. "Shein Pranassa was arrested by the guards for acting suspicious near an exterior wall," Sukhan reported. "After a brief chase, she surrendered and allowed herself to be taken into custody."

Lokelani bit the inside of her cheek to keep from cursing. "Shein Pranassa. She's in a relationship with Tanis Reynard, who used to be partners with Vala Mal Doran. I don't think that's a coincidence. Where is Pranassa now?"

"She's been detained in the guard station at the entrance."

"Mal Doran? Reynard?"

Sukhan shook her head. "They haven't been seen. Ma'am, if those three are up to something, perhaps Sri Fraiser would know…"

Lokelani shook her head. "Sri Fraiser is no longer a concern to us."

Sukhan began to say something but was interrupted by a shout coming from the wall. Lokelani looked toward it and saw a ship descending through the force field.

"More prisoners?" Sukhan said. "Already?"

"No, that's a Wayfarer ship." Ordinarily Lokelani would barely have paid attention to the supply drop-off, but the timing was suspicious. "Find Calyree and Onora. Supervise the unloading. Make sure there's no trickery."

Sukhan hesitated but gave a quick nod. She stepped around Lokelani and went into the house to find the other Cai Thior.

Lokelani narrowed her gaze at the Wayfarer ship as it descended into the wastelands. They'd never had issues with the Wayfarers, or any of their suppliers, but she wasn't about to take any unnecessary risks. Not with the Tau'ri lurking around.

CHAPTER THIRTY

CAROLYN CLOSED her eyes and counted to ten. When she reached zero, she did it again. The wall was rough against her back, and it felt like she was standing in a desert even though intellectually she knew that there wasn't even a sun to shine down on her. She used the cuff of her sleeve to wipe the sweat from her forehead and upper lip.

When her heart stopped racing, she opened her eyes and looked around to make sure she was definitely alone. She was standing on the outside of the wall. Shein's idea. The guards they were distracting had called for backup, and Shein quickly found all of her escape routes were blocked. Capture was inevitable. She was concerned about what the guards would do if they found Carolyn's radio, so she came up with a hugely dangerous, incredibly foolhardy plan.

Carolyn had jumped onto the wall and stretched out as flat as possible on top of the stone, holding her breath and praying for a lack of wind. She stayed there while Shein and Koty'r allowed themselves to be arrested, hoping the guards were distracted enough by them to not look up, then she jumped down onto the outside. The drop was only a few feet, but even a short fall could be dangerous. She'd been positive she would land wrong and break both her legs when she hit the ground. But Shein had told her the right way to fall without hurting herself and, despite the voices in her head screaming that it was crazy, she agreed. Now she was outside the walls, alone, and with no Plan B if the guys didn't show up soon. She didn't even want to risk walking too far forward because of the landmines.

"Adventure," she muttered to herself. "It doesn't matter if your father is the commanding officer, this post will give you the chance for an *adventure*." She laughed at her past self. "God, what I wouldn't give for a boring assignment right now."

She had just started to mentally list her options if the guys didn't show up when she saw movement in the sky. She looked up and watched as a ship broke through the barrier and began a slow descent toward the surface.

Carolyn pulled the radio from her pack and closed her eyes to say a quiet prayer before she hit the button. "Guys? Is that you?"

For a moment, there was only static. Then she heard a familiar Southern accent breaking through the interference. " — just barely coming through. That you, Lam?"

A grin spread across her face. "Hey, guys. Thanks for dropping in."

~#~

Cam watched the shimmering energy pass across the viewscreen, eventually fading to reveal the city stretched out below them. It was a massive sprawl of buildings from a seemingly endless variety of styles. It looked like someone had taken maps of Rome through the ages, stacked them all on top of each other, and then built it out of LEGOs. Maybe Rome wasn't right… the part of the city they were closest to seemed more Asian-inspired.

Daniel would have known, but he wasn't exactly in a position to take a look. He was in a box by the cargo hatch, waiting to be offloaded onto the planet.

A few minutes ago, Pemphero had told them that no one from the city would be close enough to hear a warning, so Cam was going to allow the Wayfarers to help unload the cargo.

"And if one of them attempts to make a run for the city?" Teal'c had asked.

"The guards wouldn't let them get close enough to say anything. Anybody starts running for the walls, they'll get a bullet in the head for their trouble."

"And how will they react when they find a stowaway in one of the boxes?" Daniel had said.

Pemphero shrugged. "Don't know."

At Daniel's sigh, Cam had patted him on the shoulder. "Don't worry, Jackson. You'll do fine. We'll poke a couple airholes in the top of the box before we leave you."

"Thanks. What could go wrong?"

Now they were moments from landfall. Cam could see people gathering near the wall of the city, hands cupped over their eyes to watch the incoming ship. The radio had been on for a while, but Cam's attention was drawn to it when the static suddenly hiccupped. He thought he heard a voice through the mess, so he used his thumb to press down the button.

"Say again, caller, you're just barely coming through. That you, Lam?"

Her voice was clearer this time. "Hey, guys. Thanks for dropping in."

Cam ducked his head and smiled, quietly celebrating the victory. One small part of their plan had gone well, at least. "Glad to hear you're in one piece. What's the situation down there?"

"Depends on who you ask," Carolyn said. "I'm on the outside of the wall. Carter and Vala are both okay. They're putting a plan in motion that will — "

Her voice suddenly cut out. "Lam?" He tapped the button a few times but she was gone. "You've got to be kidding me. What the hell just happened?"

"Altitude," Pemphero said. He had joined them on the Wayfarer ship to help pilot it through the prison's defenses, attaching his own ship to it by a towline. "We were low enough that the shield didn't interfere with the radios and high enough that the signal from the landmines didn't scramble it. Now we're too low for it to get through across the ground."

"The landmines have a signal? Is there a way we can block it from here?"

Pemphero opened his mouth, probably to say it was impossible, but then cocked his head to the side. He ran one hand over the console he'd been drooling over from the moment he took the command chair. "This *is* a Wayfarer ship. Stands to reason they might have a way to disable the landmines while they're going back and forth to unload the supplies." Pemphero began entering commands. "Let's focus on the positive. We know they're here and they're safe. And they're working on a plan. Let's run with that."

Teal'c was at the controls and set them down gently in the field of sand Pemphero indicated. Cam scanned the wall but couldn't see Carolyn.

"We unload the boxes - and Jackson - and then people from the city come to take it all inside?"

"Yep," Pemphero said, "but they always wait until the ship is gone before they come out to get it."

The ship touched down and Cam went down to the cargo area. Kourash glared at him, so Cam offered his most charming smile.

"Relax. You're about to be rid of us for good."

"And we will not rest until the universe is rid of you as well," he snapped.

"Lots of people have dibs on wiping us out. I wouldn't try jumping the line. You're doing good work here. Helping people out. Just keep doing that, let it go. We want these ladies to get their supplies just like you do, so are you going to help us unload or are you going to make them suffer? It's your choice."

Kourash bared his teeth but said nothing as the hatch door lowered. He made an unenthusiastic gesture to the others, who moved to the boxes and began the process of taking them off the ship. Cam and Teal'c took the box holding Daniel, grunting under the effort as they walked it down the ramp and placed it on the rocky ground. Cam looked up at the force field and took a second to gauge the weather.

"Well, it may look like a desert, but it's actually not bad. At least you won't bake in there." He patted the top of the box. "All right, Jackson, it's all you now."

Teal'c looked toward the city and narrowed his eyes. "Did Pemphero not say that citizens waited until the ship departed to approach?"

Cam looked and saw a shape moving toward them across the sand. "What the hell?" He put a hand over his eyes. "Is that Dr. Lam?"

"It would appear so," Teal'c said.

Cam pointed at the guard towers. "Those guns…"

Pemphero said, "Unmanned for now, looks like. Maybe there's something happening in the city taking up their attention."

"Need a distraction, just add Vala," Cam said.

"Are you certain the landmines have been effectively disabled?" Teal'c asked.

Pemphero said, "For your friend's sake, I hope so."

~#~

Sukhan arrived at the city gate, pushing through the gathered crowd with Calyree and Onora. The women near the back of the crowd had identified the Wayfarer ship and were as always speculating about what might be in the supplies this time. As Sukhan neared the front of the crowd, however, the conversation shifted to a different sort of speculating.

"What does she think she's doing?"

"It's obviously just suicide," another woman said. "Place your bets on how long it will take the landmines to burn her."

Silence fell as people saw Sukhan and her companions. The crowd parted and soon she saw for herself what they were talking about: a lone prisoner running across the sand toward the Wayfarer ship. Calyree stepped forward to stand beside Sukhan, looking to her for confirmation that they should take action. A prisoner outside the walls when a ship landed was a huge violation—enough to bring unwanted scrutiny from the guards. Their arrangement was fragile, but it had worked so far. The Cai Thior stopped situations before they became problems. They could punish the sole troublemaker and that would be the end of it. The guards, if forced to intervene, would punish the entire population. Sukhan didn't need confirmation from Lokelani about what needed to be done: this prisoner had just taken a death sentence…

And yet...

"The landmines have obviously been disabled," Onora said. "We cannot allow her to get any further or the guards will take action."

"I know."

A member of SG-1 was on the planet. Lokelani was on edge about something, and the alarms going off couldn't be a coincidence. She rubbed her fingertips against her palm as she watched the prisoner running. This had to be related to Carter.

"Sukhan," Calyree said with some urgency. She had drawn her weapon but kept it by her side. "We have to take her down or we'll all suffer."

"No," Sukhan said.

A murmur went up through the crowd. Calyree and Onora both tensed, knowing that a dangerous precedent was about to be made.

Calyree lowered her voice. "Have you gone insane?"

"No. Things have changed."

Calyree looked at the women around them. "If we don't do something to stop her right now, the guards will. And we will all be punished for not stopping it."

"Then perhaps we should do something about the guards before they become an issue."

Calyree's eyes narrowed, but she didn't reject the idea.

Sukhan caught the attention of the women closest to them. "Word of what just happened will spread to the guards soon enough. They'll station themselves at the guns to shoot that vessel down. See to it that they don't get a chance."

"What are you saying?" the woman asked.

"I'm saying the Cai Thior are finally taking over this prison. Spread the word."

Sukhan looked at the retreating figure again. A handful of people were standing outside the ship, watching her until she was close enough they could speak. Sukhan wished she had some idea of what they were saying but, after a moment, the woman stepped around the men and disappeared into the ship.

Sukhan felt something tighten in her chest. Whoever the woman was, she had just done the impossible. There was still a chance that the guns would destroy the ship before it was able to leave the atmosphere, but *that* they could do something about. At the moment she was willing to hope. Viaxeiro was no longer an inescapable prison.

~#~

"Well?"

Sam looked toward the voice. She was standing at the door to her cell, hands on the bars, trying to figure out a way to get out.

"Well, what?"

"You say you are Colonel Carter? The woman once called M'jor and Captun, the intelligence agent of SG-1?"

Sam raised an eyebrow. "I've never heard it phrased quite like that, but that is who I am."

More silence from the other cells until a different woman said, "I don't believe you. If that is true, then what are you doing here? Were you captured?"

"Sort of," Sam said. "It was part of a plan to help an old… acquaintance. Ideally we would've been able to come in with a plan, but things went haywire almost immediately. We're kind of flying by the seat of our pants here." She thumped one of the bars with her finger. "As you can see by my current predicament."

She heard the other prisoners whispering amongst themselves.

"Your plan of escape," the first woman said. "Does it include eliminating Lokelani Kiir?"

"Not originally," Sam said, "but we amended our list of goals as soon as we found out she was a Goa'uld."

More whispers. "If you *are* Colonel Carter, then we can help you get out of here."

"Great. But…"

She closed her eyes and rested her forehead against the bars. She knew that any help they provided would come with a price tag, and it was most likely going to be taking them with her when she escaped. She couldn't do that. She also couldn't make the promise knowing she would betray them when the time came to leave. She still remembered when General O'Neill had lied to Fifth, and how that deception led to one of the most powerful enemies they'd ever seen. An enemy that had worn her face.

"I can't promise to take you with me when I leave," she said. "I'm sorry, it's just not in the realm of possibility."

"Just get us out of these cages," one of the women said. "We're happy to stay on Viaxeiro as long as Lokelani is gone."

"*That*, I can promise," Sam said.

"What do you need from us?"

"I need to find the force field generator. Do you know where it is?"

"There's a device on the roof of this building. It controls several things throughout the city, I think."

Sam let herself hope. "That sounds like exactly what I'm looking for."

"We can get you to it."

Sam said, "If you can get out of here, then why do you stay?"

"Because there's nowhere to run. Escape from Lokelani, and she'll sic the guards on you. Not to mention the Cai Thior. And half the other prisoners would turn on us to stay in her good graces. Even if we got out and managed to convince a handful of other prisoners that she's a Goa'uld, there's no way we would've stood a chance against her lackeys. We stayed because we didn't have options. Removing Lokelani gives us options."

"Okay," Sam said. "Let's get out of here before she comes back."

"You heard her, ladies."

Sam heard metal grinding against stone in one of the other cells. She craned her neck in an attempt to see what they were doing, but the angles were wrong. She could only see three other cells, the women within shrouded in darkness. They reached out to each other, passing something from cell to cell until finally the woman next to Sam had it.

"We worked out this escape plan a while back, gone over it a few hundred times until we had it perfect, just in case we decided we didn't want to become her next host. We know that none of us stand a chance against a Goa'uld, but given the options… I personally would rather die fighting than have one of those snakes in my head."

"I know how you feel."

The woman placed a device on her cell door. "Look away!" she warned.

Sam covered her face as the device popped and fizzled. The cells lit up briefly in a series of quick flashes accompanied by the hiss and smell of burning powder. Sam heard something metal hit the ground and bounce. When she looked, the door had swung open and the woman inside the cell had emerged into the middle of the room. She went to a panel on the wall and flicked every switch. Sam's cell door was the fourth to open. She stepped out with the other prisoners. They stared at her, keeping their distance.

Sam offered a weak smile. "Hi."

"You came to our planet once," one of the women said. "Latona. We were attacked by Svarog because of your people. But your team helped save us. You brought peace back to our planet."

"The Sentinel," Sam said. "I remember. I thought your people didn't care about material things."

She offered a half-smile. "Not everyone is in this prison for the crime of theft."

Sam decided not to think too hard about that. It was the

exact reason she couldn't promise freedom to any of her fellow prisoners.

Another woman said, "Our world was enslaved by Cronus. Then one day, his Jaffa fled. We received word through the Chappa'ai that your team was responsible for killing him."

"SG-1 is responsible for freeing many worlds," one of the woman said, "for better or worse. False gods fell and chaos rose like dust around their corpses. But we cannot blame them for the consequences of their actions." To Sam, she said, "Come with me. I will take you to the generator. The rest of you, Lokelani is certain to discover this sooner rather than later. Stand in her way and do not let her pursue Colonel Carter."

The women nodded silently.

The Latonan woman stepped forward and offered her hand. "I'm Viona."

Sam shook her hand. "Thank you."

"Don't thank me yet. We haven't tried this before because there's a difference between being willing to go on a kamikaze mission and just plain suicide. We are surrounded by Lokelani's guards and we're currently unarmed. We may have a member of SG-1 on our side, but we still have a long way to go before we call this a victory."

She was right, of course, but Sam couldn't help but think escape was finally within her grasp.

CHAPTER THIRTY-ONE

CAM REMAINED tense the entire time Carolyn was running, certain that every step would activate the landmines Pemphero had warned them about. Through the opening in the wall, he could see women wearing matching outfits watching her escape, but none of them made any move to stop her. Teal'c noted their inaction as well.

"Perhaps it has been so long since anyone acted so brazenly, they are uncertain of how to react."

"Could be." When she was close enough, Cam moved forward to get between Carolyn and the guards, just in case they found their nerve. "Didn't expect to see you again so soon, Doc."

She was breathing heavily from her run, but wasn't panting. "Didn't have… much of a choice… had to… make sure you knew Carter's plan. Wasn't sure… how much of the message got through before the signal died."

"We got that they're okay and they have a plan."

Teal'c had retrieved water from the ship and he handed it to her. "Thank you." She took a long drink. "Carter is going to thin the atmosphere to knock everyone out. You should prepare for a quick getaway."

"Why don't we just fly over, set down in the town square, and pick up Carter and Vala? The guards didn't stop you leaving."

Teal'c said, "That would be unwise, Colonel Mitchell. If the city is indeed in a state of unrest, there would be nothing to stop the other prisoners from attempting to board as well."

"Good point," Cam said. "It might not be a riot now, but a ship landing right in the middle of the prison could push it over the edge. We're lucky they're still afraid enough of the landmines to risk making a run for it even after what they just witnessed. Any chance the guards will take an interest in us sitting out here?"

"I think the guards have more on their hands right now. But Carter and Vala can't leave yet — they have to get rid of the woman in charge. She's a Goa'uld."

"What?" Cam said.

Teal'c said, "This is a small kingdom with very little possibility of being overtaken by another System Lord. She is guaranteed a steady supply of new residents and potential hosts."

"Exactly. Tanis said it was the price of helping with the escape plan."

"So Tanis Reynard *is* here?"

"Yeah. But she's not coming with us."

Cam snapped his gaze away from the guards to look at her. "What? You mean this whole mission has been a wash?"

"On the contrary," Teal'c said. "General Landry hoped this mission would provide intelligence on the Lucian Alliance. While uncovering the location of this prison, we have established contacts within the syndicate and discovered some of how it operates. By that measure, Colonel Mitchell, I believe this mission could indeed be considered a success."

Carolyn said, "Plus the SGC doesn't have to hold Tanis prisoner indefinitely without a trial."

"You have a point there." Cam looked back toward the city.

"Get on the ship and stay out of sight. And congratulations, Dr. Lam. You just officially became the first woman to ever escape Viaxeiro."

"We're not off the ground yet."

Cam clucked his tongue against his teeth and muttered, "She just *had* to say it, didn't she…?" He shook his head. "Teal'c, get Jackson out of the box. Time for Plan K or L, or whatever letter we're up to by this point."

~#~

Tanis was the one who found the life support equipment. There were ten devices, each one looking like a pair of shoulder pads with oxygen reserves hanging off the back. A face-mask was raised up off the chest to cover the mouth and nose. Vala and Tanis each put one on and gathered enough to outfit their little rebellion.

Outside, everyone was buzzing with curiosity about what might be going on. The alarms had stopped, but now the prisoners seemed to be provoking the guards. The few Cai Thior she had seen stopped to engage in a quick, whispered conversation before running off again. Everywhere they looked, people were abandoning their storefronts and porches to see what was causing all the commotion. A few shared rumors that a supply ship had landed outside the walls and wasn't preparing to depart. If anyone noticed Vala and Tanis' strange new accessories, no one took the time to question them.

They were near Tanis' cold-water when they spotted Koty'r. She saw them at the same time and made her way over, meeting them halfway.

"Looks like you completed your part of the mission," she said.

Tanis said, "From the sounds of it, you didn't do so badly yourself. Where's Shein?"

"In custody, as expected. I followed and saw that they put her in a building near the walls."

"I know that place," Tanis said.

"I'm more worried about Dr. Lam," Vala said. "Shouldn't she be with you?"

"Plan changed. Shein and Carolyn got cornered by some guards. Shein let herself get captured, but Carolyn saw a chance to go over the wall and took it."

Vala gaped at her. "That was *not* in the plan! So she's out there somewhere? She'll die!" It was such a foolhardy chance to take... like dialing a Stargate in the middle of a firefight.

"Relax, she's fine. A ship landed right after she went over the wall. She ran out to it, and the Cai Thior just... stood there."

Tanis frowned. "They let her go?"

Koty'r shrugged. "I watched the whole thing happen. The Cai Thior ladies were there, they saw her, and they decided to just let her go."

Vala said, "Why would they do that?"

Tanis was looking at the crowd around them. "Because for all their authority, the Cai Thior are prisoners here, too. And hope can be a very persuasive thing. For some reason, your friend was able to cross the distance without setting off the landmines. That's never happened before. They could be taking it as a tipping point."

Vala said, "I'm not certain I want to give these women hope, but if it means Carolyn got to safety, I suppose I can live with it. Any word on Samantha?"

Koty'r shook her head and gestured at the sky. "I'm guessing she hasn't found the generator yet. I know I just showed up, but I imagine all hell is going to break out when she flips that switch. I'd prefer to be laying low when it happens." She nodded at the life support devices. "Did you grab one of those for me?"

Tanis handed her one. "If anyone asks you where you got this…"

"I've never heard of either of you," Koty'r said as she slipped the shoulder pads over her head. "Good luck, ladies."

They watched her flee. Tanis looked toward the entrance to the city. "If she's to be believed, your way out of here is sitting out in the salt plains. No landmines and the Cai Thior are ready to make a stand. All you have to do is run out there and you're free."

"Yeah, until those guns shoot us out of the sky."

"Still, you could be safe on the ship while the Cai Thior get this revolution underway."

Vala shook her head. "Sam might need my help. She would stay behind for me, too."

Tanis said, "Are you sure about that?"

"One hundred percent. Just like you're not going to let Shein rot in a cell while everyone else is having fun."

Tanis grinned. "A jailbreak in the middle of a jailbreak? If this has to be our last hurrah, at least you're keeping it interesting."

Vala winked and led Tanis through the growing crowd of prisoners on their way to see what was happening at the main gates.

~#~

Sam led the liberated prisoners up the stairs, pausing at the doorway to make sure Lokelani wasn't anywhere nearby. Once she confirmed the Goa'uld and her Cai Thior weren't lurking, she motioned the rest of the women up.

"This is too easy," one of the women said. "This place is usually crawling with Cai Thior."

Sam could already hear the commotion outside. The male voices indicated there was some sort of dust-up with the guards. "Sounds like they have other problems to worry about right now." She turned to the women. "Get somewhere safe. Things are probably going to get hectic before too long, and you don't want to get trampled."

The women fled, leaving Sam with Viona, who gestured toward the back of the house. "The generator is on the roof. Stairs are on the back of the building. I hope you know what you're doing, because I don't have a clue how the thing works."

Sam let her lead the way. "That's never really been a problem for me, to be honest. Goa'uld, Ori, Asgard... I've come across every kind of technology imaginable in the past ten years, and not one piece of it came with an instruction manual." Viona pushed the back door open and swept the yard to make sure no one was there before she waved Sam through. "Can I ask, just for the sake of my own curiosity, what led to you being locked up here?"

"Here as a potential host for our Goa'uld overlord, or here on Viaxeiro?"

"The latter."

Viona moved to the stairs and began climbing. "Arson."

"That's all?"

Viona smiled over her shoulder. "It may have been the residence of our world's leader. And the homes of seventeen of his closest advisors."

Sam raised her eyebrows. "Ah. That fits better."

"So we get up here, you figure out the machine, turn it off—"

"I don't turn it off," Sam said. "And I don't do anything but figure out the controls for now. I can't thin the atmosphere until I find out if Vala and Tanis found a way to keep us awake."

They arrived at the roof. The device was a huge satellite dish lying on its back like a massive bowl, with the controls on a platform beside it. The dish was low enough to the roof that it wouldn't be immediately noticeable from the ground. Sam pushed up the sleeves of her borrowed uniform as she approached the control panel. How many times had she been in this very situation? Life-and-death stakes, and a complicated array of buttons and crystals with commands she'd never seen before.

She'd done pretty much the same thing when she was a kid. Computers, calculators, her brother's remote control cars. She'd taken them apart so she could learn how to put them back together. This was the same basic thing. *These pieces were made to go together*, she told herself, *just figure out how they fit.*

The first thing she noticed was schematics for one of the tri-barreled guns in the guard towers. *Lokelani has access to their security*, she noted as she scanned the information. *I guess that settles where the loyalty of the guards truly lies.* As far as she could tell from a quick glance, it wasn't possible to disable the guns from this console. But she could eliminate their targeting systems. She found an option that shared the new command with every gun in the network and activated it. The guns could still be fired manually, but without a computer to work out trajectory and wind speeds, it would be next to impossible to hit a moving object on the ground.

"One problem dealt with," she reported.

Viona had wandered toward the edge of the roof and was squinting toward the wall. "What could that possibly be about?"

Sam saw a ship had landed in the salt plains. Boxes were collected in the shadows underneath the ship's belly, and she could see people moving around them.

"It's just a supply ship, isn't it?"

"Something is off about it. Look at the crowd around the gate."

Sam could see the crowd, and she could see it looked like they were on the verge of a riot. Half the guards looked like they were trying to settle everyone down, while the other half was escalating the issue by roughly forcing women onto the ground.

"Looks like Vala and Tanis have been busy."

She focused on the controls again. There was always some logical arrangement to how these things were set up. She was starting to see it, even if she might not know the exact meaning of each specific button. There was a screen at the top and, when she tapped a button on the lower left side, it came to life with a wall of text.

"Okay, here we go," she muttered.

She didn't know how long she had been working on the controls before Viona hissed something under her breath and ran across the roof back to the stairs.

"We're about to have company," she said.

"Damn." Sam's hands twitched, eager to grab a gun or even a zat. They should have taken the time to search the house for weapons.

Viona peeked over the edge. "It's Lokelani. Tell me you're about three *tikunra* away from figuring that thing out."

Sam said, "I'm not sure about that unit of time, but I highly doubt it."

"I'll buy you some time."

"Wait…"

Viona was already on her way down the stairs. "Dying for a cause is better than dying in a cage. Just figure that thing out! Hello, Goa'uld…"

Sam heard the sounds of a fight on the stairs. She scanned the control panel again, baring her teeth in frustration. She couldn't just hit buttons blindly. If she turned off the force field, they would all be exposed to the vacuum of space and there wouldn't be a second attempt. Viona cried out on the stairs. The fight wasn't going to last very long, and then she'd be out of chances.

"You've got one shot at this, Carter," she said. "Make it count."

Different cultures used different symbols for numbers, but they were generally more complex for greater integers. By that logic, she could determine that the numbers on the panel were meant to be read left to right, like English. So left was lower (zero) and right was higher (nine). Turning the force field off wouldn't help her at the moment, but turning it up higher… She pressed two fingers to the display and slid them up along the screen, watching as the readout went from yellow to green to red.

The change was apparent almost immediately. Sam felt as if she had just gained a hundred pounds, falling forward against the machine. She heard cries of pain and surprise as the rest of the prisoners felt the same effect. It was hard to draw breath but she forced herself to move. She got back onto her feet. Her hand skimmed along the metal of the panel, too heavy to lift, and she twisted it back to where it had been at first. The pressure let up, and she drew in a relieved breath.

She hoped the momentary shock had given Viona the upper hand, and that it hadn't affected Vala and Tanis too badly.

"Neat trick with the pressure," Lokelani said.

Sam closed her eyes. They were so close to success.

"It didn't save your co-conspirator, however. We both fell hard, but I will be able to heal the worst of this host's damage. Viona was not so fortunate." She coughed, and it was a wet sound. Apparently it hadn't fixed all the damage yet. "In a way, I'm grateful to you. Any Goa'uld worthy of a kingdom needs to face down the great SG-1, at least once. Killing you will be a rite of passage, one that I will take great pleasure in completing."

When the Goa'uld spoke again, it abandoned the pretense of a human voice and instead used the familiar hollow intonation meant to terrorize their prey.

"Turn around, Samantha Carter, so I may see the life drain from your eyes when I kill you."

CHAPTER THIRTY-TWO

VALA PUSHED herself up off the ground and checked to make sure the life support devices hadn't cracked when she fell. One moment she'd been running through the city and the next, it felt as if a two-hundred pound gorilla had jumped onto her shoulders. She'd been paralyzed for a terrifying moment before the weight went away and she was able to move again. Everyone else on the street, guards and Cai Thior and prisoners alike, had been similarly affected. She looked back and saw Tanis wiping blood from her nose.

"All right?" Vala asked.

"It's not a real jailbreak until someone is bleeding."

"That's a terrible philosophy." Vala looked toward Lokelani's home. "I think that was a message from Sam that she's found the generator."

"Sounds reasonable," Tanis said.

Vala was torn between loyalty to her friend, continuing the mission to free Shein, and her chance of escape. Tanis didn't let her suffer for long.

"Go. I'll free Shein. If you and Carter get a chance to escape, take it. Don't worry about taking out Lokelani."

"We made a promise."

"And now I'm releasing you from that promise." She sighed and looked around, then stepped closer so she could speak more quietly. "You came all this way for me. You jumped into the fire feet-first without a plan to get yourself safely out of it, and doing it risked your new home. No one has ever gone to those extremes for me. No one's ever taken a chance for me. It's what I imagine having a family feels like." She held out her hand. "You don't owe me anything. We're square."

Vala gripped Tanis' hand. "You were a great partner."

Tanis grinned. "Do you remember Ta'jicura?"

"Ugh." Vala wrinkled her nose. "Just hearing the name makes me think of the smell. Why in the world would you bring that up now?"

"I have a little vault there. It's where I store the blackmail material I've picked up over the years. You can access it using the same passcodes I used when we worked together. Your people said you could come on this mission if I gave them information on the Lucian Alliance? Well, that's a literal treasure trove. I'm not going to need it, so take whatever you think will make the Tau'ri happy."

Vala was stunned. "Thank you."

"You're welcome. Go on. Your team needs you."

"And Shein needs you."

Tanis aimed a finger in Vala's face. "And if you *ever* tell anyone that I helped out two members of SG-1, heads will roll."

"*Two* memb — " Vala caught herself when she realized what Tanis had said. She pressed her lips together and nodded. "Right. No one will hear about it from me."

"Good."

Vala blinked back the sudden moisture in her eyes. "Try to stay out of trouble… if you can."

Tanis grinned. "Try to get into trouble. Every now and again, even if just to prove you still can."

Vala laughed and nodded. "Goodbye, Tanis Reynard."

"Bye, Vala Mal Doran."

They turned away from each other and went off to save their respective partners.

~#~

"The hell was that?" Cam asked, brushing the sand from the sleeves of his uniform.

Daniel had just climbed out of the box when he was thrown to the ground. Only Teal'c had managed to stay on his feet, so he was able to watch as all the women gathered at the city's entrance fell like dominoes. Whatever happened seemed to have passed, and he could stand normally again. He offered a hand to Daniel and helped him up.

"It seems reasonable to assume that Colonel Carter and Vala Mal Doran are responsible."

"Atmospheric pressure suddenly goes crazy in the middle of an attempted jailbreak?" Cam stretched his back and grunted. "Yeah, I can see Sam and Vala's fingerprints on that one. Jackson, why don't you head into the ship and tell Pemphero he should probably be ready to make a hasty retreat. If I spot our people running this way, I don't want to lose time warming up the engines."

"Yeah," Daniel said. "It'll be nice to stretch my legs after being crammed in that box for no reason."

Cam rolled his eyes. "Hey, I *offered* to get in the damn box!"

Daniel muttered something under his breath as he continued up the ramp.

~#~

Sam carefully raised her hands from the control panel, holding them out to either side so Lokelani could see she wasn't going for a weapon. "This is a pretty incredible piece of tech to leave in the hands of a prisoner. How did you convince the guards to let you have it?"

Lokelani laughed. "Humans are so short-sighted. I didn't walk up to the guards and convince them to hand over control of the weapons and the force field. I did it slowly, over time. I offered to perform maintenance, I asked for replacement parts I didn't need, I upgraded the system until I was the only one who knew how it worked. It took a lifetime but eventually I had wrestled complete control for myself. I built my stronghold around the device."

"Clever."

"Nothing clever about being patient," Lokelani said. "But my patience is running thin, Colonel Carter. Face me and end this."

"Killing me is a little shortsighted, don't you think?"

"Silence."

The Goa'uld sounded weak and, when Sam turned around, she could see why. Blood covered half of Lokelani's face, and her left arm was hanging at an unusual angle inside her blouse. She must have taken a hell of a fall, and the symbiote was likely the only reason the host was still standing. It must have been taking most of her power to heal the damage, leaving little energy for speaking. Her posture was slumped, but the arm aiming the modified healing device was steady as a rock. There was approximately ten yards between them, too far for Sam to rush her but likely within range of the device. Sam faced her and Lokelani grinned.

"I may not be able to boast about this accomplishment, but I will have the satisfaction of knowing I succeeded where so many other System Lords failed. Ra, Anubis, even the great Apophis, none of them could claim to have killed a member of SG-1."

"Actually, Apophis *did* kill us once… and Cronus technically killed us. They were robot duplicates, but they were so much like us that I think you could make the argument—"

Lokelani hissed, "I told you to be silent!"

Sam shrugged. "Okay. Go ahead. Kill me. But when you realize the opportunity you missed, you'll kick yourself."

The healing device wavered. Lokelani's fingers tightened around it, and her eyes narrowed. Sam could see her struggling to figure out what she had missed.

"Everyone you had locked up downstairs is gone. All those potential hosts are now running around telling everyone who will listen that you're a Goa'uld. But that's the least of your problems. Unless you have a sarcophagus hidden somewhere in the house, the body you're currently using isn't going to last long. Sure, killing a member of SG-1 would be quite an accomplishment. But taking one as a host…?"

Uncertainty passed over Lokelani's features. The healing device finally wavered. It occurred to Sam that a tumbleweed slowly blowing across the roof between them was the only thing the moment was missing. She could hear the prisoners down on the ground, confused and nearly panicking at everything that had happened in the past few minutes. It wasn't a quick-draw situation. She was unarmed so there was no way to get the upper hand.

"What's the best way to avoid being hit by a car?" Sam asked.

Lokelani said, "What?"

Sam moved one foot forward, shifting her weight onto her toes. Lokelani registered the movement and brought the healing device back up. Instead of attacking, Sam unlocked her knees and let herself fall forward out of the weapon's range. *The best way to avoid being hit by a car,* Jacob had once told her, *is to stay out of the street.* She hit the roof with her hands and knees and shoved forward like a quarterback, using her body as a projectile. She wrapped her arms around Lokelani's waist and tackled her hard.

Lokelani was so surprised that she let go of the healing device. It clattered somewhere behind them. Lokelani took the brunt of the fall, the wind knocked from her body when Sam landed on top of her. They grappled briefly - Sam managed a punch to Lokelani's face, while Lokelani brought her knee up into Sam's gut. They both ended up breathless and throwing sloppy punches at one another. Sam's knuckles glanced off the rooftop when Lokelani moved her head at the wrong moment and she hissed at the pain as blood trickled down her fingers.

"What's your plan, Carter?" Lokelani's teeth were stained with blood. "Are you going to beat me to death?"

Someone else answered before Sam could say anything. "She doesn't have to."

Sam put her hands on Lokelani's shoulders to keep her down as she twisted to look toward the stairs. Sukhan was standing there, along with the members of the Cai Thior Sam had met inside. Aalid and Calyree remained next to Sukhan, while Onora spotted the healing device and went to retrieve it. Sukhan was holding a small stun weapon. Sam tensed, unsure who it was being aimed at.

"You're just in time to save me," Lokelani said in her normal, unenhanced voice. "You will be greatly rewarded for your loyalty."

Sukhan stepped closer. "Your days of giving out rewards is long past, Goa'uld. Did you truly think you could maintain such a secret? We allowed you to rule because you gave us power, because none of us felt confident we could defeat a Goa'uld. We knew about your potential hosts in the basement and didn't wish to become one of their number. But then a Goa'uld killer arrived and gave us hope." She turned her gaze to Sam. "Thank you for giving us this chance, Colonel Carter. You can step away from her now."

Sam hesitated. "What are you going to do with her?"

"They'll do nothing but provide me with a new host," Lokelani said, her voice echoing as she rose to her feet. "It was near time for me to make a change anyway. I believe you'll do nicely, Sukhan."

Sukhan reached up and lifted her hair with one hand, turning her back on the Goa'uld. "If you believe you are capable of taking me as host, be my guest."

Lokelani lunged. Sam's reflex made her take a step forward, but there was nothing she could do. Lokelani, mouth open wide, grabbed Sukhan's shoulders.

She froze. Her eyes flashed yellow and she stumbled backward. Sukhan had simply put her hand on the hilt of her sword and pushed down, raising the blade behind her. Lokelani had impaled herself on it with her attack, and now grabbed it with both hands in a futile attempt to save herself. She dropped to her knees and, a moment later, collapsed.

"I would have been a fine host," Sukhan said, "for someone far worthier than you."

Sam looked at Lokelani's body before slowly raising her eyes to Sukhan. "Vala and I…"

"As far as we're concerned, the prison is much safer without you in it." She was still watching Lokelani, as if expecting the Goa'uld to slither out. "Your vessel is waiting. If you leave now, no one will attempt to stop you."

Sam nodded and looked at the device. "I was going to thin the atmosphere. Put everyone to sleep so no one would try to escape with us."

"Some members of the Cai Thior are stationed at the wall to ensure no one tries to stop you, and no one tries to join your escape. Despite everything else going on, the majority of the women here *do* deserve to be incarcerated. The rest of the Cai Thior will take care of the guards."

Sam cleared her throat. "One last thing. Vala and I sort of promised we would help Tanis take over the prison in exchange for her help."

Sukhan twisted her lips.

"I'm not saying Tanis is the greatest person in the world," Sam said, "and to be honest, I'd probably think twice before I left her alone with anything I cared about, but they have the same goals as you. Tanis and Shein consider this their home. They'll fight to protect it. It's probably going to be rough around here for a little while. You're going to need all the help you can get to keep the peace."

"Fine. I'll speak with them."

"Thank you." Sam took a step away, but there was something else she had to know. "Not to press my luck, but why are you helping us? It can't be just because you want us out of your way."

Sukhan thought for a moment. "Every woman here was sentenced to death, shuffled away and forgotten, for a variety of crimes. Some deserved their punishment but others were simply victims of a patriarchal society quick to silence any kind of sedition. The guards and the Overseers treated us all the same. This is our chance to transform Viaxeiro from a prison into something more. We can make it into a sanctuary."

"I suppose I can respect that," Sam said. She stepped around the other Cai Thior, wishing them a quiet "Good luck" before she headed down the stairs. She stopped next to Viona's body and knelt down. Viona had given her life to protect her, and Sam didn't want to forget that. She closed the woman's eyes, rested a hand on her shoulder, and then went to find Vala.

~#~

Shein smiled when she heard the bodies fall just outside the holding cell door. She pushed herself up out of the chair and casually removed the restraints the guards had "secured" her with. The metal hit the ground just as the door swung open to reveal Tanis. She used her boot to move a fallen guard's leg out of the way and stepped into the holding cell.

"I thought you might need a hand."

"Oh, please," Shein said as she stepped around the table. "They call me Mist and Shadows on seven worlds."

Tanis grinned. "Eight now."

"What's the plan?"

"Absolute bedlam," Tanis said as stooped to disarm the guards she'd knocked out. There had only been three guards in the building, but there were bound to be more outside. "Vala and Carter are going to need help getting out of here, and the guards aren't likely to make that easy. What do you say we give them something else to focus on?"

Shein made a pleased sound in her throat. "The Cai Thior have been doing a pretty good job of taking them out already, but I'm willing to join in the fun."

They headed for the exit, armed and looking to cause some damage.

~#~

Pemphero glanced back to see who had joined him in the cockpit. Carolyn had stopped at the threshold and was staring warily at him. He smiled and flicked his hand at her in a wave.

"Hello."

"Hi." Carolyn kept her distance. "You seem a lot friendlier than the last time we saw each other. You know, right before you tried to eject me into space."

He sucked in air through his teeth. "Oh. Right, that. Yeah. Sorry. If you had just told me you were SG-1 to begin with, we could've started out as friends. I'm not trying to lay the blame on you, I'm just saying that maybe we — " He trailed off as something on his console began beeping. He leaned forward and read the display, the humor leaving his face. "How, uh, how is the plan going?"

"I'm not sure." She moved closer so she could see the display. "Why? What's wrong?"

"Oh... I'm... sure it's nothing..."

Carolyn said, "What's that you were just saying about being honest with each other?"

Pemphero said, "No, it probably is nothing." He scratched behind one ear. "But it looks like we've got incoming ships."

"Friendly ships...?" Carolyn's voice was blindly hopeful.

"Sorry. Our luck doesn't seem to be running that way. Colonel Mitchell said that you knocked out the Overseers? Well, it looks like they got fixed and sounded an all-hands alert. Every ship that was currently docked on the station is coming to see what's going on at the prison. You might want to tell your friends our time is running short. Those ships will be here in about twenty minutes, and I'm not going to stick around for them to ask questions. Clock's running."

CHAPTER THIRTY-THREE

SAM SPOTTED Vala on a running approach to the house. She held up the life support device victoriously, but Sam waved it away.

"We're not going to be needing that."

Vala dropped her arm. "I thought you found the generator."

"I did, but Lokelani isn't an issue anymore. The Cai Thior are in charge now." She looked around. "Where is everyone else?"

"Tanis is freeing Shein, Carolyn got out —"

"What?"

"Long story, they changed the plan. Last I heard, she was back on the ship."

Sam said, "So the ship *is* here for us?"

Vala shrugged. "That's what we're assuming."

Sam obviously hated the word 'assuming,' but there was little she could do at the moment. "Okay. God, what a mess… The Cai Thior are giving us a chance to make a run for it. We're not going to get a better chance."

Vala dropped the life support devices. "Lead the way, Samantha."

They ran through the city. The guards were trying and failing to keep the peace, torn between fighting the Cai Thior and trying to keep the prisoners at bay. One guard had been backed into an alley by a group of prisoners who had taken his weapon. The Cai Thior was watching the bedlam unfold without intervening. Heads turned to follow Sam and Vala as they passed. Sam had a feeling that the women she'd freed from Lokelani's basement had spread the word about their true identities.

Vala also noticed the attention they were getting. "Are they going to try to stop us or join us?"

"Neither," Sam said. "They're waiting to see if we succeed."

The crowds parted as they passed, and Sam got the distinct feeling they were running a marathon. No one was cheering, however, and getting to the wall was only half the race. They passed Cai Thior who had subdued guards, prisoners who had armed themselves but looked unsure which side they were going to join, but every woman stopped to watch as Sam and Vala passed. She could hear them whispering but only picked up a few words.

"...SG-1..."

"Tau'ri?"

"...Carter and Vala..."

"...Goa'uld killers..."

Sam looked to make sure Vala was keeping up with her. "You good?"

"Not the first time I've been literally run out of town," Vala said, only a little breathless.

Sam couldn't help smiling, but she waited until she was facing forward so Vala wouldn't see it.

A Cai Thior woman was standing at the entrance and moved to one side when she saw them. Just before they reached the wall, Sam spotted movement on a roof overlooking the entrance. Tanis was standing there, holding one of the guard's guns in her hand. Shein was standing beside her, goggles down over her eyes. Tanis grinned and hoisted the weapon in the air, nodding her head to Sam and Vala as they drew closer. Shein saluted as well.

Sam tossed off a very sloppy salute in return, not willing to sacrifice speed to do it properly. Shein said something to Tanis, and they both stepped away from the edge of the roof and out of sight. Seconds later, she and Vala passed through the opening in the wall.

They were out of the city, with only a long stretch of open land between them and the ship. Behind her, a cheer went up that seemed to echo off every building in Viaxeiro. For the first time since she was zatted in that damn bar, Sam allowed herself to believe they were going home. The mission was finally over and she could start forgetting this whole FUBAR situation—

The ship's engines fired up.

"You've got to be kidding me!" Sam shouted. She put her head down and pumped her arms, digging deep for an extra burst of speed.

Sam could see the ramp was still lowered, but now it was obscured by the dust devils being kicked up below the ship's belly. She ran into the cloud of dust, blinded by it, Vala just a few steps behind her. Sound traveled strangely in the maelstrom, but she thought she heard Mitchell's voice coming from directly ahead. Then she saw it: bursts of blue lightning followed by the unmistakable clicking of a zat gun being fired. He must have realized they couldn't see or hear him above the sandstorm and was firing into the air to guide them.

She ran for the light and, just as she began to doubt herself, someone grabbed her arm and pulled her forward. She went weightless for a moment and let herself fall limp onto the hard metal floor of the cargo hold. Teal'c loomed over her, the lower half of his face protected by a rag and his eyes covered with goggles. Even with the majority of his face covered, she could tell that he was smiling.

"Hi," she said, coughing the word out through the sand in her throat.

"It is good to see you again, Colonel Carter."

Teal'c helped her sit up and she looked toward the hatch. Mitchell and Daniel were holding onto the struts with one hand, their other arms extended into the storm. Vala appeared, they grabbed hold of her arms, and twisted to haul her inside. Vala spread her arms and legs out as if she was leaping out of the ship, yelping at the feeling of weightlessness, and wrapped herself around Daniel like a koala. He stumbled back into the wall but managed not to drop her.

"Pemphero, take us outta here!" Mitchell shouted. He slapped a button on the wall and the ramp began lifting, closing off the still-swirling eddies of sand.

Sam coughed, and Vala leaned back to see the face of her savior. She grinned. "Hel-*lo*, Daniel! My hero!" She planted a big, smacking kiss on his cheek.

"Don't call us heroes just yet," Daniel said as he put her down. "We're not exactly free and clear."

Sam wearily climbed back to her feet. "Dr. Lam?"

"She's watching over the, uh… the prisoners." Sam raised an eyebrow. "Only technically. Long story. We're going to let them go as soon as we get where we need to be."

"Okay. So what's going on? Why the rush?"

Mitchell said, "Ships. At least five, maybe more. Closing in on this location fast. Pemphero thinks the hijinks we got up to in finding this place tripped up some alarm bells."

"There were hijinks?" Vala said. "And I missed them?"

"We'll fill you in later," Mitchell promised. To Sam, he said, "You know, we would've come back for you. We were just going to haul out 'til the coast was clear. We didn't come all this way just to give up on the first try."

Sam said, "Noted, but I think we'd outstayed our welcome on Viaxeiro."

"You can tell us all about it once we're to safety."

~#~

They trekked through the ship together, joining Pemphero in the cockpit. He smiled and waved hello to Carter and Vala, then twisted back around so he could focus on taking them out of the force field.

"Colonel Mitchell," he said, "you snatched up a lovely little ship here. Think the Wayfarers would be willing to trade…?"

"Unlikely," Cam said. "How are we doing on our uninvited guests?"

Pemphero said, "They're coming in fast. Remember how I said there were at least five ships?"

"Yeah," Cam said warily.

"That was just the ships within our radar range. There's

more coming."

"How many more?"

Pemphero said, "You saw how many ships were docked at the Overseers' station? Well, everything we're doing right now is threatening their livelihood. A very lucrative livelihood, I should say. So pretty much all of them are coming to make sure Viaxeiro keeps its reputation."

"Fantastic," Cam said. "Can we outrun them?"

"I'll need a copilot so I can focus on setting the course. Which one of you wants to take a crack?"

Cam looked longingly at the controls, but he knew he was woefully deficient when it came to operating alien vessels. This was no time to learn on the job. He turned to Teal'c. "Kills me to say this, big guy, but I think I have to let you take this one."

Teal'c stepped around him to take the copilot seat. Cam went to Carter.

"Okay, bullet points. This is Pemphero. He's a transporter for Viaxeiro, but apparently he's a big fan of SG-1 so he decided to help us out. This is the ship of some nice people called Wayfarers, who supply the prison with food and sundries."

"Where are the Wayfarers now?"

"We locked them in the kitchen," Cam said. "You know. Like heroes."

Carter smiled ruefully. "Sometimes you have to find the grey areas. I assume they *aren't* fans of us."

"No, not as such. So how'd things go in the prison? Any new tattoos?"

Vala said, "No, but Tanis did give me the address of a vault where she's left everything she's gathered on the Lucian Alliance."

Carter and Cam both looked at her in surprise. "She did?" they said together.

"We *were* friends, you know."

"Wow," Cam said. "This mission might just pay off after all."

Daniel cleared his throat and gestured at the viewscreen. "Assuming of course we survive the next few minutes."

"Right," Cam said. "Always assuming that."

Vala had moved closer to the viewscreen, where the force field was just beginning to thin out and show stars above Viaxeiro. She spoke low enough that only Cam could hear her when she said, "Goodbye, Tanis. Good luck."

"Boy-ee!" Pemphero laughed, drawing everyone's attention. He let the chuckle die off slowly and shook his head. "Sorry. I'm sorry, I really am. But I just can't believe I'm SG-1's escape runner!"

"We call it a getaway driver where we come from." Cam patted Pemphero on the shoulder. "Just make sure you aren't our *last* getaway driver, and we'll all sign something for you on our way to the Stargate."

~#~

"This vessel does not appear to be equipped with weapons," Teal'c said. His voice was tinged with the slightest worry.

"It's a missionary ship," Daniel said, "what do they need with weapons?"

"Said the armed archaeologist," Cam countered. "If there are no weapons, we're going to have to focus on being faster than them."

Pemphero whistled. "Tall order, Colonel Mitchell. A lot of those ships were built for pursuit. They hunt bounties, they chase down people whose first instinct is always to run. Missionary ships aren't built for war, but they're also not really built for escape."

Cam said, "Okay, how about communication? Were they at least built to talk to each other?"

"Of course." He twisted to look around the cockpit and pointed at a small horseshoe-shaped station in the far corner. "There. Who the hell are you contacting?"

Cam said, "Hopefully some new friends."

Carter moved to stand behind Teal'c's seat. "How far is the

nearest Stargate?"

Pemphero answered her. "We're skimming by the edge of a system that has a Chappa'ai on the fourth planet. We can be there in fifteen minutes if we push the engines. Problem is, we'd have to push the engines the entire way and I'm not sure they can take that sort of abuse."

"What if we hop back over to your ship?" Daniel said.

"Sure, it's faster and the engines will get us to the Stargate. But we would lose time by docking and transferring."

Carter put a hand on his shoulder before she turned to hurry out of the room. "Set a course for the Stargate. I'll see what I can get out of the engines."

Teal'c said, "Setting a course. The first vessels are almost upon us."

"I see them," Pemphero said. "Hold on tight, folks. Inertial dampeners can only do so much."

Everyone lurched to the side as Pemphero swung the ship on a wide axis. Daniel was watching a screen which showed a cluster of vessels closing in fast on their position.

Cam was at the communication center, eyes closed so he could focus on finding sense amid the static hum. "Kimo, Adamaris. If you're listening, we could really use a hand here."

Vala said, "If those ships don't catch up with us, aren't they just going to land on Viaxeiro and make life hell for them?"

Pemphero shook his head. "Nah. One of them might land to see what happened, and it'll take them ages to sort out that mess. But all those ladies down there could kill each other and no one would bat an eye. Our job is just to get the women to the prison. Once they're safely locked away, we couldn't care less."

Daniel said, "So why are they chasing us?"

"Because escape is the one crime the Overseers won't abide. They have centuries of a reputation to protect. They'll blow this ship to pieces on the off chance we have prisoners aboard."

"Fabulous." Daniel looked at Cam. "Anything?"

"Kind of hard to pick out one voice out of everyone using this party line, Jackson."

An alarm sounded. Teal'c checked it. "The leading ships have locked onto us. They are adjusting course to intercept." To Pemphero, he said, "Are we currently at the maximum speed?"

"That's a yes, my Jaffa friend."

"Then they are likely to be in weapons range in just over a minute."

Cam grunted. "Kimo! Adamaris! A little intervention would be greatly appreciated! If you're picking this up—"

"If they're picking it up," Daniel said, "they might not want to acknowledge we're friends when everyone else is listening in."

"You're right, but if there's a chance we've got friends among the torches-and-pitchforks crowd, I'm going to take advantage of them."

Daniel seemed to accept that logic as the ship was rocked by an energy blast. Cam abandoned the radio and ran out of the cockpit to the engine room. When he arrived, Carter had already shed the jacket she'd been wearing and was crouching next to what looked like a turn-of-the-century furnace. Her forehead was glistening with sweat from being so close to the hot metal.

"How's it looking?" he asked.

"That guy up there was right about the limits of this engine. If there isn't a Stargate on this planet we're heading for, we might have to surrender just to get back to civilization."

"We may end up surrendering no matter what," Cam said.

Carter was focused on the guts of the engine. "I think I can reroute a few systems to get a boost from the engines. It's going to be a messy job, and whoever owns this ship isn't going to be very happy with us when this is all said and done. Where'd you get it, anyway?"

"We, uh, kind of hijacked it. From a group of missionaries."

"I kind of hoped you were exaggerating."

"We were breaking you out of prison," Cam said. "Rules got bent. Besides, we delivered all the supplies to the planet before we left. And we're going to let them out of the kitchen just as soon as we get where we're going."

Carter sighed.

"Yeah, I know, the apology tour starts tomorrow. Just goose those engines and we can worry about it from the comfort of the SGC."

~#~

Another blast rocked the ship, this one powerful enough that it nearly knocked Vala off her feet as Mitchell returned from the engine room.

Teal'c said, "Our adversaries are closing the distance between us, Colonel Mitchell."

"Yeah, noticed that," Mitchell said. "Carter's doing what she can."

Vala had remained frozen near the wall, trying to stay out of everybody's way, but she couldn't stay silent any longer.

"I have an idea."

Daniel said, "Ah… Vala, we're kind of in the middle of undoing your last idea."

Vala pushed her lips into a pout. He had a point, but that didn't mean she had to like it. She considered arguing but Daniel was already looking at the screens again. She decided she would never convince him and left the cockpit in search of Sam. She found the engine room by following the heat. It was easily ten degrees warmer than the rest of the ship, and she found Sam elbow-deep in the large device that took up the middle of the room.

"This would go a lot faster if people would stop asking for progress reports," Sam said without looking to see who had arrived.

Vala said, "I might know how to get enough speed for us to escape."

Sam looked up. "How dangerous is it?"

"I'm not going to lie, it is on the high side of the danger-ous scale," Vala said quickly, "but I've done it before and I survived, so."

Sam hesitated. Vala came into the room and crouched next to her.

"It's a crazy idea, yes," Vala said, "but how many times have you been in this position? How many times have you looked at a problem and just *known* you could solve it if someone just had a little faith in you. Please, Samantha, I can get us to a Stargate."

Sam looked into Vala's eyes. "What do you need?"

Vala grinned. "A zat."

"What good is a…" Sam's eyes widened. "No."

"It works."

"I know it *technically* works. I've seen it work before. But if it doesn't, we'll be stranded.

We can't take the risk."

Vala said, "If the engines burn out before we reach the Stargate, we'll be stranded anyway. Look, the energy from a zat blast has to go *somewhere*, right. All we have to do is aim it at the right place. I've done it before. I was on a ship which didn't have enough thrust to escape atmosphere. Now, I'll admit, I was just shooting the engines out of frustration, but it worked. If we already have the engines at their maximum thrust, then a zat blast will give it enough of a shove to get us away from the other ships."

As if to punctuate her argument, they were hit again by another blast. Sam wiped a hand over her face and nodded.

"Go get a zat."

Vala slapped both of Sam's shoulders with her hands, got up, and hurried out. She ran though the ship, returned to the cockpit, and grabbed Mitchell by the hips. She ignored his pro-tests as she patted him down and jerked the zat'nik'tel from the holster at his waist. She tossed a quick "Thanks!" over her shoulder as she ran back out. Sam looked surprised to see her return so soon.

"That was quick."

"I got it from Mitchell. I didn't exactly explain what I needed it for. Or ask if I could take it."

Sam said, "Okay. You're the one who has done this before, and it's your plan. Take it away."

They stepped away from the engine. Vala brought the zat up, closed one eye, and thumbed the activation switch that caused the weapon to unfold like a snake about to strike.

"Samantha, I would like to thank you for trusting me and giving me the opportunity to prove myself to you. And in that spirit, and in the name of full disclosure, I do have to admit that I've actually attempted this twice. The second time resulted in a minor explosion which crippled the ship."

"Vala—"

Vala closed her other eye and fired at the engine.

CHAPTER THIRTY-FOUR

SAM EMERGED from the event horizon and stopped on the ramp, eyes closed, and took a moment to appreciate the fact she was finally home. The familiar sounds of the SGC - distant klaxons sounding in response to the unscheduled off-world activation, the blast doors sliding open now that no threat was evident, the order for the gate room guards to stand down - calmed and reassured her that the ordeal was finally over.

Landry was waiting for them at the base of the ramp. His smile was wider, prouder, and more relieved than Sam had ever seen it, and she knew the woman standing beside her was the reason. According to Mitchell, she had been an excellent addition to the team. She had also been instrumental in making sure the Wayfarers didn't riot when the team arrived at their destination. She explained that Sam had done nothing wrong, that Vala may have once deserved to be locked up but had turned over a new leaf and was doing good work out in the universe.

"Could you really live with yourselves if you knew there was someone trapped on that planet who didn't deserve to be there?"

Kourash had grudgingly accepted that argument, but he still considered SG-1 to be blasphemous and guilty of deicide. He swore that if their paths ever crossed again, it would be as enemies. Mitchell accepted that and thanked them for the use of their ship, hurrying everyone out before Kourash and his people noticed that the engines were on the verge of failure.

Landry stepped forward as they reached the bottom of the ramp. "Welcome home, SG-1. Especially to you, Colonel Carter and Miss Mal Doran."

"Thank you, sir," Sam said. "It's good to be home."

Vala looked exhausted, but she managed a quick smile to the

general before she started for the exit. Sam watched her go and knew she was probably going to catch hell for the part she'd played in getting them captured and sent to the prison. She decided what she had to say couldn't wait for the briefing.

"Actually, General, we wouldn't be here if it wasn't for Vala."

Vala stopped and looked back at her.

"Is that so?" Landry said.

"Her advice to not attempt escape until we arrived at the prison probably kept us alive long enough to come up with a safe plan. During our time in the prison, her relationship with Tanis Reynard protected us and provided us with a lead on where we could find a storehouse of information on the Lucian Alliance. And when we were trying to get to the Stargate, it was her plan which gave our ship the boost of speed required to outrun our pursuers. She once again proved herself to be a vital and valuable member of SG-1."

Landry said, "That's good to hear. I can't wait to hear the details. But I think you've all earned a shower and a little relaxation before I put you through all that. You're dismissed."

"Much appreciated, sir," Mitchell said. "Some of us need that shower more than others." Sam looked at him and he held his hands up. "Talking about myself."

Landry fell into step with them as they walked to the elevators. "I can't help but notice you didn't bring a prisoner with you. Tanis Reynard?"

"She chose to remain in the prison, sir," Sam said. "But as I mentioned, we're confident the information she gave Vala will prove useful."

"And why is that?" Landry asked.

"Well, sir, Tanis didn't stay free as long as she did by being sloppy. I might not be the woman's biggest fan, but if she says the information is good, it'll be good."

"I suppose we'll find out soon enough," Landry said. "I get the feeling Homeworld Security is going to be satisfied with this outcome even if the information isn't exactly what we hoped for. A database is a lot easier to deal with than holding a prisoner indefinitely."

Sam said, "My thoughts exactly, sir."

The elevator arrived and Landry set the briefing for two hours from then. Plenty of time for a shower, a nap, and a change of clothes, Sam thought, not necessarily in that order. Maybe a call to Washington… Vala squeezed Mitchell out of the way so she could stand beside Sam in the elevator. She bumped her elbow against Sam's. Sam looked at her, and Vala mouthed "thank you." Sam grinned and bumped Vala's arm in response, facing forward as the doors closed.

~#~

Daniel lingered in the briefing room after the rest of the team had been dismissed. He was still wired from their last-minute escape through the Stargate. He'd asked Sam how she managed to give them that last, vital burst of speed, but Sam had simply given him a stricken look and told him he was probably better off not knowing. Given how smug Vala looked, that was probably accurate.

Landry came out of his office. "You okay, son? I'm expecting SG-10 in here for a briefing in about ten minutes. You're welcome to sit in."

"No, I'll clear out." Daniel stood and began gathering his things.

Landry stood behind his chair at the head of the table. "You did good work out there," he said.

Daniel chuckled. "I crammed myself into a box for no reason. If we hadn't happened to find a ship that could disable the landmines, Carolyn, Sam, and Vala wouldn't have gotten anywhere close to us. We fumbled and lucked our way through every step of the way."

"Seems like that was bound to happen no matter what your plan was. I got the impression Viaxeiro isn't the sort of place you can travel to in a straight line."

"True," Daniel admitted. "And along the way, we did make a lot of contacts who may prove helpful down the line. Pemphero would jump at the chance. Kimo and Adamaris would probably be open to working with us again. And Odai… well, he could go either way. But if we have matching goals, I could see him agreeing to call a truce."

Landry said, "Exactly! And if the information Vala got from Tanis Reynard pans out, we could be ready to place a mole inside the Lucian Alliance by the end of the year. And, as a bonus, Colonel Carter and Vala got to take down a Goa'uld. It wasn't pretty, Dr. Jackson, but this mission is going down as a success."

Daniel nodded. "I agree. Pemphero even said he was confident that the people chasing us would give up and go home after we got away."

"And the women left behind on Viaxeiro? Surely there's some repercussions from a prisoner finally escaping."

"Maybe. Or maybe things will continue the way they always have, but with a better situation on the ground. There's no reason for the Overseers to stop sending them shipments. It's a well-oiled machine, and now it's under the management of people who actually care about their fellow prisoners. I really believe Sam and Vala changed the prison for the better."

Landry smiled. "See? All's well that ends well."

"Mmm," Daniel said. "I'm not arguing that. I just hope our next mission is a little more… straightforward."

"You and me both, son." Landry raised his eyebrows and smiled, indicating he wasn't particularly optimistic about that panning out. He patted the back of his chair and left the briefing room.

Daniel went to the window and gazed across at the Stargate. He'd pined for the Jaffa when they were up against Ori soldiers, but now they were gearing up for war against a mixed bag of thieves, con artists, brigands, and pirates who all had their own motives and allegiances. He sighed and slipped his free hand into his pocket, patting his thigh with the files he held in the other hand. He turned away and shook his head as he walked to the stairs.

"There was a time when the worst enemy I had to face was a papercut," he muttered. "*Those* are the days I really miss…"

~#~

Though Carolyn would never admit it to the more extreme adrenaline junkies on the base, she was more than happy to return to the relative mundanity of paperwork. She was exhausted from her trip through the Stargate and, judging from SG-1's reactions, it hadn't even been one of their worst missions. If that was what counted as relaxing for them, they could keep it. She would be just fine in the infirmary.

She was on her way to the office when she spotted Teal'c lying on one of the examination beds. She changed direction to approach him.

"Teal'c? Did something happen?"

"No, Dr. Lam. But I know you would prefer to keep me under observation while I am on the base until I have fully healed from recent events."

"That's absolutely true. What changed your mind?"

"Colonel Mitchell gave me a…" He seemed to struggle over the next phrase. "Pep talk. He convinced me that my contribution to the team is more than physical strength."

Carolyn smiled. "He's right. They need you out there." She rested a hand on his arm, giving it a gentle squeeze. "Get some sleep. I'll come back and check on you in a little while."

He inclined his head and closed his eyes. Carolyn pulled the curtain around his bed and continued to her office.

She smelled what had been left on her desk before she turned on the light. A fresh cup of coffee was sitting next to the keyboard, steam still rising from the surface. She put down her files and picked up the cup. She brought it to her face and inhaled deeply. *Oh, that's the good stuff.*

It had been sitting on a slip of paper and she tilted her head to read the message. "See? I can be nice. Good work out there. Mitchell."

Carolyn laughed softly and took a seat, leaving the computer monitor off so she could fully enjoy the coffee.

~#~

A week after their return from Viaxeiro, Sam received a mission report she knew Vala would want to hear about. She checked the cafeteria, Daniel's lab, and a dozen other places before she started to worry. She was fairly sure that no one had escorted Vala off the base but there were only so many places she could be hiding. Her quarters were empty, Teal'c hadn't seen her, and Mitchell was too grateful for the peace and quiet to share Sam's concern.

She finally got a lead from an airman. He reluctantly admitted that Vala had once gotten him talking about "the deep dark secrets of the SGC." He hadn't seen any harm in telling her about some of the lower, seldom-used areas of the base.

Sam followed his directions through poorly-lit corridors which led to a part of the base even she had never seen before. A door was standing open and Sam stepped through onto a metal platform overlooking a large man-made reservoir in a cavern carved out of the mountain. Vala stood with her arms resting on the railing looking out over the water.

"My God," Sam muttered. "I always forget how amazing this place is."

Vala said, "There are actually five of them. I hear one of them has a duck."

"Really." Sam leaned on the railing next to Vala. "Do you come down here a lot?"

"Sometimes when I want to get back to nature. Since General Landry won't let me wander around outside by myself."

Sam said, "Ah, right. Well, I'll talk to him about that."

Vala looked at her, flipping her hair out of her face. "What, really?"

"You've more than earned the right to some privacy. You

don't need us babysitting you every time you want some fresh air."

Vala was stunned. "Thank you, Samantha."

"Sure." She pressed her palms together and linked her fingers. "So did you come down here to think about anything in particular?"

"Mm. The trap. My enemies got Tanis' message and figured out where to send it so they could trap me as well. I'm just wondering how long it will be before someone else tracks me down. I haven't talked about this much, but I have quite a few enemies out there in the universe."

"*No*," Sam said, exaggerating her shock. "You?"

Vala said, "I *know*, who could hate me? I'm very loveable."

Sam laughed. "So… SG-4 just got back from the address Tanis gave you. The one where she kept her records."

"Oh?" Vala straightened her posture. It was clear she was bracing for the worst. She ran her fingers over the railing, lips pursed. Her tone was fake casual, giving away how much she really cared. "Did they, um, find anything worth mentioning?"

Sam let the question hang for a moment before she took pity. "Yeah. They found a lot. Names, gate addresses, relationships between factions we've never even heard of. Major Escher was sitting in on the briefing and he looked more excited than I've seen him in years. He called it the 'Rosetta stone of intel'. Tanis may have given us the key to taking down the Lucian Alliance from the inside."

Vala grinned. "Way to go, Tanis."

"You're getting credit for it, too. We never would have gone to that prison if you hadn't pushed us. I'm going to make sure General Landry and the IOA know that."

"Wow." Vala blinked and turned her head, trying to subtly wipe at her eyes. "It's not my birthday, so I'm not sure I understand why you're being so kind to me."

Sam sighed and looked down at the water. "To be honest,

I'm making up for how I've been acting since you joined SG-1. I haven't been treating you like a member of this team. That was unfair of me. You deserve better than that. The time we spent on Viaxeiro proved that."

"What?" Vala said, honestly shocked. "Literally every plan we had blew up in our faces. Getting out was just dumb luck."

"Yeah," Sam said, "and you rolled with every punch we took. When we were captured, when we found ourselves locked up with a Goa'uld, you changed course without batting an eyelash. I'm used to fighting soldiers. Jaffa, the Ori, they make sense to me because they have strategy and they act logically. But now we're up against the Lucian Alliance. They don't make sense. They're erratic. It's hard for me to fight an enemy I can't predict. You don't predict what they're going to do. You just let them do it and form your plan later. I need to learn how to think like that."

Vala was smiling proudly. "I think I can find the time to tutor you, if you want."

"Thanks," Sam said. "Escher is going to sort through the information. Landry has already approved a mission when he finds an address that seems promising."

"Can't wait."

"Well, it'll be at least a week before he has anything usable. In the meantime, why don't you trade this reservoir for an actual lake? I'll take you out, show you around. Earth is so much more than a drab military base."

Vala bounced on the balls of her feet. "Really? Because I've heard of something called a 'mall,' and it sounds positively delightful."

Sam nodded. "Sure, I'll take you to the mall. We'll get pedicures, we'll make a whole day of it. I might even take you to Victoria's Secret."

"Who is Victoria?"

"That's the secret," Sam whispered, pushing off the railing and walking back to the door.

Vala grinned and pursued her.

ABOUT THE AUTHOR

Geonn Cannon lives in Oklahoma. He is the author of several novels, including the Riley Parra series, which is currently being produced as a webseries for Tello Films. Information about his other works and an archive of free stories can be found online at geonncannon.com.

With thanks to Jessica Johnson
for her highly valuable input into the editing of this book.

STARGÅTE SG·1.

STARGATE ATLANTIS

Original novels based on the hit
TV shows **STARGATE SG-1** and
STARGATE ATLANTIS

Available as e-books from leading online
retailers

Paperback editions available from
Amazon and IngramSpark

If you liked this book, please tell your
friends and leave a review on a
bookstore website. Thanks!

www.ingramcontent.com/pod-product-compliance
Lightning Source LLC
Chambersburg PA
CBHW011159190726

48286CB00009B/2839